BETRAYAL

Nancy Ann Healy

ISBN: 0692213546
ISBN 13: 9780692213544
Library of Congress Control Number: 2014908420
Bumbling Bard Creations, Manchester, CT

For my Mom and my Nana
The two most influential women in my life

Acknowledgements

The Alex and Cassidy series is more than simply a set of books filled with colorful characters and chaotic events. Traveling with these characters is part of a journey that continues to amaze me. It would not be possible without the love and support of my wife, Melissa, my friends, and the many readers who continue to support not only Alex and Cassidy's adventure, but mine. A special of note of thanks to my friends Natalya and Marie who so graciously and enthusiastically offered to assist with the French and Russian verbiage in Betrayal.

Throughout the Alex and Cassidy series references are occasionally made to books, films, television shows, music and actual historic events. There is so much to explore and experience in life. I am grateful to the many authors, filmmakers, playwrights, performers, musicians, leaders, journalists, teachers and friends that have sparked my curiosity and touched my heart. The influence of these wonderful people, whether from a distance or in my daily life, is something I regard as a gift. It enriches not only what I create, but the experience of creating itself. Life is a journey, not a destination. We create it every day.

Prologue

The popping sounded almost like firecrackers. The president turned slightly and smiled at the Secret Service agent beside him. "Get down!" the agent screamed. He shoved the president to his left and felt the man's body collapse into his arms. "No! Phoenix is down! Repeat, Phoenix is down! Can you hear me? Mr. President?"

"Where is that IV? Now! Hurry it up! Mr. President!" President John Merrow's eyes rolled back as a searing pain that ripped through his chest overtook his strength. He could taste the blood in his throat and his gut burned as if flames were raging within it. The voice called again, "Mr. President, open your eyes, stay with me. GET THAT DAMN LINE IN!"

"Alex…you need to tell," the president barely opened his eyes. "Didn't know that street…Mutanabbi…"

"Okay, don't try to talk. Just look at me. Look right here." The paramedic pointed two fingers toward his own eyes.

President John Merrow shook his head and let out an unearthly groan. "Tell her…..Care…Take care of…" He struggled to speak but gave over to the pain before he could finish his thought.

***

"*Que voulez-vous dire, il est vivant* (what do you mean he is alive)?" Edmond Callier screamed through the phone.

CIA agent Jonathan Krause answered deliberately as a wide sense of satisfaction gripped him. "John Merrow is a hard man to kill, Edmond."

"This is…"

"Relax," Krause responded. "He is out of commission for the foreseeable future."

"They expect him to be dead," the voice answered.

"Well, Strickland has control just as you wished. Admiral Brackett is with him now. And who knows?" he continued with contempt, "*Vous pouvez toujours obtenir votre souhait, l ami* (you may still get your wish, friend)." Krause looked at a photo of John Merrow, his best friend, the only man he had ever truly considered a brother, laughing beside him.

"I understand, Jonathan. These are the risks we all accept," Callier said.

"Yes, I suppose they are."

"You will keep me apprised?"

"Of course."

"Good. *Prenez soin de vous, mon ami. Cela passera eventuellement* (Be well, my friend. This will also pass)."

Jonathan Krause dropped the call and looked at the phone. The disgust on his face was unmistakable. He threw the phone at the wall with such brutal force that it shattered. "*Il n'y a pas d'amitié* (there is no friendship)!" he lamented. "*Pas de loyauté* (no loyalty)."

***

Chapter One

Cassidy O'Brien stood looking quietly out of her kitchen window. She smiled as she watched the woman she had un-expectedly fallen in love with chase her six year old son, Dylan, across the yard. Just a few weeks ago her morning was spent preparing for the arrival of an FBI agent after her ex-husband began receiving threats. The agent, she was told, would *protect* her and ascertain who might want to do her family harm. After years of being married to a politician she was relishing a degree of privacy in her life and the idea had both frustrated and un-settled her. When Alex Toles walked through her door that day everything changed. The FBI agent challenged all of Cassidy's preconceptions about people, love, relationships and life. In what seemed like an instant, Alex had transformed the school teacher's understanding of what truly mattered. Since that day, Cassidy had watched her ex-husband fight for his life, been held hostage by a sadistic stalker, left her job, moved her home, and all of that paled in comparison to the greatest change of all; she fell in love.

Alex Toles had stolen her heart. Alex was strong and beau-tiful, intelligent and compassionate. Cassidy admired her strength and her tenacity. She respected all that Alex had endured in her past, serving in Iraq, confronting war, facing danger, but in the end it was the agent's gentleness that had captured her heart. It was the way Alex's eyes danced when she looked at Cassidy and the way they softened when she looked at Dylan. It was the tenor in her voice when she spoke of those she

1

loved; her captain and her colonel, her brother, even Cassidy's mother Rose. And, it was the agent's playfulness and sincerity that seemed to always captivate Cassidy. It was Alex Toles' devotion and honesty that reminded Cassidy in every moment that no matter where life's path might lead, she would walk the rest of hers beside Alex Toles.

The smile on Alex's face as she chased Dylan nearly brought Cassidy to tears. The truth was that getting Alex inside would be nearly as difficult as wrangling the boy running away from her. Cassidy laughed at the thought. She closed her eyes and took a deep breath. Waking up here, heading down the stairs, brewing the coffee, watching Alex fix Dylan's cereal; these were life's simple moments and Cassidy knew they were also life's most important memories. The sudden sound of the doorbell snapped Cassidy from her private world. "Can I help you?" she asked the man standing before her.

"Mrs. O'Brien, sorry to disturb you," he smiled. He was not quite Alex's height and he had a few extra pounds. Cassidy's eyes sparkled with her question and the man smiled. He shook his head. "We haven't met….Michael, Michael Taylor." The teacher's surprise was evident. She had never met the NSA director, but as far as she knew Michael Taylor lived and worked in Washington. She couldn't imagine what would bring Alex's former captain and friend here now. She noted that the man looked exceptionally tired. "Is Alex here?"

"Yes…I'm sorry, of course…come in."

"I've been trying to reach her all night," he explained.

Cassidy sighed. "Oh, yeah…sorry, she shut off her phone." Taylor smirked a bit. "She's out back with Dylan. Is everything all right?"

"You haven't heard," he said flatly.

"Heard?"

The sliding glass door opened and a smiling Alex stepped through. "HAH…I win!"

"Alex," Cassidy's voice had a heavy tone and Alex looked up to catch sight of her friend.

"Taylor? What are you doing here? Is Cass…"

"No," he immediately interrupted her with an understanding of where his friend's fears would travel. "Your family is safe, Alex. It's not that." Alex looked at Cassidy and then back to her friend.

Taylor looked Alex squarely in the eye, summoning his strength. "It's the colonel."

"What?" Alex asked.

"You really did shut everything off," he noted. "Alex, someone shot the president last night."

Cassidy nearly fell over and put both her hands on the counter to steady herself. Alex flew to her side, pulling the teacher to her and holding her shoulders firmly. "Cass," she whispered and then looked at Taylor who was puzzled by the younger woman's reaction. "Is he…"

"No," Taylor answered. "He's alive, but it isn't good. Strickland has the reins. We need to talk, Alex." Alex nodded and gestured toward the outside. Taylor understood and headed out the back door to wait.

"Cass." Cassidy could not move. She covered her face with her hands.

"Why does this keep happening?" she asked the agent, thinking back to her ex-husband's recent car *accident.*

"I don't know," Alex confessed, guiding Cassidy's face upward.

"Alex…Chris and now John. I…."

"I know," Alex said as she pulled Cassidy into a hug. "I have to go talk to Taylor. Cassidy, listen to me, John is tough."

"What have I done, Alex?"

"Nothing. Why don't you take Dylan down by the stream," Alex suggested wiping a tear from her lover's eye.

"Alex…If he…"

"Stop. You need to stop. You did what you had to do, so did he. I love you, Cass." Cassidy drank in the agent's embrace. "We're okay. Dylan is okay. That's all that matters."

Green eyes met blue and Cassidy had to momentarily close hers to calm herself. "I love you, Alex."

"I know. Go...get Dylan." Cassidy nodded and swallowed hard, heading for the door.

***

Two Days Earlier

"I'm glad you told me," Alex said softly. Cassidy sat with her face in her hands, finding it impossible to breathe. "No secrets. Not between us. Cass..."

The teacher looked up with tear stained cheeks. "I'm so sorry, Alex."

"Cassidy, this has nothing to do with us. You made a mistake. To be honest I'm not sure I'd even say that."

"You must think...."

"What? I must think what?" Alex asked, guiding Cassidy's face to her own.

"Alex, I never..."

"Cass," Alex let out a heavy sigh. "I love you. I love you more than anything. We all have a past...so do I..."

"I should have told you."

"Probably," Alex chuckled. "But, when would you have done that? John could have told me. Cassidy, listen to me," Alex paused afraid to continue.

"Alex, please tell me what you are thinking," Cassidy pleaded.

"Honestly?" Alex sighed and finished her thought. "I think Christopher O'Brien is a selfish asshole who never deserved you or Dylan in the first place. I'm actually surprised you never did have a real affair. God knows he did."

"I don't know what I did to deserve you."

Alex shook her head. "Cassidy, you really do have that backwards."

Cassidy rested her head on the agent's strong shoulder. "I couldn't keep it a secret, not from you. To me...Dylan is your son now. I wish he was."

Alex smiled. "Well, it's a new start for us all. I have to ask you, Cass; does he know?"

Cassidy titled her head in question. "Chris? No." Alex shook her head. Cassidy had never discussed the truth of her son's paternity with anyone. She suddenly realized Alex was referring to the president. "Oh. We never talked about it. It was just that one night. He had too much to drink. I was lonely. It was before Chris ran for congress. It was at a fundraiser for the party. I saw him go off in the corner with one of John's aides. We both left feeling regretful. Never spoke of it again. At first I didn't want to think it, but Chris and I never could seem to," Cassidy paused and gathered her thoughts. "But, yes...Alex, he knows. I am sure. He has always taken an interest in Dylan. Look at him."

"That explains a lot," Alex mused.

"What do you mean?"

The agent looked deeply into her lover's eyes. "It explains why he wanted me to protect you. I wondered why he would do that. Presidents don't generally assign FBI agents to cases. He is always deliberate in what he does. I just figured it had something to do with the congressman and he needed someone he knew he could trust."

"I'm sorry I didn't tell you," Cassidy apologized.

Again the agent shook her head. "No, you couldn't. He wouldn't. But, if he knows Dylan is his son, he would go to the ends of the earth to protect him."

"You love him," Cassidy observed.

"Not like he wanted me to, no. We went through a lot together, Cass. Seeing death, it makes you...well, yes...in my own way I love him."

"I can't imagine how this must make you feel."

"What? That you slept with my friend before I knew you? Cassidy, I slept with Agent Brackett for God's sake."

"That's not what I meant."

"That you reached for comfort in a horrible relationship or that John is Dylan's real father? Cass, it doesn't matter. It doesn't change anything."

Cassidy sighed. "There were times I wanted to tell him, tell Chris; but he would use it as a weapon. I know he would. It would destroy John's presidency. It would devastate Dylan."

Alex considered the statement. "Cassidy, sometimes truth is not the best medicine. I know that's what they say. It isn't always the case. All I ask is that we don't keep secrets. I promise you there is nothing that could make me love you less or walk away."

"Well, *this* is it."

"Well, then tomorrow we leave Nicky's and we go *home*. Our home, and we start with a clean slate. Cass, when Carl Fisher had you, I thought I might never see you again. Being here with Nick and Barb, with you and Dylan, well…I just want us to be together. It's time we both think about our future more than our past. Okay?"

"You amaze me, Alex."

Alex smiled. "I love you, Cassidy."

***

"So…" Alex began as she walked beside her friend.

"Toles…"

"What the hell, Taylor? Who shot him?"

"I don't have that answer. Jordan is the last name. My best? Deep cover, military."

Alex rubbed her temple as she watched Cassidy head down the slight hill at the back of the yard with Dylan. "What aren't you telling me?"

"Alex, I don't know much. What I do know, I don't like." Alex looked at her friend. "He's into something."

"What does that mean?"

"I mean I have been looking into Congressman O'Brien's accident, Cassidy's abduction, all of it. The dots; connecting them; our old colonel is at the head of every line."

Alex shook her head. "You know there has to be an explanation."

"Well, let's hope he lives to give it to us," Taylor said.

"What connections?" Alex asked now.

"Brackett, Fisher, Krause, and Merrow, all their fathers worked on the same project." He watched as Alex pinched the bridge of her nose. "There's more." Alex nodded and licked her lips. "The president sent Agent Brackett to Congressman O'Brien. Brady picked that up in some chatter. Claire Brackett is not very quiet; about anything."

"What?" Alex shook her head in disbelief.

"You heard me."

"So?" Alex asked.

"So…The president has been sleeping with Agent Brackett."

Alex rubbed her face. "Jesus. Taylor, I don't…."

"He's into something. Whether he put himself there or not…"

"Fine. What do you need?"

Taylor stopped his own pacing and considered his next statement carefully. "Alex, the only words he's spoken….He asked for you."

"I see."

"Maybe he will…"

Alex nodded. "Fine."

"I'm leaving on the nine o'clock out of Kennedy back to D.C.," Taylor told his friend.

"All right. Book me a flight and book me back for the next feasible…"

"Alex…it's a seven hour flight to California."

"It's not a request, Taylor. If you recall I am suspended. I'm not currently on anyone's payroll."

"Cassidy is safe, Alex...I really..."

"Book it. I'll meet you at the airport. I made a promise to Cassidy. I intend to keep it." Taylor sighed as the agent gave him a faint smile. "Michael..."

"Yeah?" he asked.

"He may have his reasons."

Michael Taylor offered his friend a halfcocked smile. "I hope so," he said as he turned to leave.

Alex closed her eyes and rubbed her temples. "Me too. Colonel, what are you doing?"

***

"I'll be back by late afternoon," Alex said.

"Alex, if you need to stay..." Cassidy began when she was immediately interrupted.

"No."

Cassidy moved to the agent and took the spoon she was repeatedly tapping on the table away. "This is what you do," she said to Alex. "Is this because of what I told you about Dylan? I am all right, Alex. I really am."

"No. It's because of what I told you," the agent got up from her chair and stretched, turning away from her lover.

"What are you talking about?" Cassidy asked.

"I said that I would give you everything."

"And I told you, you already have."

"No. I haven't. I promised you when we moved that this week we would get Dylan settled and we would..."

"Alex...."

"I am not going to be him, Cassidy."

"Be who?" Cassidy looked to the ceiling and shook her head. "This *is* about what I told you."

"No. Look...There is nothing I can do right now; thanks to the good congressman reporting our relationship. I have to be reinstated in the bureau before I can make an official move to the NSA. There's no point in me staying in California. But, I have to go, I have to see him."

"I know," Cassidy said turning the agent to face her. "But there's something else."

"Cass, if he is involved in anything that led to Fisher abducting you..."

"Don't," Cassidy stopped the agent. "I don't believe that." Alex let out a heavy breath and rubbed her temples. "Alex..."

"I just need to come home Cass," Alex said softly. "I hate..."

"Okay." Cassidy knew that Alex hated hospitals and this would certainly remind her of her past. Cassidy still did not know all the details, but she did know that the IED attack that injured both Alex and the president in Iraq left more than a few physical scars. "We'll be here."

Alex finally smiled. "I need to be with *you*."

"I know," Cassidy said. "You told me; remember? John is tough."

"Yeah."

Cassidy squinted and then smiled playfully, planting a light kiss on the agent's cheek. "I love you, Alfred."

Alex laughed. "I don't know what I'd do without you Cassidy."

"Probably less dishes," Cassidy winked.

"Mm-hm...I will keep my promises," Alex said. "No matter what."

"You don't have to give me anything Alex, just come home." She kissed the agent on the cheek again and made her way toward the stove.

Alex nodded. "I will," she whispered to herself. The only thing that made the coming trip even bearable was the knowledge that she would be coming home to Cassidy.

"You'd better," Cassidy called back to Alex's delight.

***

Chapter Two

"Hi," a voice said very softly on the phone.

Cassidy sighed. "Are you there?" There was a lingering silence. "Alex?"

"Yeah. I'm here."

"Are you all right?"

"Cass...I..."

The teacher closed her eyes. There was a tone in her lover's voice that she immediately understood. Alex was hurting. "I wish I was there with you."

"I know. I just needed to hear your voice before...."

"I'm here if you need me."

"I'll be home later," Alex said quietly.

"We'll be waiting for you."

"I thought you were going to go see about school for Dylan?"

Cassidy chuckled. "I am. I'll be back before you get home."

"I should be there."

"No. You should be where you are."

Alex pinched the bridge of her nose. "I want you to...."

"I already know, Alex. Trust me there will be plenty of boring things for you to do in time, like take Dylan to soccer practice and sit through horrendous concerts and...."

"I don't think that's boring."

Cassidy laughed. "Wait." She heard Alex let out a little chuckle on the other end of the call. "Go. Do what you need to. See John. I promise I will find all sorts of boring things for you to do when you get back."

"Cass?"

"Yes?"

"I miss you."

"Give it time, Alex," Cassidy quipped, prompting Alex to chuckle. "And, I miss you too."

The agent hung up the phone and walked through the automatic doors. She stopped to show her identification when an attractive woman waved her through. Alex gave a sad smile as the woman greeted her with a warm embrace. "He asked for you," she said softly.

"Jane," Alex whispered, receiving a forced smile. Jane Merrow was a remarkable woman and Alex had always liked and respected her. The first lady had left a promising career to be with John Merrow and support his endeavors. Alex knew that Jane loved her friend deeply. The president's feelings for Alex were never his best kept secret. Alex, however, had always made it clear that she only wanted a friendship and she and Jane had grown close during the colonel's recovery from his injuries in Iraq. Alex had told the president numerous times how lucky he was to have a woman like his wife. Looking at her now, Alex mused that Jane Merrow was not unlike Cassidy. She felt her heart sink, realizing the situation at hand. And, knowing all too well the indiscretions that the president had engaged in himself, including with her lover. Regardless of how wonderful Jane was in Alex's mind; it was a fact that her friend often felt incredibly lonely in his relationship. "How is he?" Alex asked. The first lady shook her head. "Jane?"

"I don't know, Alex. He keeps talking about telling you something. When he talks. Other than asking for the girls..."

Alex nodded. "Jane, he probably...."

"Alex," the woman led the agent down the hall and away from the cluster of Secret Service agents. "There is only one other thing he said." Alex silently questioned the first lady with her eyes. "Dylan." The agent took a deep breath. "I already know. John told me years ago." The admission shocked the agent. "It was a bad time for us. A very bad time. I was…."

"Jane, I just found out myself," Alex offered.

"We never had a perfect relationship, Alex, you know that. I wasn't perfect either." First Lady Jane Merrow covered her face with her hands. "How strange you found Cassidy. He has always watched Dylan closely, wanted Chris to bring him to events, and God knows he has always loved you."

Alex sighed. "You know that I never…."

"I do," Jane smiled and took the agent's hand. "No matter, he is my best friend," she said with tears shining in her eyes. "And, I am his. He couldn't keep that secret from me."

Alex had not expected this conversation. "Jane, I….Do you know? Is he involved…"

"He is very quiet about the job, Alex. Very. Always has been. I don't know. I know that something has been bothering him. He has nightmares. Ever since…"

"I know."

Jane squeezed the agent's hand and led her down the hallway. "Come on, I don't know if he will wake up."

***

Alex opened the door to the president's room and paused. The beeping of machines, the smell of medicine and the fluorescent lights made her body shudder. More slowly than she would have imagined possible she made her way to the president's bedside. Her eyes closed momentarily as she brought her hands to her face. It was a weak attempt to still the surfacing emotions and memories brought on by familiar sounds and smells. The president's skin looked almost gray. Still, he was handsome, something she could never deny. But here his strength seemed sapped from him. It was almost as if she was looking at a shadow. "Colonel?" she whispered. He remained still, an endless beeping ringing in her ears. She took a deep breath and leaned in closer. "John?"

Two eyelids fluttered slightly, still unable to find the strength to open completely. "Lieutenant," he rasped. The faintest hint of a smile played on the president's face. "You came."

"I'm here."

"Sorry...Alex...."

Alex's mouth opened and her eyes filled with tears. "No." She saw his hand twitch and she reached for it. "Stop."

"Listen," he managed.

"John....."

"Mutanabbi...That day...I didn't know," he struggled to breathe.

"Of course not. That was my fault. I should have..."

His lips pursed as he fought to gain enough strength to continue. "No...my fault...all of it...so much you need to know."

"Tell me when you get out of here," she told him through mounting tears.

A slight laugh came from a labored breath. "You need to follow Brackett...Krause..."

"John...what does that..."

His hand squeezed hers. "Follow Krause....Good man.... best friend..."

"What are you..."

"Alex," he called to her.

"I'm here."

"Tell Cassidy...."

"Colonel...."

"Glad she found you." The agent's tears were quickly threatening to become sobs. "Waited for you."

"What are you...."

"Always love you...."

"John...."

"You love them?" He felt her tears fall onto his skin. "Dylan?"

"I do."

14

"Easy to love," he coughed. "Don't trust O'Brien."

"I don't understand."

"Krause," his voice began to fade. "You need to…."

"John, what does Jonathan Krause have to do…"

"Will never let anyone hurt them, just like you…"

"Please, Colonel…John…"

He turned his head slightly and caught sight of the crying woman leaning close to his face. His hand reached up and touched her cheek. "Always love you, Alex."

"I know."

"Be happy," he said summoning another smile as his eyes closed again into silent sleep.

Alex covered her eyes with her left hand and kept the president's in her right. "John. I am so sorry. I don't know what to do. You have to get out of here. Please." She took a deep breath wishing that someone would bequeath her with an answer, some epiphany. Alex gently released her grip on the man she long considered her mentor and best friend; the man who was the father of the boy she now considered her son. How did she get here? She inhaled and allowed the air to fill her lungs, picturing Cassidy in her mind; her refuge. She looked back at him knowing he had always loved her, and understood three things: there was some truth he needed her to discover, he did not expect to see her again, and he wanted her to take care of the son he could never really know. She bent over and placed a soft kiss on his forehead. "I love you too, John," she admitted. It might not have been the admission he had always hoped for, but it was honest and she saw his lips curl. Certain that he knew, she gathered herself and gave his hand a final squeeze. "I'll see you," she whispered before leaving.

***

The sound of breaking glass was almost deafening. Jonathan Krause looked at the cabinet now shattered in front of him.

Red streaks trickled down in spiny lines. "GOD DAMMIT!" he yelled. He moved his bloody hand to cover his watering eyes. If the world could stop spinning, it had now. And, he knew as quickly as it had stopped, soon it would begin to spin uncontrollably. "No stopping it now," he reached for the picture. Speckles fell onto the glass as his thoughts flowed freely. "Brothers, now what? He has no purpose…no courage…Jesus, John."

***

Cassidy sat on the front porch in a large wicker chair filling out what seemed like endless forms and sipping her iced tea. She had the perfect vantage point to keep an eye on Dylan who was determined to climb the small tree in the front yard on his own. She looked up and giggled at his various strategies, a running jump for the branch that was slightly over his head, a standing jump and then a stretching reach. She shook her head slightly and sighed. Alex was on her mind now. The agent would be home soon and Cassidy was certain the short trip would have taken its toll. President John Merrow was special to her lover. She did not know all of the reasons why, but she understood that the president loved Alex and that Alex loved him in her own way. Watching Dylan, Cassidy found herself looking to the heavens for guidance or perhaps absolution. John Merrow was a good man, she thought. He was far more selfless than the man Dylan knew as his father. He was gentle even though he was commanding, not unlike the woman she loved. She laughed at the irony and returned her focus to another paper in her lap. The sound of a car coupled with a familiar voice excitedly screaming Alex's name roused her from her task. As she stood, she noticed that Alex was on her phone and the pensive expression on the agent's face.

The sight unfolding in front of her as she reached the railing nearly took her breath away. Dylan was running toward

Alex. Alex scooped him up and was holding him tightly. There was no doubt now; Alex was crying. Cassidy brought her hand to her mouth. She could feel her body beginning to tremble. Something was very wrong. Almost as if in slow motion she began to make her way off the porch. Alex was kissing the top of Dylan's head and she heard her son ask with genuine concern, "Alex, why are you crying?" The agent pulled back from the boy and held his face in her hands. Her tears were falling at a pace Cassidy had only seen once before; the first night the agent awoke from nightmares about her time in Iraq. Cassidy kept her pace steady as Alex finally lifted her gaze to see her lover approaching.

"Alex?" Cassidy spoke nervously.

The agent forced a heavyhearted smile. "Go climb, Dylan," Alex suggested. He looked at her, not wanting to leave her side. "Go ahead, Speed. I'm just happy to see you. Go on." Reluctantly he turned, continually looking back at the two women he loved. Alex reached for her lover's face as her tears began to fall again.

"Alex?"

The agent shook her head. "He's gone."

It felt to Cassidy as if someone had hit her in the chest. "When?"

"Jane just called. It hasn't been released yet."

"Alex," Cassidy managed as Alex's hands caressed her cheeks.

"I don't understand, Cassidy," Alex's voice cracked and Cassidy stilled herself as she felt the strong woman collapse into her. She held her close as Alex was unable to suppress her emotion.

"I love you," Cassidy assured. "I'm so sorry, Alex."

"Cass..."

"It's okay, Alex. It's all right." Alex held onto Cassidy so tightly that she was sure she was supporting them both fully. "Let's go inside, okay?"

"I'm sorry…Dylan…"

"Dylan will be fine. He just loves you. Come on. I'll have him come inside for now. Let's just go in." Alex nodded. "Dylan!" Cassidy called him over. "Come on, we're going to go in for a bit, okay?" Cassidy smiled as her son willingly complied. She could see the concern on his small face. He loved Alex, and Cassidy could not help but think how proud she was to have a child with such a kind and gentle heart.

Dylan ran up beside the two women and looked up at his hero's face. Alex smiled at him broadly and gestured to him to climb onto her back for a ride. She felt Cassidy's hand slip into hers and she silently spoke to her friend as they headed for the front door. "Yes, Colonel, they are easy to love."

***

Chapter Three

Cassidy sat beside Alex tenderly rubbing her back as the agent held her cell phone to her ear. "Taylor?" Alex asked.

"Alex? Did you see him?"

Alex took a deep breath and swallowed hard. "He's," she paused allowing Cassidy's touch to steady her for a moment. "Jane just called me. He's gone." The silence on the phone was deafening. "Not long after I left. Announcement soon."

"Alex, I don't know what to say," Michael Taylor confessed with a stress and sadness in his voice that was palpable.

"There's more. He, he told me...Follow Brackett and Krause, something about Mutanabbi Street that day. I don't know."

Michael Taylor shifted in his chair. Alex Toles was seldom agitated. John Merrow held a place in both their lives that few could understand. "Okay. Let's just deal with that later. Alex, how are *you*?"

"I don't know."

"Are you home?" he asked.

"Yes."

"Is Cassidy with you?"

"Yeah. She's here." Cassidy kept vigil, gently caressing Alex and silently watching her struggle. Her heart was breaking at the sight before her. "I'm all right," the agent said softly. Cassidy sighed at Alex's words. That was a lie. The heartbreak seemed to pour off the woman beside her.

"Do you know," Taylor began.

"You know what I know right now," the agent said plainly.

Taylor blew out an audible breath. "Let me know…"

"Of course. I promised Jane I would be there. But," Alex looked at her lover and tried to smile.

"Alex?" Taylor called to her gently.

"Yeah…I need to talk to Cass."

"Of course."

"I'll call you later."

"All right. Alex, whatever it is….He loved you; you know that?"

Alex felt as if she were being pressed by heavy weights. It was difficult just to allow air to fill her lungs. "I know," she said quietly. "I'll…."

"Go," he said as he hung up the phone, closing his eyes in disbelief.

Cassidy called gently to the agent. "Alex, honey…." The tall, beautiful woman turned slowly to her lover. Cassidy's eyes reflected so many things to Alex now, concern, pain, disbelief, but most of all an abounding love that she could hardly process. Alex felt Cassidy's hands brush her hair aside and wipe the tear that was streaming down her cheek. "What can I do?" Cassidy asked lovingly.

The agent smiled and took the hand that was holding her face lightly. "Cass, Jane….She wants you and Dylan to come with me for the funeral."

"Okay," Cassidy said. "Whatever you need, you know that." Alex shook her head and held her bottom lip between her teeth. "What? Alex?"

"Cass…She knows." Cassidy did not understand. "About Dylan, Cass."

The teacher's mouth fell slightly open and she wiped her face with her hand. "I don't understand."

"John told her about that night."

"Why?" Cassidy looked at Alex with tears in her eyes.

The agent nodded her understanding. "Listen, I don't know, Cassidy. They've always had a...well a rocky road...but he loved her in his own way."

"Alex, I'm not sure I should..."

"He would have wanted that." Cassidy looked away. "He told me...You two are easy to love."

Cassidy shook her head. "Alex, we were never..."

"I know that. I know what he meant. He meant it for me. He was right. It's your decision. I will support whatever you want to do. There will be so much press, and you know that O'Brien...."

"Alex, what do you want me to do?"

"No. You need to do what you...."

Cassidy saw the answer in the agent's eyes that she expected. "We're going with you."

"Cass, if you..."

The teacher let out a sigh and took both of Alex's hands. "Do you love me, Alex?"

"Cassidy, you know..."

"Do you love me?" Cassidy repeated softly.

"More than anything in my life."

"Hum. Don't you know, Alex," Cassidy faltered. She shut her eyes tightly and then opened them to look directly into blue eyes that had become dark with grief. "When I said I wanted to be with you forever; I meant that."

"I know that," Alex smiled.

"You do?" The agent nodded. "That means through everything. Everything, Alex."

Alex nodded again and kissed her lover's forehead. "Cass?"

Cassidy had her eyes closed reveling in the healing that the slightest touch from this woman seemed to bring. "Hum?"

"Can we just spend tonight with Dylan?"

Cassidy pulled away slightly to look at the agent. "Of course."

"I just...I...."

"Is it because of John and Dyl…"

Alex stopped her lover's thoughts. "I need to be with my family. Both of you." Cassidy offered the agent a cockeyed smile. "Is that okay?" The agent's thought was interrupted by two fingers pressing to her lips.

"You never have to ask if it is all right for us to be together. I just hope you never ask for us to be apart."

Alex smiled. "I just hope we can get to those boring things you mentioned soon."

Cassidy closed one eye and pursed her lips. "I think I have just the remedy for that."

Alex was puzzled. She watched as Cassidy moved across the room and picked up a stack of papers and placed them squarely in her lap. "What's this?" the agent asked in confusion.

"Oh, forms, you know; school stuff." Cassidy watched as Alex thumbed through the pile and noted the look of shock on the agent's face at the number of papers before her. "See? Problem solved. You wanted boring." Alex chuckled earnestly. Cassidy had a way of knowing just what to say or do at any moment. It might only be a momentary diversion, but it was exactly what Alex needed, to see something normal in her life. She looked up at Cassidy and smiled. "What?" Cassidy shrugged in an attempt to lighten the mood.

"Do butlers do paperwork?" Alex asked with the raise of an eyebrow, referring to Cassidy's favorite pet name for the agent; Alfred. Cassidy nodded. "Really?" Alex remarked. "Well, I guess I'd better get to it, huh?" she said, setting the papers on the coffee table.

"I guess you had." Cassidy winked and started to turn away when she felt herself being pulled into Alex's lap. She looked into the agent's eyes and within less than a moment she lost herself there.

"I love you, Cassidy O'Brien," Alex said. "Thank you."

"For?" Cassidy asked, allowing her gaze to linger.

"For everything."

"Je t'adore, Alex."

"Mm...enough to share paperwork," Alex poked.

"Enough to share everything," Cassidy said seriously. Alex nodded her understanding. She felt so much pain and loss, but somehow just a few moments with the woman in her arms and she felt a warmth that she knew would help her to heal. "Everything, Alex."

"Yes, you are," Alex whispered, following her words with a tender kiss.

***

The man at the center of the room stood straight, his posture stiff and guarded. He listened carefully, expressionless. Standing over six feet tall with broad shoulders; his gray hair highlighted his blue eyes and his fair complexion. He was an intimidating presence. "Mr. President," he began, "there are expectations. You understand?"

The newly sworn in president was a far less imposing figure. Lawrence Strickland stood several inches shorter and had a soft manner about him. Always a background player, he now found himself sitting in a chair that had been held by some of the strongest and most savvy men on earth; if not always the most intelligent. What the newly sworn in president possessed was just that, a mind-blowing intellect. If John Merrow had occupied the seat with strength and honor, Lawrence Strickland would claim it with intellect. There were many differences between the two men. Colonel John Merrow believed in loyalty to his country. He understood the need for order, both to give and receive orders. His life was spent not weighing all the pros and cons, but executing plans. His life was not one guided by ambition, but ruled by a sense of duty. Once Governor Strickland was as ambitious as he was intelligent. His sense of duty to anything other than the service of his own desires was questionable. "I understand," Strickland answered.

Jonathan Krause stood at the far side of the Oval Office. His eyes scanned the room. Behind the president's desk still sat his friend's personal photos. It was impossible to control the tension in his face as his eyes narrowed to slits. Pictures of three beautiful women; Jane Merrow, Alexandra and Stephanie Merrow, all three smiling, sat beside a picture of six people, five men and one woman all in Army uniforms, giving the 'thumbs up'. Just behind it stood a photo of the president's parents. He bit the inside of his lip so hard that he could taste the trickle of blood it set forth.

"Jonathan," Lawrence Strickland looked at the man across the room. "I am sorry about John."

Krause's expression was severe. "Jonathan," Admiral Brackett said carefully, prompting a sarcastic smile from the CIA agent. "We have a great deal to do," the Admiral continued. "Sympathy will be high." Krause felt his stomach twist. 'Sympathy,' he silently thought as the admiral went on. "Congress will be hesitant not to pass any measure that the president supported. You need to capitalize on that Larry. Express how important these measures were to him; how much he was committed to our foreign relationships and security. We need that resolution amended. This will, at the very least, delay any vote. There are transactions set for next week. This will provide a needed distraction."

Jonathan Krause struggled not to release a sigh of disgust. In his mind he played his thoughts, "transactions? That's what this is, John. You and me, just transactions."

"I understand," the new president answered.

"Good. You need to address the coming European initiatives with the French Prime Minister when he calls." Strickland nodded. "Accept his wishes and open the dialogue. You need to say very little; he will understand simply by the situation at hand. We cannot allow any tighter port restrictions." Strickland again nodded his understanding. "Jonathan?" the admiral turned to the younger man. "I need you to go to Moscow."

Krause flinched slightly and the commanding admiral pursed his lips. "You know you cannot be at the funeral."

Krause understood. His relationship with John Merrow was not one that most would or could ever know about, at least not those out of these circles. His brother, at least the only man he had ever felt was his brother, was gone and he would mourn that loss alone. There was no choice. There were only two people in Jonathan Krause's life that he ever completely trusted; only two people that he could claim he truly loved. One was now gone and the other would never give him her heart. It did not change the fact that they both held his. Duty. He and his brother were destined for duty. This was his duty. There was little room in a life that was centered on following orders for love. John Merrow once told him that falling in love changed everything. The brick wall that one erects as a strong façade in a life bound by duty becomes a pane of glass when a person falls in love. The constant threat of shatter becomes a heart-wrenching reality. The CIA agent looked at his hand. The long scratches were still a fiery red from the glass he had shattered with his knuckles earlier. "Appropriate," he thought. Again, the wheels were turning. They had never stopped. Only for a few people, for a few moments. Now they would spin again and Krause wondered if that spinning could ever truly be controlled.

***

"Cassidy, be reasonable," Christopher O'Brien said through the phone.

"It's perfectly reasonable, Christopher."

"Do you really hate me that much?" he asked.

"This may come as a surprise to you, but everything I do is not about you," Cassidy answered.

"Obviously. I'd like to see Dylan when you get here."

"Of course," she said. "We're coming back Sunday afternoon. I figured you would want him to be with you Saturday."

"Saturday night?"

"Yes...."

"That's not good for me."

"I'm sorry?" the teacher asked for clarification.

"There is a dinner at Senator Levy's Saturday. I need to be there."

Cassidy shook her head and let out a sarcastic chuckle. "Of course you do."

"Don't start, Cassie."

"No, Chris...really....it's fine. Take him for the day then."

"Why can't he just stay Friday?" the congressman asked. "I'll take him after the funeral."

"No."

"No?" he responded.

"Right. No."

"Why not?" he raised his voice.

Cassidy sighed. "We are spending Friday evening with friends of Alex's."

"I don't think friends of Alex's trump Dylan's father."

"Chris..."

"Who are these *friends*?"

Cassidy moved to the front window and watched Alex boost Dylan onto the lowest branch of the small tree. "We will be with the Merrows."

"I'm sorry?" he asked.

"Christopher, you know that Alex was close to the president."

"I know they knew each other."

"Well, no matter. I'll bring him over on Saturday."

"Cassidy, we need to talk about *this*."

"Talk about what?"

"You and this FBI agent. What are you going to do when she...."

Cassidy laughed. "Chris, there is nothing for us to discuss. Give Cheryl my regards. We'll see you at the funeral."

Congressman Christopher O'Brien threw his phone across the desk. "FBI bitch," he muttered.

***

Michael Taylor stared at the photo in his hands. "Mutanabbi," he said aloud. "What the hell, Colonel? What is it about Mutanabbi Street?" He set down the picture and retrieved a file from the corner of his desk. A slight gasp escaped him as he surveyed the photo of the carnage. The street was unrecognizable. Papers littered the ground, dust lingered in the air and blood stained nearly everything in sight. "How did we even survive?" he mused to himself. "Shit. Colonel, what the hell is it about that day? What could you want Alex to know?" He sifted through the papers, searching. "Dammit!" A burst of anger sent the files soaring across the desk and he rubbed his temples with his palms. "Brackett. Follow Brackett. What the hell could Agent Brackett know?" Taylor shook his head and pushed his chair back. "Follow Brackett. Not Claire.....that's it......it's not Claire he meant."

***

Chapter Four

"*Victor, ya tam budu zavtro. Net...netu povoda tebe deystvovat. Zhdi menya* (Viktor, I will be there tomorrow. No...There is no reason for you to act. Wait for me)," Krause instructed.

"*Yesli frantsuzy ne soglasiatsa* (If the French will not comply)," Viktor Ivanov answered.

"Enough, Viktor. Edmond will handle that situation. There has been enough bloodshed," Jon Krause said.

"Do I sense hesitation, my friend?" the Russian answered.

"You sense caution, Viktor. Don't be rash. This is not the time," Krause responded. He held a large envelope in his hands, turning it endlessly. "Reaction is not the same as action."

"Very well. You must understand what we..."

Krause studied the envelope in his hand. "I understand fully. We have already taken unnecessary risks."

"You do not agree with the actions?" the Russian inquired.

"Whether or not I agree does not matter. It has opened a dangerous path that someone will want to follow."

Viktor Ivanov considered the statement. "It is not the first time, Jonathan."

"No. But it is a different time, Viktor. A very different time." Krause began to unseal the large envelope. "I will see you tomorrow."

***

"I don't understand," Claire Brackett raised her voice to the man across from her.

"What don't you understand, Claire?" her father answered.

"You had John killed?"

"Claire, I am surprised at you."

"Well?"

The admiral's temple twitched. "You almost sound as if you had feelings for the man. Did you?"

The young redhead's gaze blazed now. "What is your point?"

"Claire, what are you doing with O'Brien?"

"What do you think I am doing with the congressman?" she shot back.

"Be careful, Claire. O'Brien is hardly John Merrow."

"Now who sounds like they had feelings for him?"

The admiral stood and straightened his posture. He looked out the large window at the side of his office and considered his words. With a lick of his lips and a heavy sigh he turned back to his daughter. "John Merrow was a man of integrity, Claire. He was a soldier and a leader and he, better than anyone, understood the risks of our work. None of us are indispensable. None of us. Men like O'Brien do not see that. Men like Strickland, now."

"Well, then…you'll forgive my confusion," she said.

The admiral smiled. His daughter possessed many of the attributes that made for an excellent agent. She was highly intelligent, physically coordinated, and she was a master manipulator. The one thing that the admiral hated to admit, but was growing to understand more daily, was that his daughter did not feel a sense of commitment, but rather entitlement. That concerned him. For Claire, this was an elaborate game. Perhaps it was, but the stakes were nothing short of life and death and John Merrow was hardly the first casualty; nor would he be the last. The admiral took stock of the woman before him. She was no simple child anymore. He deliberately walked toward her and stood just a pace away. "John Merrow was like a son to me, Claire."

"Doesn't say much for my future, does it Daddy," was her acerbic reply.

"It says that we make choices, Claire. You keep an eye on O'Brien, but you keep your head where it belongs," he ordered.

"Yes, sir."

"Don't be a smart ass. You opened this can of worms when you decided to keep playing with Fisher."

"I thought you wanted things kept in the *family*," she answered his accusation with a sarcastic confidence.

"You presume many things. Fisher was cut loose for a reason."

"Well, than why get him FBI credentials?" The admiral smiled knowingly. "You set me up." He shrugged. "Why would you do that?" she asked.

"It's a reminder, Claire. You may be my daughter but you still have your orders and I have my reasons. Careful. Toles will be watching."

"You son of a bitch."

"Call it my insurance policy," he said. "Stay in line. Taylor and Toles are a dangerous combination. You keep O'Brien away from her, understand?"

"That might not be as simple...."

His gaze narrowed. "Make it easy. Toles saw Merrow before he died."

"So? Why not just take out...."

"Take out Agent Toles? Don't think I haven't thought of that. Not in our best interest. She is smarter than you think. And, there is more."

"What more?" the young woman asked skeptically.

"I'm not convinced NSA took out Fisher."

"Of course they did," she said.

"Mm. Things are not always as they appear, Claire. I thought you were smarter than that. You watch O'Brien. Threaten him if you have to."

"We did that."

"No. Threaten *him*. Make him feel it…where it hurts."

"You mean his career?"

"I mean you do whatever you have to so that he does not fire up Toles anymore than she already is."

***

Alex walked out of Dylan's room and shut the door quietly. It had been a long few days. Her nightmares were back and for the last few nights she had only been able to sleep when Cassidy would rock her. She felt like a helpless child, but she had no control over the way that the dreams would awaken her. Tomorrow they would need to leave for Washington. Dylan would need to be back Monday to start school and Alex hated to admit that she dreaded his absence during the days. She had hoped that her reinstatement to the bureau would happen quickly, but with the president gone things were more uncertain than ever. "Cass?" she called into the kitchen and heard a voice call back from below.

"Down here!"

Alex followed her lover's voice down the stairs. She stopped halfway and a smile swept over her face. Cassidy was standing behind the pool table racking the balls, a familiar long denim shirt falling down her form. "What are you doing?" the agent asked.

The teacher shrugged. "I recall…You owe me a lesson."

"Uh-huh. So you want me to teach you to play pool? Honestly?" Cassidy offered the agent a playful glance. Alex chuckled and shook her head. She needed some levity. She needed Cassidy, and somehow the woman across the room seemed to understand that. She finished the short trek down the stairs and took the triangle from the teacher's hands, allowing her hand to brush over her lover's. "Okay, first; watch." Cassidy complied happily, watching as Alex ordered the balls and shook the plastic triangle gently around them. "Now, you have to learn how to break." Alex guided Cassidy to the other end of the table and took a place behind her. "You know, I think maybe you just want an excuse to get me to hold you," Alex flirted.

"Oh? Is that what you think?" Cassidy could feel her heart beat beginning to race and she bit her lip gently to try and slow her breath. "You just get on with this lesson. I am tired of you and Dylan making fun of me," Cassidy said.

Alex leaned into her lover and whispered her instructions, "then you promise me we finish this game."

"Are you implying that I cannot resist you?" Cassidy asked keeping her eyes on the table.

"I might be implying that I can't resist you," Alex answered.

Cassidy closed her eyes. "We finish the game."

"All right," Alex smiled. "Then listen carefully. Feel that?" Alex lifted the cue in Cassidy's grip and Cassidy nodded. "Okay, now look ahead." The agent helped the smaller woman prepare, breathing each instruction into her ear. Cassidy was determined to remain focused; knowing that Alex intended to try and break her concentration any way that she could. The cue pulled back and the balls flew across the table with a loud 'click'. Cassidy jumped up in excitement. "Pool it is," Alex laughed.

The game continued and Alex settled into contentment teaching her lover. She reveled in the closeness of every instruction and could tell by the way Cassidy moved that she did as well. Watching her lover smile and cheer with excitement as she completed shots delighted the agent. In little time Cassidy was largely on her own and Alex's eyes sparkled watching the woman she loved. She stood back now as Cassidy walked to the table and lined up her shot. Alex enjoyed the competitive side she saw in her lover. Now it was the eight ball. Alex was certain that Cassidy suspected she was taking it easy on her. Nevertheless, the agent looked forward to her lover's expression when she won. Alex leaned on her cue and marveled at the intensity in Cassidy's eyes as the teacher gracefully moved the cue back and forth, just as she had been instructed. The ball flew across the table, effortlessly finding its way into the pocket. Cassidy jumped up and across the room directly into Alex's arms. The agent erupted in genuine laughter. "Geez, Cass, I wish I got you that excited." Cassidy giggled and looked into Alex's eyes. "You are so beautiful," Alex whispered.

"You let me win," Cassidy admitted with a smile, wrapping her hands around Alex's neck.

"Nah. You won fair and square. Fast learner," Alex complimented.

"Is that right?" Cassidy lifted an eyebrow.

"Um-hum."

"You're a good teacher."

"You think so?" Cassidy nodded. "I'll take that as a compliment from the best teacher I know."

"What are you sucking up for?" Cassidy flirted. Alex leaned in and kissed the woman in her arms. Hearing the sigh that escaped from her lover, Alex kissed Cassidy more deeply and lifted her onto the pool table. "You know this pool table wasn't cheap," Cassidy said with a smirk.

"Lesson two, it's called running the table."

"Really?" Cassidy questioned. Alex nodded. "Hum. Can't say I've heard that," Cassidy joked.

"Still a novice," the agent grinned, her fingers now addressing the buttons on the denim shirt as Cassidy's hands wrapped themselves gently in the agent's falling hair. Alex pulled back and whispered softly in her lover's ear, "I need you."

"Show me," Cassidy whispered back. Alex caught her breath and let her kisses trail along her lover's neck. "Alex…"

"Shhh," Alex caressed the soft cheek before her and drank in the desire she saw in Cassidy's eyes. As always, Alex was mesmerized. Right now all she felt was this woman she loved so completely; there were no words. There was no pain in this moment, no fear, only Cassidy. "Cassidy, *je t'aime plus que je ne pourrais jamais te le montrer* (I love you more than I could ever show you)."

Cassidy held Alex's face in her hands. "*Tu me le montre a chaque instant* (you show me every moment)." She felt Alex lean over her and closed her eyes. Whatever lay ahead, all that mattered was this moment. There was no choice but to surrender to the need and the desire that filled them both now. There was nothing to compare. It was not a typical moment. Nothing in their lives now was typical, and it only served to remind them that there remained one refuge; one another's arms. "Alex," Cassidy managed as Alex held her close though wave after wave of an ecstasy she once thought existed only in imagination.

"*Tu es mon monde* (you are my world)," Alex said as she felt her own body succumb. "I love you, Cass."

***

"You ready?" Cassidy asked gently. "Alex?" The agent offered a halfhearted smile and the teacher sighed. They had shared an amazing night making love, holding each other, laughing, even crying. "Why don't I go move Dylan along?"

Alex shook her head. "I'll go." Cassidy's brow furrowed slightly. "It's okay, Cass." Alex started out of the room and then turned back to look at the teacher.

"What is it?" Cassidy asked.

"Ask me when we get home," Alex winked.

"Alex?" The agent just smiled more broadly and turned to leave.

"I promise I will tell you then," she whispered as she crossed the hallway.

"I can't wait to find out," Cassidy called out.

"I knew you'd hear that," Alex called back.

Cassidy laughed. "I love you, Alex Toles," she said quietly as she closed her bag. "More than I can even believe."

***

Chapter Five

"Yes, Mr. President. I understand."

"Congressman," President Strickland continued. "Sympathy is our ally, do you really understand?"

"Of course," Christopher O'Brien answered.

"There is great sympathy for *all* that President Merrow dedicated himself to and all that he loved."

"The measures will not be a problem," the congressman said.

"No. I don't expect they will be. Nevertheless I need you in place."

O'Brien was confused. "I'm sorry; I am not following you."

"Your ex-wife; she has the public's affection."

"I'm not certain what that...."

President Strickland sighed. "Chris, it will become apparent; the relationship..."

"I did my best to compel her not to continue..."

"Congressman, I meant the longtime relationship that Agent Toles had with the president. Jane Merrow has requested Agent Toles and her family be with the Merrow family at the funeral. You really don't know much about this; do you?"

"Cassidy and I don't talk about..."

"I'm sure," Strickland chuckled. "Agent Toles saved the president's life, or that is how he told it. Be cautious. That is likely to be in the press soon and it will only increase the affection for your ex-wife."

"And who would put that in the press?" the congressman asked in frustration. The president remained silent. "I see. What do you gain by making her a hero?"

"Just take my advice. I want you to make a trip Monday."

"A trip? You do realize I am still not...."

"France. Be ready. It's time," Strickland commanded.

"France?"

"That's right. You'll get the details Saturday at Senator Levy's." The president smiled as he caressed the top of his desk, surveying the office he had coveted for so long. "This is my ship now, Congressman. Make nice at the funeral." Congressman O'Brien swallowed hard as he heard the phone click. Whatever this trip was for, the only thing he could be certain of was that it would put him at greater risk. Strickland benefited from spending so many years quietly in the background. It allowed him to leverage relationships and he had many people who owed him. Christopher O'Brien was at the top of that list and his debt was just called in as due.

***

Cassidy looked beside her at the tall, attractive woman in the next seat. Alex was contentedly watching Dylan as he gazed out of the airplane window. Cassidy could not remove her sight from the two people that she loved the most. She wondered what was going through her lover's mind. "Alex?" Cassidy called gently. She could see Alex's lip curling into the hint of a smile but Alex remained silent. She reached over and touched the agent's arm. "Honey?" The endearment sparked the agent to turn and the smile she offered Cassidy, while solemn, was broad. "What?" Cassidy asked softly.

"You."

"Me?" Cassidy asked. "I didn't do anything."

"Yes; you did." Alex kissed her lover on the cheek.

"Alex, what were you thinking about just now?"

"I was thinking…how much Dylan is like you."

"Like me? Really?"

"Um hum." Alex looked back at the boy who was oblivious to everything around him and was leaning his small face as close to the window as possible. "He is. I'm glad you are both with me," Alex confessed, prompting Cassidy to take her hand and squeeze it gently. Alex returned the warm gesture and moved to look out the window with the small boy again.

"Alex?" Dylan asked when he felt her head take up residence over his own.

"Yeah, Speed?"

"How can you fly through a cloud when you can't see?"

Alex smiled. "Well, that's a good question. I'm not a pilot."

"Do you think I could fly an airplane?" he asked.

"I think you could do just about anything you wanted, Dylan." Cassidy listened and took a deep breath, laying her head against the seat and tenderly rubbing Alex's hand with her thumb.

"But planes are really big, Alex. How can they stay up here?"

"You know, Speed. I have a feeling there are a couple of people you might like to talk to while we are in Washington."

"How come?" Dylan asked.

"Well, my friend, John…you know; the president? He had some friends who are pilots." Dylan turned wide eyed to the woman beside him. "Yeah, he did," Alex continued. "You like cars and planes, huh?" The boy nodded. "Yeah, so did John." Alex felt Cassidy's grip reflexively tighten. "There will be some people there who fly *really* fast planes."

"Can I go with them?" he asked hopefully.

Alex laughed. "I don't know about *that*, Speed. But, I'll bet you could ask them your questions." Dylan smiled and returned his focus to the window.

"Alex?"

"Yeah, Speed?"

"How come the president died?"

Alex took a deep breath and felt Cassidy's hand hold hers firmly. "Oh, Dylan; I wish I had an answer."

"Somebody shot him," he said.

"Yes."

"Why? He wasn't a bad guy, he's the president."

Alex nodded and looked into Dylan's eyes as he turned to her. "Dylan, sometimes people do things that hurt other people. I don't know why. Maybe because they are lost or sad or angry."

"But you stop them," Dylan said proudly.

The agent smiled at his innocence. "I try. People who do what I do, we try."

"Alex?" Alex just looked at him. "People shouldn't hurt other people."

"No, Dylan; they shouldn't."

"He was nice to me."

"I know he was. I'm sure he liked you," Alex assured him.

"He gave me a plane once." Cassidy looked at the pair beside her and felt her heart drop as she listened.

"He did?" Alex asked with genuine curiosity.

"Yeah. Just like his." Alex chuckled at the story. It did not surprise her. John Merrow loved planes and he loved children, especially his own.

Cassidy recalled that day well. They had been at a fund-raiser. She had lost Dylan momentarily and when she captured sight of him again, she found the president on his knees talking to her son. She had watched as President Merrow handed her son the toy replica of Air Force One and noted the wide smile on both faces as he explained the different parts of the aircraft to Dylan. At four, Dylan was just thrilled to have some attention and a toy. When the president began to rise he noticed Cassidy watching and offered her a smiling acknowledgment. It was a moment she had not given much thought to in years. Now, it seemed to her it would be a moment she would never forget. The agent felt the tension in her lover's grip and glanced across to see the tear falling down Cassidy's cheek. "Well, Dylan," Alex said. "I know that the president would be so happy to know that you remember that." Dylan smiled and looked back out the window. "Cass?" Alex turned her lover.

"I forgot about that day."

"No, you just haven't had a reason to recall it."

Cassidy shook her head. "He's like me, huh?"

The agent squeezed the teacher's hand. "Yep. Smart, sensitive, funny, good looking, and asks a lot of questions." Cassidy laughed. "Just like his mother," Alex finished. The teacher let out a sigh. "It'll be okay, Cass. I promise."

"Alex?" Cassidy asked.

"What?"

"What didn't you want to tell me this morning?"

"Oh no, nice try. See what I mean? Two of a kind." Cassidy laughed and put her head on Alex's shoulder as the agent returned her focus to the clouds rolling by outside.

***

Agent Brian Fallon sat across the desk from NSA Director Michael Taylor. "Agent Fallon," Taylor began. "Do you understand the risks involved in this?" Brian Fallon nodded his understanding. "These people; this is not your run off the mill psychos. These people are connected. Connected to everything that makes the world tick. Some might say they are the reason it ticks at all."

"I understand," Fallon answered.

"Fallon, you have three kids. Have you considered…"

"Look," Fallon said. "I do understand. I can't just walk away. Alex…"

Michael Taylor nodded. "She has that effect on people, makes them do things they once thought crazy. She's not going to like…"

"Well," Fallon began, "whether or not she likes it, she'll need to accept it."

Taylor smiled. "I'll talk to her Saturday."

"I can tell her…"

"No." Michael Taylor shook his head. "I'll tell her Saturday afternoon. Just be ready."

***

"Alex, I didn't know we were staying here," Cassidy smiled.

"Yeah, well, Jane insisted. She figured we had been here so…"

Cassidy was relieved to be at the condo in Arlington again. This place had become a sanctuary of sorts after the congressman's automobile accident. The time she had spent here with Alex had some happy memories attached to it and she suspected that no matter what the agent said; Alex was responsible for the family being here now. Tomorrow was not a day that she was looking forward to. Alex had suggested that she invite her mother to travel with them, but Cassidy declined the offer. She needed to confront her own truth. There was very little that she did not share with her mother. Her indiscretion with John Merrow was one of those few things. "Thank you," Cassidy said.

"Why don't you go up and take a rest," Alex suggested.

"What about you?"

"Cass, Dylan is already exhausted and so are you. Go take a nap with him. I have a couple of things I want to do. I'll bring dinner back; all right?"

Cassidy was reluctant but she was tired and so was Dylan. She kissed Alex on the cheek and smiled sweetly. "Where are you going?"

"Just up the road."

"Alex…"

"Don't worry. Go rest. I'll be back in a couple of hours. You won't even know I was gone."

Cassidy closed one eye and twisted her lip. She touched Alex's cheek and planted a soft but firm kiss on the agent's lips.

"I always know when you are gone," she said as she turned to make her way up the stairs.

Alex grabbed the keys to the rental car and made her way to the door. She turned back but Cassidy was already heading down the upstairs hallway. "I hope you know how much I love you," she said quietly opening the door.

"I do," Cassidy called back, soliciting a hearty laugh from the agent. "I love you too, Alfred. Don't forget dinner."

***

Alex walked up the winding hill that led toward the amphitheater. A small trolley passed by and she studied the faces within it as they gazed out over a garden of white stone. It amazed her that this place was somehow a tourist attraction. For Alex, it was a place for solitude and reflection, for memory and for grieving. Tomorrow she would visit here again within a sea of cameras and politicians, military officers and dignitaries. She had visited this place many times with her friend John Merrow before he had become the president. Just before the amphitheater she turned to the left, but not before stopping to consider the scene unfolding over the rise to her right. She could hear the click of the heels in the distance. It was the honor of an unknown soldier, a face that would not be returned yet always remembered. Alex paused. In this place she felt like Lieutenant Toles once again; that young somewhat idealistic officer who lost a piece of her soul in a busy market place in Iraq. Just over the rise to the left she could see the busy scene of preparation. She took a deep breath and closed her eyes. It was not supposed to be this way.

A few more paces found the agent ducking under a rope and standing under a tall oak tree. A few leaves were just beginning to peek out on the branches, but winter had left its mark and the mid-day sun filtered in long streaking patterns onto the ground surrounding her. She ran her hand over the top of the rough, white stone. "Jackson," Alex whispered as she traced the grooves in the lieutenant's name, Lieutenant Robert Jackson. "The colonel, I don't understand. It doesn't make sense." She looked out again to see the ropes being raised for what would be a somber event the next day. "What happened that day, Jackson? It was my fault. I should have known. There were so many signs. So many. All the chatter; why didn't I hear it? Now he tells me it was his fault...and he's gone. I don't understand. That day...why did you come with us? You never came. I don't understand R.J." Her thoughts trailed off momentarily. "Mutanabbi, Jackson; what is it about that bookstore?" Alex took in a deep breath and exhaled with some force, shaking her head as a slight chuckle erupted. "Now you will be looking out over him. Colonel, Jackson is watching over you," she laughed through some tears. "I wish you were here, Jackson. I'm tired of goodbyes. You know you said I needed to learn to love," she laughed. "I did. Took me some time. I wish you could see her R.J. And, Dylan? Crazy, he's so much like her; gentle, kind....and he's like his father." Alex closed her eyes tightly. "I'm sorry I haven't visited. I miss you. Just point me...point me there." The agent ran her hand over the stone one last time and stared at the scene just below. "Colonel," she whispered. "I don't understand."

***

Chapter Six

Jonathan Krause turned the folded paper in his hands several times before opening it again. He stared at the sheet and shook his head. "Oh, Cassie," he said quietly. "John, why didn't you tell me?" Again he surveyed the paper before folding it neatly and placing it in his jacket pocket. "How did we get here?" he asked aloud. A soft buzz startled him and he lifted the phone to his ear. "Viktor, ten o'clock. Meet me at the hotel." He hung up and closed his eyes again. After a deep breath, he silently walked across the room and made his way to pour a glass of straight scotch. He lifted his glass into the air and spoke. "To brothers. I promise, John. They'll stay safe. All of them." He brought the glass to his lips and downed the offering. "Brothers forever. You have my oath; just like my own son."

***

Friday, April 11th

Alex turned the corner and saw Cassidy sitting on the bed with her face in her hands. She was wearing a simple yet elegant back dress and Alex paused to take in the sight. Even in the most trying moment, Cassidy was beautiful. "Cass," she called gently.

The small blonde woman removed her hands and lifted her sight to the tall agent. Alex looked amazing, regal, Cassidy thought. The agent stood tall in her Army dress blues with a low heel that elevated her already considerable height. Cassidy

45

was stunned at the presentation of ribbons that graced her jacket. There was a quiet confidence about Alex that took the teacher's breath away. "You are beautiful," the teacher said simply. "And tall," Cassidy tried to joke.

"You ready?" Alex asked, gently caressing the smaller woman's shoulders. Cassidy let out a heavy breath. "The car will be here any minute," the agent said. "Do you want me to go get Dylan?"

"No. I'll get him. Meet you downstairs in a few minutes."

The agent smiled and walked from the room hand in hand with her lover. As Cassidy turned to enter the room Dylan was in, Alex spoke. "Cass, it will be all right. I promise."

"Dylan?" Cassidy called to the small boy who was sitting on the floor. "We need to get you ready, sweetie. Okay?"

He nodded and put aside his action figure. "Mom?"

"Yes, honey?"

"Alex was crying this morning."

Cassidy sighed. "She was?"

"Yeah. I saw her."

"Well, Alex is sad. She lost someone she loved very much."

He thought about his mother's words. "You were crying too."

"Dylan, I love Alex. It makes me very sad to see her upset."

"Me too," he said hanging his head while his mother clipped the small black tie to his shirt. "Should I cry?" he asked honestly.

His mother smiled and straightened his tie. "You should do whatever you feel in your heart, Dylan. It's okay to cry and it's okay if you don't cry. You do whatever you feel." Cassidy smiled at her son as he slipped on his shoes and she retrieved the small jacket laying across the bed. "Come on, Alex is waiting for us." She offered her hand to her son who accepted it willingly. "I love you, Dylan."

***

46

Alex exited the car as the driver opened Cassidy's door. She looked up at the White House, disbelief coloring her thoughts. In just a short time they would make their way to the National Cathedral before heading to Arlington; John Merrow's final journey. Alex watched as Cassidy positioned Dylan in front of her. It was difficult for the agent to fathom all that she had lost and all that she had gained in such a short time. She smiled at the woman who held her heart and put out her hand. Cassidy accepted it with a loving smile of her own. Silence seemed an ally in this moment. Dylan reached for the agent and Alex guided him between them as they entered the White House. Just through the door a young woman stood talking to the new president. "Alex," she called.

"Steph," Alex smiled. Stephanie Merrow was John Merrow's eldest daughter. She was twenty-three and a striking beauty herself; tall, with long auburn hair and hazel eyes that always seemed to twinkle. Alex couldn't help but notice how much the young woman had grown to resemble both her parents. She came even with the young woman and stopped to regard the man beside her. "Mr. President," Alex greeted.

"Captain Toles," President Strickland returned her greeting. "Been a while." Alex nodded. "I am sorry to see you again under these circumstances," he added. Alex motioned for Cassidy and Dylan to move toward the group. "Cassidy," President Strickland extended his hand with a smile. "How are you?"

Cassidy returned his pleasantries. These were circles that she had long traveled in and circles that she missed very little. "Mr. President."

Stephanie Merrow looked at the teacher and then at the small boy. She and Cassidy had crossed paths a few times on the campaign trail. "Dylan, you grew," Stephanie offered.

Dylan beamed. "I'm seven," he said. All three women laughed.

John Merrow's daughter looked at Alex and took her hand. "I'm glad you are here," she said fighting back her tears. "And

47

looking as I remember," she smiled at the uniform. "My mother is in the other room."

"How's she doing?" Alex asked.

The young woman shrugged. "Officer's wife, you know." Alex chuckled. Jane Merrow was a strong woman in her own right and she knew the role that she both needed and was expected to play. "Come on," Stephanie said as she excused the group and led them to the room where the remainder of the Merrow clan and friends waited.

Cassidy felt her stomach beginning to churn wildly. Noticing the apprehension on her face, Alex reached for her hand. Jane Merrow immediately caught sight of the group as they entered the room and a genuine smile swept over her expression. Deliberately and gracefully she walked over and took the agent into an embrace. "Alex," she said. "How he would love to see Captain Toles." Pulling back she looked at Cassidy whose face gave away her uneasiness. Cassidy had always liked and admired the president's wife and she had carried a great deal of guilt in her heart for her betrayal with John Merrow. Jane Merrow moved closer and put her hands on Cassidy's arms. "Thank you for coming with her, Cassidy." Cassidy just smiled weakly. The tall, elegant woman looked down at the boy standing between them and studied his face. "Well Dylan, look how big you have gotten."

"He's seven," Stephanie winked.

"Are you?" Jane Merrow asked the boy, receiving an enthusiastic nod. "Now, how did that happen?"

"I had a birthday," he said plainly.

"I know you did," the woman said looking back to Cassidy before returning her attention to him. "Alex tells me that you like superheroes?" He nodded. "I'll bet. Who is your favorite?"

"Batman," he said.

Jane Merrow's smile grew wider. "Batman *is* pretty cool."

"Yeah," he said looking proudly at the woman standing beside him in her uniform. "He has Alfred and I have Alex."

"Well, then," the woman said, "I would say you are both very lucky." She let out a small sigh and looked at Alex. "I'm glad you are here, all of you." Jane Merrow looked back at the small boy and then at his mother. "Alex has always been part of this family, and so are you," she said to Cassidy with a light squeeze of the younger woman's arm before turning back to the entourage seated around the room.

***

Christopher O'Brien climbed into the car beside his companion. It was a short ride to the cathedral and his mind was preoccupied now with seeing his ex-wife and her new partner; both with his son. He let out a sigh of frustration that prompted the woman beside him to take notice. "What's wrong?" she asked.

He shook his head and flashed a smile. "Nothing."

"You are thinking about her, aren't you?"

"I'm thinking about Dylan," he said.

"Yeah, I'm sure that's it, Chris."

"What is that supposed to mean?"

"Why does it bother you so much?" Cheryl Stephens asked her lover.

"It doesn't *bother* me. I'm worried about Dylan."

Cheryl shook her head. She remained jealous of Cassidy O'Brien, but she did know that Cassidy was a good mother and a decent human being. She wanted to dislike the teacher, but in spite of her efforts it remained impossible for her to do so. Cassidy had never shown the congressman's new girlfriend anything but respect and kindness. Cheryl was relieved to see that the teacher had a new person in her life. "Well, I don't know why you would worry about Dylan. Cassidy would never do anything to hurt him."

"Maybe not deliberately," he said with a tone of malice.

"Maybe you should ask yourself what this is really about," she said sharply as she turned to look out the window.

"What does that mean?"

"Just what I said," she replied. "If you don't want Cassidy back and if you know Dylan is fine...well, I guess that only leaves one possibility."

The congressman shook his head. "I'm not the enemy, Cheryl."

"No. Not mine anyway."

***

The sound of the drum cadence as it filtered through from the outside of the car was deafening to Alex. The streets were lined with people watching the procession and she mindlessly shook her head as the car passed them by. "I can't believe this," she whispered to herself. Cassidy looked over and put her hand on Alex's knee. "Cass, look."

"I know," Cassidy acknowledged softly.

Dylan maneuvered himself onto the agent's lap and peered out the window. "Alex? How come all those people are watching?"

Alex sighed. "Well, Dylan, the president is an important person. In some ways he belongs to all the people and so they all feel they have lost him too."

"But they didn't know him," he observed.

"No. Not really," Alex said. "But sometimes you can love someone that you never really knew." He was confused and the agent smiled. "I know that doesn't make sense, does it?" He shook his head and Alex leaned over and kissed the top of it. "It's true, Speed."

***

Alex and Cassidy walked past the congressman and his girl-friend toward their seats at the front of the cathedral. Dylan looked over and gave his father a small wave, receiving a smile and a nod in return. Cassidy smiled at her ex-husband and gripped her son's hand a little tighter when she felt Alex's arm wrap around her waist. The congressman struggled to hide a surfacing cringe and he slipped his hand into his girlfriend's. Cassidy chuckled within. "He'll never change," she thought silently.

***

The procession through Arlington Cemetery seemed to last an eternity. Much like the streets from Pennsylvania Avenue to the Cathedral; the sides were lined more than ten deep with onlookers. Mothers held their children as men and women alike wept at the sight of the flag draped coffin passing by. The car could not shield its passengers from the sounds that echoed outside. The drum cadence, the sound of tears as they fell from thousands of eyes, the clipping of shoes as they hit the ground in an eerily timed rhythm; it penetrated Alex's soul and transported her to another time.

Cassidy watched Alex carefully. She felt as if her soul were somehow being scorched. She could see the deep pain coursing through her lover. Part of it, Cassidy understood, was this place. Late in the night Alex had been awakened by another dream and she confessed to Cassidy that this is where she had gone that afternoon. She had come to see a friend, before she had to leave another behind. There were parts of Alex Toles' life that Cassidy could only share through the agent's recollections and there was nothing that the teacher wished more than that she could have held Alex through it all. "Alex?" she called over as the car came to a stop.

The agent turned and offered her lover a solemn smile. "Let's go." Dylan followed his mother as Alex turned to meet her new family. She paused momentarily to look up the slight hill at the tall oak tree above. She had hoped it would be many years before she would hear that drum beat again in this place.

The few short steps that they would travel to the president's final resting place seemed an endless journey for Alex. She stood a few feet behind John Merrow's family, listening to the clicks of cameras that filled the air and was amazed at how the lights from them eclipsed the midday sun. The words that poured from the minister's mouth ran over her, never making their way into her mind. She heard the sounds around her, but in her thoughts she could only speak silently to the man she considered her best friend. John Merrow had loved her beyond what was reasonable and she needed to understand why; why she was standing here now. "Colonel, why? What is this all about? You tell me these things and you leave…How can you do that now? What about Dylan?" She combed her silent thoughts for any reason.

To anyone, except Cassidy O'Brien, Alex Toles appeared the picture of confidence and control. She was Captain Alexis Toles and she emanated strength and power. The small, unassuming blonde woman who stood nearby could see every question rolling through the agent's mind. A bugle was raised and Cassidy watched as the rise and fall in Alex's chest became more rapid and shallow. John Merrow meant something to them both, in very different ways. It was over almost as quickly as it began. The time for goodbye had finally arrived. Dylan looked up and saw the tear that rolled over the agent's cheek. Alex did not change her stance, nor did she lift her hand to wipe it away. Straight and proud she stood as the trail of her tear continued. The small boy looked at the woman next to him and he reached for her hand, slipping his into hers as an innocent attempt at comfort. As the Merrow family began to turn, Alex lowered her gaze to his small eyes. His eyes conveyed without a single word how much he loved the woman holding his hand. She squeezed Dylan's hand gently and then lifted him to her hip. "Don't cry, Alex," he whispered. "I love you."

His mother looked at the pair beside her and immediately noticed the tear that was rolling over her son's cheek. His love for Alex was as great as hers. Jane Merrow looked back from her car and regarded the threesome. Alex's hand was tenderly taking hold of Cassidy's as Dylan began sliding down the agent's hip to come to rest between them, breaking their momentary affection with the grasp of each of their hands in his. Three pairs of eyes simultaneously saying only one thing; 'I love you.' "Oh John," she whispered before turning to her silent thoughts. "I wish you were here. How strange they found each other. It shouldn't have had to be this way." She slipped into her seat and smiled at her daughters. "So much lost and so much yet to be discovered," she thought. "I do you love you, John...still."

Chapter Seven

"Viktor, the admiral has things well in hand," Jon Krause said to his Russian counterpart. He had long regarded Viktor Ivanov as an impetuous man with antiquated views about the world. In Jonathan Krause's mind that made Ivanov a liability that needed to be controlled. He had little doubt that the Russian contingent of their group was the driving force behind the decision to assassinate John Merrow. That only served to increase the CIA agent's distrust of the man before him now. Ivanov was neither an agent nor was he a leader. He was, simply put, a businessman. That lowered Krause's respect another degree. Loyalty was not a word in Viktor Ivanov's vocabulary. Krause often mused that if Ivanov thought he could make more money; he would sell his own child.

"Be that as it may, Mr. Krause...You must understand that our vulnerability is much higher than yours," Ivanov said.

"Vulnerability?" Krause questioned.

"*Da. Vy ne sidite ochen blizko s nashimi, kak mne skazat? C nashimi partnerami?* (Yes. You do not sit so close to, how do I say? To our associates?)," Ivanov explained.

"Which *associates* are you referring to, Viktor?" Jonathan Krause's deliberate refusal to speak the native tongue of the man standing before him was a blatant and deliberate message of contempt.

"You do not understand the risks, Jonathan."

Krause let out a disgusted chuckle. "Viktor, this is not 1940 or even 1970. Risk is not assessed simply by one's geographic location. Killing a sitting president increases the risk to us all. The greatest risk."

"*Kakoj risk moczet bit bolshe nashey bezopasnosti* (What greater risk than to our safety)?" Ivanov snapped.

"Safety?" Jon Krause paced across the floor and shook his head. He considered the question a moment and turned. "Am I to understand you are concerned about the Russian people?" There was no response. "You are, of course, referring to retaliation. No?"

"Of course," Ivanov sputtered. "Pakistan…."

Krause cut him off abruptly. "Lines on a map do not exist anymore, Mr. Ivanov. They are not blurred. They have been erased. You seem to have missed that evolution." The CIA agent stopped his movement and glared at the man across the room. "Safety is an illusion. No one is safe. This is not a business made for safety. That is only its pretense."

"You are saying that…."

"I am saying," Krause continued, "That our efforts offer more security; strategically. They do not guarantee anyone's safety. I should think that would be clear."

"*Legko dlia Amerikantsa* (Easy for an American)," Ivanov mumbled.

Krause flew across the short distance that separated them and placed his forehead against the smaller man's. "Be careful, Viktor. Be very careful. Do not make any moves until and unless you are told. You want to know what matters right now? Security of our secrets. Exposure is our risk, and you my *friend*, have placed us in a very precarious situation." Ivanov attempted to be cool. Jon Krause was an imposing figure. The intensity in the lager man's gaze told Ivanov to tread lightly. "Now," Krause pulled back. "The transaction in France is set for next Thursday. I expect you will deal with our Pakistani friends."

"Prince Abadi will meet…."

Krause nodded. "Of course, our Saudi *friends* will handle this. Very well, Viktor. Strickland has arranged for Congressman

O'Brien to meet Edmond. I am certain he will be point on the coming exchange."

"Your new president chose that man?"

For once Krause agreed with the Russian. "Strickland is not John Merrow."

Ivanov stretched his neck in frustration. "This O'Brien, is he…"

Krause laughed. "You should be careful what you wish for, Viktor. You want to know about O'Brien? Strickland? Who they are? Why they are in this?" He made his way to the door and put his hand on it. "*Posmotrite v zerkalo* (Look in the mirror)," he said as he took his leave.

***

Alex sat in the corner of the large ballroom with Cassidy beside her and Dylan on her lap. She watched as Jane Merrow graciously made her way to each person in the packed room, thanking them and assuring each that John Merrow had valued their support and friendship. Dylan was growing a bit restless. There were very few children present and the mood remained somber. "Bored, Speed?" Alex asked. He just shrugged. "Hmm. Well, what if we take a little walk?" Dylan nodded hopefully. Alex turned to Cassidy and smiled. "Give me a minute. Okay?"

"Sure," the teacher said quietly. She watched as Alex navigated the room and made her way to Jane. There was a short exchange that ended with the former first lady motioning to her eldest daughter. Within a few moments Alex returned with Stephanie Merrow at her side. A tall man in a Marine uniform followed closely behind.

"Dylan, this is Lieutenant Colonel Moore." Dylan looked at the tall man in the uniform curiously. "He flies the helicopter that the president uses. I thought you might like to see it."

"Can we ride in it?" he asked excitedly.

The Marine smiled. "I'm sorry, Dylan, no ride today. But, you can go inside it if you would like. I'll even show you where I sit."

Cassidy smiled and began to reach her feet when she noticed Jane Merrow approaching. "Cassidy," Jane began. "I was hoping, maybe we could take this opportunity to talk. Do you think you could meet me in the study?"

Cassidy felt her heart stop in her chest momentarily and gave a nod with a forced smile. Jane gave her an understanding pat on the shoulder before turning to head toward the room. "Dylan, why don't you go with Stephanie? I'll catch up to you in a minute," Alex suggested.

Stephanie offered her hand and Dylan accepted willingly. "No worries," she said to Cassidy. "I promise we won't lose him."

"Cass, it'll be all right," Alex assured her lover. Cassidy remained uncharacteristically silent. "Honestly, it will be." Cassidy took a deep breath and shook her head. Her lips were pressed so tightly together that they were beginning to become numb. "Come on, I'll walk you over."

"Alex..."

"Cass, you can't avoid her."

"I know," she answered as Alex escorted her to the door.

"Just be yourself," Alex said softly. Cassidy sighed and entered the room were Jane Merrow was standing beside a small table, looking out an oversized window. "I'll see you two in a bit," the agent said with a wink to the former first lady.

"Thank you, Alex," Jane replied. "I thought here would be good. You can see the South Lawn from here. So, you will be able to see Dylan when they reach Marine One."

"Thank you," Cassidy said, completely unsure of what was appropriate to say to the woman before her.

"Cassidy, you don't need to worry. I didn't ask you here to confront you about John." She let out a slight chuckle. "I know it was not a love affair. Though, I know that he held you in very high regard."

"Mrs...

"Cassidy, Jane. For goodness sake, I told you, Alex is family. You are family. Dylan is family." The tall, attractive woman sighed and motioned for Cassidy to come to the window. She pointed to where Dylan had begun to sprint across the lawn, still holding Stephanie's hand and she laughed. "John always wanted to be a pilot," she said softly. Cassidy smiled at the sight of her son and then looked at the woman beside her curiously. "Oh, there were many things he wanted, Cassidy." She paused and shook her head as she watched Alex finally catch up to the group and lift Dylan onto her hip. "I am glad she found you. You know, he loved her. Truly loved her."

"Jane..."

"Oh, it's all right. John and I, well, our marriage was not so much a choice. It was more given to us."

"I don't..."

Jane laughed at Dylan's wiggling and Alex's playful nature with the boy. "He is something."

"Yes, he is," Cassidy said proudly. "He doesn't let her out of his sight."

"Mm," Jane turned her attention to Cassidy. "John and I knew each other almost from birth; you know."

"I didn't know that."

"Well, publicly the story has always been that we met through our fathers in high school. But, our fathers worked together since before either one of us was even a thought. We knew very early on what the expectation was." Cassidy was surprised at the woman's candor. "I guess somewhere along the road I fell in love with him, or at least I learned to love him as a wife. He was my best friend and I was his. That never changed. But, for John, that is what it always was. When he met Alex. Well..."

"Jane...I..."

"Cassidy, let me finish." Cassidy nodded. "I was hurt, for a long time. Alex became such a good friend to me. I think she loved him more like a brother, you know? But, she did love him. He just became so distant for so long. Part of it was Alex, but there was more." She shook her head. "He never wanted to run for the senate, for any office."

"Then why?" Cassidy asked.

"Oh, I don't know. People pushed him. He was an Army brat. The son of a decorated officer. He followed as much as he led. When he decided to kick off the campaign for president, well...he was never home. When he was, he would lock himself in his office. He didn't sleep. He tried to spend time with the girls, but..." Jane stopped and looked at Cassidy. "I know how you must feel, standing here with me." She shook her head. "Then...that time was...I did the unthinkable. I was angry and lonely. I found someone."

"Jane, you don't have to...."

"Yes, I do. It was his best friend. Funny. They are so different and so alike. I wanted to hurt him. I did."

"What happened, between John and me, it was..."

Jane put her hand on Cassidy's and motioned out the window. Alex was standing in the doorway of the helicopter and even in the distance her wide smile was visible. "She is very happy with you," Jane smiled. "I know what it was and what it wasn't. I wanted you to know why he told me about that night."

"I'm sorry," Cassidy said softly. "I am surprised."

"Yes. Well, he was my best friend, and when he found out you were pregnant; when Chris told him; I think his heart broke a little. That's when he told me about that night. Can I speak honestly?"

"Of course," Cassidy said.

"He didn't like your husband much." Cassidy couldn't help but laugh. "He wondered. Watching Dylan...Well, we both knew." Cassidy had no idea what to say as Jane walked across the room and came back holding a folded flag. "I want you to take this, for Dylan."

"Jane...I can't. Dylan doesn't even...."

Jane smiled. "I don't expect you to tell him anything. Maybe someday, maybe you can just tell him that John always wanted a son. How much John loved Alex. He would want Dylan to have this. The girls, well, they had their father." A tear escaped her eye and Cassidy instinctively took her hand to comfort her. "Your secret is safe with me. If you ever decide…to tell him. Well, you should know I will support that."

Cassidy was nothing short of stunned. She had expected that Jane Merrow would be furious. "I don't know what to say."

"You don't have to say anything," Jane replied. The president's wife had learned many things over the years about people, about life, and about love. She had given up her own ambitions to support her husband's and surprisingly she had little regret for that decision. She loved her children and she had loved him, even with all of his flaws. "Just take it, please." She walked to a small loveseat and sat. "Before he passed he told me that he loved me." She smiled. "And, he made me promise to look after all of you, the girls, Alex…you and Dylan." Cassidy struggled to breathe. "He kept saying he was sorry…over and over and over. I don't know what for. I'm sorry and take care of them. He would have done anything to protect the people he loved. Anything."

Cassidy detected a note of fear in the woman's voice. "I am so sorry," she said as she made her way to Jane. "He was always good to me, to Dylan…even to Chris."

"Hum. Well," Jane stood and readied herself. "Some might not think so, Cassidy. John was a good man. A good father. Even a good husband. He was not perfect, not at anything, but he was a good man."

"Yes, he was," Cassidy agreed.

"Come on," Jane put out her hand. "You can come take this before you leave." She set the flag on the desk. "Looks like they are headed back. I'm sure Dylan will have some stories to tell you."

"I'm sure Alex will too," Cassidy laughed. "Jane, I hope you know…"

"You don't need to say anything, Cassidy. That's how families are supposed to be." Cassidy smiled as Jane led her back through the door. "I love Alex," Jane said. "As much as he did. She was there for me during some very dark times; for all of us. And, it was a terrible time for her. She deserves to be happy." She nodded at the teacher. "And she is."

"I hope so." Jane squeezed Cassidy's hand before walking back to the large group still milling about. Cassidy let out a full breath and closed her eyes for a moment. Life felt surreal. She wondered how they had ended up here. As she opened her eyes again, Alex turned the corner. She saw Dylan looking up at Stephanie, regaling her with a story. The young woman was smiling and Cassidy could not avoid looking at her eyes. She shook her head as Alex caught sight of her. "Oh Dylan," she whispered. "What am I going to do?"

***

"Captain Toles. *Davno ne videlis, Kapitan* (It has been a long time, Captain)," a tall, thin man greeted the agent.

"*Posol, dejstvidelno davno bilo* (Ambassador, indeed it has been)," she responded as she took his hand. "Cassidy, this is Ambassador Matthews, our illustrious Ambassador to Russia." Cassidy smiled and accepted the man's hand.

"*Ocharovatel'naya, I bolee krasivaja pri personalnoj vstreche* (Charming and more beautiful in person)," he complimented. Cassidy continued to smile but tipped her head in question.

Alex shook her head in amusement. Russell Matthews had been a valued resource for the agent in her time with the NSA. She regarded him as intelligent, charismatic and most importantly, she regarded him as ethical in his dealings. "Talk about charmers," Alex laughed.

"Well, to capture you, Captain, is a remarkable feat," he nodded to the teacher who blushed at the offered sentiment.

"All right," Alex said putting her arm around her lover's waist gently. "How are you, Russ?"

"Well, I've had better weeks." The man's brown eyes seemed to turn nearly black as he spoke. "I can't believe he is gone." Alex tried to respond but she felt the weight of the conversation increasing.

Cassidy caught sight of Dylan prattling on to Stephanie Merrow with another story. True to form he was becoming more animated as he got to know the young woman better. Cassidy thought this presented the perfect opportunity to save the president's daughter and give her lover some space. She gently took Alex's hand to grab her attention and gestured across the room. The agent and the ambassador both turned to see Dylan pretending to hold a steering wheel. "I think that's my cue," Cassidy raised her eyebrow.

"Might be," Alex chuckled. "Why don't you grab hold of him? I'll meet you over there in a few minutes. Probably had his fill by now."

"I wouldn't be so sure," Cassidy giggled, seeing her son delight in the attention the Merrow sisters were paying him. "Nice to meet you, Ambassador."

"The pleasure is mine, Mrs. O'Brien," he offered as she took her leave. The ambassador turned back to Alex and sighed. "I am sorry, Alex...about John."

"I know." Russell Matthews and John Merrow had attended West Point together and had developed a mutual respect and admiration for the other. Through the years President Merrow had called on his former classmate many times as a trustworthy resource and ally, both for advice and for assistance. Matthews' placement in the embassy in Moscow drew criticism from many, but John Merrow was steadfast in his support of the former Army Captain. Most had to admit that the choice proved a wise one over the years. Matthews was a gifted communicator and negotiator. His unassuming manner prompted people to give him more information than they realized in many instances.

"Alex, I was hoping we could speak privately."

"Here?" she asked.

"Well..."

Alex moved slowly toward the far corner of the room, watching the eyes within to be certain no one was paying attention too closely. "What is it?"

"Why do you think they shot him?" he asked.

"Well, I don't know who the 'they' would be, Russ," she said flatly.

"I've heard some things, through some back channels."

Alex brought her thumb to her temple. "What things?"

"Advanced Strategic Applications, ring any bells?" the ambassador asked quietly.

"What would ASA have to do with the assassination of a president?" Alex asked, the pressure on her temple increasing.

"I don't know, except that there is talk about Pakistan and something about a meeting in Corsica."

"I'm still not sure I..."

"*Initsiativy est zdes' I vo Frantsii chrotbi kontrolirivat importom I eksportom.* (Initiatives here and in France to control imports and exports, Captain)," he said.

"*Torgovlya oruzhiyem* (Arms trade)?" Alex asked for clarification. The ambassador answered with only a glance. "You think he tried to prevent something?"

"Perhaps," Matthews answered.

Alex nodded and looked across the room to see Cassidy squatting in front of Dylan. "When are you returning?" she asked her friend.

"I leave for Moscow Monday."

"*Zdes' nelza eto obsuzdat. Pozvoni Tayloru, on ob'yasnit* (Here is not good. Call Taylor, he will explain)," Alex suggested. "It was good to see you, Russ," she reached for his hand.

"I am sorry, Alex," he said sadly as he noticed the agent's focus shift across the room. "She is lovely," he allowed his gaze to follow the agent's to the blonde woman gently running her fingers through a small boy's hair.

"Yes, she is," Alex agreed. "Speak to Taylor, Ambassador," Alex repeated, receiving a nod of understanding from her friend. "I think it's time to get a certain young man home," she winked.

"Alex," he softly called after her, prompting the agent to turn. "Be careful." Alex offered the ambassador a cockeyed smile and continued on her way. "Be careful, Alex," he repeated to himself.

***

"You should have seen it, Mom!" Dylan beamed as he climbed into the large bed.

"I'll bet it was really something," Cassidy smiled.

"Yeah. You know that it has windshield wipers? Just like our car, Mom!"

Cassidy sat down on the edge of the bed and pulled the covers over her son. "It sounds like it was quite the adventure." She contemplated the sparkle in his eyes as he finally let his head rest on the pillow. "I am very proud of you, Dylan," she said as a tear formed in her eye.

His small smile seemed to radiate the pride he felt in her praise. Alex made her way to the doorway and listened to the heartfelt exchange. "Mom?"

"What, sweetie?"

"Why are you crying?"

A slight chuckle escaped from his mother as Cassidy again witnessed the compassionate heart of her son. "I am just very proud of you."

"Why?"

"Well, because you are smart. You make people laugh." He smiled at her as her hand brushed his bangs aside. "But mostly because you are kind."

"I am?"

"Yes, you are. Today was very hard for so many people."

"I know," he said as his eyes dropped.

Cassidy's gaze narrowed as she studied his expression, seeing there the deep understanding his innocence allowed. It was not an understanding of events, but an ability to sense in all those around him a lingering feeling of loss hidden beneath adult pleasantries. "You, Dylan, made a lot of people smile today." He looked back up at her and Cassidy could see his small eyes watering. "You made people laugh and you reminded me of something."

"I did?" he asked innocently.

"Yes, you did," she smiled broadly. "That you," she paused and tucked the covers around him a bit, "are the best thing that ever happened to me." His smile began to grow. "And, Alex is the best thing that has ever happened to us," she said with a soft sigh. "I love you, Dylan," she said, placing a kiss on his forehead. As she rose to her feet she noticed his small eyes drift to the doorway.

"Good night, Alex," he called over.

The agent was still leaning against the doorway. Gray sweat pants and an FBI T-shirt replaced the formal uniform of hours earlier. The smile on her face was soft, almost as if it were whispering to them both. Alex looked at Cassidy and took a deep breath. Then she glanced to the boy with his head on the pillow. "Goodnight, Dylan."

"I love you, Alex," he said as he grabbed hold of the small rabbit nearby and closed his eyes.

"I love you too, Speed," she answered as Cassidy finally reached her and pressed into her side. "Get some sleep."

"You too. I'm gonna fly through...."

"You do that, Speed," Alex replied as she gently shut his door and turned to the woman beside her. "How are you?" she asked.

Cassidy pursed her lips. "I am all right, Agent. How are you?" she asked with concern.

"Best thing that ever happened to you, huh?" Cassidy just smiled and raised her brow. "You sure about that?"

"Pretty sure," Cassidy winked.

"Ummm…"

"What?" Cassidy asked as Alex pulled her closer.

"That thing I wanted to tell you when we got home?" Alex began.

"Yes?"

"How do you feel about a glass of wine in front of the fireplace?"

"What is going on in that head?" Cassidy asked.

"Well, you go get changed. I'll get the wine and start the fire. I think there has been enough stress and sadness for one day; don't you?" Alex smiled and placed a light kiss on her lover's nose.

"In fact, I do."

"Go change. Wine and a fire." Cassidy shook her head with a grin.

"What are you grinning about?" Alex squinted.

"Nothing," Cassidy winked. "You just surprise me sometimes."

"Yeah?"

"Umm…" Cassidy chuckled.

"What?" Alex asked as Cassidy crossed the hallway to the room that they were sharing.

"You are up to something," Cassidy called back.

Alex just shrugged. "Maybe I am," she laughed quietly.

"No maybes. You are."

"Just get comfortable," Alex laughed. It felt like the right time for a conversation the agent knew they needed to have.

It made no sense to put it off any longer. This was her family. More now than ever, it felt like it was time to embrace that.

***

"Mr. President," Assistant FBI Director Tate said as he took the seat he was offered.

"Sorry, Joshua…about the hour," Lawrence Strickland replied.

"Not at all, Sir."

"Joshua, I have been reading over some of John's notes. Where do we stand with Agent Toles?" the president asked.

"How do you mean, Sir?" Tate asked.

The president cleared his throat. "Her reinstatement is what I am referring to."

"Well, there is a mandatory two week suspension period."

"Wave it," the president replied.

"Sir, I thought that with…."

President Strickland licked his lips and considered the man before him. "There are times to think Assistant Director and there are times to act. Begin the process. I want Alexis Toles reinstated by the end of the week."

"And what would you like me to do about her transfer?" Tate asked.

"I don't think that will be a concern for you," Strickland said.

"Why is that?" Tate asked curiously.

"I have it on good authority that your agent will be returning to her roots."

"I don't understand."

"She's going back to the NSA, Joshua," the president explained.

"How could you…."

The president laughed. "Joshua. Think."

"And you *want* her to go back to the NSA?" Tate was confused.

"More control at the NSA. More military presence, so the answer is yes, I do."

"No disrespect, Sir, but…May I speak freely?"

"You may," Strickland replied.

"President Merrow considered Michael Taylor and Alexis Toles a dangerous combination for some reason."

"I am aware," Strickland said. "They are, from what I understand." Joshua Tate's eyes conveyed all of his questions. "I have put a piece in play. A new pawn to move across the board. I suspect that attention will be focused in that direction shortly," the president offered with satisfaction.

"A smoke screen?"

"Not exactly, no. A person that Alex Toles will want to follow and a different direction to lead her; at least for now. A direction that will keep them occupied while matters are settled," Strickland explained.

"You are the Commander in Chief," Tate responded indicating that he would comply.

"Yes," Strickland gloated. "I am."

***

"Hey, feel better?" Alex asked as Cassidy walked toward her.

"I do, actually."

The fire was already crackling and Alex had placed some pillows on the floor against the couch for the pair to comfortably sit together. Cassidy plopped down onto the floor and closed her eyes momentarily as she stretched out. As she opened them, she caught sight of Alex making her way over and marveled at the way the glow of the fire highlighted the agent's skin and hair. Alexis Toles was nothing short of a breathtaking sight. Cassidy smiled at the realization that her lover was every bit as beautiful in a pair of sweatpants and a T-shirt and she had been earlier in her uniform. "What are you smiling at?" Alex asked.

"Nothing, really," Cassidy said. "I'm just glad to relax, and you know I am curious what this is all about," she raised her brow.

"You? Curious?" Alex joked. The teacher's response was a light slap of the agent's thigh. "It's been a hell of a few weeks, Cass." Cassidy sighed. "I mean…it feels like years some days, you know?'

"I do," Cassidy admitted. Alex rubbed her temple and closed her eyes. "Alex, maybe we should just relax. Just enjoy the fire and rest. We don't have to talk about anything tonight."

"No, we do," Alex said seriously and instantly noted the fear on Cassidy's face. The agent chuckled and released the pressure on her temple. "No, Cass, it's nothing bad…well, I mean I don't think it's bad…it's just…well…you know Dylan and…. well… after John and then the…."

"Alex?" The agent looked at her lover a bit sheepishly. "Rambling," Cassidy smiled.

"Sorry," the agent chuckled. "I guess I don't know how to start."

"Why don't you just start and see what happens?"

"My parents have a condo in Florida. I was thinking, you know…when school is out. Well, maybe we could go down and spend a few days. Get away. Go to some of the parks. I don't know."

"Alex? You wanted to talk to me about taking a vacation?" Cassidy asked.

"No. Well, yes." Cassidy cocked her head and opened her eyes a little wider, questioning what Alex was driving at. The agent sighed. "Yes. I thought it would be good for all of us."

"It would be. I agree." The teacher looked at her lover, sensing that something else was behind all of this.

"Okay. Cass, you know how you told me you want to have more kids?" Cassidy nodded. "Well….I don't know if I…"

"Alex…"

Alex immediately stopped Cassidy's thought. "I've been thinking about that a lot the last few days."

"About?" Cassidy questioned.

"About you and me and Dylan, about us having our own family." Alex paused and closed her eyes. "Actually, I can't seem to stop thinking about it." Cassidy studied the agent as Alex's stress visibly increased. "What if I am no good, Cass?"

"No good?"

"Yeah, as a parent."

"Alex, I have to confess I am a little lost. We just went from vacation to parenting," Cassidy said gently.

The agent let out a nervous chuckle. "I have to ask my parents, Cass, to use the condo."

"Okay…."

"I don't really talk to them often," Alex explained.

"I sort of gathered that."

"Just, they never really approved…of my choices in life," the agent explained.

"Which choices?"

"All of them," Alex said as her fingers began to instinctively rub her temples.

"Alex, we don't have to go anywhere. If you aren't comfortable…"

"No, Cass. I want you to meet them. I want you to…No, I need them to know."

"To know what?"

"To know that I have a family," Alex said quietly.

Cassidy let out a soft sigh. "What are you trying to say, Alex?"

The agent nodded and took Cassidy's glass away, setting both aside and taking hold of her hands. "I want you to know who I am and why. I was hoping we could go see my parents next weekend. Nick and Barb want to give them their news about the baby and well, they've seen us. I can't just pretend…"

"Alex, this is all about me meeting your parents?" Cassidy asked.

"It's not easy for me, Cass," Alex admitted. "I don't ever want to be them."

"What do you mean?"

"I mean; what if I am like them? As a parent?"

Cassidy nodded her very basic understanding. This was the first time Alex had ventured into a discussion about her parents and even now it was somewhat cryptic. What was clear to Cassidy was the anxiety the topic caused for her lover. Working with children for so many years, it was a reaction she had grown familiar with. It generally signaled some type of abuse or neglect, or at the very least a restrictive upbringing. Cassidy had feared that for Dylan with all of Chris's preconceptions about the boy's future. It had been a major factor in her decision to leave the congressman. Listening to Alex now, Cassidy needed few details to understand that her lover's childhood had not been a happy and harmonious one.

Cassidy remained a bit unclear on where Alex was attempting to head with the discussion. She did understand that she needed to calm any doubts the agent had about Cassidy's ability to handle meeting Mr. and Mrs. Toles. And, she needed to quell the lingering fear Alex was confronting about her ability to be a good parent. "Alex, can I say something here?" The agent nodded silently. "I don't know what it was like for you with your parents. If you are worried about me, I mean what they might say or do; don't be. You are not your parents; none of us are." Alex started to open her mouth to speak and Cassidy cautioned her with just a glance. "Let me finish. I watch you with Dylan. I watch him with you. I have seen you and Nick chasing after those two little boys...Alex, I saw Stephanie Merrow light up when she saw you. Whatever it is that you are afraid of, I think you can rest easy about how you are with children."

"Yeah, but Cass, I haven't raised any of them. Cat is Nick's and Stephanie and Alexandra, I mean they were older when I met them. And Dylan, you have raised…"

"I know all of that, Alex. Don't you think I worry about whether I am a good mother?"

"Why on earth would you worry about that?" Alex asked genuinely.

"Why? Oh, I don't know. I raised my son for six years with a man that I couldn't understand and didn't agree with on anything; a man that isn't even his real father. God. Alex, what kind of person does that make *me*?"

"Cassidy, you are the best person I know and you are a wonderful mother. I don't think there is anyone that would disagree with that."

Cassidy let out a sarcastic chuckle. "Yeah, well Dylan might disagree one day."

"No."

Cassidy sighed. "The point is that I understand why you feel that way. I think you are a wonderful parent, Alex. Dylan adores you. I still am a little confused though, about…"

Alex smiled. "Seeing my parents, taking you there…it's just, well, all these things that…I…I need to do that before I can think about all of these things I can't stop thinking about."

Cassidy couldn't help but laugh. One of the most endearing things about this wonderfully strong woman that she loved was how Alex's confident demeanor could turn to an almost incoherent diatribe when she got nervous. "Alex, what exactly are you talking about?"

The agent took a deep breath and let it out with some force. "I'm saying," she stopped and repeated the same action. "I am saying that I want to have a family with you, Cassidy."

The teacher swallowed hard and put her hands on the agent's cheeks. "I want that too."

"It scares me."

"I know," Cassidy said. "It's not like it has to happen tomorrow, Alex."

"You might change your mind after next weekend."

The teacher pursed her lips and then kissed the agent's cheek. "You have endured my mother almost daily and you still want to have a family with *me*?"

"I love your mother."

Cassidy's snickered. "Uh-huh. So do I, but she can definitely be…"

"A handful?" Alex joked.

"To put it mildly," Cassidy agreed. "I didn't fall in love with your family, Alex. I fell in love with you, though I do love Nick and Barb and so does my mother. Stop worrying."

"You know, I was watching Dylan today in that cockpit," Alex began. "And, I wished I could have seen him when he was a baby. It was strange. I just…I felt like he was…"

"Yours?" Cassidy raised an eyebrow. Alex nodded. "Well, I think he feels the same way." Alex smiled and Cassidy laid her head in the agent's lap, closing her eyes and taking in a deep breath. "Alex, I wouldn't want to raise him with anyone else." Cassidy felt soft lips brush against her own. "This was what you wanted to tell me?"

"Well…" Alex chuckled.

"Hum. Can I ask you something?"

"What?" the agent asked.

"What made you start thinking about this?"

"I don't know, everything. I mean, when I was working at the house, painting Dylan's room, I kept thinking about it. But, well," Alex hesitated.

"Go on," Cassidy said enjoying the feel of Alex's hand running through her hair.

"When I came home the other day? After Jane called?"

"Yeah?"

"You handed me those papers; remember?" Alex asked.

Cassidy chuckled. "The school forms?" she asked with surprise.

"Yeah." Cassidy smiled and opened her eyes. "What?" Alex asked. "Ever since then, I don't know, I just keep thinking about us...about you. And I want to..."

"I understand," Cassidy said.

"All this craziness that's been happening. My job will always be crazy. I want to do the boring stuff, Cassidy."

"Well good. You can start with the bathroom sink next to Dylan's room when we get home."

"What?" the agent asked.

"Yeah, I think he might have shoved something in it."

Alex started laughing. "Always looking out for me; aren't you Cass?"

Cassidy smiled and closed her eyes again. "Oh, and he wants to play soccer. That boy two houses down...Jason? Yeah, he's convinced Dylan that is the coolest thing. Sign-ups are Wednesday and Thursday at the school. So feel free to wait in *that* line."

"Okay," Alex said without any hesitation.

"Yeah? Good," Cassidy smirked. "Because on Friday we need to go meet with his new teacher." She opened her eyes slightly to see Alex's mouth open a little wider and then shut again. Cassidy flashed a bright smile. "Still think you want to have more?"

"Are you trying to scare me?"

"No. You wanted boring."

"Cassidy, life with you is anything but boring," Alex laughed.

"Wait for doctor's appointments and waiting rooms and..." the teacher's list was interrupted by a kiss.

"I look forward to it."

"I love you, Alex, but trust me I think you underestimate the craziness in the boring," Cassidy said.

"Maybe. I'm good at multitasking."

"Must be the butler in you," Cassidy poked.

"Yeah, must be." Alex leaned over and kissed the woman on her lap. "Thank you." Cassidy looked inquisitively into the blue eyes above her. "I don't know if I could have gotten through today without you," Alex confessed.

"Well, I could say the same thing." Cassidy shook her head slightly. "I'm sorry, Alex, about John. I know that you loved him."

"I just wish I knew what he was trying to tell me."

"Well, you'll figure it out," Cassidy said with confidence.

"How can you be so sure?"

"I know you, Alex. You will. Just promise me you will be careful," Cassidy said, the fear in her voice unmistakable. "I don't want to lose you when I just found you."

"You worried about who will fix the sink?" Alex tried to lighten the teacher's mood.

"It's not funny, Alex." Cassidy's mood was darkening.

"Hey, I'm good at what I do. I promise. Trust me," Alex said.

"It's not you I don't trust," Cassidy admitted.

"What did I just tell you?" Alex reminded the teacher. "You trust me?" Cassidy nodded. "Then trust me when I tell you the biggest lion's den you will see me enter will be next weekend in Massachusetts." Cassidy shook her head and closed her eyes again. "Maybe I should take you upstairs. You look tired, Cass."

"No." Cassidy snuggled against the agent. "Let's just stay here for now." Alex smiled her silent understanding. "Alex, what did Ambassador Matthews say to you in Russian?"

"He said you were more charming and beautiful in person," Alex explained. "As usual, he was right."

"Je t'aime," Cassidy whispered.

"*J'espère que tu te sentiras de cette façon quand je ne pourrai pas faire fonctionner l'évier* (I hope you feel that way when I can't fix the sink)." Cassidy had drifted off into sleep and Alex smiled as she tenderly tucked the woman's long blonde hair behind her ears. Her conversation with the Russian Ambassador was invading her thoughts. Something did not feel right. She had been in and around the intelligence community long enough to know a few important things. It is not easy to assassinate a president. In fact, it is nearly impossible. Random acts of violence were seldom random at all and there were powerful interests involved in the smallest political decisions. Cassidy had a right to be concerned. Alex knew it. She had a family now. It was ironic that suddenly, as she approached what she suspected would be the most dangerous investigation of her career, she had other people to consider. The agent had two burning needs and they stood at desperate odds with one another; to understand what John Merrow was telling her, how it connected to Carl Fisher and Christopher O'Brien, and to build a life with the woman in her arms. Alex kissed Cassidy's forehead. *"Je vais garder notre famille en toute sécurité, Cassidy. Je te le promets* (I will keep our family safe, Cassidy. I promise)," she whispered.

"I know you will," a voice mumbled. "Just remember you are part of that family," Cassidy said softly.

"I will."

***

Chapter Eight

"What are you thinking, Strickland?" Admiral Brackett bellowed.

The new president sat behind his large picturesque desk and calmly smiled. Lawrence Strickland was the consummate politician. He had made his life and his career a success by consistently developing his ability to read people and he was practiced in the art of remaining cool under scrutiny. In President Strickland's world he was no elected official, no appointed commander, no entrusted leader; he was king. This was his dominion and everyone was now his subject. Not even the stately presence of Admiral William Brackett could intimidate him. He had waited a lifetime to sit on this throne and he intended to make that known. Deliberately but casually he leaned back in his chair and sighed. "Admiral, you were a naval commander for many years." The admiral watched the shorter man as he continued, still leaning comfortably back in his chair. "How many captains on a ship, Admiral?"

"One."

"Yes, I know. This is my ship. You may be a chief; you are not Captain here," Strickland said.

If the new president had hoped his show of outright cockiness would somehow rattle William Brackett, he had been drastically mistaken in his assessment of the larger man. Admiral Brackett had spent his life in this arena, nearly all of it. He had counseled many presidents. He had orchestrated wars. The admiral shook his head at the arrogance of the president. He walked slowly toward the desk and leaned over it. His eyes narrowed into tiny pinholes as he regarded the man in the chair. "To steer a ship successfully one must know what waters he is navigating. A good captain has studied the history of the waters he traverses. He looks below the surface in order to predict what perils may befall him. He follows as much as he leads and his goal is to arrive safely at his destination; whatever destination has been prescribed to him." He leaned in closer and his gaze narrowed further. "An arrogant captain will sink his own ship, Lawrence. He fails to understand that he does not control what lies beneath the surface. A captain is only a navigator." The admiral stepped away and turned his back to the president.

President Strickland sat back up in his chair and surveyed the movement of the man across his desk. Admiral Brackett was as poised as any man he had ever seen. While the president understood the veiled warning; he was not certain where the admiral was heading now. Brackett kept his back to Lawrence Strickland in a show of disgust for the president's ignorant assertions regarding power and authority. "So you are sending Christopher O'Brien to meet with Edmond Callier? Interesting choice. A young, imprudent, smug politician to meet with an experienced, connected and cautious ally. What do you hope to gain?"

"It will deter Toles. It will deter Taylor," an assured answer came from behind the desk.

The admiral let out an uncustomary animated guffaw. "It will deter them from what? Investigating?" The admiral shook his head and paced the floor. "Toles and Taylor *are* captains, Strickland. In fact, they are practiced captains. They excel in studying what lies beneath the surface. You are leading them to follow O'Brien and in the process leading them straight to Edmond and France."

"There is nothing of consequence for them to find, Admiral. O'Brien will be in Paris. The exchange will occur in Corsica as planned. It will peak their interest in his dealings, remove their focus from his accident and the assassination, at least for a time. It's simply a diversion. The money will still follow its route through Prince Abadi."

"You idiot. I know all of that. I planned it. You think this is about a simple trade of weapons through the Saudis? One deal?"

"Of course not," Strickland answered. "O'Brien can be an asset, William. He can also be the focus as we move ahead. He's a pawn to move across the board. Let him take the fall, even if Krause falls with him."

Brackett turned and stood straight. "1985."

"Excuse me?" the president responded.

"You are opening a much bigger can of worms than you realize, Larry. Much bigger. You forget how those TOW missiles made their way into Iran. You think there was one player? Two? Five? You think it ended there? Started there? Who do you think Edmond Callier is? How do you think money made its way to Nicaragua? Where do you think these insurgents learned their tactics?" The admiral took a few steps forward. "You leave me no choice."

"No choice in what?" the president asked.

"You've sent O'Brien to Paris. You will send him to Corsica."

"Why on earth would you want the congressman involved in the..."

"Do it. I will take care of the rest. Do not speak to Callier...."

"You presume," the president began, his anger rising quickly. "I do not answer to you. You forget who the Commander in Chief is," he asserted.

"You," the admiral admonished, "have no idea what a Commander in Chief does. You sit when I tell you to sit and you stand how I tell you to stand; that is if you hope to occupy that chair for any length of time."

"Are you threatening me?" Strickland rose to his feet. "Your hands are tied. You've already killed a popular president; martyred him."

"There are many ways to sink a ship, Mr. President. John Merrow was worth his martyrdom. Your fate will not be so glorious. Sit. Now. Make the move."

***

"Alex, how are you doing?" Michael Taylor asked.

"I'm okay, Taylor. Ready to go home. Any news from the bureau?"

"On your reinstatement you mean?" Alex nodded. "No, not yet, but that never stopped us before." Alex laughed. There was a great deal of truth in her friend's statement. Intelligence work was always officially unofficial. "I've been thinking about what John said to you, about following Brackett," he said.

"Yeah, I still wonder what she is looking for at the bureau. Most of my cases have not been politically…"

"Well, she might give us some hints but I don't think that's what he meant," Taylor suggested as the two friends walked along the National Mall.

Alex looked straight ahead, keeping her pace steady. "What are you thinking?"

"I think he meant the admiral, Alex."

Alex pinched the bridge of her nose instinctively. "Still involved, you think?" She turned to see Taylor's eyes widen and his head tip to the side. "I agree," Alex offered. "But Claire is still the best trail. Maybe this isn't the time for me to move back…"

"No," he said flatly. "You are too compromised to be able to follow her trail at the FBI. But, I think we have an answer."

"What's that?" she asked as they moved closer to their destination.

"Fallon."

Alex stopped dead in her tracks and turned to Taylor. She knew Brian Fallon wanted in on the investigation and she had

82

even considered bringing him in. That was until John Merrow was shot. This was no place for a man whose family meant everything to him. "No," was all she said.

"Not your choice, Alex," he reminded her.

"Taylor, no."

"Alex, it's done. He's in. He understands."

"Jesus Christ, Michael. Fallon has three kids. What the hell are you thinking?"

"I'm thinking he is a good agent. He's smart and he has an unassuming presence. He is exactly who we need." Taylor watched Alex as she pressed her tongue against her cheek in frustration and her right thumb firmly into her temple. "He's not going to let it go. Safer if he is in than if he is out on his own," Taylor surmised.

"I don't like it."

"I know. Listen, Agent Brackett...Guess who she was cuddling up to last week?" Taylor smirked a bit. "Our favorite congressman," he deadpanned.

"Brackett and O'Brien?" Taylor nodded. "Are you serious?"

"Never been more serious. Someone is scared, Alex."

"Why do you say that?"

Taylor motioned ahead for them to continue walking. "O'Brien booked a ticket to Paris for Monday." Alex stopped again. "Yeah, interesting. I agree. Particularly when you consider Brady's information that Krause was in Paris just a week ago."

"So they want us to follow O'Brien." Alex shook her head and sighed. "What don't they want us to follow?"

"That *is* the question," Taylor agreed. "We follow O'Brien," he said. "We let Fallon follow Agent Brackett." Alex sighed heavily. "You know it's the right way."

"Maybe. I still don't like it."

"Fallon's smart, Alex. He'll do well." He watched Alex as she continually pressed her thumb to her temple and decided a change in topic was called for. "Heading back tomorrow?"

She nodded. "Where's Cassidy?" Taylor took a seat on one of the long narrow steps near the top of the Lincoln Memorial.

"Took Dylan to O'Brien," she said somewhat harshly as she sat beside her friend.

"I can see you are happy about that," he joked.

"I don't trust him."

"Me neither, but he is the boy's father, Alex."

'If only you knew,' she thought silently. "Yeah, well…"

Taylor chuckled. "You know, Alex…Fallon's not the only one with something more to consider."

Alex Toles looked out over the scene before her. From her cold, cement seat she could see across the city. The towering obelisk in the center of her view stood as a reminder of the man who first headed a new nation. Just beyond, barely visible in the afternoon haze, she spotted the spire of the capitol. It was the place where men like Christopher O'Brien were sent to do the work of the people. Its halls were erected to provide for and to protect a trusting nation. It was the place Alex Toles had come to view as the ultimate paradox. It was a contrast and contradiction of all she believed in and all that she abhorred. She let out a heavy breath. She had sworn to protect all of this; sworn her life to it so many years ago. It had given her purpose, direction and focus. It had been her compass. Somewhere along the way everything changed. It all paled now in comparison to a school teacher and a little boy.

This investigation was no longer about honor or even obligation. She had been prepared to give her life for those causes since the day she walked into West Point. It was the purpose that she believed eclipsed one woman's existence. Perhaps it still did. Now, her life mattered to someone else. The safety of her family, their happiness was her objective. She closed her eyes and smiled before turning back to her friend. "Taylor, as long as O'Brien is in this mix Cassidy and Dylan are at risk."

"Yes, they are," he swallowed hard.

"Whatever I have to do, I will do," she said firmly.

"What about where it leads?" he asked.

Alex nodded, an element of apprehension on her face. The implication was clear. The trail that they were following likely led to people they trusted. The greatest risk might not be life nor limb; but the truth. She offered Taylor a sad smile. "Wherever it leads, it leads."

Taylor nodded his understanding. Two friends now sat in silence looking out over the majesty of the nation's capital. For most, it was a view that left them breathless by its beauty and artistry. For Captain Michael Taylor and Agent Alexis Toles; it was a stark reminder that everything has a façade. The most beautiful surfaces often hide an unfathomable ugliness underneath. It was their task to remove those masks so that others could build something new and hopefully more authentic. It was a task neither was looking forward to.

***

"Mom?" Dylan called from his seat in the car.

"Hum?" Cassidy inquired as she navigated a left turn.

"Do I have to go?"

An audible sigh came from the woman in the driver's seat and she forced a smile to her lips. "Dylan, your dad wants to spend time with you." There was no response and Cassidy could sense her son's tension. "It's only for the afternoon." She glanced in the mirror to see the boy tracing circles on the window. "You can tell him all about the new house." Dylan shrugged. "Oh, Dylan."

"Okay," he said.

Cassidy shook her head as a million thoughts ran through her mind. Over the last six months Dylan had become more and more apprehensive about his visits with his father. She knew that to a large degree it was because the congressman's attention was always on other things. She sensed there was something a bit more; not abuse, but perhaps something that her ex-husband talked about or engaged in that unsettled the boy. She stole another look in the mirror and resigned herself that she would find a way to coax it from him gradually. She pulled in front of the congressman's building and released her seat belt so she could turn to face her son. "Dylan," she began as she saw her ex-husband slowly heading to the car. "Daddy is bringing you back before dinner, okay? Try and have fun."

He nodded as his father opened the door. "Cassie," the congressman greeted his ex-wife.

"Chris."

"You ready, bud?" Dylan offered the man a nod and hopped from his seat. "Come on," the congressman called with a hint of urgency.

Dylan started out and stopped abruptly. He moved back to the center of the car and leaned into his mother, hugging her neck tightly. "I'll see you in a while, sweetie," Cassidy said as she reveled in his embrace.

He started back toward his father. "Tell Alex, I am going to win tonight," he said proudly; thinking about a rematch on the pool table.

Cassidy laughed. "I will tell her that."

"Bye," he smiled, now thinking about the night to come rather than the day ahead.

"Go on ahead," the congressman said to his son. "Cassie," he leaned back in.

"What?"

"What are you doing?" Cassidy shook her head and laughed. "I'm serious. What could you possibly be planning with this woman?" Cassidy smiled and looked past the man to see her son attempting to take the stairs two at a time. She chuckled and turned her attention back to the congressman. His gaze was severe, as if he were convicting her of some crime with his eyes.

She considered him silently for a moment and then her smile grew. "A family," she said simply. He stood stunned at the brief and pointed response. "Have a good afternoon, Chris," she said. "I am glad to see you up and around." The congressman stood frozen, staring blankly at the woman in the car. "The door, Christopher?" she reminded him. He started to speak and Cassidy turned away. "I'll see you around six," she said as she fastened her seatbelt and turned the key in the ignition.

Christopher O'Brien shut the car door and stepped back onto the curb watching the woman he still regularly referred to as his wife pull away. "That's my family, Agent," he muttered. "My family."

***

"Nicky called," a tall, slender older woman said as she hung up the phone.

"Oh?" a man in a large arm chair answered.

"They are all coming Saturday, Nicolaus," she told him.

"Who would that be?" he asked.

Helen Toles took the paper from her husband's hand and placed it on the table beside his chair. She looked at him sternly. At seventy, Helen Toles' hair had begun to turn from its once deep black to a faint gray. She stood 5'10 without the aid of any heels; the addition of which generally placed her nearly eye to eye with her husband. She remained a strikingly attractive woman with cobalt eyes and high cheek bones. There was no denying that Alexis Toles resembled her mother; if not in her manner and lifestyle, certainly in her physical presence and appearance. "Nick," she said in a deep voice. "Alexis is bringing her new friend."

"So, Nicky is bringing the family, then?"

"Nicolaus," Helen repeated. "Please think about Alexis."

"Alexis has made her choices, Helen. I can't change that. Do you really think she should be carrying on with this woman; a woman who has a child?"

"Nicky says she is lovely," Helen raised an eyebrow.

"Don't worry," he said. "I won't berate our daughter if that's what you are afraid of."

Helen Toles sighed. Her husband was as obstinate as he was handsome. She sometimes wondered where the idealistic young man she once knew had disappeared to. She still remembered the first time she had seen him at a friend's wedding more than fifty years ago. He was twenty-six and had just finished his law degree at Harvard. Immediately, he caught her eye just as she had captivated him in the distance. It was Friday, November 22, 1963. While a nation sat glued to images on television screens of a fallen president; two young people began the journey of what would become a lifetime. Helen shook her head and put her hand on his shoulder as he retrieved the paper from beside him. "I'll make you some lunch."

He grasped her hand and held it for a long moment. "That sounds fine," he said continuing to focus on the paper before him.

Helen Toles momentarily turned back to glimpse her husband placing the paper in his lap and rubbing his temples. She sighed and shook her head wondering when he would accept their daughter for who she had become. "So different," she whispered to herself as she made her way into the kitchen, "and so much alike."

***

Chapter Nine

Monday, April 14th

Alex sat drumming on the steering wheel endlessly. Cassidy smiled and raised her eyebrow at the tall agent. "It's only school, Alex," she let out a slight chuckle. "He'll be home in a few hours." The agent huffed, remaining fixed on the large brick building across the street. Alex shook her head and mumbled something as she turned the key in the ignition. "You know, I'm going to start to think the only reason you keep me around is so you can get me to make tacos while you watch Batman and play pool with Dylan," Cassidy joked.

"I can't help it," Alex confessed. "I'll just...."

Cassidy reached over and grasped Alex's arm lightly. "I know you'll miss him." It had been a difficult few weeks with so many upheavals and the death of President John Merrow had taken a great toll on Alex. Having Dylan home kept the agent occupied and Cassidy understood that in some way this felt to the agent like another loss. She smiled as Alex finally turned to her. "Come on, you said you wanted boring."

"What are you planning?" Alex narrowed her gaze playfully.

"Me?" Cassidy feigned innocence. "Nothing," she laughed. "*But,* there are still a boat load of boxes to unpack in the garage. That ought to keep us both busy."

Alex rolled her eyes. "FANTASTIC!" she exclaimed sarcastically.

***

"Mr. Callier, it's a pleasure to meet you," Congressman O'Brien greeted the older man.

Edmond Callier studied the congressman. He searched the eyes before him intently and watched as Christopher O'Brien offered him a sly smile. 'Smug,' he thought. "Yes, Congressman, please...sit," he gestured to an arm chair seated at the table.

"So, Mr. Callier, I understand that you have concerns over some of the current legislation in our House...I am here to assure you..."

Callier interrupted, "assurances do not exist, Mr. O'Brien. I think we both know that. I am, however, interested in your plans."

"I don't know if I understand....Senator Levy made it clear that you would be looking for..."

The older man rose from his seated position and walked across the room keeping his back to the congressman. "Senator Levy is not my concern. The legislation will take care of itself. Sympathy for your fallen leader is the only assurance of that needed." O'Brien watched as the man calmly poured himself a drink and continued. "However, I am interested in your plans on this initiative for, what was it called? Oh yes, more *oversight* on intelligence. And on the campaign funding bill I have heard so much about. How do you plan to rectify that?"

"Neither is even in debate. That bill has not even been completely crafted."

"Ah...but it would restrict the bundling of campaign donations; would it not? Further than it already does?" Callier kept his back turned and lifted the small glass to his lips taking a healthy sip and grimacing slightly as he felt the burn glide down his throat. "And, it would make distinctions between foreign corporations; even those with American subsidiaries; no? And, if I understand correctly is would place more legislative power over your investigative agencies."

"Well, yes..."

"These cannot come to pass. We already have challenges with the reluctance of our Israeli partners to act as intermediaries. The fluidity of funds cannot be compromised," Callier continued as he lifted the glass again.

"Mr. Callier, I can assure you that the negotiations…."

Callier shook his head and turned, "*N`assurez pas ce que vous ne pouvez pas. C'est la preuve d'un imbécile. Vous négociez ce que vous pouvez et vous achetez ce que vous devez. Ce qui reste après que n'a qu'une seule autre solution* (Do not make assurances you cannot. That is the mark of a fool. You negotiate what you can and you purchase what you must. What is left after that has only one other solution)."

Congressman Christopher O'Brien's posture stiffened and he looked at the table to gather his thoughts. "I am sorry, Mr. Callier, I do not speak…"

"I am sorry, I assumed…that charming ex-wife of yours spoke fluently."

O'Brien looked up in shock. "How do you know Cassidy?"

The older man smiled and spoke softly. "*Seul un fou pourrait laisser filer une telle femme* (only a fool would let such a woman go)." He lifted his eyebrow as the congressman shifted in his chair. "I have met Cassidy, Mr. O'Brien, many years ago. A man does not easily forget a charming, beautiful woman who possesses intellect." He took a long pause before finishing his thought, "at least not an astute man."

"Well, Cassidy is many things…."

The older man set his glass down. "I think that we are finished here, Congressman."

The stern look on the older man's face prompted the congressman to reach his feet swiftly. "What is it," O'Brien asked, "that you would like me to convey to President Strickland?"

With a nod Callier answered. "If he cannot deliver; assurances will be provided." The man opened the door to the conference room. He paused and looked at the congressman sympathetically. "I am sorry for your loss, Mr. O'Brien."

"Thank you. The nation will recover."

"Yes, I am sure. I was not referring to the loss of your president." O'Brien looked at him and Callier smirked. "Have you heard of Jean de La Fontaine?" The congressman shook his head. "I see. Not the lover of poetry then. Another difference from your former wife." Callier turned around, retrieved a piece of paper and wrote something on it. He handed it to the younger man who looked at it curiously. "He once said, '*Toute personne chargée de puissance va en abuser sinon également animée par l'amour de la vérité et de la vertu, peu importe que ce soit un prince, ou l'un du people* (Anyone entrusted with power will abuse it if not also animated with the love of truth and virtue, no matter whether he be a prince, or one of the people)," Callier recited the passage in French. "Look it up."

***

Cassidy opened a large box and pulled out a blue photo album. "What you got there?" Alex asked. Just as Cassidy was about to answer Alex's cell phone rang. "Tate," she said quietly. Cassidy blew out a breath and nodded her understanding as Alex walked out of the living room. "Assistant Director," she answered.

"Agent," he responded professionally. "Your reinstatement is set for Monday."

"Thank you Sir. I assume it is formally approved?"

"It is."

Alex pursed her lips and took a deep breath. "Then, I am afraid I need to tender my resignation." The agent slowly wandered back into the living room and stood in the doorway, glancing over to see Cassidy flipping through the pages of the album.

"Agent Toles…"

"Sir, I have decided to accept a position with another agency. I will send you my formal letter this afternoon," she said somewhat coolly. Joshua Tate nodded his understanding on the other side of the line. "Sir?"

"I understand, Agent," he answered.

An awkward silence ensued and Cassidy looked up to Alex as the agent ran her tongue over her lips. "Thank you for your support," Alex said as genuinely as she could manage.

"Of course, Agent." Alex was ready to hang up when the assistant director's voice continued. "Alex," he said in what was almost a whisper. "Just," he swallowed hard. "Well, I wish you the best."

The agent was certain there was something else that Joshua Tate wanted to say which piqued her curiosity. "Thank you," she said as she hung up the call, sitting down on the sofa and putting her face in her hands.

Slowly, Cassidy made her way over and placed her hand on the small of Alex's back. "What is it?"

"My reinstatement was approved."

"Isn't that a good thing?" Cassidy's own apprehension about Alex moving back to the NSA was something she had tried desperately to suppress in front of her lover. Working as an FBI agent posed many risks. The NSA conjured images and ideas of secret agents, spying on civilians and worst of all, imminent danger. The thought of losing Alex was terrifying to Cassidy but she was determined to be supportive. "Alex?"

"It is a good thing," the agent said with a reassuring smile. "I need to call Taylor."

Cassidy nodded her understanding as Alex stood and made her way out of the room. She put her face in her hands and took a deep breath. "God," she sighed. A sudden rattling sound from the side table startled her and she watched her cell phone gently glide across it. "Now what?" she muttered.

***

"Why the change?" Krause asked rubbing his forehead.

"Strickland is an idiot," Admiral Brackett answered.

Jon Krause held the phone in front of his face and rolled his eyes. Moving it back to his ear he shook his head and chuckled. "He's arrogant. I told you that from the beginning."

"What did Viktor say?" the admiral inquired with notable concern in his voice.

"He's spooked. Worried about Callier. Worried about the French commitment to our operations."

Admiral Brackett paced the floor of his small office. "Is he talking action?"

"It's clearly an option for the Russians."

"Jesus Christ, Jon."

"I think you can rest easy for now. He won't like this change though, delaying the transaction again to deal with O'Brien. What about Edmond?"

The admiral sat behind his desk, twirling a pen mindlessly in his fingers. "Edmond agrees. O'Brien is a liability."

"Sending O'Brien to Corsica…it's an exposure risk. If he…"

"Jon, call Edmond. He will explain. We need to put O'Brien in line. He's no longer an asset. Go to London. Mitchell will meet you there. Edmond will deal with Mercier. Corsica presents an opportunity to put this to bed. I'll inform Sparrow. Sparrow will get the documentation we need."

Jon Krause took a deep breath. "Are you sure that is a wise decision?"

"There's no choice. Contact Edmond first. We need a trail to O'Brien that is verifiable. Strickland remains a wild card." Krause chuckled. Lawrence Strickland was the opposite of John Merrow. The decision to remove President Merrow may have stitched closed one tear in the network but in the process it effectively infected everything else with an unpredictable virus. "Krause, we need to handle this situation quickly."

"Well, Admiral," the CIA agent began. "Have you an antidote for hubris?"

William Brackett's temple twitched as he considered his response for a moment. The final decision to assassinate John Merrow came from him. He listened to the players and their concerns and he took the necessary action. Now, he hated to admit Krause's words stung. Strickland was not dependable, O'Brien was not trustworthy and both had only one agenda; the furtherance of his career. That made them dangerous players that needed to be controlled quickly. "You brought O'Brien into this," the admiral reminded the agent.

"Did I?" Krause countered. "I set up what you asked. I positioned where you dictated. I believe that I cautioned the chosen…"

"Yes, I recall," Brackett admitted. "London, Jon. O'Brien is going to Corsica next week. Work with Agent Mitchell. Make it happen. I want him removed from this."

Krause let out a heavy sigh and tossed the phone aside. "My pleasure this time," he said.

***

"I don't know, Taylor," Alex said. "There was something in Tate's voice."

"You think he suspects…"

"I don't know what I think," Alex said abruptly. "What about Fallon?"

"Not much yet. Brady's digging more on Brackett's time with DCIS. Fallon seems to think her purpose at the bureau was not initially about you. Something about an investigation in 2008 with the DEA regarding a chemical attack on the Saudi Embassy. Sound familiar?"

"We looked into some of that when we were investigating Al Asad," she recalled as she heard Cassidy's voice approaching.

"No…No…I understand," Cassidy said with her phone to her ear. "Of course."

"Taylor, I gotta go," Alex said noting the expression on Cassidy's face as the teacher hung up her own call.

"Everything okay?" he asked.

"I don't know. Keep me posted. I'll head in Thursday and touch base with Brady." Alex disconnected her call and looked at the teacher. "Cass?"

"It's Dylan." The agent's heart stopped and she immediately went pale. "No," Cassidy gave a nervous chuckle. "He's all right. We need go to the school."

"What's going on?"

Cassidy shook her head. "I'll explain on the way."

***

Alex and Cassidy walked into the school office and Alex immediately caught sight of Dylan sitting on a small chair in the corner. His eyes were slightly red and his clothes were covered in dirt and grass stains. He looked at the two women as they entered the room and immediately cast his gaze on his feet. An attractive woman dressed in a blue pantsuit emerged from a frosted glass door and smiled. "Mrs. O'Brien?"

"Yes," Cassidy answered.

"Sorry we meet this way. I'm Dr. Bell. I guess Friday was just too long to bring us together," the principal said with an earnest measure of reassurance. Cassidy smiled halfheartedly. "Follow me," she said with a smile. "Sit down, please." Alex fidgeted in her chair as the principal extended her hand.

"This is my," Cassidy paused and thought for a moment. "Partner?" she looked to Alex who smiled nervously, "Alex Toles."

"Nice to meet you Ms. Toles," the principal greeted warmly. "So, as I told you, there was an incident on the playground between Dylan and another young man. He was, as I am given to understand, taunting your son."

"It's not like Dylan to hit someone," Cassidy said plainly.

Dr. Bell nodded. "I don't doubt that. I understand that Dylan did try to walk away. Apparently, George pushed your son. That's according to some of their classmates."

"And then Dylan hit him?" Cassidy urged the principal to continue.

"No. The boy said something to him. Dylan would not share with me what it was and neither would George. Whatever it was; it resulted in a brawl." Cassidy sighed and shook her head. Alex bit her bottom lip. "Both the boys will have detention tomorrow. I think, in light of how upset Dylan was when I spoke with him; well....I know it's been a difficult time for him. This hasn't been the best first day. I thought, maybe a fresh start tomorrow would be best. George's mother assured me she would speak to him and get to the bottom of things."

Alex swallowed hard as Cassidy maintained control. "I appreciate that. Alex and I will have a talk with Dylan when we get home." The teacher's voice was even but strained and Alex could tell that Cassidy intended to be firm with Dylan. It reminded her a bit of her own youth.

"He seems like a very sweet boy," the principal smiled.

"He is," Alex answered bluntly without hesitation. Cassidy tried not to giggle, completely aware that Alex's reaction was to defend Dylan.

Principal Bell nodded. "Let me know, please....what you discover?" she urged.

"Of course," Cassidy assured. The principal opened the door and Cassidy and Alex stepped through. "Let's go," Cassidy called over to the boy who would not look up to meet her gaze. Cassidy kept her pace steady as Dylan fell in behind and looked up sheepishly to Alex. The agent offered him a faint smile. She had asked Cassidy for boring. As she watched Cassidy enter the car and Dylan climb in his seat; she realized she had been right. Dull would never be a problem in this family.

***

97

The silence in the car lingered. Alex looked over at Cassidy who was looking out her window and noted the tension on the smaller woman's face. She looked into the rear view mirror and tried not to laugh when she was met with the exact same expression on Dylan's. His words startled her. "I'm sorry, Mom." Cassidy let out an audible sigh and was about to speak when he continued. "You're mad."

"Dylan, you know better than to hit anyone," she answered.

He kicked at the seat in front of him. "I had to."

"You had to?" Cassidy uncharacteristically raised her voice. Alex reached over and grasped the teacher's hand. "You don't ever *have* to hit someone."

"He called you gay!" Dylan yelled.

"That's no reason to hit someone," Cassidy answered immediately.

"Yes it is," he said. "He said you can't be a mom."

Cassidy was still aggravated by the entire situation. Alex licked her lips and finally dared to speak. "Dylan..."

Cassidy interrupted. "Dylan, do you know why he said that to you?"

"No."

"Well, Dylan. You know that Alex is a girl and so am I," Cassidy began.

"So?" He kicked at the seat again.

"Stop kicking the seat!" Cassidy demanded.

"Dylan," Alex interjected. "I am gay."

"No you're not," he said. "You're Alex."

Alex shook her head and finally saw Cassidy start to chuckle. "I guess we have some things to talk about, huh?" Cassidy looked at her lover. Alex smiled. "Dylan," Cassidy continued. "You can't hit people. You understand that? Even when they say something about me."

"I know," he muttered.

"Mm...Why don't we get a pizza and head home?" Cassidy suggested to Alex.

"You're not mad?" he asked his mother hopefully.

"No, I'm not mad." He perked up in his seat and smiled. "But I'm not happy either," she went on. "I think we need to talk about some things. And I don't want you fighting. No matter what he said; hitting him was wrong."

Alex kept her focus forward. "Your mom is right, Speed."

"I know," he whispered. "I'm sorry."

Alex smiled. "Speed, some people don't understand. Somebody like your mom being with somebody like me."

"You mean because you're like a superhero and Mom is a teacher?"

Alex laughed and Cassidy covered her face with her hand. Dylan was so innocent and it was nothing if not endearing. "No. I mean because I am a girl and so is your mom. And when that happens some people call it gay."

"Oh," he said taking the statement in. "Why?"

"I don't know," Alex confessed.

"That's stupid," he said.

Cassidy shook her head. For a moment she had begun to worry about explaining things to her son. There was nothing to explain; had the other boy called her any name Dylan would have responded in the same way. He had no idea what 'gay' even meant. As they drove now she realized that George probably didn't either. He had probably heard someone else say it without even grasping what it meant at all. She and Alex could prepare Dylan for some of what he might hear and they needed to do that, but she would never be able to make him understand why people said it. She chuckled and looked at Alex; her first visit to the principal's office. It was a milestone, a rite of passage in parenting, and unlike the many that had passed before it; this one she was sharing with someone else. Her distress over her son's fisticuffs dissipated into an overwhelming sense of gratefulness and she squeezed the hand that held her own.

"Is this what you meant by chaos in the boring?" Alex asked. Cassidy nodded and raised her eyebrow. "Sign me up," the agent smiled.

***

Chapter Ten

Wednesday, April 16ᵗʰ

Agent Steven Brady rifled through the papers that were spread across his desk. He held one up and examined it closely. Letting out a strong sigh he placed it carefully on top of the heaping pile and retrieved another. Brady shook his head and pushed his chair away from the desk with some force. He pulled at the short hairs on the top on his head and grimaced. "It can't be," he muttered, running his hand over his face and pulling at his lip. "Shit." The agent picked up his phone and waited. Hearing the voice on the other end, he spoke. "Michael," he began softly.

"Brady?" Michael Taylor answered. There was no question that something was troubling the younger man. It was more than unusual for Steven Brady to address the director as Michael. That informality was reserved for two things; personal time and issues that were sure to produce emotion. "Brady, what?"

"Well…Admiral Brackett," Brady paused. "Listen, you said that the president mentioned Iraq to Agent Toles."

"Yes, he did." Brady paced the floor of his small office, holding the phone with one hand and continually rubbing the other over the top of his head. He stopped for a moment behind the desk and glanced down at the two papers set atop his pile. "Brady?" Taylor called with some impatience.

"What exactly was your mission there?" Brady asked.

"In Iraq?" Taylor asked in confusion.

"Yes, in Baghdad. Your team; what was the mission?"

"I told you before, we were assigned to assess threats. Assess movements in and around the city that would pose a danger to our forces or the new government."

"And?" Brady asked.

"And liaise with the locals. Strengthen their trust, help rebuild local commerce in order to stem insurgents."

Brady swallowed hard. "What was it called?"

"What?"

"The operation. Did the operation have a codename?" Brady asked.

"Well, of course," Taylor offered. "Brady, what the hell does this have to do with…"

"Please, what was the name?

Taylor pursed his lips and tightened his jaw, "SPHINX, the codename was SPHINX."

Steven Brady collapsed into his chair. "I think you need to see this."

"Brady, what the hell is going on?"

"Remember when you said Merrow was at the head of every…"

"Jesus, Steven…just tell me!" Taylor interrupted.

"SPHINX…as in the creature for which you must solve a riddle."

"I suppose," Taylor said.

"There's the riddle," Steven Brady paused and approached his friend and mentor carefully. "That mission; that's not what SPHINX's objective was."

"What the hell are you talking about?" Taylor yelled in frustration.

"Brackett, Merrow, according to this, that had to be a front." Brady picked up one of the papers. "I have to dig some more…"

"Brady, what the hell are you saying?"

"ASA…money filtered from SPHINX to ASA."

"The Russian arms manufacturer?" Taylor asked.

"That would be the one. Somehow SPHINX was linked to funds that landed at ASA. Money filtered through a Swiss account. ASA was the destination. Brackett's directive. I can't tell what was brokered. I think…"

"What?"

"I think it was weapons shipped into Baghdad through Jordan. It would have been in what appeared benign shipments," Brady explained.

"Christ, Brady. Alex is coming there tomorrow to touch base. She's not official, not until next week…I…"

"I won't say anything," Brady said.

"No. Tell her. Give her what you have."

"Do you really think that's…"

Michael Taylor exhaled and interrupted his friend. "Steven," he said quietly, "this is Alex's. No one knows the contacts we used during SPHINX better. If it was a cover for what you suggest, Alex will be able to unravel it the fastest." He stopped and took a deep breath. "She has the right. She's blamed herself all these years; give it to her."

"Sir, with all due respect. Agent Toles has just…."

"Toles can handle it. Trust me. She'll find it anyway. If she thinks we kept it from her…Well….You need to keep following the admiral's trail. There's more there. If SPHINX was a cover, our operations were not the end of it. If John knew that," his thoughts trailed to a whisper.

"All right. What about the younger Brackett?" Brady asked.

"That's well in hand. Follow the admiral and O'Brien. Anything new on that front?"

"Not yet. Separate pile," Brady chuckled in an attempt to relieve the palpable tension.

"Keep on it."

"Taylor?" Brady inquired.

"Yes?"

"If the president was…"

Taylor felt his stomach lurch. He looked out his window at the trees that were beginning to bloom. "If John knew...well," Taylor swallowed hard. "It's hard to kill a president from the outside."

Brady nodded silently. There was nothing more to say. Whatever SPHINX was, it likely would tell a new story about Admiral William Brackett and President John Merrow. "Maybe he didn't."

"There's only one way to know. Give it to Agent Toles."

***

"I don't understand," Christopher O'Brien said to the president.

"What don't you seem to comprehend, Congressman?"

"Why would you want me to go to Corsica? I just got back," O'Brien replied.

President Strickland smiled. "Christopher, you wanted in. Right?" O'Brien looked at the president but remained silent. "You wanted to be in the center of it all. Now you are. We financed your campaign. We set you up on the right committees. We charged you with certain legislative goals. All of that, Christopher is just a screen. The legislation won't stop or start anything. It can complicate things, but we do not operate from a legislative position. The risk is exposure. You can no longer stay on the sidelines. Your missteps with Chairman Stiller... Well, he is more determined than ever to increase oversight at the CIA and the NSA and follow through with the port restrictions. Even the National Security Council is on his docket. People do not trust you, Congressman."

"What do I have to do?" O'Brien asked.

"You have to convince our partners that their investment is secure. And that you are invested."

"I don't understand."

"You will. You will get directive. Corsica next Thursday, Chris. The cover story will be a meeting with several foreign corporations that provide us with military equipment; to hear their concerns over the legislation. Be prepared for them to ask for your assurances."

"Sir, Callier did not want assurances."

Strickland laughed. "Edmond Callier regards you as a fly. He has no reason to believe you. Stiller spoke with the French Prime Minister on Monday before you arrived. Callier is well aware of that."

O'Brien was confused. "How would...."

"You are naïve, Congressman. Stiller has had a close relationship with the French Prime Minister for years. Their daughters attended the same university. Don't be fooled. Either you immerse yourself fully or..." O'Brien looked at the president as the man took a seat in his large leather chair. President Lawrence Strickland nodded at the questioning he saw in the younger man's eyes. "Or they will swat the fly," he said hitting the top of his desk for dramatics. "You need to learn how to make the right friends, Congressman. Corsica. Get ready."

***

Friday, April 18th

Alex Toles sat at the kitchen table pouring through files. The full cup of coffee to her left had gone cold. She set down a paper and rubbed her eyes with the palms of her hands. There was a trail here; she was sure of it. The problem was that all of the breadcrumbs seemed to abruptly end. There was little doubt in her mind that Steven Brady was right. SHPINX was indeed a project; not simply a codename for a military operation. What she couldn't figure out was whether John Merrow or anyone else in the unit knew about it. It made sense that whomever was behind SPHINX wanted intelligence on the local merchants. There would be no better way to ship arms than to bring them in through general commerce. She remained uncertain who the weapons were destined for and who was actually selling

105

them. If the goal was to equip the local police and army; why wouldn't the unit simply have been informed? She moved the palm of her hand to her temple and pressed forcefully. Her eyes were tired, her head was throbbing and her concentration was continually interrupted by thoughts of her parents. "Shit," she whispered, running her hand over the length of her face.

The agent sensed the hand in front of her and slowly opened her eyes. "I think you need a break," Cassidy said bluntly. Alex released a heavy breath and accepted the two ibuprofen in the teacher's hand. She watched the coffee mug be lifted and replaced with a large glass of water. "Alex…"

"Cassidy, I have to know."

"And you think your answer lies in there?" She pointed to the pile.

"I don't know," Alex snapped back.

"I see," Cassidy stood firm. "So….you sitting here with this all afternoon has nothing to do with the fact that your mother has called three times since last night?"

Alex looked up, her eyes nearly on fire. "My mother has nothing to do with this."

Cassidy nodded and pursed her lips. "Alex, I have no idea what is going on; what you are looking for. I do know you. And this is not just about that pile," she gestured to the full mug in her hand. When Alex was focused she had a habit of unconsciously lifting her coffee or her Diet Coke to her lips as she read. Cassidy had observed that when Alex was pouring over files during the investigation into Carl Fisher. Alex was clearly unfocused. There was no doubt that whatever Steven Brady had given the agent was troubling her, but there was more to it and Cassidy was sure of that. Helen Toles had called the house three times since the night before and Alex avoided her call each time. Cassidy had finally picked up and spoke with the woman herself. "Alex, just call her back. She was very sweet on the phone."

"I need to deal with this. That's all," Alex answered sharply.

"Fine. I have to pick Dylan up." Cassidy looked at the agent who was already feeling guilty for her impatience. The teacher set the mug in the sink and turned back. "Take those," she nodded toward Alex's hand and left the room.

Alex pinched the bridge of her nose and looked down at her hand. She silently scolded herself for losing her temper and took the pills as Cassidy had directed. Her eyes scanned over the pile in front of her and she collapsed back into the chair. There was something here. She knew it. She just had to find it. The agent looked to the ceiling and a chuckle escaped her. She wasn't going to find it; not now. Cassidy was right. She couldn't concentrate. Gently her thumb caressed her temple. Lifting her gaze she noted the time on the clock. It was still too early for Dylan to come home. "Dammit," she looked at the pile and cursed it and herself. Cassidy wasn't even going to remind her. They were supposed to meet with Dylan's teacher and the principal. "Brilliant, Toles," she admonished herself. Swiftly, she gathered the papers in front of her and put them in her briefcase. Grabbing her jacket and keys, she headed for the door. "I hope she doesn't give me detention too."

***

"They're sending me back to France," O'Brien said as he watched the tall redhead climb from her bed.

"I know," Claire Brackett replied. The congressman rolled to his side and reveled in the view that stood before him. "See something you like?" she cooed.

"I'd like it better back here."

"I'm sure you would," she quipped. "Why do you think they are sending *you*?"

O'Brien collapsed back onto the pillow and put his arms behind his head. "I don't know something about immersing me; making the right friends. That's what Strickland said."

Claire Brackett let out a roar. "And you believe that?"

"Why else would they send me?"

"You might be handsome, but you certainly are stupid," she shot.

"Excuse me?" he sat up.

"They are setting you up," she said as she pulled a black sweater over her head.

"How do you know that?"

"Because they are sending the sparrow in to take care of it," she shrugged.

"The sparrow?" he laughed. "Claire, that sounds like some spy movie. How would you even know what they are planning?"

She licked her lips and winked as she seductively made her way back to the bed and straddled her lover. She hovered just above him planting a soft kiss on his chest. "I know," she said placing another kiss on his throat. "Because," she kissed him on the nose. "I am the sparrow." She lifted her eyebrow and kissed him passionately.

***

Alex called to Dylan to stay in the yard before turning to her lover. "I'm sorry, Cass," she said as she made her way behind the teacher, wrapping her arms around Cassidy's waist.

"I have to admit, I was surprised to see you walk through that door," Cassidy smiled as Alex's head came to rest on her shoulder.

"I screwed up."

Cassidy turned to face the agent. Gently, she placed a kiss on Alex's cheek. "No. You didn't."

"You were right," Alex conceded.

"Really?" Cassidy lifted her eyebrow playfully.

"All right, you don't have to rub it in," Alex smiled.

"Alex, I know that you are worried about whatever is in that briefcase." Alex started to speak and Cassidy put her finger to the agent's lips, "and, I know you are nervous about tomorrow."

108

"I just don't want them to make you feel...."

Cassidy stretched to meet the agent's lips. "Stop worrying about me."

"Mm-hmm. She wanted to know what you and Dylan liked or didn't; you know to eat," Alex said.

"You called her?"

Alex shrugged. "On my way to the school. She'll probably make everything she knows how to make." The tone in the taller woman's voice gave away her embarrassment. Cassidy laughed. "She wanted me to invite your mother."

"Oh Lord," Cassidy laughed. "And?"

"Up to you."

"Uh, Alex...my mother..."

"I think you should," Alex said.

"Why? You think she can protect you?" Cassidy joked.

"Maybe," Alex admitted. "You have Barb. At least someone there will like me."

Cassidy laughed. "I'd say there will be more than a few people there that *like* you."

"Really? Who?" Alex asked.

"You are impossible, you know that?"

"I am sorry, Cass," Alex said softly. "I shouldn't have snapped at you."

"I have a feeling it won't be the last time," Cassidy kissed the agent's cheek.

"Still, I...."

"You know you can always make it up to me later."

Alex's grin widened. "Oh? What did you have in mind?"

"Well," Cassidy ran her hands up the agent's back. "Downstairs?"

"Yes?" the agent urged.

"There's a pool table..."

"Uh huh," Alex swallowed hard as Cassidy's hands reached her neck.

"Well, it seems that the table somehow got shifted..."

"Oh?"

"Yeah...and it seems that your favorite mother-in-law bought us a couch for the room; you know so she could watch Dylan play."

"What?" Alex asked.

"Yes. So the table needs to move back even farther. She's having it delivered Tuesday." Cassidy smirked and ducked under Alex's arm. She started toward the refrigerator when she felt a grip on her jeans pull her backward.

"Well, you know we could just move it the same way it shifted," Alex breathed in her ear.

Cassidy closed her eyes. "And how would that be, exactly?"

"Well, that will require another lesson," Alex nipped the teacher's ear.

"Are you saying I need more instruction?" Cassidy asked playfully, feeling Alex's kisses trail along her neck.

"No, I fell in love with a teacher for a reason."

"Alex..." Cassidy lost her breath completely as the agent's hands ran across her stomach.

"You teach me every day," the agent said softly. "*Je suis désolée* (I am sorry)."

Cassidy turned in the agent's strong arms. Tenderly, she caressed Alex's cheek and saw a faint smile creep across the agent's face. "*Tu n'as pas à être désolée, mon amour. Je serai toujours là* (You don't have to be sorry, love. I will always be here)." Alex bent down and kissed her lover gently. Cassidy pulled back and smiled. "I will look forward to the lesson," Cassidy whispered in the agent's ear. "But, I still need you to move the table."

***

Chapter Eleven

Claire Brackett looked left and then right, checking her surroundings completely. Across the street a blue sedan sat inconspicuously. The driver shifted in his seat and watched as the young woman climbed into her vehicle. "What are you up to, Brackett?" Brian Fallon wondered aloud. He studied the car carefully as it began to pull away from the curb. Patiently, he waited as the car carrying the young woman reached the corner of the street. Slowly he pulled his sedan out, leaving enough distance between them to ensure that no one would suspect his presence. He glanced in the rearview mirror and gasped. "What the hell?" Quickly, he refocused his attention on the car a block ahead, glancing back to confirm the sight he still needed to process. "O'Brien, what are you doing with Brackett now?" he mumbled as he turned his full attention ahead. "I will figure your game out Claire; believe it."

***

Saturday, April 19th

"Did the road move again?" Cassidy asked the woman sitting in the driver's seat. A soft chuckle escaped from her mother who was seated behind her.

"What?" Alex asked a bit defensively.

"You've moved that mirror at least five times in the last fifteen minutes," Cassidy observed. "And, I'm pretty certain that windshield is cleaner than it has ever been." Alex had a habit of fidgeting when she was nervous. She forced an unconvincing smile and reached for the radio when she felt Cassidy's hand take hold of hers, placing it gently to rest on the teacher's knee. There were few things that could rattle Alex Toles. Her parents remained at the top of that very short list. Gently, but firmly Cassidy kept Alex's hand in her grasp. Alex Toles was a woman with many layers and even in the most difficult moments, Cassidy loved her completely.

"Ready?" Alex asked as she pulled into the driveway of 122 Pond View Road. Cassidy smiled feeling the warmth of Alex's hand which was uncharacteristically trembling. Dylan was already opening his door and Rose struggled to contain her amusement at his enthusiasm when he caught sight of Cat running toward them. "Dylan," Alex started to call, but the two boys were already in a sprint toward one another.

"It will be fine," Cassidy reassured the agent. "Come on."

***

"I was surprised to get your call," Michael Taylor said to the man in front of him.

"I'm sure," the man answered.

"So? What is it that you wanted to discuss?" Taylor asked. The NSA Director of Domestic Affairs was curious and skeptical of the man that stood before him now.

"Agent Toles," the man began.

"What about her?" Taylor asked stoically.

"There are things that she needs to know, Director. Things you should both know."

Michael Taylor bit his bottom lip and his eyes narrowed. "What *things*?" The taller man nodded and retrieved a piece of paper from his coat pocket, handing it to the NSA director. "I don't understand," Taylor offered as he studied the paper.

"That's all I can give you," the man answered, "at least now. There are answers there, or at least that is where you can find the trail."

"Even I don't have access to…."

The taller man began to turn to make his exit and stopped. "Few have access. I can't help you with that. I am certain Agent Toles will have an idea," he suggested.

"You are suggesting we break into a top secret," Taylor began and was immediately interrupted.

"If you want the answers, Director Taylor, you will need to search the sources." The taller man turned and walked away. He continued his thought without slowing, "be careful, Taylor, both of you. Send Toles."

***

The day was progressing far more smoothly than Alex had anticipated. Bringing Rose along proved a godsend for the agent. Cassidy's mother expertly navigated the rocky waters of conversation with Helen and Nicolaus Toles. Alex chuckled thinking that Cassidy's mother could charm the pants off a president or a punk with equal ease. It was a trait that Rose McCollum had passed onto her daughter and Alex was amazed at the ease with which Cassidy had engaged Helen Toles. She laughed at the thought as she watched her brother chase after a wobbly thrown football. Cat and Dylan had become engaged in an impromptu football game, albeit a wobbly one. It gave Alex and Nick an excuse to leave the female dominated conversation inside the house to "instruct" the boys. In true form, brother and sister had decided that a game was in order; Nick proclaiming that it would be "epic".

Alex bent over and whispered to Cat while Nick mimicked the same action with Dylan. They met in the middle of the yard; Nick offering his sister a smug smile. In an instant Dylan was off with a shot. Alex chased down Nick and sacked him,

113

but not before he had a chance to launch the ball high in the air forcefully. Cat took off after Dylan who was determined that this was his moment. Dylan held his arms out and watched the ball sail toward him. It was right there; right in his small grasp and he jumped slightly to meet it. He felt the ball in his arms and then he felt his body thrust to the ground. Alex hopped to her feet just as the small boy tumbled backward. Like a bullet from a gun she was off to his side. "Jesus, Nick!" she scolded, looking at the trail of blood running down Dylan's face.

"I caught it Uncle Nick!" he proclaimed.

"I guess you did," Nick tried not to laugh.

"You're not supposed to catch it with your face," Cat said plainly.

"I still caught it," Dylan insisted as Alex swept him up and headed swiftly for the house. The agent's heart was racing faster than she could remember. Cassidy shook her head as a pale faced Alex stepped into the kitchen. "I caught it Mom!"

"I can see that," Cassidy said calmly.

"Good Lord, Alexis," Helen Toles began. "What did you do to that boy?"

"What? I didn't….Nick….."

"Hey, he caught it," Nick shrugged.

"Honestly, Alexis. He is just a boy." Alex sat Dylan in a chair and Cassidy accepted a wet rag and some ice from Alex's mother.

"I told you we'd win," Dylan winced at Alex through a few silent tears, determined to stay tough.

"Dylan," Alex began when her mother cut her off.

"Alexis, let the mothers take care of this. You two have caused enough grief for one day," she pointed to her children.

Alex looked at Cassidy sheepishly and was met with a reassuring smile. She felt Nick's hand leading her away and shook her head. "What happened?" Nicolaus Toles asked as his children entered the living room.

"Casualty," Nick explained, flopping back onto the couch.

Alex sat in a chair close to the doorway, trying to listen to the conversation a few rooms away. "Alexis," her father began, prompting her to meet his gaze. "Boys will be boys. If you *had* children you would know that."

Nick looked at his sister and bit his lip. "It was my fault," he admitted in an attempt to change the subject. "I threw it too hard."

"Just toughening him up," Nicolaus Toles said firmly. "Cat can handle it. He's a Toles."

"It wasn't Cat that got hurt," Alex said.

"Oh?" her father inquired.

"No," she said.

"Your *friend's* son, then?" he asked as he continued to peruse the magazine in front of him.

Alex felt his words cut through her. "My *friend?*"

"Well, yes, what else would you call her?"

Nick scratched his eyebrow and looked to his sister in hopes of calming what he knew was a rising storm. "She's my partner."

"I don't understand, Alexis. She's a teacher, isn't she?" her father answered.

"You know perfectly well what I mean," Alex responded sharply.

"I don't know why you are getting so upset," her father said coolly. "I'm sure the young man is fine."

"The young man has a name."

"Alex?" a voice called from the door. The agent turned to see a small, slowly bruising face approaching.

"Hey, Speed; you all right?" Alex asked as Dylan reached her.

He nodded and looked at Nick. "Sorry, Uncle Nick."

"What do you mean Dylan? You caught the ball," Nick praised.

"Yeah, but I didn't make the touchdown."

"Not your fault, Dylan," Nick assured him. "It was a bad throw."

Dylan smiled as Alex's finger made its way to his lip. The agent sighed and gave the boy a crooked smile. "Mom wants you in the kitchen," Dylan said taking hold of the agent's hand.

"Uh-oh, am I in trouble?" Alex asked quietly.

"Not with Mom," he said. "Maybe with your mom," he tried to whisper.

Nick snickered as he watched his sister nervously move to her feet. "Good luck," he smirked.

Dylan pulled at Alex's hand. "I'll be right there," she said, encouraging him to continue onward. Alex stopped in the doorway and looked at her father. "That young man?" Alex looked squarely at her father as he dropped the magazine slightly to meet her gaze. "His name is Dylan…and he *is* my son."

***

"Brackett. What are you doing?" Brian Fallon ran through possibilities in his mind as he watched the young woman enter a small building on L Street. The gate rolled up and the red-headed agent walked in. "What the hell are you doing in this neighborhood?" Fallon mused. He was frustrated with keeping his surveillance at a distance. All of the younger agent's actions clearly indicated that she was engaged in something below the radar; possibly even from whomever she was working for. He pulled the sedan over into a small adjacent alley and made his decision. Somehow he would gain entrance to that building. Claire Brackett had information. Time was not always an ally. That was a fact that Brian Fallon understood clearly. He needed to get closer. There was no other option.

***

Alex sat at the dinner table listening to her brother and father talk about business. Her mother and Rose talked about children, and Cassidy and Barb occasionally broke in with their own tales about the two boys. Cat and Dylan were laughing at the far end of the table. Alex found herself wishing she could shrink somehow and be part of their conversation. She felt completely alone and her father's words and tone kept pouring through her mind. It reminded her of when she was younger. Why didn't she play with the other girls? Nicolaus Toles sought to correct that with a paddle and a thick stick. When she announced her acceptance to West Point her father rolled his eyes and left the room. The only time she had ever introduced her parents to a lover, her father refused to call the woman by her name. It was Ms. Johnson. She felt the tension building in her back as she played with the food on her plate mindlessly.

"So we have some interesting news," Nick's voice broke the agent's silent memories.

"Oh?" Helen Toles smiled.

"Well, it seems we'll need another chair at the table soon," Nick smiled.

"Why?" his father inquired. "You make a new *friend?*" Alex felt the words like a knife in her back, knowing they were directed at her.

Barb responded. "Not exactly, Dad."

"Oh…You're pregnant!" Helen Toles erupted with delight, receiving a confirming nod from her daughter-in-law.

"Well, about time we added some more grandchildren," Alex's father said bluntly.

Barb caught sight of Alex's forced smile as Nicolaus Toles stared at his daughter harshly. "It will be quite the full table this time next year," Barb offered. "Seems like everyone's family is growing," she smiled at Alex.

"Umm…always thought Alexis would be the one. When you have a daughter you just expect…" Alex's father began.

"It's wonderful news, Barb," Rose interjected, pretending she had no prior knowledge.

"Alex might surprise you yet," Barb looked at her father-in-law.

The agent nearly choked on her water and Cassidy gasped slightly at Barb's assertion. "I don't think Alexis…" he began.

Barb was growing tired of Nicolaus Toles and his hurtful rhetoric. She was well aware of the way it affected both Alex and her husband at times. Alex and Cassidy were family, her family. Cassidy had quickly become the sister Barb had always wished for and she regarded Dylan every bit as much Alex's son now as she did Cat her own. The Toles family had a way of avoiding honest conversation and talking in circles. In the few instances that Alex had joined the family in the last few years; she had always been the target of her parent's veiled insults. After the last get together, two years earlier, the agent had deliberately stayed away. Barb recalled that evening well. Helen Toles had admonished Alex for not taking a stronger role in the family. She should be married by now and raising her own family. The agent's father had bluntly stated his disappointment in Alex's choices. She could have had everything. He'd worked his whole life to make sure she would have everything and she had spit in his face. At least Nick was normal, he explained. Alex had calmly risen from her seat and excused herself. She had not returned since, not even at the holidays. "Well, we are all lucky to have Dylan," Barb continued without missing a beat. "But frankly, I hope Cassidy talks Alex into at least one more," she winked at the teacher.

"One more?" Alex's father looked at his daughter-in-law.

Nick looked at his wife to caution her but she had reached her limit. "Yes, you know, a baby." Cassidy learned her forehead on her hand as Alex's jaw flew open.

"Mom? Are you having a baby?" Dylan lisped through his split lip.

"No," Alex and Cassidy answered simultaneously.

"Awww," he huffed and turned back to Cat. "How come you get one?"

Nick and Rose both started laughing. "Time for dessert, I'd say," Nick interjected.

"Yes, it is," Alex said looking for any means of escape. "I'll take care of that."

"You?" Helen Toles questioned.

"Yes, Mother. I do know how to get plates and cut pie," Alex responded offering her hand to Cassidy who accepted willingly and followed Alex to the kitchen.

"I'll help," Barb offered.

"Yeah, thanks," Alex whispered to her sister-in-law. "Think you've *helped* enough."

"I know," Barb giggled with some satisfaction as they entered the kitchen. "I thought he was going to hemorrhage right there!"

"You do know Dylan is not going to forget that?" Cassidy raised her eyebrow at Barb. Barb just shrugged.

"Yeah she knows," a man's voice called from the doorway. "It's part of her master plan," Nick laughed.

Alex remained silent, retrieving small plates and forks and placing them on the counter. Cassidy looked at the agent who had begun to pinch the bridge of her nose with some force. "Let me take those," Barb said reaching in front of Alex as Nick grabbed the pie and motioned to his wife to follow.

"Alex," Cassidy said softly. "I'm sorry if…" Alex smiled and looked at woman she loved standing just a few inches away. Helen Toles was making her way toward them and stopped just shy of the kitchen to see her daughter lean forward toward Cassidy. She watched and listened curiously in the distance.

Alex sighed and kissed Cassidy's forehead. "What was that for?" Cassidy asked.

Alex shrugged. "I don't care what they think."

Cassidy's eyebrows lifted and she pursed her lips. "Yes, you do care."

"Maybe," Alex smiled earnestly. "I just want to get this over with, Cass, and go home."

Cassidy nodded and rubbed the agent's arm. "I know that made you uncomfortable."

"Cass, I am *always* uncomfortable here."

"I'm sorry," Cassidy looked down sadly.

"I am sorry if they made you feel like…"

"Alex, I am fine. Dylan is having a great time with Cat, bloody lip and all. Don't worry about us."

"I do worry, Cass. *You* are my family. I just wish they could…"

"Come on," Cassidy prompted the agent.

Alex pulled the teacher back gently. "For the record?" she began. "What Barb said did not make me uncomfortable. My father, well…" Cassidy smiled and Alex sighed. "After this, I wouldn't blame you if you ran back to New York."

Cassidy laughed and planted a soft kiss on the agent's lips. "Sorry, Agent, you are stuck with us."

"Hum. You know this means we will have to come back here, right?"

"I think I can handle that," Cassidy said.

"You might want to rethink that when it's my turn to make that announcement."

"You can't change who they are, Alex."

"I know. I just wish they would stop trying to change me."

"Come on," Cassidy encouraged.

"Cass?"

Cassidy turned around. "Hum?"

"Thanks."

The teacher winked. "Enough stalling, Alfred. You got out of cutting that pie. It's not going to eat itself."

Helen Toles stood straight and walked into the doorway, stopping the pair in their tracks. "Could I have a moment with Alexis?"

Cassidy looked up into the agent's eyes, witnessing the insecurity in them. She squeezed Alex's hand and smiled at the agent's mother. "Of course," she said, leaving the Toles women alone in the kitchen for the first time in more than two years.

***

Brian Fallon approached the rear of the abandoned three story building carefully. It was not uncommon in this part of the city and yet another reason Claire Brackett's visit here was perplexing. This part of L Street was noted for drug deals and gun sales, not a place a DCIS or FBI agent normally ventured. This was a beat cop's territory. Agent Fallon was glad he could claim that title on his resume; that and all that went with it. This was his turf. He looked to the left and saw the rickety fire escape that climbed the height of the building. "Worth a try," he muttered. He pulled on the bar and it fell just above his head. With a heave he pulled himself up the ladder and onto the first stair. The smell in the alley was both suffocating and familiar. It was a blend of human excrement, dirt, stagnant sewer water and rotting wood. Fallon had deemed it the 'hopeless' smell when he worked his beat. He exhaled the stench and continued upward.

Reaching the second level he noticed a window where the boards had been pried away, hanging loosely on a nail. Clearly someone had made this an entrance at one time. "Likely a junkie or a homeless person," he mused. He shook his head as it filled with the images of despair he had so often encountered in alleys just like this one. It was time to focus on the task at hand. Carefully, he lifted the board and spun it upwards, peering into the blackness beyond. "Here goes nothing," he whispered. He cautiously draped his foot over the widow frame, hoping it would be met with solid ground. Feeling a firm presence beneath him, he reached around his side for his small flashlight. With a deep breath, Brian Fallon began his exploration of the building. He walked as if treading on glass, keenly aware of every sound around him and equally attuned to the need for silence in his maneuvering. Several feet away he could see light peering through the floor boards. He let out a heavy breath dreading the next move. Sliding onto his belly his senses were immediately filled with the scent of must and mold. He swallowed hard and squinted to peer through the crack that opened several inches in the floor. "Well, well, Agent Brackett...who is? What is that, Claire?" He rested his forehead against the floorboard and strained to focus as another figure came into view. "Son of a bitch, Tate."

***

"Mom, I really shouldn't leave Cass...."

"Sit down, Alexis," Helen Toles directed. "I think Cassidy can handle herself." Alex sighed and took a seat at the small kitchen table. She rubbed her hands together, twisting her knuckles, and wringing them tightly. "You are going to get arthritis is you keep doing that," her mother warned. "Always a fidget."

"You wanted to talk to me about fidgeting?" Alex asked pointedly.

The older woman sighed. "She's lovely, Alexis."

"I'm sorry?"

"Cassidy. She is a lovely woman," her mother said flatly.

"Yes, she is," Alex agreed with his mother's appraisal.

"Um-hum...and you think you can do right by her? And Dylan?"

Alex immediately pushed her chair back. "Look," she began.

"Sit down, Alexis," her mother instructed firmly. "For once just sit down and listen to me." Reluctantly, and with a heavy, audible sigh, Alex complied. "What you do; it's dangerous, isn't it?"

"It can be," Alex admitted.

Helen Toles nodded. "Alexis, you were always focused on what you were doing. You never had any interest in family."

"That's not true," Alex answered. "I never felt I had one."

"That's ridiculous," her mother responded.

"Is it?" Alex asked. "I never fit in here. You made that clear."

"I see," Helen Toles answered. "And, now?"

"I still don't belong here."

"Alexis, you are my daughter. You belong here more than anyone." Alex was shocked by her mother's words as the older woman stood and shook her head. "I don't understand, Alexis. Your father...well..."

"You don't have to explain," Alex said sadly.

Helen Toles turned and placed her hand on her daughter's cheek. Alex struggled against the tears that suddenly began to well in her eyes. She felt transported. They had been distant for many years now, Helen and Alexis Toles. It had not always been that way. Before the agent hit her teenage years, Helen Toles had been her refuge. She had bandaged the skinned knees and comforted the young Alex after any one of her father's many reprimands. Alex's decisions as a teenager to pursue sports, to dress casually and to avoid dating frustrated her traditional mother. Helen Toles had harsh words for the teenage Alex; words that stung more than any paddle her father had ever lifted. They were words that somehow seemed to wash away all the happy memories of years past. Now, the gentle touch of the older woman's hand seemed to convey a comfort Alex had all but forgotten.

"You love that woman in there," Helen said plainly. "That little boy; Alexis, he worships you; like you once did your father." Alex tried to hold her tears, feeling as if she were a small child again. "If you want a family you have to take care of them. Don't be so reckless." Alex looked at her mother whose eyes had grown misty. "Time is a teacher, Alexis. I don't really understand. I can't tell you that I do." Alex began to open her mouth to speak when her mother continued. "But, two years is too long. You can't get them back. Just remember that," she smiled. "Now, come on, there won't be any pie left." Helen Toles started to move when the feel of Alex's hand startled her.

"Mom?" Helen Toles smiled. "Why does he hate me?" Alex asked without looking at her mother.

"Oh, Alexis. Hate you?" The older woman sighed. "Is that what you think?" Alex's tears were now visible and threatening to break through her cool exterior. "Could you ever hate Cat?" Alex shook her head. "Nick?" Alex shook her head again. "Dylan?" Helen Toles crouched in front of her grown daughter. "We all have our demons. That man in there has never hated a living soul, least of all you." Alex did not understand. "Someday, maybe you will understand, Alexis. Give him some time."

"He's had years."

"You ran away, Alexis. A long time ago. You left. That is how he sees it." Alex swallowed hard as her mother wiped away a tear that had managed to roll down her cheek. "Don't be so reckless, Alexis. It will get tough. That's life. You can't run away when you have a family, even when you want to." The agent looked at her mother who had a twinkle in her eyes. "Believe it or not, Alexis, I love you." She kissed her daughter's forehead and gathered herself. "Now get yourself together and meet your family in the dining room."

***

Chapter Twelve

"Alex...Alex," Cassidy gently shook the woman lying next to her. "Wake up, it's a dream. Alex..." Alex had curled up into a ball and was mumbling something unintelligible. It was a scenario that Cassidy had grown familiar with. One that had seemed to play out in their lives regularly in the last few weeks. One night Cassidy would find herself waking the strong agent and rocking her as if she were a small child, comforting and reassuring her that the images and sounds in sleep were only dreams. Another night would find Cassidy gently wrapped in Alex's arms as she struggled for her breath, awakened by some nightmare of a shadowy figure and a knife. This new life together was always a dance; a balancing act that each seemed to understand intrinsically. "Alex," Cassidy gently called again as the taller form beside her finally collapsed into her arms. Cassidy stroked the agent's long hair and kissed her head softly. "It's all right. I'm here. You're safe," she assured her lover, believing that Alex had again traveled to that day on Mutanabbi Street.

"I don't understand," Alex said through a few remaining tears.

"What? What don't you understand?" Cassidy asked, placing another gentle kiss on the agent's head.

"She's wrong."

"I don't understand. Who is wrong?" Cassidy was confused.

"He does, Cass. Why does he?" Alex asked.

"Honey, I don't know what......."

"He does hate me. He's never...."

Cassidy sighed and closed her eyes. She shook her head and pulled the agent closer to her. "Your father doesn't hate you."

"Then why? Cass, why?"

It was so hard for Cassidy to understand this part of Alex's pain. The closer that she and Alex became the more she understood that their childhoods had been drastically different. While Cassidy was no stranger to loss; she was keenly aware that she had been fortunate to know the love of both of her parents. Her father's death had been devastating, but her mother had been deliberate in comforting, reassuring and nurturing Cassidy; always making a point to allow the young girl the time and the patience to grieve and to recall her father. Witnessing the insecurity and pain in Alex's eyes as she spoke of her parents broke Cassidy's heart. She had seen that same expression on so many children's faces in her classroom over the years. Looking at the strong woman she loved so deeply lying in her arms, reduced to the fears and the longings of a child, Cassidy felt a mixture of sadness and anger. "Alex, listen to me. Your parents don't hate you. They don't. They just don't understand."

Alex took a deep breath and laid her head on her lover's chest. "I'm sorry."

"What on earth are you sorry for?" Cassidy asked, perplexed by the agent's apology.

"I really shouldn't be carrying on like I am."

"Like you want your parents to approve of you?" Cassidy smiled. "I don't think that ever really changes for any of us."

"You don't?"

"No," Cassidy said flatly. "I don't."

"I'm sorry about Dylan."

"Alex, Dylan is fine. In fact, I think he is rather proud of his war wound."

"I never meant for him to get hurt."

"It happens. I doubt it will be the last time," Cassidy laughed. "Truthfully, I was more worried when I saw your face than when I saw his."

"Huh?'

"At least he still had some color. I thought for sure we were going to be picking you up off your mother's kitchen floor." She kissed Alex's head. "And so did your mother."

"You like her; don't you?" Alex asked.

"Your mother?"

"Yeah."

"I do. *But*, I don't like seeing you upset," Cassidy's tone became strained. "Alex, I think you just need to give them some time."

"Maybe."

"Did you tell them about the job?"

Alex sighed and sat up. "No." The question prompted a conversation that the agent knew was inevitable, but was dreading. She had talked to Michael Taylor late in the evening and she was not looking forward to delivering the news to Cassidy that she would be away for a few days, possibly longer. Without any conscious thought the agent's hands lifted to her face. She pressed the bridge of her nose with her index fingers before allowing them to come to rest on her cheek.

"What is it?" Cassidy asked. Alex's thumb reached her temple, pressing firmly and she swallowed hard in an attempt to summon the words she needed to speak. Cassidy nodded and closed her eyes. The signs were all there. Something was on Alex's mind and it wasn't simply the family visit they had been discussing. "Just tell me."

"I have to go away Tuesday," Alex said.

"Away to?"

"I can't tell you that, Cass." There was no response. Alex turned to look down at her lover. Cassidy's eyes were closed and she had hold of her bottom lip with her teeth. "Cass..."

"How long?"

"I don't know. A few days. Maybe a week." A silent tear escaped Cassidy's eye and Alex set out immediately to quell her lover's fears. "I'll be fine, Cass. It's just to look into some files. That's all."

"Files? But you can't tell me…"

"No. I can't. Trust me it is safer if you don't know." Alex wrapped her arm around Cassidy's waist and laid down beside her.

"Safer? Is it safe, Alex?" Cassidy asked. Some nights she would wake and swear she felt Carl Fisher slumping onto her foot. Memories of her time with the sadistic stalker were still fresh and although she was able to suppress them during the day, her dreams still had a mind of their own. She shuddered. With Alex close, Cassidy felt safe. They had only spent one night apart since that awful day in New York and Cassidy had not slept at all without the agent beside her. The thought of days or longer without Alex to hold her through her night-mares was unsettling. Alex's career posed risks. That was a real-ity that Cassidy knew she had to accept. It remained a reality that terrified her.

"I promise, Cass. I will be back before you know it."

Cassidy felt the agent's arms pulling her closer. "Alex…"

"I promise, Cass."

***

Monday, April 21st

"Taylor, who the hell gave you this information?" Alex demanded.

"Alex…."

"Look, you did not fly to New York with this, you did not call me on a Saturday night with this on the say so of some civil-ian analyst desk jockey and we both know it." Michael Taylor paced the small office. "And just what the hell was Fallon doing following Brackett into that building? Jesus."

"Enough, Agent," Taylor turned on his heels. "Brian Fallon is a seasoned agent and a former cop. You know that better than anyone."

"Yeah, and you know as well as I do that this is not about street thugs or even serial killers. The people we are dealing with make the likes of what Fallon has dealt with look like characters on a kids' cereal box."

"Interesting analogy."

"Taylor...."

"Look, Toles, just trust me it's good information on both fronts."

"Fine. What am I looking for?"

"Something on SPHINX. Something about the colonel. I'm not certain."

"Do you trust the source?" she asked

Taylor nodded and groaned. "I trust he has his reasons. I believe there is something there to find, yes."

Alex nodded and sat on a small desk chair. "What about Fallon?"

"Agent Fallon is following up on Assistant Director Tate as we speak," Taylor answered.

"I thought he was following Brackett?"

"He is, but whatever Brackett and Tate were discussing, Fallon was able to make out one word that repeated on the paper from his location."

"What was that?" Alex inquired.

"Corsica."

Alex picked up a file from the desk beside her and opened it. "You think Tate is involved with the French?" She pulled out a paper and studied it.

"Who knows? Fallon couldn't tell what it was. He was pretty certain that Corsica was written on it several times. That's all he saw, other than a few other minor words he could discern from that distance."

"Nothing is minor," Alex cautioned.

Michael Taylor laughed. He had forgotten Alex Toles' propensity for searching what seemed to others to be minor details. "See something in the word 'and'?" he joked.

Alex remained focused on the paper in her hands, her eyes scanning slowly across the document. Without lifting her sight she answered, "Yes, actually I do."

"See something?" he asked her to clarify her statement.

"Have Fallon call me when he is done with his surveillance of the assistant director."

"Toles?"

Alex placed the document in her hands back in the file and stood. "This had better not be some joke about little green men," she warned.

The NSA director shook his head. "What? I thought Mulder was your hero?" he joked.

"Uh-huh. For the record, I'm more inclined toward his partner."

"Really?" Taylor chuckled.

"Yeah."

"Alex, whatever is there; you have to get in first."

"I'll get in," she said assuredly.

"I don't have to remind you that we don't have John to…"

"No. You don't."

Taylor grew pensive. "I don't have authority to get you that clearance. Technically, you are not military personnel. What are you going to do?"

Alex smiled and placed her hand on her friend's shoulder. "It's better if you don't know, Taylor."

"Plausible deniability?" he asked kiddingly.

"For all of us," she answered seriously.

"Alex, he did say," Taylor stopped himself.

"What did this informant say?"

"Be careful. He said to be careful."

"Well, I feel so much better knowing he cares," Alex remarked sarcastically. "I've got some things to do before tomorrow. If Fallon…"

"I'll make sure you are the first to know."

Alex nodded. "Taylor?"

"Yeah?"

"The ands; they mean there are many. Even if John was at the head of the trail, there are a lot of forks in the road. Watch Brackett."

"Which one?" he asked.

Alex shrugged. "Watch everyone."

***

"Alex."

"Jane. How are you?"

"I was surprised to get your call so soon. Is everything all right? Cassidy? Dylan?"

Alex smiled, accepting a seat on a large sofa. "They're fine. Other than a split lip."

"Good Lord, teaching Cassidy hand to hand are you?" The woman laughed.

The agent offered a broad smile. "Not Cassidy; Dylan. But that might not be a bad idea."

"Alex, you didn't fly here for a brief afternoon chat. What is going on?"

"I don't know."

"I see," the former first lady responded. "Well, what do you know?"

"Jane, John wanted to tell me something. Something about Iraq."

The older woman across from the agent nodded. "That's not all, though, is it?"

"I honestly don't know," Alex said. Jane Merrow stood and walked across the room. Alex watched her as she moved. She was graceful and poised even in the midst of difficult situations. She had seen Cassidy take on that persona as well. It was a skill, not unlike Alex's mastery of language. The agent had a proclivity for observation and memorization. Jane Merrow, much like Cassidy O'Brien, had a natural ability to relate to people. It enabled them to command any audience in a manner that to most seemed effortless. Alex admired both women. It was her job to observe and to dig beyond the surface and Alex was adept at peeling back the layers. As graceful as Jane Merrow appeared, Alex could see the anxiety pouring off her friend in waves, much like those that rise off pavement on a summer day. "Jane?"

Jane turned and looked at her friend. "Alex, we both know presidents don't get randomly shot." Alex felt her jaw tighten. The frank admission of the woman before her surprised her. "What is it that you need from me?" Jane asked.

"I need clearance."

Jane Merrow covered her mouth and considered the agent's statement. "Military, I assume?"

Alex nodded. "I can't tell you much more than that. I..."

Jane held up her hand. "I don't want to know, Alex. I don't need to know the details."

"I wouldn't ask if," Alex began.

"I know that."

"Can you..."

The former first lady smiled. "I still have my connections, Alex."

"I know it's..."

Jane shook her head. "Where?" The agent sighed. "Alex, I have to know where."

"New Mexico."

"Holloman?" Alex nodded. Jane understood. "I assumed it would be an Air Force installation if you were coming to me."

"Jane, if I thought there was another way..."

"Just tell me this; do you think you can find out? Why they killed him, I mean?"

Alex looked at her friend and pursed her lips. "Do you really want that answer?" The former first lady nodded. "Then, yes," Alex said. "I have to know."

"You're worried about Cassidy and Dylan, aren't you?"

"Yes, I am."

"Alex, I would never..."

"You and I both know there is no such thing as a perfect secret," Alex said.

"He's gone, Alex. Do you really think Dylan could be..."

The agent slowly began to rise from her seat. She paced across the room, considering her next words carefully. "O'Brien is in this, Jane. That's bad enough on its own. If he ever were to..."

"Alex, you don't think Christopher O'Brien would use his son as leverage?"

The agent let out her breath and turned to face her friend. "Yes, I do. If he knew Dylan was John's; I think he would use either of them."

Jane Merrow covered her face with her hands and shook her head. "When do you need it?"

"Yesterday," Alex chuckled slightly.

Jane nodded and headed toward the large wooden doors at the far end of the room. "I'll make the call. Alex?" The agent looked at Jane who now had her hand on the large brass doorknob. "No matter what you find," Alex listened intently, "he loved you. He loved his family." She opened the door and turned back, "Dylan too. Don't forget that."

Alex forced a crooked smile. She held her breath until Jane had left the room and released it as she closed her eyes. She did not want to come here, but Jane Merrow was someone she trusted, at least as much as she trusted anyone these days. The former first lady had the one connection that Alex knew would provide anything without explanation. It was her only choice and she would use it to her advantage. "Colonel, what the hell are you leading me to?"

***

Tuesday, April 22nd.

Alex walked with Cassidy to the bus stop and looked down at the small eyes gazing up into hers. "I'll see you in a few days, Speed." Dylan swung his arms around Alex's neck tightly. "Whoa," Alex said. "I won't be gone that long, I promise." Dylan pulled back and looked at the agent with great apprehension. Alex caught his eyes as they wandered in concern to his mother and she mentally slapped herself for missing the obvious signs of his fear. Dylan had been quiet the last two days. She and Cassidy dismissed it as nerves about the new school, but it was clear to the agent now what was bothering him. No matter how brave Dylan tried to be; he was afraid. The agent knelt down and put her hands firmly on the boy's small shoulders. "Dylan, no one is going to hurt your mom. I promise."

He looked at her and Cassidy caught her breath at the sudden realization of what was disturbing her son. The last time Alex left, Carl Fisher had arrived. They had tried to shield Dylan from as much of that reality as possible. Dylan was very perceptive and extremely attentive. He might not have known all of the details, but he was aware that someone had hurt his mother, and he certainly understood that it had happened as soon as the agent had set off on her last "working" trip. Cassidy understood his anxiety. She would never have admitted it to Alex, but she had been experiencing a deep sense of foreboding ever since the agent announced her latest travel plans. She smiled over the agent's shoulder at a pair of small eyes. "It's okay, Dylan. I will be here when you get off the bus. I promise," Cassidy attempted to reassure her son.

Alex took a deep breath and squinted at the boy. She too had fought to reconcile the need to leave. Images of Christopher O'Brien at her door had awakened her in the middle of the night. But, they could not allow Carl Fisher to control their lives forever. She understood that too. Still, she had thought to make some arrangements, if only to put her own mind at ease. "Would you feel better knowing that Grandma will be here this afternoon?" Alex asked. Dylan nodded and Alex felt Cassidy's eyes on her. "Good." She watched Cassidy kiss Dylan on the cheek as the bus pulled up.

"Promise?" he asked his mother.

Cassidy smiled. "Promise." She waved and turned to witness the concern in Alex's eyes as the agent gave Dylan a thumbs up. "Grandma?" Cassidy asked.

Alex shrugged. "Just humor me."

"Worried about me?"

Alex put her arm around the teacher's waist as they made their way back toward the house. "I'll just feel better knowing Rose is here."

Cassidy sighed as they finally reached their door. "You really can't tell me?" The agent shook her head. "Promise me you will be careful." Cassidy knew Alex as well as anyone ever had. There was little doubt in her mind that wherever her lover was headed; there were risks.

"Cass, I will be back."

Cassidy nodded as the agent grabbed the bag behind the door. "I know this is just something," the teacher's words were cut off by a gentle kiss. She placed her hands on the agent's face and looked into Alex's steel blue eyes. "I'll never get used to this."

"Neither will I," Alex confessed.

"I love you, Alex."

"Mm….tacos."

"What?" Cassidy asked.

"If you love me, you'll make tacos when I get back."

"Is that right?" Cassidy raised her eyebrow.

"Yeah."

Cassidy was ready to quip back at the agent when she felt a pit in her stomach rise into her throat. "Just come home. You can have tacos every night if you want."

Alex smiled and kissed the smaller woman again. "I'll call you as soon as I can. I love you, Cassidy. You know that?"

"I do."

The agent let her lips linger on Cassidy's forehead. She made her way to the car, threw her bag in the trunk and looked over at her lover. "You might want to practice your shots. I moved the pool table but, uh...I think it might be slightly off center still. Might need to be adjusted when I get back."

Cassidy bit her lip to stifle a laugh. "I'll keep that in mind." Alex winked and stepped into the car. She backed out and stopped one last time to glimpse the woman she loved. "Just come home, Alex," Cassidy whispered to herself. "Please."

***

Brian Fallon jimmied the lock pick in the door and looked cautiously to each side. "Time to find out what you are up to Tate." He quietly closed the office door and made his way behind the desk. With the assistant FBI director away and Claire Brackett markedly absent from the office, this was his opportunity to dig a little deeper into the pair's meeting. He hoped that the assistant director might just be bold enough to leave something in his office. After all, he was at the top of the heap in the bureau. Joshua Tate had little reason to fear an internal investigation. Fallon was certain that no one suspected he was working for the NSA. He was fully aware that his unassuming presence and his amiable nature was often mistaken as weakness, or even a lack of intellect. That had proven to be advantageous more than once. He silently wondered if anyone realized what truly lay underneath the surface. "And what do we have here?" The agent lifted a paper and shook his head as his eyes scanned it. He retrieved his cell phone and promptly snapped several pictures. "Who is playing who here, Claire?" he smiled. "Oh, Alex, wait until you get this."

***

"Claire Brackett is up to something."

"You think she'd cross her father?"

Jon Krause laughed. "She'd sell her firstborn if she thought it'd serve her."

Agent Ian Mitchell sat across from the CIA agent, his thick British accent making him sound ever more distinguished than he knew to be true. "Do you plan on apprising the admiral?"

"No."

"Any idea what she is up to then, Jon?" Mitchell asked.

"The admiral is setting up O'Brien."

"To remove him?"

"In a manner of speaking," Krause responded. "It isn't his intention to remove him physically, but to compromise him."

"And Claire?"

Krause shrugged. "She won't allow that."

"Sleeping with the enemy now?" Mitchell asked. Jon Krause nodded. "So then; what?" Krause smiled and the MI6 agent nodded his understanding with satisfaction. "You think she will remove the contact?" he asked. "Ah…You want me make certain the role is filled."

"You always were quick, Ian."

"Who is the contact?"

"Doesn't matter," Krause answered.

Ian Mitchell understood. "This congressman of yours, he and the Brackett girl; they were the downfall; weren't they? His, I mean."

"They were the catalyst, yes."

137

"Why not just kill him?" Mitchell asked. Krause sighed. "I see. More painful this way. I understand, Jon. If it had been Elliot they killed….I…"

"I know," Krause answered. "I made a promise, Ian. A long time ago. We all did."

"Yes, we did. When?"

"Thursday. Corsica."

"I'll make the arrangements," Mitchell answered. Krause gave a slight nod of appreciation and moved to take his leave when he felt his friend's hand stop him. "Jon, if what you suspect is true. You know what that means." Ian Mitchell was part of the same unique brotherhood as Jon Krause. He was a ghost made of flesh; a man who had few verifiable connections and yet had traveled to nearly every inch of the globe. It was an elite group. They were men who spoke many languages, endeared world leaders and then assassinated them. They traded in arms and they laundered money. They could buy elections and sell entire governments. They were the ghosts engineered by men who believed themselves gods. These *ghosts* possessed rare skills and enviable talents; abilities very few could lay claim to. The reality was that gods sometimes underestimated their minions. A ghost is a dangerous adversary, even for a god.

"Ian?" Krause began. "There will be company."

"You sound certain."

"I am."

Mitchell nodded. "I'll be certain they see him." Krause smiled. "Jon, be careful. It is *in* the family now." Krause understood. This had been his *family* all his life. He felt a crawling sensation creep through his body. He'd accepted what he'd been given with open arms. He wondered now why his eyes had not followed that same path.

***

Chapter Thirteen

Alex sighed and turned her back from side to side. She hated flying and was relieved to be able to stretch the length of her tall form. The motel room seemed cold compared to home. The sooner she completed this task, the better. In spite of the teasing she endured about her pension for spy movies and *The X-Files*, Alex did not truly enjoy the undercover aspect of her profession. Most people in the intelligence community regarded the NSA as a place lined by endless desks and computer screens; a high tech, low risk brand of intelligence. She laughed as she retrieved her uniform and shook her head. The NSA engaged in as much espionage as any intelligence agency. Their focus, and this was always troubling to her, was listening in on private conversations and communications. Unfortunately, Alex had learned that there was often reason to do so. There were people with agendas, all kinds of agendas. Some were zealots, others were entrepreneurs; both posed risks to the safety and welfare of the country and its citizens.

Slowly, she unzipped the long garment bag that held her Army uniform. Alex was no longer an inconspicuous agent. The press coverage of Cassidy's abduction and the continued focus on her presence at President John Merrow's funeral meant that someone would almost certainly recognize her. There would be no aliases. She needed her military credentials to be reinstated and to appear authentic. Jane Merrow knew the one person who could do that and would do so without hesitation.

Matthew Waters was that person. Waters had followed his father's footsteps in many ways, attending the Air Force Academy, flying planes and serving his country with distinction. There was one thing he loved above all else and that was his sister. Alex learned that firsthand when she and John Merrow were at Walter Reed recovering. Jane Merrow's brother was a major then. He had climbed the ladder quickly and now held the rank of Brigadier General. Alex was well aware that Jane Merrow was Matthew Water's light. The pair often reminded Alex of her and Nick. She was certain that he would want answers about the president's assassination and that Jane's request would be granted without question. Alex held up her uniform and closed her eyes for a moment. Today, she would again be Captain Alexis Toles. It was a role she missed at times. Today, she wondered where it might lead her.

***

"So....It is O'Brien that is headed to France."

Brian Fallon nodded. "It would appear so."

"Interesting," Taylor pondered the information. "Why would Tate know that? Brackett?"

"I think so, yes. Sir?"

"Yes, Agent?"

Fallon's jaw tightened and he licked his lips. "He came to you."

Michael Taylor pushed the chair away from his desk and stroked his chin as he considered his response, taking several moments to gauge the man before him. Agent Brian Fallon's expression was unwavering. It was impossible to discern what Fallon was thinking and Taylor found himself wondering what it would be like to play poker with the generally affable agent. The director's eyes narrowed slightly as the tension in his jaw increased. "He did."

"Does Agent Toles know this?" Fallon asked calmly.

"No."

Looking to the ceiling, Brian Fallon shook his head. "Sir, if Agent Toles…."

"Agent Toles is acting on information from an informant. That is what she knows. That is all she knows. Just as I do not know from whom she attained her needed credentials."

"Why would Tate come to you?" Fallon asked with some concern. "Playing both ends against the middle? Did he tell you about O'Brien?"

The NSA director smiled genuinely. "Agent Fallon," he paused and offered the agent a long stare. "Everyone in this game plays both ends against the middle." Fallon remained stoic as the director measured his response. "Perhaps the assistant director expects that Alex will uncover more in New Mexico than just information on an old project. I don't know. Perhaps he does not wish to compromise Agent Brackett. What his agenda is; I can't say."

"What if it is a trap?"

Taylor shrugged. "Could be."

"You sent Toles into a potential trap without telling her that?" Fallon's voice rose slightly.

"Agent, it is always potentially a trap. That is what we do. Agent Toles knows what she is doing. She does not need the identity of the informant distracting her from her objective."

"So, what about O'Brien? I go to France?" Fallon asked.

"You go nowhere. Stay on Brackett and Tate."

"Brackett is likely already in France."

"Distinct possibility, yes," Tate replied.

"And we just pretend that doesn't matter? Don't you think that could be the lead we need? At least you should tell Alex."

"Agent Fallon, listen to me. Agent Toles did not want you brought into this mix at all. You are an intelligent and savvy investigator but this is not typical police work. Connections run deep. People make a career of assessing one another in this business. If Tate is compromising himself in any way, he will be cautious what he gives and to whom. He's throwing breadcrumbs. Why? I don't know. That is not our focus...not yet, anyway. Toles needs a clear head." The NSA director stopped and took a sip from his coffee cup. "I assume you already sent her the information."

"I did."

"Fine then. I am certain Alex will follow the trail to France."

"She's in...."

Taylor laughed. "Agent...Trust me. You stay on the trail within the bureau. I'm sure you are right; if Brackett is MIA, she went ahead. The question is why. Follow that. If she's gone take the opportunity."

"You want me to go into her personal life? Her private quarters; I mean?"

"There is no such thing as privacy in this business. Yes."

***

"Cassidy?" Cassidy was pacing the kitchen, wiping the counter for what Rose counted as the tenth time. "You could perform surgery on that counter it is so clean," the older woman grabbed her daughter's hand and stopped its motion. "I'm sure Alex is fine."

Cassidy released the towel in her hand and let out a nervous chuckle. "I'm sure she is."

"This isn't just about her being away; is it?"

The teacher shook her head, made her way to the small table at the far side of the kitchen, and slumped into a chair. "She was so upset before she left." Rose followed her daughter and took a seat at the table, resting her face gently on her hand as she listened. "I thought they were nightmares about Iraq."

"But?"

"I don't understand, Mom. How can a parent treat their child that way?" She looked out the back door window at Dylan as he ran across the yard chasing a soccer ball.

"Are we still talking about Alex here?"

"What?" Cassidy turned her attention back to her mother.

"Uh-huh…Cassie, what is going on?"

Cassidy covered her face with her hands and shook her head. She could feel the tears beginning to sting the back of her eyes. "She thinks he hates her."

"You mean Alex? She thinks her father hates her."

"Why wouldn't she?"

Rose chuckled "Cassie….parents are just people."

"I know that," Cassidy said, returning her gaze out the door.

"You can't change who his father is," Rose chimed.

Cassidy nodded and pursed her lips. A soft smile began to take shape as she watched her son raise his hands over his head triumphantly. He was quite obviously engaged in a make believe match of some kind and clearly he was the victor. Unconsciously, she shook her head, "no, I suppose I can't." Her mother studied the younger woman's expression as Cassidy slowly turned toward her. "We need to talk."

***

Claire Brackett smiled as she rose from the bed and made her way toward the large chair across the room, retrieving her clothes along the way. "You should visit more often," the man behind her said.

"You think?" she answered coyly.

"*Oui, quel meilleur endroit pour apprendre sur l'amour,* (Yes, where better to learn about love)?" he asked.

"Love?" Claire Brackett laughed as she slipped her arms through her blouse and picked up the jacket on the chair. She gently reached into the deep pocket of her coat and fondled the cool plastic she felt there. A devious smile of satisfaction crept onto her face as she expertly placed her left hand in the large bag next to the chair. She flipped the long, black cylinder into her hand. "You think this is love?" she cooed.

The man in the bed stretched his hands behind his head and closed his eyes, *"Ah, qu'est-ce que l'amour? Seulement un moment commun entre deux âmes* (Ah, what is love? Only a common moment between two souls)." He sighed, a contented smile gracing his pale face.

Claire Brackett twisted the long cylinder gently. Feeling it click firmly into place; she turned slowly. *"Et l'amour, comme tous les moments tire à sa fin* (and love, like all moments come to an end)." She looked at the figure sprawled in satisfaction and raised her eyebrow. The weight in her hand was almost as seductive as the expression on his face. Her finger found its destination and carefully applied the needed pressure. *"Mieux vaut avoir aimé et perdu que ne jamais avoir aimé du tout* (Better to have loved and lost than never to have loved at all)."

His eyes opened slightly only to capture a brief glimpse of the figure now hovering above him. "Why?"

The redheaded agent stroked his cheek and shut his eyes. "Love is a fool's game, Elliot. And I am no fool." She kissed his forehead and retrieved her bag. *"Il n'y as qu'un seul coté a jouer, un seul* (There is only one side to play on. Only one)," she whispered as she closed the door behind her.

***

"Captain Toles."

"Major. Thank you for taking the time," Alex responded. There was a unique presence about Alex Toles when she donned her uniform. It was confidence. The simple truth was that Alex felt most comfortable as Captain Toles. There were still times she regretted her decision to give up her military career and join the FBI. She often wondered what made her feel so strongly about her service. It had been that way from the beginning and her time in Iraq had only served to strengthen the feeling.

"Is this for an investigation, Captain?"

Alex smiled. The Major's demeanor immediately told her that he recognized her and not simply by the badge she was wearing. She had decided that she would be as forthright as she felt was prudent in this endeavor. "In a manner of speaking, yes, Major."

Major Gregory Black nodded his understanding as he gestured for Alex to follow him down a long, narrow hallway. "I only met him a couple of times," the Major said solemnly as they reached a metal door at the far end of the corridor. Alex offered him an appreciative smile. "He was a reasonable and honorable man," the Major offered. Alex nodded as he held the door open for her. "If you need anything," he said.

"Major?"

"Yes, Captain?"

"If you don't mind…this visit…"

"You don't even need to ask, Captain." Alex smiled and watched him leave.

***

Rose McCollum fingered the rim of her wine glass as she regarded her daughter closely. Cassidy was uncharacteristically wringing her hands in her lap and had not raised her eyes to meet her mother's in long minutes. "Cassie…"

"I know," Cassidy said in a hushed voice.

"What is it that you think you know?"

A heavy sigh escaped the younger woman and she shook her head. "I can't imagine what you must think of me."

"Cassidy Rose McCollum," Rose chastised playfully. Cassidy's eyes flew open at the sound of her name through her mother's laughter. "What I feel is some relief."

"What?"

"Oh for heaven's sake, Cassie. I can't tell you how many times I wondered how a blockhead like Christopher O'Brien could father such a beautiful child. I just thanked God he seemed to inherit your genes." Rose moved from her seat to sit beside her daughter on the couch. She placed her arm around Cassidy's shoulder as her tone softened. "Everything happens for a reason, Cassie. Everything. That little boy upstairs, there is your reason."

Cassidy leaned her head against her mother as a few tears trickled over her cheek. "What do I do now?"

Rose smiled and brushed her daughter's hair aside. "Do you need to do anything?"

"I don't know."

"Mm…. Cassie, what is it that you want to do?"

"I don't know."

"Yes, I think you do know," Rose said as she firmly took hold of her daughter's shoulders and guided her to come face to face. "Have you talked to Alex about this? Telling Chris, I mean."

In spite of all of their close relationship, Cassidy was still amazed by her mother's perceptiveness. "No."

"Why not?"

"Honestly, so much has been happening. I just…"

"I know, Cassie," Rose said softly.

"I should be worried about Dylan…I mean Chris is…"

"Dylan hasn't wanted to be with his father for months, you know that. Who else knows?" Rose asked.

Cassidy took a deep breath and covered her eyes. "No one except Alex…..and Jane."

"Cassie, did he know?" Cassidy nodded her head and Rose sighed. "You can't hide it forever. Secrets will drain your soul over time. Sometimes we hide things with the best of intentions and we create unforeseen consequences."

"Dylan will never forgive me."

"Dylan has what he has always needed, Cassie."

"I guess I was lucky."

"What do you mean?" Rose asked in confusion.

"Well, look at Alex. Look at Dylan with Chris. I have you. I had Daddy. I certainly haven't lived up to that mark, have I?"

"Lived up to what? Your father and I?" Cassidy nodded. Rose shook her head. "You think we were the Cleavers."

"We were happy. I was happy. I was loved," Cassidy said.

"You were happy and you are loved. Dylan is happy and Dylan is loved," Rose said turning her eyes downward.

"What? Mom, what is it?"

"You were so young when you lost your father."

"You lost him too."

Rose returned her gaze to her daughter. "You know, you are very much like him in some ways." Cassidy smiled. "Smart, strong, willful, and beautiful."

The younger woman's smile began to fade as she noted her mother's eyes slowly closing. "Mom?"

"He certainly did love you, Cassidy....your father. From the moment you were born his eyes were fixed on you whenever you were in the room." There was a sadness in the older woman's voice and Cassidy began to feel her heart ache. "The truth is I lost him long before you did. Long before."

Cassidy's mind began racing. She could not imagine what her own confession had spurred in her mother. How could this be happening? Her family had been close. She remembered so many moments with her parents at the beach, in the yard, at the playground. Her heart sank, certain her mother was about to reveal that her father had been much like her own ex-husband. Could history have repeated itself, she wondered? "Mom?"

Rose took a deep breath and let the air fill her lungs with courage before releasing it. "What do you remember, Cassie? When you think back? What do you recall about the three of us together?"

"I don't know....the beach. I remember the swing at the playground. He would take me on Sunday morning and sing to me, teach me songs. Sitting at the picnic table in the yard. The dinner table...."

"Mm."

"Mom...what? What did Daddy do? He had a mistress?"

"He did." Rose saw the crushing weight of her words fall on her daughter with a force that seemed to instantly diminish her stature. "His mistress was not a woman, Cassie." Cassidy looked up at her mother, waiting desperately for her to continue. Rose let out another heavy breath as a compassionate but apprehensive expression overcame her. "His mistress was a bottle. It was an infatuation I could never compete with."

***

"Fallon?"

"Alex?" he answered his phone in surprise. "Are you all right?"

"Yeah...fine," Alex answered as she reviewed the file in front of her on the long metal table. "This message you sent me on my phone...Tate is Taylor's informant? Is that what this means?"

Brian Fallon looked past his own desk and nodded silently to himself. "Yeah...it's in the files I sent."

"I don't have my laptop here. How do you know?" she asked. Agent Fallon smiled at a woman as she passed his desk. He picked up his coffee cup and began to make his way past the cadre of agents seated in similar stations. "Fallon?"

"Yeah...."

"Where are you?" Alex asked.

Fallon shut the door to the small kitchenette. "At work."

"At the bureau?"

"Yeah, where else would I be?"

"Fallon, why would Tate go to Taylor?" Alex pulled another file folder in front of her as she awaited the answer.

"I don't know. You haven't seen what I sent?" There was no response. Alex's eyes were preoccupied on a piece of paper in front of her. She studied the words one at a time, *Special Project Helix Installation Nigeria Axis–SPHINX.* "Alex?"

"Yeah....Sorry."

"You didn't see what I sent?" Fallon repeated.

Alex took a deep breath and let her fingers play over the words on the paper. "No. I changed and came straight here. There's more? I mean than Tate?"

"Yeah, Alex, the Corsica thing; it looks like they are sending O'Brien."

Alex's finger lingered over the words on the paper. "Interesting."

"That's all? Just interesting? I think Brackett went ahead."

Alex allowed her finger to slowly travel down the document in front of her. Even here, the document had been heavily redacted. That was one of the beautiful things about her job; for some reason people seemed to think the removal of key words protected their information; as if only those who owned black Sharpies could crack their secret code. They called it sanitization. Alex called it a challenge. It was like chess. The black marks were the unseen moves. The rest of the words on the paper were just like your opponent's board. If you studied it closely enough you could almost always predict what was to come. She smiled. "I'm sure she did."

"So, what are you going to do?" he asked.

"Well, they aren't sending the congressman on a mission."

Fallon was confused. "I don't understand."

Alex retrieved the small camera from her pocket. It looked inconspicuous enough. People would be amazed, she thought, at the things that existed in reality. Just a pack of mints. She opened the cover and popped a mint in her mouth, carefully triggering the shutter and photographing the document on the table. "He is the mission, Fallon."

"What do you mean?"

"Not here. When is he due to arrive?" Alex asked.

"Thursday, at least that is what I gathered. I should follow Brackett to Corsica."

Alex laughed and retrieved another page. She studied it for a few moments and then took another mint. "She won't be in Corsica, at least not yet."

"What are…"

Alex shook her head. Fallon was a terrific agent but this was a landscape he had a great deal to learn about. "You can never look too much. Trust me. Keep digging."

"Are you…"

Alex closed the file and turned to replace it in the tall metal cabinet behind her. "I'll be there by Thursday…more, Fallon, I need more."

He sighed as the door to the small room he had found moderate privacy in opened. "Yeah, I understand. Glad you are doing well," he said. "Tell Cassidy I said hello, all right?"

Alex chuckled as her hand reached the red button on the panel next to the heavy steel door. "I will do that, Fallon. Watch yourself."

"Will do," he said with a smile directed at the agent walking past him.

"See that you do," Alex cautioned.

***

"Alex?" Cassidy picked up her phone.

"Hey, sorry I missed saying good night to Speed."

"It's all right," Cassidy said as she collapsed back onto the king size bed, feeling the empty space next to her. "Is everything okay?"

Alex unplugged the small drive from her computer and shut the top. There was a somber tone to Cassidy's voice that immediately concerned the agent. "Cass, what's going on?"

Cassidy took a deep breath and closed her eyes. "I'm all right. I just miss you."

Alex was certain that was true; when Cassidy did not want to burden the agent with something she always answered truthfully, just not fully. "I miss you too. You don't want to tell me what's wrong?"

"I told my mother."

"Ooookaaayy....."

"About Dylan, Alex."

Alex let out an audible sigh as she began packing up her files and piling her bags on a chair. "And?"

"She was great."

"Of course she was. So, what's wrong?"

"Alex, it's okay, really."

Alex made her way to the double bed and flopped into the middle of it. "No. Not okay. What's up?"

"She just told me some things."

"What kind of things?" Alex was now truly curious.

Cassidy pulled Alex's pillow to her and inhaled. "About my father." The agent could feel the tension pouring through the phone. Cassidy adored her parents. She waited for a moment and was ready to ask another question when Cassidy continued. "Seems she dealt with a mistress too for many years."

The agent was stunned. In the few conversations that she and Cassidy had about their childhoods, Cassidy had always painted James McCollum as Super Dad. Alex wondered a couple of times if the man might actually have sported a cape and if that is why Dylan loved superheroes so much. If *she* was shocked by the statement, she could not imagine how Cassidy must have reacted to her mother's admission. "Cass, I..."

"Yeah...thing is it wasn't a Stephanie, Barbara or Violet."

"I don't understand," Alex said carefully.

"Nope. It was more like Scotch, Bourbon and Vodka."

"Cass, everyone has their..."

"Demons? Yeah, I know. Parents are people, right?"

Alex's heart sank. "I wish I was there."

"Ummm, still can't tell me where you are?"

The agent laughed and rolled to her side. "Strangely enough, I think I can."

"Really?"

"Yeah, I'm in New Mexico."

"I thought you were headed off to Moscow or Beijing or something," Cassidy joked, feeling her tension ease slightly at discovering Alex's whereabouts.

"Nope, sorry. Dry, dusty New Mexico."

Cassidy couldn't resist her next question. "Find any evidence of an alien invasion?"

Everyone, even Cassidy, knew that Alex loved *X-Files* and James Bond. They did not all know her infatuation with comic books, and even Cassidy had yet to discover the agent's strange pension for old Bing Crosby movies; though Alex suspected that little nugget would reveal itself to the teacher's great amusement when the holidays rolled around. "No. No aliens. But, the truth is out there, Cass."

Cassidy laughed. Just hearing Alex's voice was comforting and she loved their banter. "Any idea when you will be home?"

"If all goes as planned I'll be home by the weekend." The teacher closed her eyes again. It was clear in Alex's voice that she was certain it would not be sooner.

Cassidy bit her lip to quell her fear. "Alex, whatever you need to…"

"I should be home by Saturday, Cass. I actually had a good day."

"I'm not sure what that means, but if it means you get home sooner rather than later; I am all for it."

Alex took a deep breath. "I'll try to call you in the morning, okay?"

"Okay?" Cassidy asked.

"If you don't hear from me….for a day or two; I don't want you to worry," Alex explained.

"You know I can't promise you that."

"I know," the agent laughed. "I had to say to say it, though. You gonna be okay there with Rose?"

"Yeah, just get home, Alex."

"Tell Dylan I miss him, okay?"

"I will."

"Cass?"

"Yeah?"

"I," Alex stopped and caught her breath. She had no idea what awaited her in France. She knew it involved Christopher O'Brien and Claire Brackett and Alex knew that spelled trouble. "I love you, Cass."

"I love you too, Alex."

"Take some time with your mom, okay?" Alex suggested.

"I will. Alex?"

"Yeah?"

"Promise me you…"

"I'll call you in the morning," Alex promised.

"I can't lose you, Alex."

The fear in Cassidy's voice was unmistakable. "I'll be home soon. I promise," Alex answered. "Get some sleep."

"You too."

"And Cass?"

"Yeah?"

"Remember, you promised tacos."

Cassidy giggled. "I did."

"Love you."

"I love you too, Alfred."

***

Chapter Fourteen

Thursday, April 24th

The sound of breaking glass filled the small apartment. The tall, fair haired man closed his eyes tightly and fell to his knees next to the bed. His hands reached across the large form still tucked away under a sheet. Grasping the sheet forcefully, Ian Mitchell's anger turned to sobs. "No...No....No...." He kept repeating the words as if willing the man in the bed to listen. The blood stained wall was still not enough to convince his mind that the scene before him was a reality. "God dammit, Elliot. Who did this? Who could do this?"

Mitchell lifted his hands to his face, rubbing with such force that it left long finger trails down the length of his cheeks. Slowly he regained his footing and began to pace the small room, searching with his eyes. His hands scoured each surface for evidence of who might be responsible for the death of the man in the bed. A small crumpled paper lying near the door caught his attention. Carefully, he unrolled it and brought it toward his face. His eyes narrowed to slits as an angry sigh escaped his lips. "So...you were the one that was going to meet O'Brien, Elliot." He turned back to the man lying cold in the bed. "I told you to be careful of her. Foolish." A maniacal chuckle escaped his lips. "Well, won't they be surprised this evening."

***

"Brady, you didn't have to come."

Steven Brady stretched his legs out and lifted them onto the small table at the center of the hotel room. "Really, Toles? And let you have all the fun? I don't think so."

"Is that what this is?" Alex questioned. "Fun?"

Brady shrugged. "Could be if we catch the smug son of a bitch up to something." Alex nodded and gave her friend a halfhearted smile as she laced up her boot. "What?" Brady asked, seeing her expression. "You said it yourself, O'Brien is being set up."

"Yeah. He is."

"So, I should think you would be glad to catch him...even if it is a set up. Christ knows he put himself in the middle of all this." Alex kept her eyes on the laces of her boot. "Toles, what? What are you worried about? Telling Cassidy about O'Brien?"

Alex shook her head and let out the hint of a chuckle. "No. Not at all."

"Then I really don't understand," Brady said as he sat back up and leaned forward. "What is it?"

"Brackett."

"You mean the admiral?" he asked.

"No." Alex finished tying her boot and sighed. "I mean Claire."

"What; did Fallon find something at her apartment?"

"Only what I already told you. She's definitely into it with the congressman and she definitely headed here to France."

"Her father probably sent her," Brady surmised.

Alex stood and stretched her back. All the travel had made her stiff and while she would never admit it to her compatriot, she was feeling anxious about following O'Brien into whatever he had gotten himself involved in. "I don't think the admiral sent her ahead."

"I don't understand Alex."

"Brady, I think our friend Agent Brackett is trying to play both ends against the middle."

156

"Why?"

"Shit," Alex said shaking her head. "Why wouldn't she? Think about it. What if Claire is the one who arranged O'Brien's accident?"

"So?"

Alex looked at Brady and bit her lip, considering how to continue. "You think she'd want *him* to know that? Just think how deep she is in this, whatever *this* is. She was sleeping with Fisher at some point, sleeping with the president right before he was assassinated, and now she is sleeping with O'Brien. Where do you suppose Fisher got his FBI credentials?"

"I assume Agent Brackett."

"Yeah, but Claire couldn't get those on her own. Even as a DCIS agent she wouldn't have that kind of authority," Alex offered.

"You have got to be kidding me. You think her father got those credentials for Fisher? Why would he help a liability?" Brady asked.

"To take out insurance on a bigger liability," Alex raised her brow.

"Jesus, Alex."

"Look, Brady...in those files I got at Holloman...William Brackett is mentioned over and over again. It's going to take me some time to discern it all. It's heavily redacted, but trust me, SPHINX runs deep. Admiral Brackett runs deeper. Claire is as loose a cannon as Fisher was and that spells trouble."

"Yeah, but what does SPHINX have to do with this?" he asked.

"Directly? Maybe nothing. Indirectly, I suspect everything. It's the key to unlock the door, Brady. That's what SPHINX is; the key to unlocking a secret door. But, if we manage to unlock it; I suspect we will find a whole bunch of other doors with Admiral William Brackett greeting us at every one."

"SPHINX was years ago," he said. Alex's posture stiffened slightly and she shook her head. "Well?" he asked urgently.

"What? Why would Brackett set up his own daughter? I get that she is a wild card, Toles. But if you think he's worried about covering up SPHINX…I mean Claire was just a kid. What could she possibly know?"

"About the project? Probably nothing specific," Alex said grabbing her jacket off a chair. "But now, with everything she is doing…Well, she could lead us somewhere he does not want us to go. I'm more worried about what he is trying to keep us *from* than what he seems to want to lead us *to*. Brady, SPHINX; do you know what it stands for?"

"No. Only that it was the codename for the project. Even Taylor wasn't certain what the call letters stood for."

"Yeah. That's the thing about being a soldier, Brady. You don't always ask the right questions. SPHINX stands for Special Project Helix Installation Nigeria Axis."

"And?"

Alex pinched the bridge of her nose. "You're the one who found this in the first place. You've been dealing with the arms trade for how many years now? Think about it. Helix is a spiral. Installation; putting something in place. Nigeria; what is Nigeria known for, Brady?"

"Money laundering," he answered.

"Mm… and Axis?" He looked at her inquisitively. "It's an imaginary line that a body rotates around. Imaginary boundaries, spiraling around Nigeria." Brady shrugged. "Brady, there is a veiled meaning in every project code you know that. These people always think they are smarter than the rest of us. Think about it. What is a SPHINX?"

"My ancient mythology is a bit rusty Toles, but if memory serves it was a mythological monster that presented riddles," he answered, not following the importance.

"Yeah, and SPHINX is the riddle. What happens when you can't solve the riddle of the sphinx? What does the sphinx do if you fail, Brady?" Brady rolled his eyes slightly. "Brush off that rust."

"I believe it kills you and then eats you."

Alex nodded. "This is a game to these people, Steven. It is more than the code name of a project. The project, if I had to guess, is a lot more far reaching than we know. Claire Brackett has put a lot at risk with her recklessness. She has her hand on the door. If we unlock it...."

"Okay, okay...but if the admiral is using Claire..."

"The question isn't what the admiral might want Claire to do. It's what Claire is going to do. Claire Brackett is not one to be rejected, denied or outdone. If she wasn't Admiral Brackett's daughter she'd be the feature in an episode of Nancy Grace for sure, and not as a victim." Brady smiled as Alex began to button her jacket. "What?" she asked.

"I swear, Toles...I don't know how you do that."

"Do what?"

"Figure out all of this shit."

"It's what I do," Alex said plainly.

"Yeah," Brady laughed. "Where are you going? You want to leave already?"

"No, just going to step outside for a minute. Be ready when I get back."

Steven Brady leaned back in his chair and shook his head. Alex Toles never ceased to amaze him. She saw things in color where others only saw black and white. He ran his hand over his head and sighed. It was evident to the NSA agent that Alex was concerned. Secretly, he hoped she was wrong about the potential risks in this assignment, but there was no denying that was seldom the case. He closed his eyes and took a deep breath. "What the hell are we into?" he muttered.

***

"Are you ready?" Claire Brackett asked.

"What on earth do I need this for?" the congressman balked.

159

Claire Brackett ran her hands along the buttons of Christopher O'Brien's shirt. "Trust me. You want that."

"Claire, I am not a…"

"Do you need a lesson in how to use it?" she asked with a sly smile.

"I know how to fire a gun, Claire."

"Do you?"

"Yeah, pull the trigger."

"Oh, you are brilliant, aren't you, Congressman?" she hissed at him.

"I can handle myself," he said nervously.

"Oh, yes…I can *see* that," she smirked, buttoning his jacket slowly. "I'll be close by."

"I thought you said that this would be a rouse?"

"I said I took care of the primary party," she answered as she turned to retrieve her own sidearm.

"Then why the…"

"There are always back up players, Christopher." He looked at her, his eyes glistening with apprehension. "You don't seriously think," she began, "that we are the only ones who know you are here?"

"What does that mean?"

"It means," she explained as she slid her arms through her leather coat, "that someone is always watching. Who that someone is will determine whether you need to use that," she gestured toward the pistol in his hand, "or not. Now let's go."

***

Jonathan Krause held the phone to his ear and listened to the message as it played. The voice was thick with rage and the CIA agent immediately knew there was danger ahead. "Krause. Mitchell. You were right. Sparrow seems to have left the nest. I am on my way. More than your congressman will fall."

Krause swallowed hard. "What the hell did you do Claire?" He grabbed his gun and hurriedly made his way to the door. "Ian, be careful. Shit…John, I wish you were here."

***

"Cassie?"

"Hum?"

"Are you going to tell me what is going on in that pretty head of yours?" Rose asked.

Cassidy laughed. She had spent the last two days talking about nearly everything with her mother. Rose's admission that Cassidy's father had struggled with addiction throughout most of their marriage was difficult for her to comprehend. To Cassidy, her parents had what seemed a storybook love affair. That had been the imagination of a ten year old mind. She wondered how she could have romanticized something that had clearly caused so much pain within her family. It was a revelation that set her thinking about her own son and who he was. She tried to convince herself she could lead him to believe he was someone else. Now, it seemed clear to her that the truth was something he deserved and it terrified her. Christopher O'Brien was not Dylan's father. His father was a man with flaws as well, but Cassidy was beginning to realize that the flaws of the real man, and even her own shortcomings, would be far more palatable for Dylan than a secret revealed after many years. "It's nothing," Cassidy assured her mother.

"Cassie, I know you better than that. I know you're angry…"

"No, Mom; I'm not angry with you at all," Cassidy said as she plopped onto the sofa. She listened as Dylan played above their heads in his room. "Batman returns," she shook her head. "I swear he becomes more like Alex every day."

Rose smiled. "He loves her."

"Yes, I know."

"Cassie, what is it? Is it your father?"

"No," the teacher sighed. "You are right though, Mom."

"About?" Rose asked.

"Well, secrets can have unintended consequences."

Rose nodded. "I'm sorry, Cassie."

"No...it's all right, Mom. Really, it is. I understand. I even appreciate it. I really do." Cassidy reached over and took her mother's hand.

"Then what? You want to tell Dylan about his father?"

"I want to tell Chris. I'm not certain how to tell Dylan, Mom. He's seven. But, yes; I do. For a lot of reasons." A faint smile slowly played on Cassidy's face.

"Oookaaay?" Rose squinted. "What aren't you telling me?"

"Alex and I had a talk before she left."

"About?"

"About having a family together," Cassidy answered. Her mother bit her lip to contain her smile. "You don't seem surprised."

"Should I be?" Rose asked.

"I thought you might think it was awfully soon for us to be talking about that," Cassidy admitted.

"Well, are you talking about it or did you already do something about it?"

Cassidy laughed heartily and rolled her eyes, soliciting a wink from her mother. "I just think that we should have an honest slate before that happens...if it happens."

"Uh-huh," Rose muttered.

"What?"

"Cassie..."

"What?" Cassidy asked again with some urgency.

Rose snickered. "*If* it happens?"

Cassidy was about to deliver a smart retort when her phone rang. She looked at the screen and smiled. "Alex?" Rose patted her daughter's shoulder and left the room to give her some privacy.

"Hey," the agent said quietly.

"I didn't think I would hear from you."

Alex took a deep breath. "Guess I missed you."

"Huh. Really?"

"Yeah, maybe a little. Hey, is Speed there?" Alex asked hopefully.

"Yeah, hold on. He's in his room being Batman."

Alex laughed as she heard Cassidy call to Dylan. She could hear him bounding down the stairs and Cassidy's command to 'slow down' in her ear.

"Alex?"

"Hey, Speed. Whatya doin?"

"Mom told me to clean the Batcave."

Alex fought her inclination to laugh out loud. Cassidy was inventive. She had been determined that Dylan was going to clean his room before Alex got home and she had clearly taken the perfect approach. "So, is the Batcave shipshape?"

"Almost," he said. "Batman had Alfred to help."

"Yeah, I know. I'm sorry. I will be home in a couple of days though."

"Promise?"

"Yeah, I promise. You helping your mom?"

"Yeah. Grandma is making sgetti tonight," he told her.

"Wow. I can't believe I am missing that," Alex said with disappointment.

"So, come home."

"I wish I could, Speed. I'll be back before you know it and then you can show me the new and improved Batcave."

"Okay," he said quietly.

"I love you, Dylan," Alex said softly.

"Love you too, Alex," he replied. "Here's Mom."

"Hey," Cassidy said. The line was quiet. "Alex?"

"Yeah, I'm here."

"What's wrong?" Alex sighed. She hated being away. In the past she had enjoyed the constant travel her job entailed, never really wanting to be at home. The fact was she didn't really feel like she had a home. The risk, the excitement, and the fast pace of her work left her with little time to think about what she might be missing. Now she needed to still her emotions and focus on her job. She missed Cassidy and she missed Dylan. She needed to hear them both before she headed off to her assignment. "Honey? Are you okay?" Cassidy asked.

"I'm fine. Just tired. How are you doing? I mean with your mom and…"

"I'm all right. I will be better when you are home, though," Cassidy admitted.

"Me too. I can't talk long, I just wanted to call while I had a minute."

"Alex…are you sure everything is okay?"

"Yes. I'll be home Saturday morning if all goes well here."

"In New Mexico?" Alex didn't answer. "I see," Cassidy continued.

"Don't worry, Cass. Okay?"

"Too late."

Alex chuckled. "I'll see you in less than forty-eight hours."

"You'd better."

"Then you can fill me in on everything. Plus I think I recall something about tacos," Alex reminded her lover.

"You and your tacos. I'll see if the chef is available that day."

Alex was grateful for the levity. "Will the chef have an apron?"

"What the chef will have is a butler."

"Yeah…I got it."

"Alex…"

"I promise, Cass. I will be home by Saturday." Cassidy remained silent. "Cass?"

"I'm sorry, I just miss you."

"I know. I miss you too. I love you, Cass."

"I love you too, Alex. Just come home soon."

"No place I'd rather be. See you soon." Alex closed her eyes and hung up the call. She couldn't shake the sense of foreboding that seemed to be coursing through her. "I swear, Cass," she said to herself. "I'll be home."

***

Chapter Fifteen

The pier was dimly lit, casting shadows along its planks that took on the appearance of ghostly figures. Christopher O'Brien shivered. The air felt crisp but the chill running up his spine was produced by something else altogether. This was not his world. He traveled in a world of suits and ties, tuxedos and cigars. The only guns he saw were those in the hands of Secret Service agents and policemen, occasionally in testimony, or on a tour of some manufacturer. Now, he felt the pressure against his hip as if it were a cancerous growth. The weight in his deep jacket pocket centered in his mind. Why would he need a gun? She had told him this was taken care of. No one would be meeting them. Whoever was watching, hoping to catch Congressman Christopher O'Brien engaging in illegal activity would be left wanting. What hadn't she told him? The sound of his breath releasing echoed in his own ear and he heard the woman behind him beginning to chuckle.

"You really are a stuffed shirt," Claire Brackett observed.

"I didn't hear you complaining about it earlier," he snapped.

The tall redhead laughed and kissed him on the cheek, not as an endearment but to remind him that she remained in control. "Just do what I told you. Wait by the pole. If all goes as planned no one will show. Look at your watch and shake your head as if you are annoyed."

"What about you?"

Brackett pulled out her sidearm. "I will be here."

"With that? Jesus, Claire. Just what are you expecting?"

"The unexpected."

***

"Dylan…come on."

Dylan made roaring sounds as he pushed his toy Batmobile across his floor. "I have to park the Batmobile, Mom."

Cassidy rolled her eyes. "Of course you do. Grandma has dinner ready. Finish up and come down," she said as she turned back toward his door.

"Mom?" Cassidy stopped and allowed her eyes to fall upon her son who was carefully placing his car in a make believe garage. "Is Alex chasing bad guys?"

The teacher considered her answer for a moment, noticing that his eyes still had not lifted to meet hers. She walked to his bed and sat on the edge. "Dylan, come here." He complied slowly, still looking at his feet. "Are you worried about Alex?" He shrugged. "Are you worried about me?" He shrugged again. "Sweetheart?"

"If Alex is chasing the bad guys; what if they come here?"

Cassidy sighed and pulled him onto her lap. "Dylan, no one is going to come here." He nestled against her and chewed on his bottom lip; his eyes fixed on the hand that held him. The abrasions from Cassidy's altercation with Carl Fisher had healed, but in Dylan's mind they seemed to be fresh. Alex's absence unsettled him. Cassidy had felt his presence in the doorway of their bedroom the night Alex had left and called him to her. Even with his grandmother home and all of his mother's assurances, he had not slept in his own bed since the agent's departure. Cassidy did not tell Alex, afraid it would distract her and keenly aware of the anxiety that knowledge would produce. To Dylan, Alex had become his parent and more; his best friend and their protector. "Dylan, we are safe. I promise."

Dylan looked up at his mother with watering eyes, "but Alex isn't here. What if the bad guy comes again?"

"Listen to me, Dylan. Alex is doing what she needs to do to keep us all safe."

"She is?"

Cassidy nodded. At the moment the fear she held was solely for the agent. "Yes."

The boy hopped up and headed to the small book shelf at the far side of his room. His mother studied him curiously. He seemed to be focused on something and Cassidy nearly lost her breath when she saw the object that commanded his attention. He ran his small hand over the toy airplane and stared. "Will the bad guys shoot at Alex?"

Cassidy caught her breath and closed her eyes for a moment to gather her thoughts. "Why would you ask that?" He picked up the long white airplane that his friend, the president, had given him and turned to his mother with questioning eyes. Cassidy immediately understood. "Sweetheart, Alex is very good at what she does." His skepticism was evident. She gestured to the toy in his hands. "You know, it was your friend the president that sent Alex here to help us." He looked up at her in surprise. "Um-hum. He wanted to make sure that we were safe and he sent the best protector he knew."

"But, then he died," Dylan said sadly.

"Yes, Dylan, he did."

"Mom?"

"What, honey?"

"If Alex was with him..."

"Dylan, come here. Alex would not have been with him, even if she wasn't with us. And, he wanted her to be with us."

"Why?" he asked.

"I guess because he loved Alex, just like you and I do. And, because he liked you very much. And, he knew that Alex loved us just like we love her."

"He did? Like me?"

"Yes, Dylan. He did."

"But what if that bad guy wants to hurt Alex?"

Cassidy ruffled his hair and pulled his face to meet hers just as her mother reached the doorway. Rose looked on as her daughter tenderly touched her grandson's cheek and she saw the younger woman's eyes soften. "Dylan, has Alex ever broken a promise to you?" He shook his head. Cassidy smiled. "The truth is sometimes bad things happen, Dylan. Sometimes even to the people we love." Cassidy's thoughts momentarily turned to her own father. It mattered very little what his shortcomings had been. Losing a parent produced unimaginable pain. And, losing John Merrow had set her thoughts in a new direction. There were things she needed to set right. The fear, her fear, Dylan's fear of losing Alex was real, but Cassidy understood now more than ever that even if Alex had a desk job; there were never guarantees. Her own father was all the proof she needed of that fact. What Alex did for work was attached to dangers and Cassidy was certain that the agent tried to shield her and Dylan from that reality as much as she could. It was a reality that the teacher would need to learn to accept and learn to make some peace with for all of them to feel safe. She smiled at her son. "That's why Alex went away. To keep the people she loves safe. And she loves you very much."

"She loves you too."

"Yes," Cassidy giggled. "I guess she does."

"Mom?" Cassidy opened her eyes wider, encouraging him to continue. "I don't want Alex to die."

She pulled him to her chest and took a deep breath. "I know, baby. You have to trust Alex, okay? Why would you be thinking about that, Dylan?"

"Cause Alex has a gun."

Cassidy kissed his head. He had asked a lot of questions about the president before Alex left. He didn't understand everything. He did understand very clearly that a 'bad guy' killed someone he thought of as a friend, and that had happened with a gun. "I know she does, but what did Alex tell you about that?"

"She doesn't want to use it."

"And?" Cassidy urged.

"It doesn't make her a hero."

"That's right."

"I still think she is a hero," Dylan said proudly.

"So do I, Dylan."

"Mom?"

"Hum?"

"Can I sleep with you tonight?"

***

"What the hell would he be doing here?" Brady wondered.

Alex looked out the windshield and shook her head. "I don't know. I don't like it."

"A pier? I mean, Toles; does that make sense to you? Seems like a bad spy movie." Alex clenched her jaw and focused on the pier ahead. "Toles? I thought Fallon said the email on Claire's computer indicated they wanted him framed."

"That's what he said, yeah."

"Does it look that way to you?"

Alex sighed. "I don't know what it looks like, Brady. That is why we are watching."

Brady shook his head. "You think Brackett is with him?"

"Yeah, I do and that's exactly what worries me," Alex said. She pressed on her temple with her thumb and bit her lower lip. "Claire, Claire," she whispered. "What is your game?"

***

Ian Mitchell pulled up alongside a small building that stood on the narrow road to the pier. "Well, Congressman, I wonder if she has a bullet for *your* back," he said as he loaded his Glock

30 and placed it is his holster. "We'll just see, Sparrow, where you fly to now."

***

"Here he comes, Toles." Brady gestured out his passenger side window as the congressman emerged from the cement façade across the long pier. "What the hell is he carrying?"

"I don't know. Just keep an eye on O'Brien," she said as she carefully opened the car door.

"Where the hell are you going?" he grumbled at her, trying to keep his voice low.

"Just stick with O'Brien, Brady. No matter what, you stick with O'Brien. Understand?"

"Toles," he cautioned.

"Something doesn't feel right here," she said holstering her HK 45.

"I'm coming with you."

"The hell you are," she said leaning back into the car. "This is what we do. I saw something over there on the right. I don't think we are alone, Brady."

"I will back you up."

Alex was growing impatient. "Follow O'Brien and Brackett. We can't lose them. I can take care of myself."

"You aren't James Bond, you know," Brady reminded her.

Alex shook her head and chuckled. "No, he didn't speak as many languages…I don't think."

"Toles…seriously…."

"Brady, don't make me sorry I brought you."

"Taylor sent me."

Alex was already moving away from the car and edging herself closer to a large pile of stacked pallets. It seemed her best hope for concealment while she moved closer to O'Brien. Seeing wasn't enough. She needed to hear, to know who was behind all of this and why. John Merrow and Christopher

O'Brien were linked to her family. That presented very real dangers for the people she loved. One way or another she was getting to the bottom of it all. "Come out, come out wherever you are," she whispered, sensing another presence nearby.

***

Ian Mitchell walked deliberately toward the tall pole that held a dim light. He had been in these exact situations thousands of times with only one exception; the woman who murdered his best friend was here also. Like all ghosts, Agent Ian Mitchell was a master at appearing confident and remaining emotionally distant. His stride gave away no emotion to the man that had begun to tremble just paces away. Mitchell would sweep in, sweep away any evidence of his existence, and glide away as quickly as a cloud carried by the wind; seen one minute and invisible the next. "Where is your friend, Congressman?" he mused to himself.

Christopher O'Brien felt his throat go dry and his hands tingle in fear as he watched the approaching figure. No one was supposed to show. Claire had arranged that. "Calm down," he told himself as he desperately tried to tame the beating of his heart. He felt in his pocket, fondling the hard, cold plastic that rested there. He caught his breath as the figure came even with him and he forced his stance erect.

"Congressman, we meet at last," Mitchell smiled, extending his hand.

***

"What in the hell? Shit. Mitchell." Brackett retrieved her side-arm and readied herself. If Mitchell was here then he likely knew about the meet and its purpose. The question was who had sent him. Brackett shook her head and released a heavy sigh. "Couldn't have been Mercier," she said aloud. "Unless he told you before…" It didn't matter. She needed to get O'Brien out of the area and fast. The question was how to do so without compromising herself in front of Mitchell. The redheaded agent stretched her neck and dropped the gun to her side. She skulked along the edge of a cement barrier, just peering over its top. "Just be ready, Congressman," she said as she licked her lips. "It's show time."

***

Steven Brady heard the car door opening. "Thank God you came to your senses," he began as he turned to the driver's side. He jumped at the smile that greeted him.

"Agent Brady," the man smiled. "Well, we meet again."

"Meet again?" Brady knew the man and knew him well. He had sorted through dozens of files on this agent. "We have never met, Agent Krause."

"Oh, I forgot. I had the advantage that day."

"What the hell are you doing here?" Brady asked apprehensively.

Krause nodded and gestured out the front window. "O'Brien and Brackett are not alone, Brady; look."

"What the…"

"You need to get out of here," Krause ordered.

"I can't. Toles is…"

"I'll take care of Agent Toles. You get to the other side of the pier. If Brackett and O'Brien make it that far; follow them. Go."

Steven Brady was no coward but Jonathan Krause was nothing short of a legend in intelligence circles. He traveled in the upper most echelon. He was an anomaly; known and yet untouchable. "I am supposed to leave Toles with you? I don't think so."

Krause snickered. "You are over your head, Brady. I will get Agent Toles out of here," he said as he began to reopen the door.

"Why would you help Alex?"

Krause winked. "Over your head, Agent. Trust me, if O'Brien and Brackett make it to their car, you'll want to follow. Don't make me tell you again," he said coolly.

Brady swallowed hard and moved into the driver's seat. He watched as the tall CIA agent expertly made his way closer to Agent Toles. "What the hell is going on?" he asked himself.

***

"You're here alone then?" Mitchell asked, catching sight of a shadow off to his left.

"Of course."

Ian Mitchell smiled. "Relax, Congressman. Were you not expecting me? You look as though you have seen a ghost."

The congressman fidgeted with the case in his hands. "This is…uh, what you came for, I believe."

"Is it now?"

"I'm sorry?" O'Brien asked.

"What's in that case, Congressman. That is what I came for?"

"I was given to understand…"

Mitchell laughed as he kept tabs on the shadow that was edging closer. "You were given to understand what exactly, Mr. O'Brien?"

"Well…I…President Strickland made clear that you would…"

"Have you seen another ghost, Congressman? You seem to have gone white again." O'Brien swallowed hard and attempted to steady himself as Mitchell turned his attention away. "BOO!" he yelled in the direction of the cement barrier.

Claire Brackett popped up, gun held securely at her side, just concealed by the three foot high barrier. "Ian. What brings you to Corsica?" she fluttered her eyelashes.

"I came at a friend's request. Didn't expect to see you, Claire. Daddy send you to protect the little flower here?"

O'Brien bristled at the statement. "Claire is only..."

"BOO!" Mitchell barked at the congressman causing him to leap backward a pace. Brackett tucked the gun in her pocket and kept her hand firmly on it. Deliberately and seductively she walked toward the pair, winking at the congressman along the way and hoping he would understand that as her subtle signal to be ready. "Daddy won't be happy that the sparrow flew so far from her nest," Mitchell said.

"Oh....I like to think of myself more like a falcon," she cooed.

"Really? A messenger bird, is that it?"

She allowed a slight sarcastic laugh to escape her as she moved closer. "Strong, beautiful, commanding," she said moving closer to the MI6 agent as the congressman seemed to remain planted in place.

"Strange," Mitchell said. "I see you more as a gull. You know; what do they call them? A dump duck?" Claire Brackett seethed at his insult and tightened her grip on the gun in her pocket. A few feet away Christopher O'Brien did the same. She moved only slightly and before she could retrieve her weapon, found Mitchell's aimed at her.

"Now, Ian; is that any way to treat family?"

***

"Shit!" Alex growled, looking across the short distance that separated her from the threesome. "Shit," she repeated. The taller man was pointing his weapon at Brackett and O'Brien. She focused her gaze on the congressman. "Christ, Claire you gave that imbecile a gun?" O'Brien was aiming directly toward the unknown figure now. Alex withdrew her sidearm and grasped it firmly with both hands, swiftly moving in a sideways motion toward the unfolding scene. "Dammit," she groaned as she pressed forward. "O'Brien!" she yelled as she moved closer.

***

POP. POP. POP. POP. Four quick pops lifted Steven Brady from his seat. He looked in the rear view mirror. It was dark. Someone was falling toward the ground. He couldn't make it out. He shifted his gaze out the side window and saw Brackett lifting something. "Shit. Alex, where are you? DAMMIT." He considered his options for a split second. Jonathan Krause's words were still ringing in his ears. The breath in his lungs fell forcefully out of his mouth in a large rush as his foot connected with the gas pedal. "Better be right, Krause."

***

"IAN! NO!" a voice bellowed. Alex shifted her gaze slightly to try and see who the voice belonged to.
POP. POP.
"IAN!" the voice called a second time. "TOLES!" POP. POP. Krause fired his weapon toward Brackett as she pulled the congressman to his feet. "STOP!"

***

It felt like glass, sharp glass. Searing pain traveled down one arm and it seemed as if might never stop. Connecting with the ground felt like falling twelve stories. In the distance there was a faint voice. "Christ, Ian; what were you thinking? Get out of here...GO!" It sounded muffled somehow; far away. The warmth that Alex felt traveling down her back seconds ago suddenly turned cold. It was eerily familiar and she fought to keep her eyes open when the voice returned. "Toles. Jesus. Just hang on. Hang on." The voice was vaguely familiar but she couldn't place it.

"What?" Alex struggled to speak.

"Toles...just relax. I'm gonna get you out of here," the voice promised.

There was noise all around but it was becoming harder to discern. "Brady?"

"Fraid not, Agent. Hang in there."

"I don't," Alex tried to open her eyes. She could see the hint of an outline in the falling lights but everything was swirling now.

She heard a clicking sound and then the voice spoke again. "It's me. I need a favor.....no....no, it's Agent Toles....Calm down...Just calm down and listen to me." There was silence for a moment before the voice continued. "I know that....I can get her there....No, I won't. Just listen. Do you have a way to get to Cassidy...I sent Brady off......I will....I'll explain later...Just get her there." Another click. "Hold on tight, Agent," was the last thing Alex heard before her world went dark.

***

Chapter Sixteen

"**A**m I dreaming? Cass? Are you there? Cassidy?" Alex wasn't certain if her words were only in her head or if she was actually speaking them. It was dark. Her head was pounding and she felt cold, incredibly cold. There were voices. She strained to listen. She struggled to remember. "Where the hell am I? Who's? Cassidy....."

"You need to settle down, Agent." There was that voice again. "I'm going to get you to Cassidy, Agent Toles."

"Cold."

"Yeah, you're in shock. Just relax," he said filling a syringe from a small bottle.

"Thinks I was in New Mexico."

"I know, Agent. I know more than I should. You're gonna be fine. I promised."

Alex could hear the words but it was hard to understand what they meant as the pain began to encompass her body. A sudden sharp pinch and the words from the deep voice began to fade into a gentle tone. It was so familiar and so comforting. The agent began to relax as the voice echoed in her mind. "Cass..."

***

"Where the hell did they go?" Steven Brady yelled from the front seat of his car. Reaching the far side of the warehouse, there was no evidence of Christopher O'Brien or Claire Brackett. "Shit!" The NSA agent bristled at his own actions.

"What the hell were you thinking, Brady?" he chastised himself. "DAMMIT!" He threw the car into reverse and hit the gas pedal with force. "Alex...I hope you are there."

***

"What?" Michael Taylor asked for clarification. "When?" He rested his forehead against a closed fist and exhaled the breath that he had been holding. Slowly, he replaced the phone to his ear. "Brady hasn't checked in. What do you mean....Are you certain? We'll need an extraction.....How the hell did..." The NSA director nodded his silent understanding to the voice on the other end of the call. "Yeah, I'm here......You want me to call her...I don't know if that's wise. Someone should warn her..... Are you sure? How far out are you?" Taylor shook his head and sighed. "Fine, I'll work on Brady. Keep me in the loop."

***

"What in the hell were you thinking?" Claire Brackett screamed.

"He was pointing a gun at you!"

"Jesus Christ, O'Brien!"

"What was I supposed to do? What are we doing in here anyway?"

Brackett gritted her teeth and groaned. "We're waiting."

"For what?" the congressman asked.

"For the smoke to clear, you idiot."

"Look. Claire...I'm done with this. We..."

"You," she said as she moved to take a menacing position over him, "are just beginning."

"I need to get back to...."

"You aren't going anywhere, Congressman. You'll be lucky if you leave this pier."

***

Light was just beginning to peek through the tiny slits in the blinds as Cassidy rolled over. Dylan was sprawled across the bed and she smiled at the contented expression on his face. She stretched and looked over at the alarm clock and sighed. It was not even 6:00 a.m. yet. Occasionally, right about now, Cassidy would awake to find a tall, sweating agent hovering over her sporting a toothy grin. "One more day," she said to herself as she planted a soft kiss on the sleeping boy beside her. "Coffee now."

The teacher reached over and retrieved her cell phone. She smiled as she opened the text message from Alex. "Cassidy. I can't explain. I know Rose is with you. Someone is on their way to pick you up. Just be ready, please. You'll understand then. Please, trust me. Pip." Cassidy froze. This was impossible.

***

Christopher O'Brien had been prattling on, mumbling for hours about how he needed to get back to Washington. The cement floor was cold, it was damp and he was growing increasingly tired of his surroundings. He was feeling a bit emboldened by the earlier altercation with his ex-wife's new lover, and a bit gratified as well. His constant chatter, albeit nearly inaudible, was grating on Claire Brackett's nerves. The congressman stretched his legs out in front of him and rested all of his weight against the wall. He closed his eyes, recalling the episode hours ago. "See what you get," he sighed as a smirk swept over his face.

"You really are not very bright. Are you?"

"Excuse me?" he asked.

Claire Brackett shook her head. "Krause."

"What about him?"

"Get up, Christopher," she demanded.

"Are we finally leaving this hell hole?"

Brackett licked her lips and nodded. "I'm leaving this hell hole." The congressman looked at her and a new wave of fear overtook him. She laughed. "If, by hell hole you mean this dank warehouse, yes, we are leaving. Assuming you can shut up long enough to follow what I tell you."

"And then?" he asked, struggling to lift himself from the floor.

"I have a plan. Just be quiet and wipe that smirk off your face." He grinned a bit wider. "You think if Toles dies all will be well?" She shook her head. "Either way you went from a nuisance to enemy number one."

"She's just an agent."

"You think so? My father had the President of the United States assassinated; on the basis of a suggestion. He won't kill Alex Toles. Why do you suppose that is, Congressman?"

"Who knows, Claire?"

"Mm-hum…Well, all I know is that whoever *she* is connected to is powerful enough to worry my father. No one worries my father."

"No one even knows…"

"Everyone who matters knows we were here or they will within hours. You just keep your mouth shut and do what I say and maybe we will both live long enough to get back to Washington."

***

"Mom?" Cassidy gently shook her mother from her sleep.

"Cassie?" Rose blinked and rubbed the sleep from her eyes as she pulled herself to a sitting position. Cassidy's expression frightened the older woman. "Cassie, what is it?'"

"I don't know," Cassidy faltered.

"I don't understand."

"I got a message from Alex's phone."

"What did she say?" Rose asked.

"It wasn't from her."

"Cassie, that doesn't make sense."

Cassidy could not stop trembling. "No. It doesn't, but in a way…"

Rose reached out and took the younger woman's hand. "Cassie, who was it from?"

"An old friend."

"Of Alex's?"

"No, of mine. It's hard to explain. I just know someone is on their way here. Something is wrong. There is no way that…" She stopped as her body began to shake more violently.

"Sweetheart," Rose pulled her daughter closer. "Alex, she'll be all right."

"What if she's not? Mom? What if she…."

"I don't believe that, Cassie. You shouldn't either."

Cassidy took a deep breath and nodded. "I packed a bag. Can you…."

"I'll do whatever you need, you know that. But, what makes you think you…"

"I can't explain it. Pip…if he was with Alex, from what Alex told me…I can't explain, Mom."

Rose pursed her lips and sighed. "Okay. I'll get Dylan up. You do…."

Cassidy rose from her seat on the bed and headed for the door. "All I can do is wait. That's all I can do." She left the room with her hand on head. "Alex, is this what it was like for you?" Suddenly, Cassidy realized what it must've been like for the agent when she realized that Carl Fisher had managed to capture Cassidy. The difference was that Alex moved heaven and earth to reach her. Alex knew what calls to make, where to go; Cassidy was helpless to do anything but wait. "Alex," she pleaded.

***

"Where am I?" the agent asked, sensing familiar surroundings.

"You're in good hands, Agent Toles."

183

"Where's Brady?" she asked, still struggling to pry her eyelids open.

"Still in France, Agent."

"What do you mean?" Alex tried to move and immediately fell back.

"I need you to listen to me, Agent. Don't try to open your eyes. Just listen to me."

"Who…"

"Agent Toles. SPHINX…it's just a start. Do you understand?"

"I don't…."

"Lie low for now. I promise I will help you. But," Jon Krause paused and closed his eyes as he gathered his thoughts. "I made a promise, Agent Toles. Not just to him."

Alex strained to concentrate on the voice. "Who? Cassidy….I …."""

"She'll be here soon, Toles. Lie low. For now."

"John," she rasped. "Why did you leave?" Alex fought to stay awake as a tear slipped out from under her eyelid and slowly descended the length of her cheek.

Krause watched as the female agent's expression began to relax again and sleep began to overtake her. "You'll get there, Agent. Follow SPHINX. Follow John." He leaned in closer to her. "This is much bigger than you or I, Agent Toles. Just….. Just tell her Pip brought you here. She'll understand. Then you will too." He started to leave just as two men in scrubs began wheeling the gurney away. He stopped them momentarily. "Take care of her. She's…"

"Easy to love," Alex muttered as she felt herself being carried away.

Jon Krause nodded his agreement. "Yes, Agent. She is."

***

Dylan sat at the kitchen table spooning his cereal into his mouth as if in a trance. Cassidy watched him and silently wondered how she would explain her leaving without upsetting him. "Cassie," a voice broke through her private pondering. "A car just pulled up out front," Rose whispered in her daughter's ear. Cassidy closed her eyes, licked her lips and nodded her understanding. "Do you want me to," Rose began.

"No," Cassidy answered. "I should answer it."

Rose attempted to offer her daughter an encouraging smile. The older woman's own apprehension had grown in the last hour. She didn't know much about Alex's job. She did know there were dangers attached to it and she did know that Alex meant the world to her daughter and her grandson. "God, please just let her be okay," she softly whispered.

"Keep praying that, Mom," Cassidy called back as she headed for the door.

Cassidy's hand was trembling so fiercely that it was difficult for her to grasp the door knob and turn. She had been filled with a sense of dread ever since Alex had climbed into the car to leave a few days earlier. Now, she confronted her worst fears. Where was the agent? Was she hurt? Did someone take her? Was she dead? She shook her head slightly trying to banish all of her questions and opened the door. "Cassidy," a soft voice greeted her. Her eyes grew wide and then narrowed in an attempt to process the sight before her. "Not who you expected, I guess," the woman said reaching for Cassidy's hand.

"Jane?"

"It's a long story," Jane smiled genuinely.

"Alex…is she…"

"No. But, we need to get you to her."

Cassidy nodded and then began to speak, "Jane…is Alex…."

"I'll explain on the way; what I know anyway. Which isn't much, Cassidy. It could be a couple of…"

"I already packed."

"He called you then?" Jane asked.

Cassidy searched the woman before her silently with her eyes. "How do you know…"

Jane Merrow smiled. "Oh, Cassidy. We all have our secrets. You thought it was only you, huh?" Cassidy's composure relaxed slightly. She was still terrified of what she might find when she reached Alex, but it was clear that Alex was alive and that put her greatest fear at bay, at least for the moment.

"What am I going to tell Dylan?" Cassidy was visibly worried about how Dylan would react to her departure.

"Why don't you let me lead?" Jane suggested. She gently rubbed Cassidy's shoulder.

Cassidy led Jane the short distance to the kitchen. Dylan had taken possession of one of his action figures and was playing at the table. "Look who I found," she announced as light-heartedly as she could manage.

"Hello, Dylan," Jane called over to receive a smiling wave. The former first lady turned and faced the older woman at the counter whose jaw had dropped several inches. "You must be Rose," Jane greeted warmly. "Alex speaks so highly of you. Nice to finally meet the legend," she winked.

"Mrs. Merrow, I...."

"Please...Jane. I told Cassidy already, Alex is family; so are all of you." She tightened her grasp gently on the older woman's hand and released it. "Dylan," she said as she made her way to him. "Could I borrow your mom for a bit?"

He looked up at her and shrugged. "I have to go to school."

Jane fought a genuine laugh. "Do you like school, Dylan?"

"Sure," he said.

"I promise I will get her back as soon as I can."

The small boy looked at her and nodded. "Alex comes home tomorrow."

Cassidy tried to quell her rising emotions, still unsure what was truly happening with the agent. Jane remained intent on the small boy, keeping his attention firmly focused on her. "Well, that's why I am here. Your mom and I are going to go help Alex with a couple of things and then your mom will bring her home as soon as she can."

"Alex is working," he explained. "She catches bad guys."

"I see. Kind of like a superhero, huh?" Jane remarked gesturing to the figure in his hands.

"Yep," he said proudly.

"Well, do you think you could take care of your grandmother while your mom and I go meet Alex?" He nodded. "Good. I know how proud she will be of you for doing that, Dylan." He smiled at her. Jane put her hand on his small cheek and nodded her appreciation, taking a moment to look at a familiar expression. He looked a great deal like his mother, but that bluish hue in his eye, the way it twinkled; that, she thought, that was John. "Alright, then," she continued, regaining an upright position. "Let's get you to that agent so we can get you both home."

Cassidy nodded and headed to her son. "Dylan, I'll call you later today, okay?"

"Okay," he said.

Cassidy looked down at him and kissed his forehead. "I love you, Dylan."

"Mom," he moaned, a bit embarrassed by her affection in front of their visitor. His response solicited a slight, but genuine giggle from his mother as she turned to Rose.

"Cassie, is Alex…"

"All I know is she is alive," she whispered. "I'll call you as soon as I know more," Cassidy assured her mother.

"Tell Alex we love her," Rose said with a tear of concern forming in her eye.

Cassidy smiled. "I will, Mom."

"Ready?" Jane called back as Cassidy picked up her bag and nodded. "It was lovely to meet you, Rose. I'm sorry it is this way. I promise I will make sure they both get back here safe and sound."

Rose smiled. "I appreciate that, Jane."

Jane corralled Cassidy with the soft grip of her arm. "Come on, I'll explain what I can on the way."

***

"What do you mean?" Admiral William Brackett bellowed.

"What part did you not understand?" Jon Krause answered through the phone.

"You expect me to believe that Claire…"

"I don't care what you believe, Admiral. The facts speak clearly. Claire killed Mercier."

"That's ridiculous, Jon. Why would Claire kill Elliot?"

"To keep him from meeting with O'Brien perhaps?"

William Brackett paced the floor of his spacious study. "Why hasn't Callier called?"

"Perhaps he doesn't know yet," Krause offered. "I'm tired of cleaning up after your daughter, Bill."

The admiral's anger was rising fast. "You listen to me, Jon…"

"No, Bill. You listen to me. I have no idea what your daughter's game is. She has compromised us again. You put her in play. You put O'Brien in this and you positioned Strickland…"

"You know better than anyone how I felt about John."

Jon Krause peered into the small hospital room. "Doesn't matter. Has she called you yet?"

"No," the admiral answered curtly.

"You know where she will head?"

The admiral took a deep breath. "Back here, I would suppose."

Krause shook his head. "She'll cover her tracks, Bill. You taught her well. She knows no one can pin her or O'Brien. Agent Toles is a ghost in this now too. I'd be careful."

William Brackett responded coolly. "If I didn't know better, Jon, I'd think you just threated me."

"No. No, Admiral Brackett. Just a friendly caution. We are *family* after all, aren't we?"

A brief pause ensued as the admiral considered his answer. "Yes, Jon; we are. I will handle Claire."

"You do that," Krause answered smugly as he hung up the phone. He took a long look through the small window at the woman lying in the bed a few yards away. "Good luck with that

Admiral," he snickered. "I think you may have just met your match."

***

Cassidy was still trying to process everything that the former first lady had told her, which was not much. Only that Jon Krause had reached Alex in time to get her out of a bad situation, that Alex was hurt, and that her old friend 'Pip' and the Merrows had known each other for many years. It had been quiet in the car for quite some time and Cassidy was becoming increasingly anxious. They had just passed the sign for Hanscome Airforce Base and Cassidy's worry was growing by leaps and bounds. "Cassidy?" Jane called over, prompting the teacher to lift her head. "I'm sure Alex will be all right. Jon would have told me if..." Cassidy forced a smile in recognition of Jane's attempts to put her fears at rest. In truth, she was preoccupied with thoughts of Alex and sitting with the former first lady made her more nervous. She had been wrestling with how to divulge the truth about Dylan's father to everyone that mattered and a part of her was worried about what the woman seated beside her might think. Jane Merrow was as adept as any agent had ever been at reading people. It was both a talent and a skill; a skill she had needed to master in order to survive the military echelon and the political landscape her life handed her. Cassidy's expression was transparent. "Cassidy?"

"Hum?"

"What is it? I know you are worried about Alex. But there's something else. Is it Jon?"

"No. I don't know what she's going to think about that, though," Cassidy sighed.

Jane nodded and took in a deep breath. "He is a good man. Complicated, but a good man," she said quietly, looking out the window of the car.

"Jane?" The former first lady turned her attention back to the teacher. Cassidy wanted to speak openly but her anxiety over Alex's welfare superseded that need now. "Thank you."

Jane just smiled and clasped Cassidy's hand as the car pulled up to a gate and the back window rolled down. "Ma'am," a young airman greeted. Jane flashed a card. "Have a nice day."

"Thank you, Airman," she said with an acknowledging smile and rolled up her window. Jane tightened her grip on Cassidy's hand and looked over to her. "Anything you need, or Alex...all you ever have to do is ask."

Cassidy felt a genuine smile manifest. Jane Merrow had a calming presence. She took a deep breath and returned Jane's gentle squeeze. The unlikely pair occupying the back seat of the black sedan shared more than one thing in common; not the least of which was a deep love for the woman that awaited their arrival.

***

Cassidy walked down the long, narrow corridor beside the former first lady. She wondered how in the world her life had changed so dramatically in such a short period of time. Her fear was increasing with each step that brought her closer to the agent. She still had no idea what she would find. The idea of Alex helpless, Alex hurt, or Alex in pain was nearly unbearable. Images swirled through Cassidy's thoughts as she attempted to steady her nerves. A tall, somewhat slender man in an officer's uniform greeted them just shy of their destination. She noticed a smile sweep across Jane's face as he extended his embrace. "Janie..."

"Matt," Jane hugged him and pulled back. "How is she?"

The tall man looked at Jane and then turned to Cassidy. "You must be Cassidy." Cassidy forced a smile and nodded.

"I'm sorry, Cassidy," Jane began. "It was so crazy that day... So many people...You remember my brother, General Matthew Waters?"

He extended his hand and gripped the teacher's firmly. "Just Matt," he said before continuing to address them both. "She's out of surgery." Immediately, he noticed the color drain from Cassidy's face. "She's going to be groggy," he said. "The bullet went in through her upper chest and lodged in her shoulder. They had to remove it. Thankfully, it didn't do any major damage. The force of hitting the ground might be the worst for her with her back injury."

"Is she..." Cassidy began as her body again began to shake.

"The surgeon assures me, she'll make a full recovery. She was lucky she had on a vest. The second shot," a grip of his sister's hand stopped his explanation.

"Matt..."

"She's right in here. She's been asking for you since she got here," he said leading them to the door of Alex's room. "I don't know if she's awake."

Cassidy was already pushing the door open. Alex had her eyes closed and her face was pale. Cassidy took a deep breath and covered her mouth with her hand, attempting to stifle her mounting tears. She made her way to the agent's side and looked down on her. There was a large bandage wrapped around Alex's right shoulder and an IV ran into her opposite arm. The monitors beeped steadily in Cassidy's ear as she brushed the agent's hair gently out of Alex's face. She leaned down and placed a tender kiss on the agent's forehead. "Alex," she called softly. Alex licked her lips and an inaudible groan escaped her. "It's okay," Cassidy continued. "I'm here."

Alex still couldn't open her eyes, but the voice penetrated her. "Cass?" she managed. She had been calling for Cassidy for hours, sometimes imagining that her lover was already sitting beside the bed.

"It's me." Alex reached with her left hand slowly and Cassidy took hold of it. "You're all right."

"Mm....sorry..." Cassidy's tears escaped in a sob as the agent's fingers entwined with her own. "Don't cry," Alex whispered hoarsely.

"Alex..."

"It's okay. Where's Speed?"

Cassidy smiled and kissed the agent's hand. "He's fine, Alex. He's with Mom."

"Mm." Alex wanted to speak but the sedation from surgery was still making it difficult.

"Are you in pain?" Cassidy asked trying to control her tears.

Alex shook her head 'no'. "Drugs," she tried to explain. Cassidy stroked the agent's hand and kissed it again. Alex could feel the warmth of her lover's tears as they fell onto her skin. She needed to see Cassidy and more than that, Cassidy needed to see her. She willed her eyes to open, if only as slits, and slowly the beautiful face she adored came into focus. "Missed you. Need my tacos," she forced the hint of a smile. Cassidy's sobs mixed with a heartfelt laugh as Alex's eyes met hers. "Love you, Cass."

"I love you, Alex. You scared me."

"Sorry," the agent strained to reply. "Tired."

"I know. Sleep. I'll be right here."

"Cass?"

"What, love?"

"How did..."

"I'll explain later. Jane brought me." Alex smiled as her eyes closed again.

"Cassidy?" Alex's grip tightened on the woman and Cassidy understood Alex had her own fears now. The agent hated hospitals. They reminded her of the past; a past that often plagued her dreams.

"It's me. I'm not leaving. I promise." As Cassidy's words registered the agent began to relax. "I can't lose you, Alex,"

Cassidy whispered as she sat in the chair beside the agent's bed-side, never releasing the hand that held her own. Seeing Alex in the bed helpless, even for a moment, resurfaced all of the teacher's fears. She had never loved anyone the way she loved Alexis Toles. Alex was everything; the piece that completed the puzzle of her life. It was a piece she wasn't certain she would ever find. "Alex, you are everything to me. I can't lose you. I thought you left me," she confessed through her tears.

Sleep was claiming the agent quickly but she managed one word. "Never."

***

Chapter Seventeen

"**I** need you to send Dimitri to meet me," Claire Brackett said. Viktor Ivanov ran his tongue over his teeth and considered her request. "Viktor?"

"I heard you. Why not Mercier?" he waited for her response.

"I don't think Elliot will be meeting anyone soon."

"Interesting."

"Viktor...."

"The sparrow has sprouted teeth, then?"

"I need a cover," she said.

"That man; he is with you?" Ivanov spoke with obvious contempt.

"*Da. On so mnoy* (Yes. He is with me)."

"*Berlin, v etot vecher. Hotel Adlon* (Berlin, this evening. Hotel Adlon)."

Brackett nodded. "Understood."

"And, little Sparrow?" Viktor Ivanov took a brief pause. "*Ne dumaj choeto bezplatno* (Do not think this is a free pass)." With those words Claire Brackett heard the phone click and go silent.

"Well?" Christopher O'Brien asked impatiently.

"We are going to Berlin." Before the congressman could comment the redhead continued, "And you...you will owe the Russians your freedom, Congressman."

"What does that mean?"

"It means we are going home." She noted the relief on his face and chuckled. "And, it means you will have a debt owed."

"You...."

She laughed and kissed him. "You have no idea, do you? Just stop trying to lead, Christopher. That is not what you were chosen for."

"I am a..."

"You are a pawn on the board. Meant to follow. The sooner you accept that, the safer we will both be," she told him.

***

"Cassidy?" The teacher picked her head up from her hands and glanced across to the attractive woman making her way through the door. "I brought you some coffee," Jane said softly. Cassidy accepted the offering with a smile. "You look exhausted." The morning had worn on Cassidy. There were calls she needed to make but she did not want to leave Alex's side. "Why don't you just go get a little air?" Jane suggested. Cassidy let out a heavy sigh. "I'll stay with her."

"Actually, I do need to call my mother and Alex's family." Jane was a bit surprised by the latter part of Cassidy's statement, but pleasantly so. Alex's estrangement from her parents and the effect that sometimes had on her relationship with her brother was no secret to Jane. She could sense Cassidy's reluctance to leave as the teacher reached her feet and began to caress Alex's forehead tenderly.

"I promise, I will stay right here. Go on."

"I know...what if she wakes up and I'm not....."

"Cassidy," Jane placed her hands on the shorter woman's shoulders. "If Alex wakes up, I will let her know you stepped out to call Rose. She'll understand." She leaned in and whispered to the teacher, "Go on." When Cassidy turned her eyes had filled with tears and Jane took her immediately into a warm embrace. "I know."

"I can't lose her."

"I don't think there is a force on earth that could make that happen anytime soon. Not if Alex has anything to say about it." Jane smiled and placed Cassidy squarely in front of her. She let out a sigh and smiled. "Loving them...it's hard. They live a different life, Cassidy. That is who they are." Cassidy nodded. She had realized that from the moment she met Alex. And, she knew that loving Alex Toles was its own rollercoaster ride. Jane looked over at Alex asleep in the bed. "She loves you. And, Alex," Jane paused and turned back to Cassidy. "Well, John would have told you that she is the most loyal person he ever met. In that way, they are so much alike." The older woman fought her own tears. She missed her husband. "It makes it difficult not to love them," she chuckled. "They don't give their hearts, though...not easily. You have hers. I could tell the moment I saw her at the hospital that day. I'd never seen that expression on her face." She looked back again at the agent and then patted Cassidy's hand. "I watched the three of you at the cemetery after John's funeral. Strange. Seems to me you were meant to be together somehow." Jane winked at the teacher. "Go. I'll bet she is still sleeping when you get back. If not; I promise to keep her in that bed."

Cassidy allowed a quiet laugh to escape her. There was truth in that statement. There was no way Alex was going to want to stay down, or in this place one second longer than she had to. "Thanks," she said to the woman in front of her. "I still don't know why you are so kind to me."

"Oh? Well...love doesn't come with conditions, Cassidy. Alex means a great to my family. Dylan, well...he is part of that family in his own way and that means you are too."

Cassidy nodded her head. Jane was truly a remarkable woman and the more time she spent in the former first lady's presence, the more she understood the love affair people had with her. She was controlled, like all good political spouses. But, she was much more, at least when it came to those that she loved. Cassidy suspected Alex would describe her much the same way; loyal. As she reached the door, Cassidy turned back to see Jane smiling down at the agent and whispering something. There had been so much loss and so much change for them all. It seemed some days as if years had passed within what was only a matter of days. Perhaps, she realized, they too needed a moment.

***

"I still haven't heard from Brady."

"You're worried," Agent Fallon surmised.

"I am."

"What about Alex?"

Michael Taylor stretched his neck from side to side. "She'll be on her feet before you know it. If I know Alex, before she should be."

Agent Fallon pursed his lips. "What happened?"

"I don't know."

"How did you know she was hurt if Brady didn't…"

Taylor cut off Brian Fallon's questioning. "This is not the FBI, Agent Fallon. It's a different game altogether. I told you that.'

"Interesting that you call it a *game*." Fallon's voice dripped with disgust.

"Why? What would you call it?" Taylor rose from his chair and paced across the floor. "I have known Alex Toles a long time, Agent. A very long time." He turned back to face the man still seated and brought his hands to a point in front of his face. "What do you know, Agent Fallon? About Agent Toles?"

"I'm not sure I know what you mean."

"Mm." Taylor sat on the arm of a large chair, took a deep breath and put his hands on his knees. "Agent Alexis Toles…. when I first met her she was Lieutenant Alexis Toles. I was her captain and the man you know as President John Merrow was our colonel."

"I know that," Fallon replied.

"Yes, but I suspect that is all you know. Alex," he sighed, "Alex is the most intelligent agent I have ever known." Fallon had always considered his partner intuitive and capable. He had to admit he was surprised at the definitive sound in the NSA director's appraisal. "Ahh…that surprises you a bit? Well, Agent, did you know that Alex can speak and translate thirteen languages?" Fallon felt his mouth open slightly. "Uh-huh. Not three, not seven; as she so modestly is reluctant to admit. Thirteen in total." He laughed. "She says seven because it is seven she can interact with as if sitting across from you and I in conversation. She has eidetic memory. Did you know that? She can see things that others will not. She holds degrees in linguistics, psychology and forensic psychology, which I might add she had completed by the age of 29. And that isn't all." Fallon swallowed hard. "Before her injury, she was scouted by the Olympic team. She's as good a sharp shooter as any I have known and I would not want to face her hand to hand. She is the real deal. The shit spy movies are made of."

"Okay….But what does that…"

"Alex Toles spent five years at the Pentagon, Fallon. She was placed there by John's predecessor. She continued to work there as an NSA agent into John's presidency. She doesn't even know why; why he wanted her there."

"Why?" Fallon asked the obvious question.

"Because Alex, as smart as she is, as fit mentally and physically as she is, possesses something few people in this field do, Agent Fallon; integrity. He trusted her. She was a barometer for what was wrong and what was right. She helped keep him honest in a job that demanded anything but that. More than that, Agent; John Merrow loved Alex."

"What does that have to do with…"

"It has everything to do with everything, Fallon. To most people in the intelligence community this is a game. It is a game of wits and physical prowess. They lack integrity. They speak of loyalty but they would sell out their own brother for a chance to get ahead. This is all just a challenge to most. Alex is an anomaly. She is loyal and she is humble. It's what made him fall in love with her."

"You are telling me that the president was in love with Agent Toles?" Fallon asked doubtfully.

"I am. She has powerful friends, not just the president. Friends who would give their life for her; for her happiness. It is something she earned. And, it is one of those friends that called me." He thought about the woman who placed the call. "I dare say she may be more powerful than any of us could imagine possible."

"Are you one of those friends, Taylor?"

Michael Taylor smiled. "There are few things I would sacrifice myself for anymore, Agent Fallon. I've seen too much. Alex Toles remains one of them. Whatever we are into here, John wanted us to dig in. It's big. It's dangerous. And Alex is in the thick of it."

"What about Brady?"

Taylor nodded. "Time will tell. If he's not dead, he is laying low somewhere."

"You think he's dead?"

"I don't know. I'm not Alex. I can discover information, she's the one who sees the picture."

"So, what from me?"

"I want you to search through Alex's old NSA case files. And I want you to keep working the congressman's accident," Taylor explained.

"Spying on Alex?"

"No. But, there is a trail. Heard of Advanced Strategic Applications?" Fallon nodded. "I want you to see if it appears in her previous investigations….anywhere. And, I want you to see if it appears beside Jonathan Krause or William Brackett."

"Krause and Brackett I understand. The Russian manufacturer, why?"

"An old friend has some suspicions about the president's death."

"What are you saying?" Taylor laughed at Fallon's innocence. "Are you saying that the assassination is somehow linked to O'Brien?"

"It's all linked, Fallon. I just don't know how. I need Alex back for that. Dig. Use whatever resources you have....but make sure they are trustworthy."

"What about Cassidy?"

"She's with Agent Toles. Book yourself a flight to Connecticut next week, Fallon. You'll feel better when you see them."

"You think I'm...."

"I think," Taylor said as he made his way back to the chair behind his desk, "that Agent Toles has many powerful friends, Agent. She's lucky."

"What about you?"

"I have my own stones to turn over. Go easy with Toles... she'll want to jump right back in."

"Director?"

"Yes, Agent?"

"Do you know? Who shot her, I mean?" Fallon tried to control his anger.

"No. Perhaps Alex will shed some light on that."

Fallon nodded. He couldn't be certain what was really happening. His head was spinning with endless possibilities. Foreign companies, presidents, assassinations; how could they all be connected? He shook his head hoping to clear the jumble that had amassed within it. "Alex, I hope you can make some sense of all of this."

***

"No. I'll call, Barb."

"Cassidy, I can call Helen if," Barb Toles said through the phone.

Cassidy had one more call she needed to make. She had saved it for last and it would be the most difficult yet. Part of her wanted to accept her friend's offer to call Alex's parents, but she felt it was both her place and her responsibility. They were together. They were committed. When the roles had been reversed; Alex had dealt compassionately with Rose and Dylan. Now it was Cassidy's turn. "No. I'll call her Barb, but thanks."

"You sound tired. Do you know when…"

"I don't know. You know Alex. She'll want out the minute she wakes up. We'll see what the doctor says."

"Are you alone?" Barb asked.

Cassidy smiled. "No. One of Alex's friends is with me."

"Okay, you have Rose call us and let us know…we'll…"

"I will."

"We love you both," Barb said.

"We love you too," Cassidy hung up her phone and took a deep breath. She took hold of Alex's and sighed. Slowly, she allowed her finger to press the contact and she waited for a voice to answer the line.

"Alexis?"

"No…"

"Cassidy?" Helen Toles asked. "What's wrong? Is it Alexis?"

Cassidy wasn't certain why but the sound of Alex's mother's voice began to break down her emotions. She took in a deep breath and let it out slowly. "She's okay," she began. She heard Alex's mother release her own sigh of relief. "But, she…"

"Cassidy?" Helen softly urged. Cassidy's tears had begun to flow again and in spite of her efforts she could not seem to control them. "It's all right, dear. Tell me what happened."

Cassidy sniffled and massaged her forehead, attempting to will her own words. "She was shot."

"Oh dear God; she's all right though?"

"Yes," the teacher managed through her tears.

"Where are you, dear?"

"We're at a military hospital."

"Is Alex there with you?"

"I just stepped out to call. She's sleeping....they had to remove the…"

"Tell me where you are, Cassidy."

Cassidy licked her lips and tried to calm herself. "Hanscome Airforce Base."

"In Bedford?"

"I don't know, Helen…I…."

"Is Dylan there too?" Cassidy could hear the concern in Helen's voice.

"No, he's with my mom."

"Good. We can be there…."

"No…I don't know how long she will even be here. She won't want to stay when she wakes up."

Helen Toles let out a soft chuckle. It was clear now that her daughter was not in imminent danger. It was also clear that the young woman on the phone was distraught, and moreover that she knew her daughter quite well. "I am certain that's true. What can I do for you?"

"Nothing. I wanted you to know. As soon as I can I will have her call you."

"Well…."

Cassidy laughed through her tears. "I promise, Helen. I will have her call you."

"I know you will. Right now, I think I am more worried about you, dear."

"I'm all right," Cassidy said weakly.

"Cassidy," Helen Toles smiled and shook her head on the other end of the phone. "She is very lucky to have found you."

"I don't know about that, Helen."

"I do. Don't worry too much about arguing with my daughter to call," Helen said, momentarily lightening Cassidy's mood.

"You have Rose call me when you know what is going on. I'll assume you already spoke with Barb?"

"Well….I did….But I…."

"You don't need to explain. That's how sisters are. I know that is how she thinks of you." Cassidy smiled. Helen Toles was still a bit of a mystery to her, but Cassidy was certain of two things; no matter what had happened in the past, Helen loved Alex and Alex, in spite of her protests, loved her parents.

"I'm sorry I had to call with such…"

"I am just glad you are both safe. You've had quite the time."

"Yeah….I guess we have," Cassidy admitted as her tears began to subside. "I should get back…"

"You tell Alexis we love her."

"I will."

"And Cassidy?"

"Yes?"

"Take care of yourself too."

Cassidy nodded as she disconnected their brief call. She had only been gone a few minutes but the time apart felt like an eternity. The short trek back to Alex's room was filled with overwhelming emotion. Knowing that Alex would be back to herself should have been a relief, but in some ways it seemed to terrify Cassidy. She took a deep breath and opened the door. "Hey," a grumbled voice called.

"You're awake," Cassidy said almost to herself.

"Looks like."

"I'm sorry…I needed to…"

Jane smiled and squeezed Alex's hand. "I'm going to leave you two alone," she winked at the teacher as she passed. "I'm going to go find that brother of mine."

"Thanks, Jane," Cassidy smiled.

"Don't thank me," she whispered. "You're going to have your hands full with that one."

"Hey!" Alex tried to yell after her friend but her voice cracked.

Cassidy raised an eyebrow. "You starting trouble already?" she asked as she made her way to Alex.

"Me? Never." Alex coughed out as she reached for her lover's hand.

"Mm...How are you feeling?" Cassidy asked, stroking the agent's forehead.

"Kinda like a truck hit me, backed over me and then hit me again." The teacher nodded. She was finding it difficult to look in the agent's eyes, fearing her emotions would get the best of her again. "Cass? Hey, I'm okay." Cassidy nodded again. "Cass, look at me."

"I can't," Cassidy whispered.

Alex closed her eyes. She understood. When she had seen Cassidy for the first time after the incident with Carl Fischer, Alex thought she might literally fall over. It was overpowering; the relief, the guilt, the fear, most of all the love she felt running through every inch of her. "I'm sorry, Cass. I'm okay, really."

"I know."

"Hey, don't cry."

"I can't help it, Alex."

"Listen, it's not that bad."

"Alex, someone shot you. I'd say that qualifies as *bad*." Things were still fuzzy for the agent. She could remember pieces, but between the painkillers and the pain itself it was still difficult to see anything clearly. "Alex, what happened?"

"It's still cloudy. I remember this voice...deep voice...I thought it was Brady, but..."

"You mean you thought Agent Brady shot you?" Cassidy was confused.

"No, got me out of there. I can't remember how I...just that voice. Must have been a dream."

"What did this voice say, Alex?" Cassidy asked, finally looking at her lover.

"Something...I was calling for you. I remember that." Cassidy smiled and ran her thumb gently over Alex's hand as she held it. "Said to tell you Pip brought me." The breath instantly left Cassidy's body and she covered her mouth with her hand. It confirmed what Jane had told her. "Cass, what? I'm sure it was just a dream."

"I don't think so, Alex."

"What?"

"Pip….Pip is an old friend of mine," she looked into the agent's eyes and sighed. "Alex, Pip…that was Jon's nickname. It's all I ever called him when we were in France."

It took a moment, but then the pieces began to fit together in Alex's brain. "Krause…..it was Krause."

"Alex, I swear I have no idea why he…"

"No, it's okay Cass, I think I do. Doesn't matter right now."

"Jane told me he helped you, but…What if he shot you, Alex? What if it was Jon…"

The pieces were moving about in Alex's brain and she closed her eyes to allow them to come together. "It wasn't Krause, Cass."

"Alex, I know you can't tell me….I just….I…." Cassidy's tears seemed to have a mind of their own.

"Shhh, not now. Doesn't matter now…Okay?"

"I'm sorry, you are the one in the bed and I am…."

"You are perfect. I'm the idiot who got shot."

"Alex, don't joke about…"

"I'm sorry." Alex kissed the teacher's hand. "Just get me home."

"You just woke up."

"I know. I hate these places."

"Alex…."

"Come on, Cass."

The door opened and a short dark haired woman entered. Alex smiled. "Captain Toles, I did not think I would be seeing *you* back in a military hospital."

"I'd say I missed you, Major, but…."

The woman laughed and shook her head. "I see the pain-killers didn't help much with keeping you quiet."

"Yeah....so when can I go home?"

"Alex," Cassidy cautioned.

"You must by Cassidy," the other woman smiled. "She hasn't stopped talking about you since she got here. Even in her sleep. I give you credit. Takes a tough woman to handle the ornery Captain, here."

Alex shot the woman a look of playful disgust. "Cassidy, meet Major Jennifer Garrison. You can thank her for that scar on my back."

"Actually, you can thank the shrapnel for the scar on your back, Captain. You can thank me for the fact that you are still able to be so annoying."

"Funny," Alex said.

Cassidy was perplexed by the interaction. The two women seemed like much more than casual friends but she did not get the feeling that they had been lovers. Sensing both her emotional stress and her understandable curiosity, the major offered an explanation. "Captain Toles and I, we go way back. She was the most difficult patient I had my first year as an active surgeon. Prepared me for anything that would follow. I guess I should thank you for that."

"Yes, you should. So let me go home."

"Alex," Cassidy cautioned again and Alex let out a sigh.

"OOO....She's good, Alex."

"So, Major...when can Alex..."

"All right. You can go home tomorrow; *if* your vitals stay within the appropriate range tonight," Alex started to perk up slightly. "Uh-uh...and *if* there are no signs of any infection."

"No problem," Alex said definitively.

"Hold on," the Major cautioned. "Alex, you have to take it easy." Seeing the glint in her friend's eye Jennifer Garrison held up a finger. "First of all, that bullet was no joke. You lost a lot of blood. If that agent who brought you in hadn't been so thorough, you might not have been so lucky." Alex sighed. "And, when that medication wears off, I suspect you are going to find there is more pain in your back than in your shoulder."

"Why?" Alex asked, vaguely recalling connecting with the ground.

"You have four broken ribs along with, what I am sure is substantial inflammation. I mean it, Alex. You go home. You rest. You read. You watch TV. You do a puzzle."

"I got it. I got it."

Cassidy shook her head. "Major? Is there…"

The Major smiled. "I wish I could give you something for the attitude, Cassidy." Cassidy tried not to laugh. The brief interaction with the surgeon had helped to relieve some of her tension. Although she knew Alex would be difficult to keep down, she had to admit that selfishly she wanted the agent home. "What I will give you is some antibiotics, pain reliever, strict instructions…and I'll make certain that you have some anxiety medication."

"What do I need that for?" Alex asked.

"That's not for you, Captain. That's for her." Alex frowned and Cassidy offered the Major a smirk of appreciation.

"Thank you," Cassidy said.

"I'm not sure I'd be thanking me, but you are welcome. She'll be back on her feet in a couple of weeks."

"What about work?" Alex asked.

"I said a couple of weeks. Do I need to check your hearing now too? Maybe you hit your head," the Major leaned over her patient and pulled on Alex's ear.

"Hey!"

"You, behave, Captain. No offense, I'd like to *not* see you again anytime soon."

"None taken," Alex shot back. "Hey," she called after the major. "Thanks, Jen." The major smiled and winked as she left.

"Alex, you have to …"

"I promise, Cass. I just want to go home." Alex was drained and being in a hospital bed unsettled her.

"I know. I want you home."

"Yeah? Does that mean I get my tacos?"

Cassidy smiled as a tear rolled down her cheek. "Alex, as long as you are safe you can have tacos every night of the week."

The agent touched the teacher's cheek. "I'm sorry, Cass. I know…"

Cassidy shook her head. "No…stop…I just can't help it. I just found you…I…"

"Don't let Jen scare you, I promise I will behave."

Cassidy chuckled but then grew serious. "I love you, Alex. More than I think you know."

"I know."

"You do?"

Alex nodded. "What time is it?"

"Why? It's 3:30. Oh my…"

"Good, then I can call Speed," Alex said. "At least I can keep my promise. I'll be home tomorrow."

Cassidy smiled. Alex amazed her sometimes. She could see the agent wincing at the slightest movement, but the mere thought of talking to Dylan lit her from within. Cassidy wondered what they would tell him. "Alex, he is going to want to…."

"We're going to tell him it was an accident."

"Alex…."

"Cassidy, he doesn't need to know….not this."

Cassidy looked to the ceiling and pursed her lips. There was a fine line between protecting Dylan and lying to him. There was already one enormous secret that would need revealing. "No, Alex. We aren't. We are going to tell him that you were smart and that is why you were not badly hurt."

"Cassidy…"

"Alex, no. I understand, I do. You are the one who said no more secrets. No more secrets, Alex. Not in our family, please."

"All right. You're right." Cassidy was right, trust mattered. "So…can we call him?"

Cassidy laughed. "Yes."

"Okay," Alex put out her hand for the phone.

"As long as you promise to call you mother afterward."

"My…." Cassidy raised an eyebrow. "I promise."

✳✳✳

Chapter Eighteen

"Dimitri," Claire Brackett greeted the man before her. Dimitri Kargen nodded his greeting. The Russian SVR agent was tall and rugged with jet black hair that stood in stark contrast to piercing green eyes. He was familiar with the younger female agent standing before him and he was cautious. "Sparrow," he said, "that you would call my uncle tells me much. What is it, little sparrow, that you have done?"

Brackett pursed her lips and narrowed her gaze. She slowly walked toward her Russian counterpart and as she reached him, she allowed a sly smile to begin to creep across her face. "Now, Dimitri….Why do you assume I *did* anything at all?" She reached out for him and his hands swiftly and firmly grabbed hers, placing them back at her sides.

"I do not know who you think I am. I am not a lovesick Frenchman and I am not your American president." He stopped momentarily and let his eyes travel over to the smaller American man standing in the corner of the hotel room. He shook his head and snickered. "I am not so foolish, Sparrow."

"Does it matter, Dimitri?" He watched her without changing expression. "Well?" she continued as she stepped away from the man a few paces. "You have little use for my father, we both know that."

"So, then…you killed Rooster because he was your father's arm…"

"No."

"Mercier; you did kill him; no? And the admiral says what to this?"

Brackett walked directly up to the man whose posture remained rigid and whose expression remained stoic. "I don't know what my father says. He made a mistake."

"Is that so?" Kargen asked.

"It is."

"You refer to the death of your lover?"

"You mean the president?" she asked and then smiled. "No, Dimitri. That is all part of our game and I am certain you were thrilled with that outcome." Kargen tipped his head upwards and his eyes narrowed further. "No. No...My father does not see my value."

Kargen allowed the hint of a smile. "Backed you into a corner, did he?"

"Umm," she looked across to the congressman. "I needed my own insurance. You understand."

"So, you want that I make it appear a Russian intervention." She shrugged as Kargen continued to regard the man across the room. "Your father will know..."

"Yes, he will. And I want him to....But to the rest of our world it must look as though it was a deal gone wrong. We were never there. An..."

"I understand. That is easy. What will not be so easy, Sparrow, will be the favor you will one day return."

Claire Brackett inhaled deeply and nodded. "I would like to think we can make agreeable *arrangements*."

The Russian laughed. "The arrangement is, when I call... either of you," he looked at the man in the corner who was clearly stricken by fear. "You will answer. That is the only arrangement."

"Fine," she agreed.

"Good," he replied. "What of the American?"

"Toles? She'll live, I am sure."

He shook his head. "The sparrow has truly fallen from the nest then."

"What do you mean?"

Kargen licked his lips and gloated. "The man...NSA... Mitchell has him."

"Why would Ian..."

"That is the question."

"Where?" she asked.

"You will go home, Sparrow. That is not your concern," he told her.

"It is if...."

Kargen took a deep breath and made his way to the congressman. He stopped, standing just in front of Christopher O'Brien, close enough that the congressman could feel the heat of the larger man's breath on his face. The SVR agent looked the congressman straight in the eye as he continued. "There are many things here, Sparrow. We will do as you ask and you will do as expected. *Nablyuday za etim vnimatelnom Vorobey* (Watch this one closely, Sparrow)."

"*Eto, ya mogu kontrolirovat* (That, I can control)," she said assuredly.

He did not answer right away as he searched the eyes before him coldly. "*Dva bezdushnix cheloveka opasnee drug drugu, chem ostalnomu miru. Ya Sovetuju vam, bit ostorosznoj.* (Two who are absent of soul are more dangerous to one another than to the rest of the world. I suggest you be careful)."

Brackett nodded, though she was unsure what the Russian meant. "When should..."

"You will leave Sunday night. I will need that time to secure things as you wish."

"Dimitri," she began.

The Russian turned and reached the door in a heartbeat. "Enjoy your time together here," he said with a smirk. "I will speak to you." With that, he was gone.

"What the hell, Claire?" O'Brien asked as the door shut.

"Shut up, Christopher. He will make it look as though the deal was interrupted by the SVR; that you were never here."

"How…"

"He will."

"And your father?"

"Oh, I am certain he knows everything by now, but that is exactly how I want it."

"Claire….If Agent…."

She laughed and collapsed onto the bed. "You were never here, Congressman. And, my father will know I took control. Relax…it's time for a changing of the guard."

***

"Coffee?" Ian Mitchell asked.

Steven Brady bristled. "What is it you want?"

"Why do you think I want something, Agent Brady?" The NSA agent shifted in his chair uncomfortably, his left hand bound to it securely. "I am not such a terrible host; am I?" Mitchell smiled. "So, Agent…coffee?" Brady nodded. "We have things to discuss. I want to be certain I have a *captive* audience."

Brady watched as Mitchell politely handed him his coffee. "I suppose I should thank you then?" Brady asked sarcastically.

"Well, that is courtesy, after all," Ian Mitchell smiled and took a seat across from the American agent.

"You really should let me help you with that," Brady observed, nodding in the direction of the bullet wound on the MI6 agent's arm.

"This?" Mitchell shrugged. "A scratch."

"What is it you want to discuss, then?"

"You have a family, Agent Brady?" The NSA agent shifted again. "Relax," Mitchell smiled. "Brothers? Sisters? Children?" Brady nodded. Mitchell stood and paced across the floor. "As do I." He stopped his movement and turned back to the agent in the chair. "What would you do to protect your family?"

Brady's answer came swiftly. "Anything."

"Yes, and if your father; if he killed your brother…if your sister; if she killed your brother…what then?" Brady watched the man before him carefully. Ian Mitchell's jaw had become taut and his eyes seemed to have grown a shade darker. The MI6 agent nodded and made his way back to the table. "A question, Agent." Brady narrowed his gaze as Mitchell continued. "Agent Toles, is she your family?" Brady was confused. "Agent?"

"Not as…"

"But is she your family, Agent Brady?" Brady sighed. "You love her, not as a partner, not as a friend, as a sister?"

There was a bond between agents that few could understand. It was similar to what soldiers often formed during war. Facing violence and death, lies and betrayals required a trust that sometimes seemed to supersede traditional family. Brady began to understand the questions. "Yes, she is."

Mitchell took a deep breath. He made his way to the agent and knelt beside him. Brady momentarily felt his body stiffen. The British agent pulled a key from his pocket and held it in front of the American. "I don't think we will be needing that anymore," he said.

Ian Mitchell began to remove Brady's restraints. Steven Brady looked to him with questioning eyes. "I don't…"

"You would trust me? If I leave you tied to a chair?" Brady nodded his understanding. "Families can be complicated, Agent Brady. They can change. I did not bring you here to kill you. I brought you here to help me."

"Agent Toles…"

"My brother has that well in hand," Mitchell assured.

"You mean Krause. Agent Toles and I have been…."

"You think you understand things you do not, Agent. Your sister, I promise you she will be safe. He will ensure that."

"Why? What does Alex…"

Mitchell laughed. "Families are complicated, Agent…but those who deserve our loyalty will always have it."

"Are you telling me that Alex is…"

Mitchell shook his head. "Agent Brady, it would serve you to drink your coffee and listen to what I have to say. This is not as simple as it may seem to you. I suspect we have similar goals, as does my brother. Not everyone in this family shares that vision. You understand?"

"You want me to believe that you and Jon Krause have the same objective as Alex and me?"

"Hum. Well, yes…perhaps not for all the same reasons, but yes. To betray the trust of those you claim to love…"

Brady was not certain what was happening but two things had become clear: Ian Mitchell was not a threat to him and Ian Mitchell wanted his help. "I'm listening," he said.

***

Cassidy reached the front door when the agent stopped suddenly. "Alex?" Cassidy turned and took hold of Alex's arm, concerned that she might be faltering. "Are you all right?" The agent looked forward blankly and Cassidy could see her trembling. "Alex?"

Alex looked off to the side and noted Nick's car. "Cass…"

Cassidy took a deep breath and let it out. She quietly pulled Alex aside on the front porch. "Alex, they were all worried. I didn't know Nick would be here." Alex nodded. "What is it?"

"Dylan…"

Cassidy understood immediately. She had shared the same concerns when they first arrived at Nick's after her abduction by Carl Fisher. "He will be all right when he sees that you are all right. Didn't you tell me that once?"

Alex looked down at Cassidy and smiled. "Using my own words against me, huh?"

"Did it work?" Alex nodded. "Come on, you need to get inside and get off your feet." The lack of protest from the agent assured Cassidy that she was correct. Alex was still weak, she was tired, and Cassidy knew the reality of attention from all that awaited them inside was adding to the agent's stress. Alex stopped her as she was about to open the door again. "Alex?"

"Thanks," the agent said.

"Let's go," Cassidy winked as she opened the door.

"ALEX!" an exuberant voice bellowed. In seconds Dylan was barreling down the hallway.

"Dylan James! SLOW IT DOWN!" Rose called.

Dylan paid his grandmother no mind and headed for the agent, plummeting straight into her. Seeing Alex wince, Cassidy began to pry Dylan away but she stopped when she noticed that Alex was pulling the small boy closer. "You're home," he said still holding onto the agent.

"Looks like it, huh?" she said, trying to keep her balance.

He pulled away slightly and studied her arm in the sling, his small face dropping in what was quite obviously a mixture of concern and fear. Cassidy and Alex had explained that Alex had gotten hurt, but that she was safe and would be home the next day. They left out most of the details, but when Dylan pointedly asked if someone shot Alex, they answered truthfully. Alex had hoped it would be a conversation that could wait for her arrival home, but Dylan had been worried since Alex had left and Cassidy was determined they would neither lie to, nor keep it a secret from him. It had been a difficult conversation for them all, made more so by the distance between them. The small boy looked at the agent and whispered, "Does it hurt?"

Alex smiled, and although she could feel the pain traveling through her body with the slightest motion, she squatted to meet his eyes directly. "Only a little, Speed. I'm pretty tough," she winked.

Dylan wrapped his arms around her neck and Alex took the opportunity to lift him onto her with her good arm. "Alex," Cassidy warned. The agent looked at her lover and shook her head. The message was clear. Cassidy sighed in protest but remained silent as the agent gritted her teeth and propelled herself and the boy forward onto the couch a few yards away.

"Alexis," a familiar woman's voice called.

"Mom?"

"You sound surprised," Helen Toles said as Nick followed her into the room; Barb and Cat close behind.

"You didn't say anything when I called you yesterday," Alex reminded her.

"No. I didn't," she turned to the blonde woman who was laying her jacket across a chair. "Thank you for that, Cassidy." Cassidy smiled.

"You didn't have to come," Alex started.

Dylan was pressed up beside the agent and Helen took note of how her daughter's hand absentmindedly continued to run through his short hair. "Of course, I did," her mother answered. "I was worried about you." Helen looked back to Cassidy. "All of you."

Alex heard the sincerity in her mother's voice. Between the boy next to her and her mother's words, she began to struggle with her own emotions. Cassidy studied the scene and sighed softly. "How about I go make us all some cocoa? Dylan?"

"I can do that," Barb said. "Sit down and relax."

Cassidy winked at her friend. "I've been driving for over three hours. I need to stretch," she said. Alex looked up at her lover, silently pleading for her to stay. Cassidy just raised an eyebrow. "So, Alex; what do you say? You and Dylan want some hot chocolate?" she asked, leading the agent. Dylan just nodded, staying close to his hero.

"Sounds great. Maybe we can watch a movie, Speed." Alex said. He nodded again. Helen looked at Cassidy and mouthed the words, 'thank you.'

"All right, we'll be back. Cat, do you think you could help your dad get a couple of things outside?" Cassidy asked.

"Cassidy, Rose and I will go return the rental. Cat? How about we to go for a ride?" Nick asked. Cat shrugged. "Go get your jacket."

"Thanks," Cassidy said as she made her way to the kitchen with Barb. "Sure you don't mind?" she asked her mother as they passed one another.

"Nope. I cannot watch anymore Batman, Cassie. I actually dreamed I was Catwoman last night. It was not a pretty visual."

Cassidy laughed and touched her mother's arm. "I see."

Rose called ahead to Nick. "How about we pick up pizzas on the way back?"

"Works for me!" he answered as Cassidy handed her mother the keys to the rental car.

Rose leaned into Cassidy. "When you see what Helen brought, well, you won't need to cook for a week." Cassidy was grateful for her family. And, she was glad Helen had come. As much as a part of her wanted to simply be with Alex, this gave her some time to process her own emotions; or perhaps to avoid them a while longer. She kissed her mother on the cheek and made her way into the kitchen.

"Cocoa and pizza it is, I guess," she said.

***

Helen Toles sat down across from her daughter in a large chair. Alex was still ruffling Dylan's hair and every so often she would kiss the top of his small head. The older woman watched contentedly and curiously as the tender display continued to unfold. "Speed," Alex whispered. "Why don't you go get one of your action figures? You can show my mom." He looked up to her, his eyes conveying that he was torn. "Secret? I'll be right here. Plus, you know Mom; she might use too much milk." Alex raised an eyebrow. Dylan finally smiled and scooted himself off the couch. He had missed his mother too, and part of him was happy to have an excuse to see her.

"He's adorable, Alexis."

"Yeah, he is," she agreed as she watched Dylan sprint from the room. "Like his mom," Alex said softly as if to herself.

Helen smiled. "How are you feeling?"

"I'm okay," Alex answered as her thumb pressed her temple.

"Alexis, you have never been a good liar. At least not to me." Alex looked at her mother in surprise. "You're worried."

"I am." Alex let go another sigh. "I didn't want to tell Dylan."

"No?"

Alex shook her head. "Cass...well, she's handled it so well. All of it."

"She loves you, Alexis. So does that little boy." Alex looked at the older woman and then closed her eyes. "What is really bothering you?" Helen asked her daughter.

"I shouldn't have...."

"Shouldn't have what?" The agent exhaled, looked at her mother and shook her head. "Alex," her mother continued, soliciting a surprised glance from the agent at the use of Alex's preferred name. "They love you for who you are." Alex nodded again. "You're not used to it; having to think of someone else first." The agent reluctantly smiled. "Mm...not so easy; is it?"

"No," Alex agreed, "it isn't."

Her thoughts were abruptly interrupted by a lively voice. "I got Batman, the Joker and Spiderman, see?"

"My favorites," Alex said.

"Yep." He turned to the older woman in the chair when a voice called to him.

"Dylan?"

"Coming Mom! I'll be right back." He sprinted off again as the two women in the room laughed. In what seemed like an instant he was back.

"Geez, I guess Speed was the right name," Alex mused.

"Yep. I'm fast and cool." Alex and Helen tried to contain their laughter as the small boy turned to the older woman. "Ummm....Mom said...do you want some cocoa too?"

"I would love some cocoa, Dylan."

"Okay. Mom!" He started to turn and stopped abruptly looking briefly to Alex and then back to the older woman in the chair.

Helen pursed her lips thoughtfully. "I guess we need to figure out what you should call me." Alex's eyes grew wide as Dylan leaned back into her legs. Cassidy reached the doorway ready to ask where the fire was at with all of Dylan's yelling and stopped as Helen began to speak. "What would you like to call me, Dylan?" He shrugged, afraid to answer.

"You are Alex's mom."

"Yes, I am," she smiled.

"Alex is," he stopped again.

Alex pulled him a little closer. "I'm your Alfred." He looked to Alex and his small face became serious. "What is it, Dylan?" Alex asked, beginning to grow concerned.

The small boy shook his head. "Mom said…"

"What?" Alex asked again. Dylan leaned in and whispered in Alex's ear. "That's true, Speed. You are."

He turned and looked back at the woman in the chair. "Alex is my mom too," he said. "I just call her Alex."

Helen fought her amusement at his innocence, seeing the pride that he had in his declaration. She glanced at her daughter and leaned forward to regard the boy more closely. "Well then, that would make you my grandson, wouldn't it?" He looked at her a bit sheepishly. Alex held her breath, amazed at her mother's response. "But, only if you want to be." He nodded. "Then, that is settled," she said.

"I can call you Grandma?"

"Well, Cat does sometimes, but usually he calls me YaYa."

"How come?" Dylan asked.

"It's Greek, Dylan," Alex explained, "for Grandma. It's what I called my mother's parents."

"Okay. Then I would have a Nana, a Grandma and a YaYa."

Cassidy felt Barb's hand come to rest on her shoulder. "You have no idea how huge that is," Barb whispered. "Not just for Alex, either." Cassidy nodded. She did have an idea. She had heard it in Helen Toles' voice the day before on the phone. She was a mother. Alex was hers. Cassidy could not imagine the pain of separation from a child. She smiled and led her friend back toward the kitchen.

"I guess it's cocoa all around then, Speed," Alex said.

"MOM!" he yelled again as he sprinted off. "Alex and YaYa both want cocoa!"

Alex looked at her mother. "Thanks, you didn't…"

Helen Toles looked directly into her daughter's eyes. "Alexis, when Cassidy called me yesterday, well, I stopped breathing. I don't know how to explain to you what that felt like; that call. It was like that day…"

"I know."

"But," her mother continued, "One thing was different." Alex was confused. "It wasn't a stranger on the line. It was Cassidy." Alex smiled. "She is really quite…"

"Easy to love?" Alex chuckled.

"Yes, Alexis, she is."

"Tell me," the agent smiled.

"Something tells me I don't have to."

***

Nick walked through the garage entrance way, carrying three large pizza boxes to find Barb, Cassidy and Helen at the table talking. Barb looked over and smiled at her husband. "Hope you guys are hungry," he said.

"I'll go get Alex and Dylan," Cassidy offered. She made her way quietly into the living room, zooms and crashes filling the air from the second Batman movie of the afternoon. She stopped just shy of the couch and smiled at the sleeping pair. Two, half full mugs of cocoa sat on the coffee table with the remote between them. Alex had moved slightly to her side to accommodate the small boy lying against her. His head was tucked under her chin and he was partly on top of her. Cassidy couldn't imagine how the agent was handling that with her broken ribs, but the pair seemed completely content as they were. She took a deep breath and walked toward them, bending over and kissing each gently on the head. Neither seemed to stir the slightest bit and she chuckled. Just as she was about to make her way out of the room, she felt a hand grab onto hers.

"Where are you going?" the agent asked sleepily.

Cassidy moved closer and kissed the agent's forehead again. "Nick just got back."

"Mm," Alex mumbled.

The teacher giggled. Alex was exhausted and so was Dylan. "Just sleep. There is enough food here to feed the entire Army." Cassidy started to pull away again and Alex pulled her closer. "What is it?"

"Stay here."

Cassidy closed her eyes and felt Alex's words wash over her. "Alex, everyone is..."

"Cass," Alex pleaded.

"Alex, I think the couch is full," she smiled. Alex gently pulled the boy to rest on top of her. "Alex, your ribs." The agent opened her eyes slightly and tipped her head. Cassidy sighed as Alex scooted closer to the back of the couch. The teacher finagled her way beside the agent and her son. "Your friend the Major would not approve of this, you know?" Alex felt Cassidy's head come to rest next to Dylan's as her leg wrapped around the agent's. "Nick and..."

"They know how to eat pizza," Alex assured her lover.

"They are going to come..."

"Let them," Alex said plainly. Cassidy closed her eyes and breathed in the agent. "Wish I could hold you," Alex whispered. Her bad arm was resting atop her hip and her free arm was supporting Dylan who remained partly on his side.

"You are," the teacher answered.

"I love you, Cass." Cassidy reached her arm around the pair beside her, both to steady her balance and her emotion.

Rose peeked into the room and smiled. Helen walked up beside her and mimicked the response, noting that Cassidy's mother was beginning to cry. Alex's mother wrapped a comforting arm around the woman beside her. "Been tough for all of them."

Rose took a deep breath and nodded. That was true. She could see it on Cassidy's face. For all of her pretenses, the teacher remained rattled. But, there was something more. "I have never seen Cassie so happy," Rose said. "I can't imagine if we lost her..."

Helen closed her eyes. It was apparent to Alex's mother that her daughter loved these people in a way Helen had never seen and that they loved her just as much. Rose loved the agent as much as she loved her own daughter and looking at the three bodies sprawled across one another Helen understood. They just fit. It was evident in every interaction. Alex and Cassidy were a family. She smiled and patted the shoulder beside her. "What do you say to some pizza?"

Rose smiled and nodded her agreement. "I think we'd better find where Cassidy keeps the ibuprofen while we are at it."

"Are you not feeling well?" Helen asked with concern.

"Oh no, I am fine," Rose chuckled as they headed for the kitchen. "But, I don't think it will just be Alex in need of pain relief when they wake up." Helen laughed at Rose's assessment.

"I wish I could tell you that someday she'll realize she's not invincible," Helen said.

"If anyone can teach her that..."

Helen laughed in agreement. "It will be Cassidy."

***

Chapter Nineteen

The day had been exhausting for both Alex and Cassidy, but each had made the silent admission that the love of their family was both needed and welcome. It was surprising that after a short rest, the living room conversation with their family had easily spiraled into late evening. When they had gone to check on the two young boys, they found each sprawled in his own beanbag chair sound asleep. Nick had moved in to wake the pair when his sister stopped him. In spite of protests, Alex and Cassidy insisted that they allow the boys to just *be*. Normalcy was something everyone needed now. Dylan had been shaken by Alex's injury and his contentment in the moment was enough to convince both women that this was exactly what he needed. Helen and Rose both raised eyebrows at their daughters' insistence, but realized an argument was futile. Though neither wanted to admit it, Cassidy and Alex were secretly glad when Rose decided to spend one more night in the guest room.

Alex woke up unexpectedly and was surprised to find an empty space where Cassidy would normally be. She slowly moved and stopped to catch her breath. Her injuries were far more painful and debilitating than she intended to let on, and she grimaced as she struggled to find her feet. It was unlike Cassidy to be up in the middle of the night unless a nightmare plagued one of them or Dylan made his way into their room after a dream of his own. The agent sighed and gently stretched, feeling the soreness that seemed to rack every inch of her body. Slowly, she made her way out of the room, ready to head downstairs. She thought perhaps Cassidy had gone to check on the boys. A faint light from Dylan's room stopped her and she changed direction.

Cassidy was standing in front of Dylan's bookcase. Alex couldn't tell what she was looking at, but it seemed that the teacher was focused on something. "Hey." Cassidy did not respond, merely shutting her eyes tightly and fighting to draw in a full breath. "Cass?" The agent bridged the distance between them and put her hand on her lover's shoulder. "Cass?"

Cassidy turned very slowly on her heels. Once she managed to force her eyes to meet the agent's, Alex immediately noticed the swollen redness. "Alex, I can't do this."

The agent's heart stopped. This was her greatest fear come true, losing Cassidy to her own stupidity. She kept telling herself that she did what she had to do. That is why she ran into the situation with Brackett and O'Brien. She was keeping Cassidy and Dylan safe. These last two days Alex had grown unsure of everything; everything except Cassidy. If keeping Cassidy in her life meant quitting her job, she would do it. She would find a way to protect them somehow. She remembered everything now about France and about the shooting. "Cassidy, I'm sorry. I know this has been hard. I need to tell you…"

"Alex, please…."

"Cass, no please. I said no secrets. I have to tell you…"

Cassidy shook her head and put her hands on Alex's chest. "No. I need you to listen to me, please?" Alex licked her lips and nodded as the knot in her stomach and the ache in her heart began to outweigh the soreness in her body. Cassidy turned away to gather herself. "When I got that message and I was waiting," she paused and took a deep breath. "Jane came and we were in the car, she took my hand…"

"Cassi…."

"Alex, please, let me get this out. I didn't know….what I would find. Where you were," she stopped and stilled herself.

"I sat with Jane. I thought about Dylan, and you and me; everything my life has become." Cassidy exhaled and nodded, taking a pause to calm herself. "I love you, in a way that I don't even understand some days, Alex. I didn't think it was possible to love someone like this....to..."

Alex reached out again and touched Cassidy's shoulder. "Cass," she whispered.

Cassidy finally turned to face the agent. "I can't lose you, Alex." Alex searched the eyes before her. "I can't do this anymore," Cassidy said softly. Alex let out a heavy sigh and nodded, closing her eyes. She suddenly felt the warmth of Cassidy's palm on her cheek. "You are my family, Alex, you and Dylan. I have to tell him." Alex opened her eyes in confusion and looked at her lover. "I'm not sure how we tell Dylan, he's seven." Cassidy trembled as she continued, but the resolve in her voice was clear. "I don't know what Chris will do, Alex. Dylan...Dylan is not his. I looked at Dylan tonight. I could see John. I could see *you*. I could see my mother, but Chris?" Cassidy shook her head. "He may have been a part of Dylan's life, even though Dylan thinks Chris is his father....Somehow, he just never made it to Dylan's heart."

Alex sighed in relief and kissed Cassidy's forehead. "Are you sure?" she asked. Cassidy nodded.

"Alex, I'm not going to lie to you. Sometimes I hate what you do, the danger. It scares me. Only because I don't want to lose you." Alex understood. "But, I made my choice to be with you. All the things we've said to one another, this family...We can't move forward with that secret. It's not fair, not to you, not to Dylan, not to Jane or me." She chuckled sarcastically, "not even to Chris." Her voice dropped and Alex heard the unusual contempt in it, "and I don't want him in our family." Cassidy looked up at Alex and smiled softly. "I love you."

"I love you too, Cassidy. More than you know." She paused and pinched the bridge of her nose.

"What is it?" Cassidy asked.

"I'm glad you want to tell him. There's something I have to tell you."

"Alex?"

"Cass, you are not going to like this. Let's go back to bed, okay?"

"Alex, you are scaring me."

"No more fear, Cassidy, just the truth. I promised no secrets. I meant it. Please?" Cassidy nodded. "No matter what, you need to know that nothing is more important to me than you and Dylan. Nothing."

"I have a feeling I might need some of that anxiety medication," Cassidy offered with a deep breath as she followed the agent back to their room.

***

"What are you telling me?" Jane Merrow asked pointedly. Jon Krause sighed deeply and looked to her with heavy eyes. "Are you telling me that Congressman O'Brien shot Alex? Is that what you are telling me, Jon?" The fury in her voice seemed to increase with every syllable. "Just what the hell is going on here? What does this have to do with John?"

"Jane," he began carefully as he slowly bridged the distance between them. "I did what I could where John was concerned. This isn't about John. It's Claire and it's O'Brien."

The former first lady closed her eyes tightly and grabbed onto the agent's arms. "I know you did what you could."

He pulled her closer and kissed the top of her head. "I have to see Toles."

She pulled away abruptly and questioned him fearfully, "Jon...I don't..."

"I have to. I need you to work with Matt..."

"Jon...."

"Listen to me," he said softly as he pulled her closer again. "Claire killed Elliot."

"What?" her voice echoed her disbelief.

"This is spiraling, all of it. I need Toles. Ian and I...."

Jane shook her head and turned, covering her eyes in frustration. "Jon, what the hell was he into? This isn't simply..."

"Jane, John was trying, trying to change things...I don't know...that is not what my role is. You know that. I know enough, enough to..."

Jane Merrow looked up into her friend's eyes. "You're afraid for them, aren't you?"

"Yes. I am."

She nodded and covered her eyes again. "O'Brien...he's not part of the..."

"He is self-serving, Janie...if I could..." She looked at him conveying her concern. "I won't, but I'd like to," he told her.

"You need to be careful," she warned him.

"This is who I am."

"You should tell her, Jon."

"Tell who, what?" Krause asked.

"Tell Cassidy about O'Brien."

He chuckled. "No....Toles will tell her."

"Alex knows?"

"I'm sure your good agent has put the pieces together by now about O'Brien. I need her. She and Matthews are tight. She can get closer..."

"I can't lose you, not any of you...not after..."

Krause heard the panic in Jane's voice. "Call Matt. Tell him I am in."

"You know once you cross this line..."

"I'm already over it, Jane. Mitchell and I are in. I will find out what John was doing, why the Russians were so...where SPHINX leads."

"Just promise me, Jon...no matter what, I promised him...."

"Jane, I will do whatever I have to. I won't let anything happen to Dylan or Cassidy," he said emphatically. "I'll do whatever I can to protect Agent Toles, but I can't keep her out of this. That is not who she is. You know that too. This is what we do, Jane. It's what we were built for. Brackett and O'Brien have to be controlled and there are…well, I have to see her. She'll have questions."

He turned to leave and Jane grabbed his arm. "If you did," Krause stopped, searching her eyes for her meaning. "I mean… if the congressman were to….well, I would not shed any tears." He nodded. "If you are going to see Alex, I am going with you."

"Jane, you risk compromising…"

"Jon, they both deserve to know what we are headed into."

"Cassidy is not in…."

Jane took his strong face in her hands with a deep understanding. She leaned into him and spoke softly, "we don't choose who to love, Jon. We both know that. But, who we love….This effects them both. Dylan…and Alex is her…"

He closed his eyes and leaned into the gentleness of her touch. "I know."

She pulled back and looked at him as her tears glistened. "You are good man, Jonathan."

"I wish that were true."

"It is," she said quietly as she turned to leave.

***

"Brady?"

"Sir," Steven Brady answered.

"Where the hell have you been?" Taylor blared through the phone.

"I was detained."

"By what?"

"Not by what, by whom." Taylor rubbed his hand across his forehead and prepared himself for the coming conversation as Brady continued. "Toles, how is…"

"Agent Toles is already home, Brady. Seems she has some very unlikely friends."

"Seems we all do, Sir."

"Explain," Taylor said pointedly.

"I will when I get back. What I do know…well," he paused. "O'Brien shot…"

"I'm aware," the director said. "He and Brackett arrived back in D.C. late this evening."

"Does Alex know?"

"I haven't spoken to her yet. How did you get…"

"Seems the Brackett clan has made more enemies than friends," Brady explained.

"And this new ally you've found?"

Brady took a deep breath. He anticipated Taylor's skepticism. He still had a fair degree of his own. "He has his reasons."

"I see."

"Sir, I need Toles."

"She has been ordered home for two weeks," Taylor responded.

"I don't need her in the field. I need her eyes."

Taylor sighed. "For?"

"Russia, ASA, Nigeria, U.S. Congressional Campaigns. Even my source isn't completely sure how they all…"

Michael Taylor understood. "I have some ideas. I'll see you in New York Wednesday morning. Just get home Agent Brady, with everything you have. I'll be certain Agent Toles gets the pieces."

***

Tuesday, April 29th

"What in the hell were you thinking, Claire?"

"Oh please…."

Admiral William Brackett's cool exterior had long since vanished. "You…you stepped so far over the line…"

The tall redhead smirked. "Oh, now Daddy, watch your heart." She leisurely took a seat on the sofa in his private office and reclined. "We were never there."

"You know as well as I do that everyone who matters knows exactly…"

She shrugged. "What is it that bothers you, Daddy? Are you that afraid of Agent Toles? Or is it Jon?" His face tightened further and began to flush. "Or is it Edmond? No? Maybe it's the idea that *you* are not in control anymore." He shook his head. "You set me up, tried to back me into a corner. You taught me better than that." She paused again and gloated. "Never corner a cobra," she offered smugly.

The admiral shook his head. "Claire, you are more naïve than you are brash. A cobra?" She tipped her head and smiled with satisfaction. "A sparrow is more dangerous than a cobra, Claire." She looked at him quizzically. "Not as smart as I thought you were. I spent a fair amount of time in Southeast Asia… if you recall. Cobras, they are not the dangerous animal you portray. They are large and easily visible. And, unless provoked they do very little harm. Corner them, they hiss. They are solitary animals; unlikely to get close enough to do any harm to anyone. Even when cornered they prefer escape." The admiral looked at his daughter as her expression gradually became uneasy. "Sparrows, sparrows are small and unassuming. They are social animals. They can easily get close. They don't need venom. They are charming and appear innocent. They can win over a human heart. They can listen silently or sing their tune."

He moved toward a bookcase in his office and turned to her. "A sparrow or a snake, Claire?" She stared at him blankly. "I see. So then, *you* are the cobra." He chuckled. "The Russians? Dimitri? That's where you went?" She continued to stare at the older man as he reached for a tattered book on the shelf. "I used to read this to you when you were small. You may not remember." His hand affectionately caressed the binding and he smiled at the cover. "Rudyard Kipling. I think you should revisit it." He handed her the worn copy of *The Jungle Book*. "Dimitri, Claire; do you know his handle?" She looked at the book in her hands and back to her father. "Mongoose." He smiled at his daughter and pointed to the book in her hands. "Rikki Tikki Tavi, it's in there." He shook his head. "Read it."

***

Chapter Twenty

Wednesday, April 30th

Alex walked into the kitchen and spied Cassidy dancing and singing slightly off key to an unfamiliar tune. The teacher was clearly oblivious to the agent's presence and Alex took the opportunity to lean in the doorway and enjoy the show. She could faintly hear the music playing in Cassidy's ears and covered her mouth with her hand to keep from laughing. The past couple of days had been stressful. Alex was still in considerable pain, Dylan was waking often with nightmares of his own and Cassidy was reeling from everything. Watching her lover now, Alex felt as if the weight that had been pressing in on them all had finally begun to lift.

Cassidy spun around on her heels to grab a towel and caught sight of the agent. It startled her enough to scream and she jumped nearly a foot backwards. "Alex!"

The agent could no longer contain her laughter as she made her way to Cassidy, whose face had flushed to a bright shade of pink. "You are adorable." Alex smiled and wrapped her good arm around Cassidy, who buried an embarrassed face into the agent's chest. Alex kissed the top of a shaking head. "You've got some moves, there." Cassidy pushed back and snapped the towel at the agent, poking at her cheek with her tongue in mock disgust. She pulled out her ear phones and tossed the player on the counter. "What?" Alex asked innocently. She mocked a little groove of her own and winked at her lover.

"You're funny."

The agent made her way back to the teacher and pulled her close. "Maybe I should take you dancing."

"You are enjoying this, aren't you?" Cassidy asked. Alex shrugged and smiled. "That's what I thought." Cassidy started to pull away but Alex pulled her back, slowly swaying them together. "What are you doing?" Cassidy grinned.

"I thought you wanted to dance."

"Alex, there's no music."

"No?"

Cassidy looked up into the agent's eyes and smiled. "Are you sure you didn't hit your head when you fell? I don't recall them telling me...." Her words were abruptly stopped by a soft kiss. She took a deep breath as Alex pulled back. "Alex..."

"Yes?" the agent asked as she leaned in for another kiss, running her hand gently through the teacher's hair.

"This is not a good idea."

"What's that?" the agent mumbled as her lips traveled slowly along Cassidy's neck.

"You are supposed to be relaxing..."

"I am relaxed," Alex whispered heavily into her lover's ear.

Cassidy sighed. "If you don't stop..."

"Mm?"

"Alex..." Cassidy's hands were gripping the agent's head and she was finding it increasingly difficult to stand on her own power. "We shouldn't..."

"No, we shouldn't," Alex mumbled, pushing Cassidy against the counter.

"Your arm..."

"Cass?"

"Mm?"

Alex ran her hand slowly along Cassidy's side to the top of her jeans and released the button. "Stop talking," she whispered. Alex lost herself in the woman she loved. She had no thought of the days that had passed, no sense of any physical pain. In this moment there was only Cassidy and she suddenly needed to feel closer to her, to hold her, to touch her, to remind herself that this was everything in her world; this beautiful, wonderful, compassionate woman. The simplest moments with Cassidy took Alex's breath away and she never wanted to let one slip by. "I need you."

Cassidy tugged at her bottom lip, unable to form a coherent thought as Alex tenderly explored her body. There was something in the agent's touch that told Cassidy that this was a moment Alex needed as much as she did. She had missed the closeness that they shared in the last few days. It wasn't desire that fueled her. It was exactly what Alex had said. It was need. It was the need to know that Alex was real, that she was honestly safe. It was a need to know that she was part of Cassidy; the part that moved her beyond reason or logic. Alex looked into Cassidy's eyes and as she touched her gently, tears began to roll down the teacher's cheeks. "I never want to be without you," Cassidy managed as she moved in time with her lover.

Alex took a deep breath and let the hint of a smile grace her face. "Never," Alex whispered. There was something in the way Cassidy held onto her now that Alex understood was not simply passion. There was fear. The fear of losing this; losing each other. In their short time together both had looked that fear in the eye. Alex could feel the reality washing over them both now. Most of the time it felt like an eternity that they had been together, but in truth they had just found one another. "You are everything to me, Cassidy. I promise, I am not leaving you." Cassidy gave over to the agent completely, unable to form words, she pulled Alex so close to her that she was certain even air could not exist between them. "I'm here," Alex promised. She felt Cassidy collapse into her; the teacher's tears racking her violently. "It's okay, Cass."

"Alex...I thought I'd lost you."

The agent closed her eyes and held her lover against her as tightly as she could. Cassidy had been focused on taking care of everyone else. The anger the teacher felt over Alex's revelation about her ex-husband and the shooting prevented her from confronting the depth of her own emotions. Being close to Alex, feeling her, destroyed the wall Cassidy had managed to erect. Now that it had crumbled Alex understood that she needed to help Cassidy feel safe again. "Let it go."

"Alex…"

"Come on." Alex put out her hand. Cassidy looked at the agent and sighed. "Let me hold you now."

"I need to," Cassidy began to protest.

"You need to stop trying to take care of everyone else, Cassidy. Let us take care of you," Alex said lovingly.

"I'm not the one…" Alex smiled and stopped the thought with a kiss. She took Cassidy's hand and led her to the couch and removed her sling. "What are you doing?" Cassidy grabbed the agent's hand.

The agent guided her lover down beside her and put her arm around her, holding Cassidy close. "I told you. You have held me all week. I am holding you now."

"Alex…"

"Cassidy, just rest. Sleep with me for a while. I am not leaving," she whispered. Cassidy's tears were still falling freely as she nestled against the agent and caressed the hand holding her. "I can't lose you either," Alex admitted as she let her eyes close. "Je t'aime, Cass."

"Je t'adore, Alex."

***

The sound of the doorbell startled the agent from her sleep. Cassidy was not beside her. She wiped the sleep from her eyes and forced her feet to the floor, slowly making her way toward the hallway. Willing her eyes to open, she noted the time on the clock and smiled. "She went to get Speed," she mused as she reached for the door handle. She squinted as she looked into the afternoon sun. "What the?"

"Alex."

"Jane?"

The former first lady smiled. "I know that this is a bit unorthodox. I have my reasons."

Alex nodded. "No, you know you are always welcome," she stopped to regard the man approaching.

"I know...Alex," Jane began, suspecting that the agent might bristle at his presence. She was surprised to see Alex's shocked expression begin to soften as quickly as it appeared. Alex opened the door wider and gestured for the pair to enter. "I would have called..."

The agent shut the door and let out a sigh. "It's all right," she said. She looked directly at the tall man now standing in her hallway. "I guess I owe you a thank you."

"You don't owe me anything, Agent Toles." Alex nodded.

"Alex? Is..."

"Cass will be back soon. She went to get Dylan. I assume you are not here to see her, though."

"Actually, we are here to see you both," Jane replied.

Alex raised an eyebrow. "Well, coffee?" she offered as she led Jane and Jon Krause to the kitchen.

"How are you feeling?" Jane asked with concern.

"Better." Alex went about starting a pot of coffee and then looked to the tall CIA Agent. "So, you won't mind if I ask you this, Agent Krause....Before Cassidy gets home." He smiled his understanding. "Did you do it for him or for Cassidy?"

"Agent Toles...John was my brother, maybe not biologically, but....there is a lot we need to discuss. I promised to protect you...all of you."

"So that's why you took out Fisher?" Jane looked to Alex and then to the CIA agent in confusion. "Well?" Alex asked.

"Figured you would put that together," he smirked.

"So?"

"John called me right after you called him." Alex looked at him and nodded. "I was already on my way."

"That doesn't answer my question," she said plainly.

"Both, Agent."

Alex sighed as she heard Dylan's voice outside. "I'll be right back. I think it might be best if Cassidy finds out we have visitors from me."

"Of course," Jane answered.

The agent made her way back into the hallway and was quickly greeted by a sprinting seven year old. She squatted down and accepted his greeting. Cassidy caught the expression on the agent's face. She looked back out the door and noted the black sedan parked on the street. The teacher's raised eyebrow met the same expression from Alex. "Dylan, Mom and I have some company. Do you think you could go watch something downstairs for a little while?" Alex asked. He shrugged his agreement and started off toward the door.

"Hey," Cassidy called after him. "That doesn't mean you don't have to do your homework."

"I know," he called back as he descended the stairs.

"So," the teacher began as Alex moved toward her. "Who is our company?" Alex licked her lips. "Alex?"

"Jane." Cassidy opened her eyes wider in an effort to implore Alex for more details. "Okay…and Krause." Cassidy leaned in closer in disbelief. "Cass?"

"Pip is here?" Alex shrugged. "Why?"

Alex let out a heavy breath. "Cass, he did save me…and he was John's best friend… and…"

"And what?"

Alex released a sigh and took Cassidy's face in her hands. "And he cares about you."

"Alex, that's…"

"Look, Cassidy, whatever it is they want to tell us…"

"Tell *us?* Alex, what do I have to do with any of this?"

"Cassidy, you are Christopher O'Brien's ex-wife. Dylan is, well John's…and now there is me and what happened in France…"

Cassidy rubbed her face with her hands. "Alex…"

"Let's just see what they have to say, okay?" Alex suggested gently.

Cassidy caught the faint smell of coffee in the air. "You're making coffee?" The agent stopped and looked at Cassidy. "I think I might prefer wine," Cassidy quipped. Cassidy's hand affectionately squeezed the agent's and Alex found herself feeling grateful for the morning they had shared.

***

"So, what are you saying?" Alex looked at Jane.

"Alex," her friend implored.

"You are telling me that there is a government within the government? Is that what you are saying?"

"That is what we are saying, yes, Agent Toles," Krause intervened.

Alex pinched the bridge of her nose. "For what purpose?"

He nodded and pulled out his chair, taking a moment to pace across the kitchen toward a window. "That's really the question; isn't it?"

"Krause, what the hell does that mean? You don't know the objective? You work for these people, don't you?"

"Alex," Cassidy put her hand over the agent's to calm her.

Jon Krause looked at Jane who offered him a halfhearted smile of encouragement. "Agent Toles, John and I…we were raised to be who we are. To do what we do. Do you understand? The objective? We took orders. Orders to protect our country. That was the objective."

"Protect the country? Selling arms to warlords and drug dealers? You are telling me he knew about all of this?" Krause nodded. "Why? Jesus Christ," Alex pulled away from Cassidy's touch as her anger began to burn hotter. "So, now what? You want my *help*?"

"Yes," he said.

Alex let out a sarcastic chuckle. "Why now?"

Jane looked at Cassidy and then made her way to Alex. "Alex, listen to me. We are pretty certain that John was working against The Collaborative."

"The what?" Alex asked.

"The Collaborative," Krause repeated.

"The Collaborative?"

Jane took Alex's arms. "Alex, please….please, sit down." Reluctantly, Alex complied. She looked at her friend as Cassidy gently stroked her back. "Listen, for a long time there have been people working to root out the source; determine who is really pulling the strings." Alex looked at Jane skeptically as the former first lady continued. "Matt…he never went that way. Even when our father tried to convince him to take a role in Admiral Brackett's office at the Pentagon, he refused. Things didn't make sense to him. John…He called Matt that Saturday. Left a message. They never spoke."

"All right, what does this have to do with O'Brien?" Krause started to answer and Alex stopped him. "What about Cassidy and Dylan?"

Krause looked at Cassidy and smiled. "I'm sorry, Cassie," he said honestly. "O'Brien is nothing more than a pawn. The admiral chose him, among others. He fit a profile; ambitious to a fault, adept at storytelling; a convincing liar." Cassidy shook her head and rolled her eyes as he continued, "he was easy to manipulate."

"And now?" Alex asked.

"Well, Claire Brackett has tipped that on its head. Look, Agent Toles, I will tell you everything I can. I don't know as much as I know you would like to believe. I can tell you about transactions, players…orders," he stopped. "We are all pawns. Nothing more."

Alex studied his expression. "Why? What changed?" She looked at him and caught his gaze drift to the woman beside her. Alex chuckled and shook her head.

"They killed my brother, Agent Toles."

Alex sighed. "So, where do we start? We both have something to protect."

"SPHINX."

"What do you know about it?" she asked.

"Not a lot. Enough to know it leads somewhere deeper than even I have been."

"What did he want me to know about Iraq?"

"I don't know, Agent," Krause admitted. "He would never speak about that; never. SPHINX leads to something deeper. It was not my operation, not part of my duties."

"Okay...what do you want me to do?" she asked.

"Matthews."

"The Ambassador?"

"Yes," he answered.

"Jane is closer to Russ..."

Krause looked at Alex. "No. Jane needs to be out of this part."

"Why not just come to me, Krause? Why involve Cass?"

"Cassidy is involved, Agent, no matter whether you or I like it that way. Dylan, well no matter whether they think he is O'Brien's or John's or...."

"You're worried they might use him as leverage. Against who?" Krause looked at her blankly. "Shit. Against me?"

"Maybe. Against anyone."

"And Cassidy?" Alex asked.

He sighed. "Agent Toles, I came here because I don't intend to let anything happen to Cassidy or Dylan. Now, after John; after what happened in France; this is the only way."

"This is crazy," Cassidy muttered as she put her face in her hands.

"Cassidy," Alex whispered. "I won't let anything happen to you or Dylan."

"What about you, Alex?" Cassidy's voice raised a decibel.

The agent attempted to smile. "What did I tell you, earlier?"

"I know, I know this is a lot," Jane said quietly. "You deserve to know, Cassidy. John tried, my father tried to keep me from it. When John came home from Iraq, things just didn't add up. Not for me. It wasn't just PTSD. It was something else. I heard him on the phone screaming at someone about murdering innocent people. That's when I went to Matt. That was the first time I heard of The Collaborative."

"Jesus," Alex muttered. "Cass, maybe I should step…"

"Don't you dare, Alex," Cassidy cautioned.

"Alex," Jane said. "Cassidy is safer with you than she would be without you and so is Dylan."

"All right. Cassidy doesn't need all the details. Krause?" He nodded his agreement. "Why don't we take a walk," Alex suggested. "Let Cassidy and Jane breathe."

"Alex," Cassidy stopped the agent as she went toward her jacket on the back of a chair.

"It's all right," Alex kissed the teacher. "Better we know. We'll be back."

***

"So, this 'Collaborative'," Alex asked as the two agents headed back toward the house from their walk.

"Yes?"

"What is it?"

"Exactly what it sounds like, Agent. A group. A group of politicians, military leaders and businessmen. They move merchandise, they remove liabilities and place assets."

"Who?" Alex asked.

"I suspect the list is much longer than we have time to cover. The Russians, French, British….it's grown even in the time that I have been in the CIA."

"ASA?" He confirmed her question with a nod. "And?"

"Technologie Appliquée, Source System Innovations, among others," Krause offered.

"So, O'Brien was in France for some trade as a set up. And…"

Krause chuckled. "Brackett changed that course."

"Krause, how deep does this go? If the president…" He just offered a cockeyed smile and sighed. "Jesus Christ," she shook her head. "And what if we do find out who is pulling the strings? What then?"

"We start pulling some of our own, Agent. We are not alone in this."

"You mean Matt?"

"Yes, but there are others across multiple agencies. The Admiral's decision to assassinate John, his trust in his daughter, it has fractured trust in him. Now is the opportunity, before he has a chance to repair the cracks." Alex stopped their movement and the taller man smiled. "I don't expect you to trust me, Agent Toles."

"But you trust me?" Alex tipped her head.

"He did," Krause looked toward the house. "She does." He turned back to Alex and she firmly held his gaze. "Whatever you think, Agent….There are only two people I have ever trusted completely. They both trust you. That's enough for me."

"You love her?"

Krause laughed. "Agent Toles…"

"Nah, don't even bother," Alex said as she began moving again. "She's easy to love."

"Yeah…"

***

Cassidy and Jane were sitting in the living room sipping wine when the two agents entered. Alex raised an eyebrow and looked at Krause who chuckled. "Something wrong with my coffee?" she asked trying to lighten the mood.

The teacher sipped from her glass. "Unless you would like to peel me from the ceiling," Cassidy looked at Jane who tried to suppress a giggle, "I think my beverage choice is the most advisable."

"I see," Alex answered as the doorbell rang. "Jesus, who could that be now?" Cassidy shrugged, anticipating her mother or some friend of Dylan's and took another sip of her wine. "I'll get it," Alex offered somewhat playfully. "You just relax." The agent's mind was rolling through a million scenarios and she was relieved to see that Jane had successfully eased some of Cassidy's anxiety. This was their reality now. Alex had feared that whatever her friend the colonel had been involved in, it was connected to much of her work at the NSA. Her biggest concern now was how all of it connected to Cassidy and Dylan. She was still unsure about Krause, but something told her she needed to follow him. She would, she told herself, remain guarded where his motives were concerned. She let out a breath as the doorbell rang again. "God, these kids are impatient," she laughed as she opened the door, expecting one of Dylan's friends.

"Agent Toles," the cocky voice greeted.

"What the hell are you doing here?" Alex's voice dropped to a low hum.

"On your feet I see?" The agent stared at the man, pressing down her rising temper.

"Alex, who is it?" Cassidy made her way into the hall and saw the congressman in the doorway.

"Get out," Alex warned him harshly as her hands began to push toward him.

"Alex, no," Cassidy pulled the agent back. Alex complied but left her stare to bore into the man still outside the door. "What do you want, Chris?" Cassidy asked dryly.

"I want to see my son, of course," he answered smugly.

Cassidy nodded. "You are not welcome here."

"Like it or not, Cassie…Dylan is my son too."

Cassidy let out a sarcastic chuckle. She had not intended to have this conversation now, nor had she anticipated it would be here. Looking at the man before her she could not recognize him. He was a stranger. He was a fraud. He was the person who nearly cost her the family she had just found. The contempt she felt for him was profound. "What you are Chris, is a lying, manipulative, opportunist."

"I'm his father, Cassie." He looked at the agent and smirked. "I don't think the agent here can make that claim."

"No?" Cassidy stepped directly in front of her ex-husband. "You shot Alex," she whispered with venom.

"I have no idea what you are talking about, Cassie. See, this is what I was afraid of. You are delusional. Dylan needs to be with…"

Alex moved in quickly and grabbed the congressman by the shirt. "I will end you, O'Brien."

Cassidy pulled the agent back again. "Alex," she whispered, "he's not worth it."

"Well," he said, brushing the wrinkles from his shirt. "A court might not agree with that, Cassie."

"Mm. Is that a threat?" the teacher asked. He raised an eyebrow. She moved in again and whispered directly in his ear. "You are not the only one who can keep secrets, Christopher."

"What is that supposed to mean?"

She shook her head. "You think you're the only one who had any affairs?" His face dropped slightly and Cassidy suddenly felt a sense of empowerment. "Dylan had a father, it was never you…not even when I wanted it to be."

"You have lost your mind, Cassie."

"Have I?" She nodded and looked at Alex whose gaze remained fixed on the congressman, ready to intervene at any second. "I don't think so, Congressman. I think you should leave….now."

"This isn't over, Cassie." He looked at the agent and felt his temper boil. "You, bitch," he muttered as he leaned toward her.

"I wouldn't do that," a voice beckoned from behind the teacher. A strong hand took hold of the congressman's, squeezing with a force just shy of breaking every bone in the hand it held. "You should leave."

The congressman looked up. "You're a fool, Krause. When the admiral...."

Jon Krause laughed. "You're nothing, Chris. Smug, stupid and small."

"So, what? I suppose you are Dylan's father? I should have known that....All that..."

Krause shook his head. "Unlike you, O'Brien, if Dylan was my son, I can promise you, nothing would keep me from them...."

The congressman snickered and looked at Cassidy. "I never took you for a slut."

Alex's fist flew and met immediately with the congressman's face, dropping him where he stood. She stood over him ready to continue the assault when Cassidy pulled her off. "Enough!" Cassidy yelled at them all.

The congressman reached his feet and stroked his jaw. "Fine. I will ruin you," he said to the group.

Krause shook his head. "Asshole," he slammed the door.

Cassidy grabbed hold of Alex. The agent had raised her fist without thinking and the pain coursing through her made her unsteady. The teacher smiled slightly and shook her head, "Alex..."

"He deserved it."

"I guess he did," Cassidy admitted. "Come on, let's get that back in the sling where it is supposed to be, huh?" Alex reluctantly nodded. Cassidy looked up at the CIA agent and smiled sadly. "Pip, I...."

He gently touched her on the shoulder. "It's all right, Cassie."

"Krause, you should have stayed out of sight," Alex said with a hint of genuine concern in her voice.

"I hate that guy," he muttered.

"Well, I guess we have more than one thing in common then," Alex smiled, looking to Cassidy with a raised eyebrow.

"What the hell was that?" Jane asked emerging from the downstairs. "I heard the commotion. I thought I should keep Dylan out of the...."

"Yeah," Cassidy looked at the former first lady.

"Cat's outta the bag, Jane," Alex said.

"What?" she asked.

Krause continued the thought for the agent as Cassidy gently replaced Alex's sling. "That was O'Brien. He knows...Dylan isn't his."

"Does he *know*?" Jane asked fearfully.

"No," Krause laughed. "He thinks Dylan's mine."

Jane looked at Alex and then at Krause. It was clear to Cassidy that a singular thought was passing between all three. "What?" the teacher asked. "I had to..."

"It could be advantageous," Jane said, receiving a nod from Krause.

"Am I missing something?" Cassidy asked.

Alex reached for the teacher's hand. "He thinks Krause is Dylan's father."

"But Pip told him..."

Alex smiled. "He thinks it's Krause."

"But, Alex...what are you saying?" Krause looked at Alex and smiled knowingly. He gestured to Jane and the two left the room silently. "Alex?"

"We let him think that, Cass."

"No. Alex, we agreed...."

"I know that. Listen to me, it gives Krause a reason for being here. He's exposed. We need him as much as he needs me," Alex offered an explanation.

"And tell Dylan what?"

"I don't think we need to tell Dylan anything just yet. I don't think O'Brien will make a public case. He's too concerned with..."

"His image? Yeah, I know," Cassidy said. "Alex, this is crazy."

"I know it is."

"I thought you were going to kill him," Cassidy said.

"I probably could have."

"Did I put Dylan in more danger?" Cassidy asked nervously.

The agent shook her head and pulled Cassidy to her. "No, in fact I think he might be a bit safer now. Krause is…well, he has a reputation."

Cassidy shook her head in disbelief. "God, Alex…How did I end up here? I should have left him so long ago. None of this…"

"None of this is your fault, Cassidy; none of it. Do you hear me?" Cassidy nodded and sighed. "If you had, I might never have found you." Cassidy looked up at the agent and offered the first hint of a smile. "We'll get through this."

"I know."

"Cass?" Alex asked as the pair began the short trek back to the kitchen.

"Yeah?"

"Why do you call Krause, Pip?"

Cassidy laughed. "Later, Alex."

***

Chapter Twenty-One

"What?" Claire Brackett asked.

"You heard me," O'Brien answered.

The female agent laughed heartily. "Oh, now this is rich."

"I'm glad you are so amused, Claire."

"Oh, come on. The perfect little school teacher isn't so perfect after all," she laughed again. "Krause? Really? Can't say I would have imagined *that*." He glared at her. "Oh, Chris; are you actually hurt?" she mocked.

"Claire, Dylan is not...."

"So what?" He shook his head. "You know what I think?"

"No. I don't."

"I think," she cooed. "You are just like me." He stared at her blankly. "You aren't fooling me, Congressman. What is it that has you so upset? The fact that the boy is not yours?" His jaw stiffened. "Um-hmm," she smiled. "That's what I thought."

"Claire..."

"The fact that she actually was with someone else." Brackett's smile grew and she nodded. "Not the picture perfect Christmas card after all," she teased.

"Shut up, Claire."

"Oh, Chris," she pushed him back on the bed. "Do you really miss her that much?" He looked up at her and licked his lips. "No?"

"Do you miss Agent Toles?" he shot back.

"Oh....I think we both know we are where we should be."

"Where is that?" he asked.

"Congressman," she whispered as she unbuttoned his shirt. "Love or power?"

"What?" he asked trying to focus as she undressed him.

"It's a simple question. Love or power?" She pulled back slightly and regarded the questions in his eyes, smiling seductively. "One thing my father did teach me, Congressman; you cannot have both. Either you love or you love power. Which is it?"

His expression changed slightly and revealed the slight twinkle in his eye. "He is my son, Claire."

"No, he's not," she grinned. The congressman's head was spinning and his heart was racing with the attractive agent methodically seducing him. "Emotional entanglements equal compromise. Information equals power," she whispered in his ear and then began leaving a trail of kisses down his chest. "You are free of one." He closed his eyes momentarily until he felt her absence. Opening his eyes, he found her hovering above him. "So?" He kissed her fully and she pulled away with a smile. "That's what I thought."

***

Alex sat at the kitchen table weeding through a stack of documents with Brian Fallon watching closely. "What is it you think is in there?" he asked.

"I don't know what's in here, Fallon. If I did I wouldn't be sitting here looking at this mess."

Fallon picked up a piece of paper and shook his head. "There's more blacked out on this than there is written."

Alex kept her gaze focused on the paper. "And?"

Her partner shook his head. "Anyway, you are supposed to be resting. Cassidy is going to kill me when she finds us here."

"Nah, she won't. I was given clearance to do puzzles."

"What?" he asked.

"I said, the doctor told me I could do puzzles," Alex smirked.

"I doubt that this is what she meant." Alex shrugged. "So," Fallon began. "You think President Merrow was involved in something."

Alex clenched her jaw as her thumb moved to press on her temple. "I don't *think* anything."

"I don't understand."

Alex sighed and finally lifted her gaze. "Fallon, he was. What it was and what he was doing; that I don't know. It got him killed, so whatever it was, it wasn't good."

He looked back down at the sheet of paper in his hands and began studying it again. His brow twitched and he squinted in concentration. "Alex?"

"Hum?"

"You never knew Admiral Brackett?"

"The Pentagon is a big place, Fallon." Her partner sneered at her. "*Really* big," she opened her eyes wide for effect and laughed.

"Alex?"

"What?"

"Look at this." Alex accepted the paper from her partner's hand and began to study it. She scanned it several times before riffling through a stack of papers in front of her and retrieving another page. "Do you think it means anything?"

"Son of a bitch."

"I guess that means yes," he surmised. Alex pressed the heels of her hands into her temples and let out an audible groan. "Alex," Fallon began cautiously. "There's a lot blacked out there...."

"Yeah, there is. Sometimes what is missing tells the story, Fallon."

"What would Somalia have to do with Merrow?" he asked.

"Specifically, you mean?" He nodded. "Nothing...probably. But, it's certainly an interesting path to follow."

"This is from 2004, Alex."

Alex nodded again and set the papers down. She pulled out her chair slightly. "Yeah….Fallon, let's just say that SPHINX was more than a mission to work with the locals and assess potential threats. That's just what we were told."

"You mean when you were in Iraq?"

Alex got up from her chair and walked to the back door, needing to move and a brief change of scenery. "Let's say that our efforts were just a bonus to the actual objective."

"I don't," he began as his partner pressed on the bridge of her nose with some force. Alex felt sick. "Toles?" The agent kept her back to her partner. She rubbed her eyes and attempted to process her suspicions. "Alex?"

"Fallon, look at the second page." He retrieved the second page of the document and focused on it. His eyes traveled slowly over the paper but he remained unsure what it was that Alex wanted him to notice. "You see that word; the one that looks out of place? Look, Fallon. What word looks out of place?"

"WASHTUB?"

"Yeah, right, WASHTUB. Do you know what WASHTUB was?" He remained silent, shaking his head.

Alex turned slowly. "It was a CIA project in the 1950s."

"You really do watch too much *X-Files*," he rolled his eyes.

"It's not a joke, Fallon. WASHTUB was the codename for an operation that planted fake Soviet arms off the coast of Nicaragua. It was part of an effort, disinformation. The intention was to tie the Guatemalan government to communism. The objective was to overthrow the Guatemalan president."

"Alex, what the hell would that have to do with anything in Somalia or Iraq?"

"Do you know, Fallon; what two of the most lucrative businesses in the world are today?" He stared at her. Alex chuckled and looked to the ceiling. "Arms and drugs, Fallon….arms and drugs."

"I really am not following you."

"Do you know what prompted WASHTUB?" she asked him.

"I would imagine it has something to do with communists. I do recall a bit of that in my history lessons," he smiled.

"Mm." Alex let out another heavy sigh. "Bananas."

"Excuse me?"

"Bananas."

"Alex, you lost me."

"Fallon, the world is and has always been about money. Today it's drugs and weapons....back then, well in Central America it was bananas....and guns."

"Okay?"

Alex walked back to the table and pointed to the two pieces of paper. "If you want to keep your customers happy, you keep them in control. The money flows to them; the money flows to you. Right? Let's say WASHTUB was repurposed."

"What?" Fallon was perplexed.

Alex sat down. "Back in the 1950s Fallon, there was a move to reform land ownership in Guatemala. Ever heard of United Fruit?"

"Fruit? Alex...."

Alex shook her head. "Doesn't matter the details. The point is, Fallon, the president of Guatemala committed to redistribute land ownership away from United Fruit and back to the Guatemalan farmers; to reduce dependency on foreign business. That was not a popular platform. It got him ousted....and the CIA was central in ensuring that. It's about money."

"I still don't...."

"Well, the attempt was to tie him to the communists. Follow?" Alex laughed. "Same deal, Fallon. You want to keep moving your guns? Keep moving your drugs? What do you do?" He shook his head. "You tie your opposition to your enemy. 1950s it was communists. Now? It's terrorists."

"Why WASHTUB?"

"Back then, it probably had more to do with the submarine cover story they used...who knows? NOW, great word... WASHTUB. Wash it clean."

"You mean money laundering." Alex raised her eyebrow in confirmation. "You don't actually believe that SPHINX is about running guns?"

"A lot more than guns I suspect."

"And President Merrow?" he asked.

Alex sighed. The picture was coming into clearer focus, at least part of it. She couldn't be certain what it meant yet and she couldn't be certain how far back it went; but John Merrow's need for her to dig was beginning to make sense and she did not like the way the puzzle was coming together. "I think," Alex said as she rose to her feet again and made her way back to the window. "I think, that John was CIA. And, I think that our small team's work served a different purpose than Taylor and I were led to believe."

"You think John Merrow was running…."

"I think we need to keep looking. Somalia, Yemen, Chile, Hungary….All mentioned. You're right; there is a lot blacked out. There is still enough visible to see in the light of day, Fallon." Alex rubbed her face and shook her head again as her voice dropped to a whisper. "Jesus, John."

"Alex…John Merrow…"

"Fallon, in this business no one is ever who they appear to be, no one."

"What does that say for us?"

Alex nodded. "I don't know, Brian. I really don't know."

***

"Toles, you seriously think John was working under CIA directives?" Alex blew out the breath she had been holding as she watched Brian Fallon's car pull away. "Hey, Toles….you there?"

"Yeah, Taylor…I'm here."

"You ask Krause?" Taylor asked.

"No. Not yet," she answered.

"You think Jane knows?"

Alex sighed again. "She might suspect."

"Even if you are right. What would that have to do with Mutanabbi?"

"I think you know. I think we were set up."

"Jesus.....You think it's all related? I mean to the assassination?" Taylor felt sick.

"Taylor, you and I both know it's all related."

"We can set up additional taps...look at..."

Alex took a deep breath. "Listening and reading isn't going to solve this one, Taylor."

"Toles..."

"You and I both know there is only one way to dig into this one."

"You want to go off the grid." There was no response. "Toles..."

"*I* can't go off the grid, Taylor. At least not right now and I can't break this on my own. We need someone closer."

"You want to use Krause. Toles, how can you be sure you can trust him?"

"I'm not sure. I am sure that's the best choice we have if we want to find out what is really going on." She paused and felt the weight of her suspicions falling on her. "If I want to keep Dylan and Cass safe."

"You don't think O'Brien is CIA?"

Alex laughed. "Hardly, but he's connected to Brackett."

"Toles....You don't think the colonel was still CIA...I mean when...."

"Taylor, once you are a spook you are always a spook."

Michael Taylor took a deep breath and tapped his pen on the edge of his desk. "You think the CIA is controlling the White House?"

"Yeah. I do. That's not what has me worried." Alex shook her head. "Who is controlling the CIA?" Taylor chuckled. "Something amusing?" Alex asked with some impatience as she watched Cassidy's car pull into the driveway.

"No. I just wonder why you aren't the one sitting here."

"Me and desks, never a good combination," Alex reminded him.

"Yeah, I know," he laughed. "Surprised *you* never went to the agency."

"They never asked," Alex said. "I have to go. Taylor?"

"Yeah?"

"Keep Fallon on Tate and Brackett."

"Why? Do you…"

"Get Brady on the congressman's accident."

"Toles…"

"There's more there. I know it. Tate had to have a reason to come to you. Leave Krause to me. Trust me, Taylor. Just trust me."

"You are about the only person I do trust," he said.

Alex laughed as her hand reached for the door. "Yeah."

"Toles, take it easy…will you please?"

"Be careful, Taylor," she said as she hung up the phone.

***

Cassidy watched as Alex stood over Dylan in his bed. The agent had been unusually quiet all day and Cassidy was beginning to wonder what had prompted the change in her lover's demeanor. Alex had been looking forward to Brian Fallon's visit. When Cassidy returned in the afternoon she was surprised to find the agent nearly silent. At first, she dismissed it as fatigue and physical pain. Alex was always quiet when she was in pain, but when the agent's mood persisted Cassidy began to grow more concerned. "Alex?" The agent didn't answer. Alex kept her silent watch over the boy. Cassidy let out a deep sigh and made her way to the agent's side. "Alex?" she whispered as she gently turned her lover. "What is going on?" The agent managed an unconvincing smile. "Alex…"

"I'm sorry, Cass."

"What?" Alex turned back toward Dylan. "Alex, what hap-
pened while I was gone today?" The agent shook her head and
Cassidy gently began to guide her away from Dylan's bedside.
"Let's go."

"Cass…"

"Come on." Reluctantly, Alex followed Cassidy to their
room and took a seat on the edge of the bed. "Spill."

For the first time in many hours the agent smiled. "I'm all
right, Cass."

"Liar." Alex laughed a bit harder. "Something happened,"
Cassidy raised her eyebrow.

"I think I'm just tired," Alex said.

"Uh-huh…and I am the Pope."

"Well, in that case Your Eminence…"

"Alex…"

"I don't want to talk about it."

"Don't want to talk about it or don't want to talk about it
with me?" Cassidy asked.

Alex pulled the teacher to stand between her legs. "Don't
want to talk about it."

"I'm worried about you."

"Don't be."

"Alex, you are never this quiet."

"Cass?"

"Yes?"

"Do you ever wish you could go backward?"

Cassidy nodded and wrapped her arms around the agent's
neck. "I used to."

"But not now?"

"I don't know. When Chris showed up here yesterday, in
that moment, yeah…I wished I could go back, but then what
did you tell me?" Alex shrugged. "If I did, maybe there would
be no Dylan at all; maybe we wouldn't be together now."

Alex rested her head against her lover's chest. The feel of Cassidy's fingers running through her hair calmed the agent. "Do you trust him?"

"Who?" Cassidy asked softly.

"Krause."

The teacher pulled back slightly and looked into Alex's eyes. "Pip was a good friend to me, Alex. He saved you...so, yes, I guess I trust him."

"He's in love with you."

"I don't think..."

"No. He is."

Cassidy smiled. "Well, I love *you.*"

"I know," Alex leaned back into Cassidy and held onto her waist.

"Alex? Please tell me what's wrong."

"You are the only person I trust, Cass."

Cassidy took a deep breath. There were many things that she did not know about her lover's work. She was becoming more aware by the day that Alex's work meant sometimes uncovering truths that were painful. It demanded seeing the worst in people and as much as Cassidy knew that Alex's job was important, it was also evident that it took its emotional toll. "You can always trust me, Alex...no matter what."

"I know I can."

"You can tell me...you know...anything."

Alex let out the hint of a chuckle and rested her face against Cassidy's chest. "I think John was working for the CIA when we were in Iraq." Cassidy remained silent and kissed the top of the agent's head. "I think," Alex increased her grip on Cassidy's waist. "I think we were responsible for helping to move guns, move weapons to insurgents." Cassidy let out a soft sigh of understanding and kissed the agent's head again as Alex continued. "I think...Cass, I think we sold those people the weapons...that day. I think it was us."

Cassidy felt the warmth of Alex's tears through her blouse. "I love you, Alex."

"Cass, he knew...he knew we were..."

Cassidy was beginning to understand just a bit of what was troubling the agent. "Alex, even if....even if that is true, I don't believe that John would ever do anything that he thought would hurt *you*."

"Doesn't matter, Cass. Does it? It's like O'Brien, right? He didn't know that Fisher was..."

Cassidy stopped the agent's thoughts. She pulled Alex to face her and placed a soft kiss on the agent's lips. "Alex..."

"What if I do that?"

"Do what?"

"What if what I am doing...what if it got you hurt; or Dylan?"

A soft smile took shape on Cassidy's face and she caressed the agent's cheek. "Alex Toles." Alex looked into the teacher's eyes and Cassidy immediately saw her fear. "You listen to me, right now. Everything you do is to protect us. I know that and so does Dylan."

Alex swallowed hard. "I'm going to quit."

"What?"

"The NSA, Cass. I'm going to quit."

Cassidy nodded and pursed her lips. She looked directly into her lover's eyes and shook her head. "No. You are not."

"I made my decision, Cassidy."

"Alex, I would love to know that you are safe every day. That is the truth. But, you are not going to leave behind something you believe in because something *might* happen."

"Cassidy...."

"Alex..."

"What about when we want to have a family?" Alex rose to her feet. "Am I supposed to endanger all of you?" Cassidy covered her mouth and shook her head. "Nothing is more important to me than you and Dylan. Krause can handle this. There are other things I can do. I'm not...I can't risk...."

Cassidy crossed the room and took Alex's face in her hands. "I want you to listen to me, Alex."

"Cass..."

"Please, I want you to listen to me, right now." Alex looked at Cassidy's expression and reluctantly assented. "You cannot protect us from the world, no matter how much you try. You didn't create Carl Fisher." Alex started to interject and Cassidy cautioned her with a glance. "My father walked out the door one day Alex, and he never came back. He drank too much and he suffered the consequence and so did I." Alex listened intently, seeing the conviction in her lover's eyes. "Life happens. I chose you. I love you. I know who you are. Only one thing scares me more than losing you or Dylan," she paused and ensured Alex was looking at her. "The only thing that scares me more than that is seeing either one of you unhappy. You are not Batman, Alex. No matter how much you want to be. But, you are meant to do what you do. You love it. It's part of who you are. I know that too."

"Cass, all I need is you and Dylan."

Cassidy shook her head. "Alex, you have us. We love you because you are you. I'm not going to stand here and tell you that part of me doesn't wish you would quit..."

"Then why..."

"Let me finish. I have never been more frightened than I was when I saw Pip's message on my phone; not even when Carl Fisher was standing over me with a knife." Cassidy stopped for a moment to take a deep breath and took Alex's face back into her hands. "If there comes a time when you want to quit because in your heart that is what you want, I will support you with all that I am. But, I will not support you walking away from what you believe in because you are afraid of losing us."

"Cass, I just....If I ever hurt..."

"Alex, just love us. That's all."

"I do."

"Then, stop this," Cassidy said softly.

"I trusted him, Cass. I loved him like a..."

"And he loved you."

Alex shook her head. "He lied to me."

"Maybe he did, Alex. Doesn't mean he didn't love you."

"He put us all at risk. Even if he didn't intend...I won't do that to our family."

Cassidy sighed. "When did you decide this? This quitting?"

"While I was watching Dylan."

"And, you think you can just let all this go?" Alex stared blankly at her lover. "Mm-hum...that's what I thought. Alex, that is not in your nature." She kissed the agent and smiled.

Alex took a deep breath and let it out as Cassidy closed her eyes and leaned into the agent's embrace. "Cass?"

"Yeah?"

"I blamed myself." Alex swallowed hard.

"I know."

"That day..."

Alex's body began to shake and Cassidy pulled her to the bed to sit. She had grown familiar with Alex's nightmares but the agent had never truly explained what happened in any detail. "Go on," Cassidy said gently.

"There was this family...I....well, I worked with their daughter, teaching the young people English; you know?" Cassidy encouraged Alex with a smile. "Awad, he owned this bookstore. Sabeen and I, we would teach the children there." Alex stopped. "There were always people in and out, so many people." The agent closed her eyes as the memories flooded her consciousness. "It's mostly outside, you know...the market-place. I was so focused on Sabeen and the..."

"Alex..."

"I was...too focused on her and the kids. I wasn't paying attention. I thought John wanted me there to help....Awad, he got shipments. They ran a small clinic out back three days a week. I helped carry them, Cass. So many times. I helped carry them that morning. I thought they were books and medical supplies…I thought…."

Cassidy closed her eyes with a new and painful understanding. It was beginning to make sense to her now. Alex suspected that she had unknowingly carried the very materials that were used in the attack that injured her. Now, there was the possibility that John Merrow might have had a hand in all of it. "Alex, you couldn't have known."

"No, Cass. I should have known. I was too busy paying attention to Sabeen. Don't you understand? I didn't pay attention to John; where he was going, who he was meeting with. I didn't pay attention to Awad." Alex rubbed her face with force. "Twenty people died, Cassidy. Twenty. Three of my best friends, eight children and Sabeen. Sabeen triggered it…He threw her out. She was the trigger. His own daughter. I never saw it coming until that moment…not any of it."

Alex's body began to shake noticeably and Cassidy pulled her close. "Alex, I'm so sorry."

"What if I am so busy looking at you that I miss it? That you and Dylan…that I don't see Krause or Taylor? Or Jesus…who knows? For who they really are."

"Alex, you are not a twenty something naïve girl." Alex looked at Cassidy in amazement. "Well?" Cassidy continued. "You loved this girl?"

"That was….I thought…."

"Alex, we both have a past. You loved her?" Alex nodded. "And you think that blinded you?" Alex didn't answer. "Maybe it did." The agent looked back to Cassidy who smiled. "Love does that sometimes. It makes us see the best in people. It makes us hopeful."

Alex shook her head. "Don't you understand? John, it just makes it worse…it's my fault."

"No. It isn't." Cassidy laid back and guided Alex to her chest. "Alex, I loved Chris once. I didn't know who he was. I saw what I wanted to see. Maybe I saw what I needed to see. Do you think it's my fault that Carl Fisher did what he did? Do you blame me for Chris shooting you?"

"Of course not."

"You loved someone. You trusted them. You are not responsible for what they did. The only thing you are guilty of, Alex, is loving; that's all."

"I can't lose you, Cass."

"You're not going to lose me, Alex. It's different now, for both of us."

"What do you mean?" Alex asked.

"The way I love you; it doesn't close my eyes. It opens them."

Alex propped herself up and looked at her lover. "I just want to keep you safe."

"You do."

Alex's voice dropped to a whisper. "I promise you…"

"You don't need to make me any promises. I already know."

Alex closed her eyes and let Cassidy hold her, much as she did after a nightmare. Her mind was racing. There was little doubt in the agent's mind that following this trail would be dangerous, for all of them. John Merrow was her best friend. He was Dylan's father. In so many ways, he had been and was her family. Alex struggled to reconcile what she knew had to be the truth and what she felt in her heart. She contemplated everything Cassidy had said. It was one of the things Alex loved and admired most in the woman lying beside her; Cassidy was thoughtful, compassionate, and honest. She had the type of intelligence that no one can teach; the kind that comes from the heart. Throughout the entire day the agent had only one thing on her mind, protecting the family she now had. It was something she had never dreamed possible. In these last days, seeing her mother embrace Dylan, watching Nick chase Cat, drinking coffee with Rose, and now holding onto Cassidy; she realized how much her life had changed. Her mother had told her she couldn't run anymore. Now, after hearing Cassidy's words, it suddenly all seemed to make sense. Cassidy was right. She couldn't quit. She couldn't run. Her eyes had been opened like never before and what had opened them was her love for the woman beside her.

"Cass?"

"Hum?"

"How do you feel about vanilla cake?"

Cassidy smiled and kissed the agent's head. "I like it."

"I know. I think maybe we should have one."

The teacher chuckled, amused by the shift in Alex's train of thought. "Is that right?"

For Alex, it made perfect sense. She was never good at being direct with personal requests. Vanilla cake was the best way she could think to convey that she wanted to spend her life with Cassidy. "Yeah, unless you don't want to."

"Actually, Alex, I don't think there is anything I would like more than to share vanilla cake with you."

"Good. Maybe we can talk about it tomorrow."

"Does that mean you are not quitting anything?" Cassidy questioned.

The agent snuggled closer. "No, but I do think it is time for new beginnings."

"Every day is a new beginning with you."

"I love you, you know, Cassidy?"

"I know you do, Alex. I love you too. I just hope you don't get disappointed in the *boring* stuff you keep looking forward to."

"Cass, life with you will never be boring."

Cassidy laughed. "I'll take that as a compliment."

"You should."

"Get some sleep, love."

"Thanks, Cass."

"I have no idea what you are thanking me for."

"Vanilla cake."

"I'm not baking it," Cassidy said plainly.

Alex chuckled as her eyes grew heavier. "Well, you know...
we..."

Cassidy shifted and kissed the agent's forehead. "Go to
sleep, Alfred."

Alex smiled and let her eyes fall shut. For the first time in
many days she looked forward to her dreams knowing they
would be filled tonight with images of a school teacher and a
little boy, and maybe a little vanilla cake.

***

Chapter Twenty-Two

"**T**oles, are you sure?" Jon Krause asked through the phone.

"Yeah, I am," she said.

"It makes sense."

"Krause, was he? CIA, I mean."

"Agent Toles, the agency is a strange place. There are webs within webs. It doesn't matter what his designation was, really. If you are asking me if he was taking orders outside of ASOW, then yes, I'm certain that was so. Anything on SPHINX specifically stand out to you?"

"No. But WASHTUB was mentioned in those documents more than once."

Krause sighed. "Historically?" he asked.

"I don't think it was a historical reference," Alex offered. "I suppose it's possible. I pegged it as a laundering operation." A lingering silence ensued as Alex stepped onto the back patio. "Krause? What are you thinking?"

"What if it was a historical reference?"

"That would be a relief, I guess."

"Would it?" Krause asked. "Toles, what if WASHTUB was part of SPHINX?"

"Well, that's why I figured it was a convenient…"

"No, Agent. What if WASHTUB was part of SPHINX?"

"WASHTUB was over fifty years ago." Krause did not answer. "Krause, operations don't last fifty years." The silence continued. "Do you realize what you are suggesting?" she asked.

269

"Yeah, I do and I suspect that you already had that suspicion yourself."

"Krause, who exactly is Admiral Brackett?"

"That's a very good question, Agent Toles. He's simply The Admiral. FBI, ATF, CIA, NSA, DOD, and USSS; he can pull strings just about anywhere. He knows the alliances and he keeps that very close to the vest. I need you to talk to Matthews. What I can tell you is that there is a massive Russian influence in all of this. The congressman's accident, John's," he took a moment and continued. "Moving merchandise has been my job for years. Making certain it arrives at its destination, ensuring the funds follow accordingly, whatever that means. My field work has been largely limited to business transactions."

Alex interrupted. "Matthews mentioned ASA after John's funeral."

"ASA isn't the only interest. What did Matthews say?"

"Something about weapons and Corsica, and thinking John might have tried to prevent something. Maybe he wasn't preventing at all."

"Or maybe he was. Guess it was inevitable we both ended up in France," Krause chuckled uncomfortably. "There are things we need to discuss when I get back. If you don't hear for me..."

"Be careful," Alex cautioned.

"You almost sound like you care, Agent Toles."

Alex sighed. "Cassidy does." There was no response. "There's been enough loss for her...I don't..."

"Deal with the ambassador," he said. "I have a feeling he may know more than he is actually telling you. Given your suspicions about John..."

"You think Ambassador Matthews is CIA, don't you?" Cassidy asked. The silence gave her the answer. "Jesus, Krause."

"Not uncommon, Agent. I will look for clarification on the point, but yes."

"What is? Uncommon, I mean?" she tried not to chuckle at the absurdity in the conversation.

"I'm headed out of the country," Krause explained. "Talk to Matthews. He would not be the first operative placed as a diplomat, believe me."

"Yeah, I do believe you. That's what worries me."

"I'll contact you when I can, Agent. Just be safe."

"Yeah. Krause?"

"What?"

"Watch your back. I'd hate you to get caught in one of those webs," Alex said.

***

Cassidy made her way down to the kitchen and found a note in front of a full coffee pot.

Morning,

I didn't want to wake you or Dylan. I just had to run a few errands. I know what you are thinking, but I am okay. I might even be back before you see this, which would probably be a good thing. Don't be mad.

Thanks for last night.

By the way, I was kind of hoping for tacos tonight.

Je t'aime.

"Tacos," Cassidy giggled. "What is it with you and tacos?" she mumbled as she poured herself some coffee and caught sight of a sleepy boy walking into the kitchen. Dylan made his way to her side and collapsed against her hip. "Still tired, sweetie?" He nodded. "Why don't you go watch some cartoons? I'll make you some breakfast." Dylan rubbed his eyes and looked lazily up to his mother. "Are you feeling okay, Dylan?" Cassidy asked with some concern. She felt his head and frowned at his sniffling. "Come on," Cassidy said, putting her coffee down and leading her son to the other room. "I think this is going to be a quiet day." She plopped him onto the sofa and covered him with a blanket. "Maybe this will at least keep Alex quiet," she mused. "She wanted boring."

Cassidy heard the front door and headed into the hallway. Alex was juggling two large grocery bags and her keys. Picking up her pace, the teacher reached the agent and relieved her of the bags. "What are you doing?"

"Thanks," Alex said as she placed a gentle kiss on her lover's forehead and followed Cassidy into the kitchen.

"Alex, you are supposed to be taking it easy."

"Am I in trouble?" Alex raised an eyebrow.

Cassidy set down the bags and turned, immediately noticing the slight wince that accompanied her lover's pleasantries. "What am I going to do with you?"

"I have some ideas on that particular subject," Alex winked.

Cassidy laughed. "You," she shook her head, "are wobbling as it is. Let's get you settled in with Dylan."

"Why? Where's Dylan?"

"Sick on the couch."

"What do you mean he's sick?"

"He has a little fever. Probably a cold." Alex looked at Cassidy skeptically. "He's okay, Alex. Come on." Cassidy took Alex's hand and led her to the living room.

"Speed?" Alex looked at him. "You okay?" He nodded and offered her a weak smile.

"Come on," Cassidy urged. "Let me help you get your jacket off." Alex turned pale and began fidgeting with the zipper on the jacket. "Alex? Are you okay?" The agent stared blankly at her lover. "Are you getting sick too? Are you cold?" Alex shook her head. "Oooookaay..." Cassidy chuckled. The agent sat down next to Dylan and pulled the covers over both of them.

"Maybe I am a little cold, Cass."

"Uh huh," Cassidy tipped her head and shook it slightly. Alex fidgeted on the couch for a second and then stood back up. "You're right. I should take it off." Cassidy raised her eyebrows at the agent as Alex maneuvered the fleece jacket off and gave the teacher a grin.

"You must have hit your head when you fell. I think I will have to ask the major about that." Cassidy rolled her eyes. Alex just shrugged and kissed Cassidy's cheek before plopping back down beside Dylan. "Did you get my note?"

"Which note is that?" Cassidy asked playfully.

"I bought all the stuff."

"What stuff?"

"You know, for tacos," Alex said nudging Dylan slightly.

"Oh? Is someone making tacos?"

Alex bit her lip and opened her eyes wide. Dylan scooted into her side and looked at his mother. "I like tacos," he said.

"I suppose that means I can expect a day of cartoons then too?" Alex smiled again. "I give up," Cassidy laughed. "You two relax."

"Where are you going?" Alex asked. "Don't you want to watch cartoons with us?"

"Tempting, Agent Toles, but…No. I have some things I need to do myself this morning. Starting with putting away those groceries you brought home."

"I thought we were going to spend the day together?" the agent asked with a hint of disappointment in her voice.

"We are. You wanted boring, right?" Alex nodded. "Well, Dylan is sick, you are still in pain," Alex started to object and Cassidy immediately intensified her gaze. "You two need to relax. Both of you." Dylan wiggled closer to the agent and put his head against her. "I need to do some laundry and run to the pharmacy, all that boring stuff you seem to cherish. Then I will make you two some tacos and then, maybe I will watch some crazy movie with you."

Cassidy looked down at the pair on the sofa and smiled. Alex was unconsciously playing with Dylan's hair and Dylan's eyes were closing slowly as he cuddled against her. The teacher gestured to her son and immediately saw Alex's expression change. "Cass, he's hot."

"I gave him some Tylenol a while ago. He just needs to rest, and so do you."

Alex laid back and guided the boy next to her. "I should help you."

"You are helping me; keeping him quiet and keeping yourself out of trouble."

"Okay. I just want to take care of you both."

"I know you do, Alex. Sometimes, maybe it's my job to take care of you. That's how it works." Alex sighed her compliance. "No files today, okay? Just take it easy; for me?"

"That's playing dirty," Alex frowned.

"I know. Did it work?"

Alex laughed. "Yeah."

Cassidy kissed the agent's forehead and then her son's. "No files. Cartoons and rest. Promise?"

"I promise, but we all have tacos together later, right?"

Cassidy laughed. "Deal," she said heading out of the room.

Dylan had fallen asleep and Alex whispered to him as if he were really paying attention. "She has no idea, Speed."

"I may have no idea what you are up to," a voice called back. "But, don't think I am not watching you."

"Watch away," Alex said slyly to herself.

"I will," the answer came. "You want those tacos, you'll behave."

***

"Alex," a muffled voice called to the tall agent sleeping beside him.

"Hey, Speed."

"I don't feel good."

The agent forced her eyes open and focused on the blue eyes searching hers. "What's wrong, Speed? You are burning up." Dylan rolled his head to the side and rubbed his ear. "Is it your ear?" He nodded. "Okay, I'm gonna go find Mom, alright?" He nodded again and let his small head fall onto the couch. Alex looked back at him briefly and headed into the kitchen where Cassidy had begun her taco preparation. "Cass?"

"Hey, did you have a good rest?"

"Cass, Dylan's ear is bothering him. He doesn't look so good. He's burning up."

Cassidy sighed. She wiped her hands on a towel and cupped Alex's pale face in her hands. "Ear infection," she said. "Do me a favor and put that away," she gestured to the cutting board. "I think we might be headed to the doctor." Alex nodded sheepishly. "I'll go see," Cassidy reassured. "Looks like your taco night might be on hold."

Alex nodded again and started cleaning up the kitchen. The day was not going exactly as she had planned or hoped. She fought the deep ache in her stomach thinking about the expression on Dylan's face. She couldn't bear seeing him in pain, even for a minute. A voice broke her silent pondering. "I'm going to take him."

"Let me get my jacket," Alex said.

"Alex, why don't you just relax? Who knows how long it will take. He's okay. He just needs an antibiotic."

"Cass, if you are taking Dylan I am going with you." Alex was firm and Cassidy knew an argument would be pointless. "We can do tacos tomorrow. Let's just take care of Dylan." Cassidy smiled and kissed the agent's cheek before turning to retrieve Dylan. "Never a dull moment," Alex whispered.

"Not in this family," Cassidy called back.

***

Alex stood outside the small clinic absentmindedly toying with the zipper on her jacket as she spoke on her phone. "I can't get there.......I don't know how long we will be, a while....... Yeah, I know..........I am sure. Not even a question......You know where it is? Okay....Can you pick up something for....

okay......I will. Thanks." The agent hung up her phone and faced the afternoon sky. "Never boring," she mused and headed back through the automatic door.

***

Michael Taylor paced the floor as he listened carefully to the voice at the other end of the call. He let out a sigh. "You need to get in there. They are likely to cover more tracks if the admiral figures out that you are onto anything...That's a huge accusation. You'd better be sure that he was CIA before..... London too? Shit....I can do that. If you are certain I will contact Brady...If you are right, shit......watch yourself......I'll be in touch." The NSA director disconnected the call and flopped into his oversized chair. "Jesus, Colonel. Who are you?"

***

Alex walked in the door with Dylan close at her side. "Feeling punkie, huh, Speed?" He nodded. "Well, guess what?" He shrugged. "I heard that there is a Batman movie waiting for you in the family room, all ready to go." Cassidy raised her eyebrow inquisitively at the agent. Alex just smiled and continued. "Mom says you need to eat to take your medicine." He nodded. "Maybe not tacos...how about some really awesome chicken soup?"

"Alex?" Cassidy asked.

"It's nothing. Why don't you go into the family room with Dylan and I will bring some in for all of us."

"Alex, where did you get chicken soup?"

The agent shrugged and then winked. "I have connections, Cassidy. Powerful ones, remember?"

Cassidy shook her head and rolled her eyes playfully. "I do remember," she laughed. There was no point in pressing Alex for details. The agent had a way of taking care of things; big things, little things, anything that she could. Cassidy suspected that seeing Dylan sick was almost as painful for Alex as it was for her son. Alex would call the White House for chicken soup if she thought it would make Dylan feel better. It was one of the agent's most endearing qualities and one of the many reasons Cassidy had fallen so deeply in love with Alex Toles. "Why don't you let me get the soup, though? You go sit with Dylan."

"Nope," the agent said as she scooted mother and son toward the family room. "I slept for hours earlier. You have been going all day. Go sit with Dylan. I promise; I can heat soup."

"Uh-huh...don't burn anything, Agent...like yourself," Cassidy joked.

"Cute, Cass." Cassidy laughed. "Go on."

"Okay, I give, you can be the chef."

"Thank you," Alex said dryly. "Is that a promotion or a demotion from butler?"

"I'll let you know after I eat the soup," Cassidy called back.

"You just wait for dessert," Alex gloated quietly.

"Oh, I will be waiting with bated breath," a voice answered from the distance.

The agent shook her head and laughed. "Oh no," she thought silently to herself, fully aware that Cassidy expected a comeback. "I'm not giving it up that easily."

***

Dylan was sitting on Cassidy's lap watching another movie while Alex fussed about in the kitchen cleaning up from their dinner. "Is your ear any better, sweetie?" Cassidy asked as she tenderly brushed Dylan's hair to the side.

"Kinda," he answered quietly.

"Do you want to go upstairs?" He shook his head no.

Alex stopped in the doorway and watched in silence as Cassidy kissed the small head against her. For a moment she was frozen. It was a simple moment. Alex realized as she watched the two people she loved more than anything, it was all the simple moments that seemed to matter to her now. Every minute with Cassidy and Dylan was an adventure; an adventure that had more meaning and held her interest far more than any crime she had ever solved. The last weeks and the last days had driven home with crystal clarity to the agent that Cassidy and Dylan were the center of her world. She never wanted either to doubt her love, honesty or her commitment. They had almost lost each other more than once already. Alex still struggled to grasp the responsibility she felt to keep this family safe. "Hey," Alex called softly. "I brought some dessert."

"Dessert, huh?" Cassidy asked as she laid her head on top of her son's.

Alex made her way slowly to the couch and set down a small pastry box on the coffee table. "Yeah. I got something special for you both." Dylan looked up to Alex and she winked at him. Cassidy looked at the agent curiously. Alex reached in the small box she had placed on the table and pulled out an even smaller box. She looked at Cassidy and smiled and then looked at Dylan. "This is for you, Dylan." He accepted the box and opened it slowly. "That's a Saint Alexander Medal." He pulled the small, slightly tarnished silver medallion from its home. "See, it's a tradition in our family. Nicky and I both have one. This one belonged to my grandfather Papas. When I was old enough my mother gave it to me."

"What do you do with it?" Dylan asked.

Alex smiled and pointed to the small piece of silver in the boy's hand. "You don't have to do anything with it. It moves from each parent to their child. That's just how it works. I was hoping you would accept it from me." Dylan was still a little confused. Alex chuckled slightly. Her palms were sweating and she was unsure exactly what the perfect words were now. She took a deep breath and pulled another small box out, this time from her pocket. She looked at Dylan and smiled. Then she looked at Cassidy. "See, I kind of hoped that you and your mom, well," Alex took another deep breath and looked at Cassidy. Cassidy immediately felt her body begin to go weak.

"Alex?" Cassidy's voice faltered.

"I know it's not the most romantic thing, Cass, but it isn't just you and me. It's all of us together." Cassidy covered her mouth with her hand, understanding clearly now where Alex's thoughts were headed. "I know that you tease me about wanting to do all the boring stuff, but the thing is...nothing is ever boring with you. I love you both and I want to do all of it. Everything." The agent paused and looked at Dylan who was listening carefully, but with evident confusion. "Dylan, you know I love you," he nodded and Alex pointed to the small medal that was still in his hand. "I never thought that I would have a son or a daughter to give that to. Now, I have you. I was hoping you would be my family." He looked at the agent and his eyes grew wide. "What I mean is," she stumbled slightly on her words. "I would really like it if you would give me permission to ask your mom....well," Alex was sure that she had never been so nervous. She didn't dare face Cassidy yet. "See Dylan, your mom's dad isn't here. So, that makes you the man in her life. And, you are the biggest part of her. So, would it be okay if I asked your mom to marry me?"

Dylan's mouth fell open and he nodded. "You're gonna get married?" he asked hopefully.

"Well, that sort of depends, I guess. I mean I bought vanilla cake...well, actually cupcakes," Alex said, turning to Cassidy whose tears had begun a swift descent over her cheeks. "Hoping that your mom would say yes." Alex opened the small box and put it in Cassidy's hands. "Maybe it is crazy, Cass, but I don't want to wait to ask. I don't need to think about it. I never want to lose you or Dylan. There is always uncertainty for me at work, with my parents, but not here, not with you. I want..."

Alex's rambling was stopped abruptly by a smiling school teacher's kiss. "Yes," Cassidy barely managed to whisper.

"Did you say..."

"Yes," Cassidy repeated cupping Alex's face in her hands.

"I ummm....I..." Alex looked to Dylan who was bouncing just slightly in spite of his aching ear. "I mean...I guess then..." Alex took the ring out and tried to put it on Cassidy's finger. Cassidy guided her trembling hand. "I mean...you know....If you don't like..."

Cassidy smiled and kissed Alex again. "Rambling."

"It's an emerald."

"It's beautiful, Alex."

"It was..."

Before Alex could finish her thought Dylan interrupted them. "So when are you gonna get married?" he asked.

Cassidy laid her head on Alex's shoulder and chuckled. "I don't know, Speed. I guess we'll have to think about that," Alex said.

"Alex?" he asked a bit tentatively.

"Yeah, Speed?"

"Does this mean I am really your son now?" he asked, pointing to the medal.

Alex took a seat next to Cassidy and pulled Dylan to sit between them. "Dylan, you don't need any medals or any rings to be my son. I just wanted to make sure you wanted me to be part of your family as much as I want you to be part of mine. I wanted you both to know that you are the most important part of me. So, that's why I gave you the medal." He nodded and rubbed his ear. "Still, hurting?" Alex asked. She could see his reluctance to answer. "Too much for a chocolate cupcake before bed?" Dylan smiled but Alex could tell he was reaching his limit. She looked across to Cassidy and sighed. "How about we save that for tomorrow?" He nodded again. "All right, come on." Alex motioned for Dylan to climb onto her back. "Let's get you some rest." She stopped momentarily and turned to look at Cassidy who was following close behind. "I know it wasn't exactly the most…"

Cassidy looked at her son resting his head against Alex's shoulder. "It was perfect," she whispered. "Let's go, I am still waiting for dessert," she winked.

***

Cassidy was sitting on the bed playing with the ring on her finger when Alex finished tucking in Dylan. The agent stopped and caught her breath. Cassidy's eyes were glistening with tears and Alex could feel her own misting now. "I hope you like it." Alex could see Cassidy's lips curl into the hint of a smile, but the teacher did not respond. "Cass?" the agent called gently as she made her way to the bed. "Hey…"

"I would marry you right now if I could," Cassidy said softly.

"You would?" Cassidy nodded. "Cass, are you okay?"

"I can't believe you. The way you asked with Dylan…"

"Yeah, I'm sorry. I probably should have thought about…" Cassidy's kiss quelled any speech or possibility of thought for the agent. "What was that for?"

"It was perfect, Alex, every minute of it."

Alex took Cassidy's hand. "Do you recognize it?" Cassidy searched the agent for her meaning. "It was your mom's."

"Alex, this is Mom's emerald? From my Nana's ring?" Alex nodded. "How did you? When did you…"

"When we were staying at Nicky's," Alex said.

"How did you get…"

"When your mother was telling me about her bed, how you always wanted it but he didn't…she told me about the ring. She said she offered it to him but he didn't want it."

Cassidy closed her eyes. "It's the only thing I wanted that was Nana's."

"I know. I asked her if I could have it to…"

281

"You asked my mother if you could marry me?" Alex shrugged. "When we were staying at Nick's?" The agent shrugged again. "Really?" Cassidy was amazed.

Alex laid back on the bed, guiding Cassidy along. "I didn't really have to ask. It was all over my face, I guess." The admission caused both women to giggle. "I love you, Cassidy," the agent said softly. "More than I think you can understand."

"I understand, Alex."

"You do?"

Cassidy climbed over the agent and looked down at her. "Yes, I do."

"I imagined I would do something more romantic," Alex confessed.

"It was incredibly romantic."

"Yeah? That's what you dreamt of? Little boys with ear infections and some insane woman rambling on her knees?"

Cassidy chuckled. "No. It isn't at all what I imagined."

"I'm sorry, Cass, I wanted it to…."

Two fingers pressed firmly to the agent's lips. "It was more romantic and more meaningful than any daydream I could ever have." She moved closer to the agent and searched Alex's blue eyes. "I love you, Alex."

Alex closed her eyes as her lips met her lover's. The tenderness in Cassidy's touch felt like the soothing sensation of cool water on a warm day. Gently, it carried Alex along. At the same time it produced a fire within the agent that she was certain could never be fully extinguished. As Cassidy's lips traveled over the agent's throat, Alex moaned and arched her back. "Cass…"

Cassidy's hands gently lifted the agent's T-shirt and began to explore the softness of her breasts. "I want you, Alex."

Alex felt a shiver of excitement pass through her and pulled Cassidy back to her, kissing her passionately. "You have me, Cass."

Cassidy pulled back slightly and looked into Alex's eyes. "I don't have words."

"You don't need any." Alex swiftly but tenderly pulled Cassidy over and underneath her. Softly, more softly than Cassidy could have imagined, Alex let her kisses travel across Cassidy's neck and throat, lingering gently but insistently. Deliberately and gradually Alex allowed her hands to explore her lover. "You are everything to me, Cassidy." She looked into the teacher's eyes as their bodies moved perfectly in time with one another. "Everything," she whispered in Cassidy's ear.

It was difficult for Alex to believe that they could grow closer, but each time she felt Cassidy willingly give herself over, she fell deeper under the spell that seemed to bind them. Making love to Cassidy was as tender as it was passionate, and it was powerful. Alex found herself wishing she could lose herself here. "Don't let me go," Cassidy begged as her body began to tremble and quake. "Alex…."

"Everything, Cassidy," Alex assured. Cassidy held onto the agent tightly, needing to feel the safety of Alex's arms as a new rush of emotion and physical sensations pounded over and through her. "Je t'aime," Alex whispered as Cassidy's body finally submitted fully.

Tears fell swiftly between them. Cassidy held Alex's face in her hands and searched her eyes in silence. "No words," she finally repeated.

Alex smiled. *"Tu n'as pas a dire un mot. Je veux juste t'aimer.* (You never need to say a word. I just want to love you).

"I hope you know that I want to give you…."

The teacher's words were met with a soft and simple kiss. "Everything. You give my life purpose. You've given me everything…Cass?" Alex asked as Cassidy's head came to rest on her chest.

"Mm?"

"You're sure, right?"

"That I want to marry a butler?" Hearing her lover's response, Alex let out a relaxed chuckle. "I'm sure, Alfred."

"Thank you, Cass."

"For what, love?"

"For giving me everything."

Cassidy moved herself slowly over the agent. Her eyes sparkled as she offered Alex a seductive smile. "*Pas tout a fait, Amour* (not quite everything, love)." She kissed Alex and whispered in her ear. "*Mais, je te promets, je le ferai* (But I promise, I will)."

Alex closed her eyes and reveled in the feel of Cassidy close to her, kissing her, touching her, loving her. "Everything," she whispered with a new understanding of what that word meant.

***

Chapter Twenty-Three

Brian Fallon sat quietly sipping his coffee, regarding the man seated across from him. "You'll have to forgive me."

"You don't trust me, Agent Fallon. Well, I would say that you don't have much choice now."

Fallon took a deliberately long sip from his coffee and let it linger on his lips. As slowly as his hand would allow he moved the cup back to the table before allowing his gaze to meet the eyes fixed on him. "Assistant Director, I don't understand why you called me here. Agent Toles may be my friend, but she is no longer with the bureau."

"No, she is not. And neither are you, Agent."

"Assist…."

"Don't bother, Agent Fallon. I understand. I also understand your reluctance to believe me. I already spoke with your boss. Director Taylor is why I called. I have been at this a great deal longer than you, Agent. I worked in the field once. I had a partner. The kind of partner you don't forget."

"So that's your reason…"

"Listen to me, Agent Fallon. You think you know more than you really do, both you and Toles."

"You do realize that the idea of a sitting president as a CIA agent sounds a bit," Fallon raised his eyebrow, "farfetched."

"Maybe to you."

"Okay. What's in this for you?"

Assistant FBI Director Joshua Tate shook his head. "For me? Nothing, Agent." Fallon stared blankly at the man he had known as his mentor and boss. "There comes a time, Agent Fallon, when we have to make a choice. What do you believe in? What are you going to do about that?"

"So, you are making a choice?"

"Fallon....I knew John Merrow for many years. Our daughters grew up together. When he called me six months ago... well, I didn't ask questions. He was the President of the United States. He was a friend. Do you understand?"

"So, *he* told you this, then?"

"No, he didn't. He was cautious, concerned about Brackett's placement at the FBI. He did not tell me all the reasons why. Something deeper. I only know that he wanted her controlled. He didn't want Toles to discover her roots. Brackett is, well... her need to get close to Agent Toles; it prompted your assignment to the O'Brien case."

Fallon nodded. "I think there might have been more than that to it, Assistant Director."

"I'm sure, but Brackett concerned him," Tate maintained.

"Why?"

"I don't know that. It wasn't often you could read John Merrow. He was concerned, Fallon. The last time I saw him....I suggested he tell Agent Toles everything."

"Everything about what?" Fallon asked.

"What he was doing with the French...and others."

"And what was that?"

"I don't know much Agent Fallon. I was told what I needed to know. Large disbursements of cash ran through several congressional campaigns this last season. Far more than years earlier. The money, most of it moved through Nigeria before it made its way to Swiss accounts."

"And..."

"I don't know what the sales were. Not specifically. What was being sold concerned the president enough that he called me."

Brian Fallon rubbed his hand over his head. "Why do you think he was a spook?"

"I don't think it, Fallon. He was. His whole life. Look in that file. I can tell you this...you think Director Kearn controls the CIA?" Tate laughed. "Admiral Brackett, Agent. He *is* the agency as it actually operates. Whatever the agency even is."

"What does that mean?"

"Agent Fallon, lone gunmen do not get close enough to presidents to kill them. This isn't 1865."

"So, the president was an intelligence operative that was killed by the CIA?" Fallon scoffed. "I thought Alex watched too much *X-Files*."

Tate chuckled and shook his head. "You're a good investigator, Fallon, but you are certainly naïve."

"Why not bring this to Taylor yourself?"

"I did that once. People are watching both of us, Fallon. You and I have a reason to be here together. Be careful. Look at that file. Get it to Agent Toles. You are into something here; something much bigger than any of us can understand. It got a popular president murdered."

"That's a strong accusation."

Tate stood and released an audible breath. "It's not an accusation. It's a fact."

"If he knew someone might try and eliminate him, why wouldn't he...."

Joshua Tate forced a solemn smile as he interrupted Fallon's question with his answer. "I told you, Fallon. We all have to make choices."

"You think he chose to die?"

Tate scratched his eyebrow. "Either you follow what you believe in Agent, or one day you believe in nothing." He started to walk away as Fallon opened the file. "You have a family, Agent. People you love. So did John Merrow. So do I. Why did you choose this?" Fallon looked up and watched as the taller man nodded again. "Be careful, both you and Toles. I will do what I can where Agent Brackett is concerned. Who she answers to, well…I'm not sure of that anymore."

Brian Fallon looked back into the file as Tate walked away. His eyes scanned it quickly and he shook his head. "What the hell is going on?"

***

Cassidy woke up and reached across the bed to find Alex absent. She rolled over and looked at the clock. "5:30?" she groaned. The agent was still forbidden to go running and Cassidy wondered where she might have gone. Reluctantly, she left the comfort of the bed, threw on her robe and went in search of the agent. Dylan's bed was also empty. The living room was still dark and she continued curiously to the kitchen. The coffee pot was on and a juice container sat open on the counter. Cassidy laughed. "Still tired," she mused. It was unlike Alex to leave anything undone. She popped the juice back in the refrigerator and shuffled herself down the hallway. The faint sound of the television echoing from the family room caught her attention. Cassidy stopped in the doorway and smiled. Alex was lying sprawled out on the couch with Dylan nestled into her, his head tucked under her chin. She took a moment to study the scene, noting the remote that had fallen to the floor and the way Alex's hand held her son gently. She shook her head in both amusement and deep affection for the pair. Quietly she walked over and kissed the agent's forehead. "Alex," she called gently.

"Hum? Cass?"

"Yeah, what are you doing down here?"

"What time is it?"

"It's only 5:30. What…."

Alex opened her eyes slightly and gave a weak smile. "He wasn't feeling good."

"I didn't hear him," Cassidy said feeling a bit guilty.

"I know, you were sleeping so soundly when he came in. I didn't want to wake you.

Cassidy knelt down beside the couch and brushed the hair from Alex's eyes. "You didn't have to....you could have woken me up." The agent smiled and took Cassidy's hand. "What?" Cassidy asked.

Alex swallowed hard. "He's my son too, Cass."

"Yes," Cassidy said softly. "He is."

"Cass?" Alex asked. Cassidy noted a hint of fear in her lover's eye.

"What?" Cassidy asked with some concern.

"It was real, right?"

"What?"

"Last night. I mean you said yes....I didn't just....well...you know...I..."

"Did you ask me something last night?" she asked playfully.

"What? Well....yeah...I..."

"You are tired," Cassidy observed. "Yes."

"What?" Alex answered.

"Yes, Alex. I said yes," Cassidy laughed. "Come on. Come back to bed."

"Dylan...."

"Did you give him anything?" Alex nodded and the teacher kissed her head. "He'll sleep. Come back and sleep with me for a while." Alex wiggled her way off the couch and covered the still sleeping boy. She stood over him, watching silently. "Alex? Are you all right?"

"Yeah. Is it weird, Cass?"

"What's that?" Cassidy asked as she wrapped an arm around the agent and pressed into her.

"I don't know. I just....I can't believe sometimes it's all real."

"What?" Cassidy asked.

Alex turned and looked at her lover. "You."

"I know."

"Sometimes, I think I will wake up and it will have been just a dream."

Cassidy did understand. "Well, it is a dream for me Alex; you, Dylan."

"Is it?"

"What do you mean?" Cassidy asked.

"I never want to disappoint you."

Cassidy took the agent's face in her hands. "Impossible."

"I hope so."

"Come on." Cassidy pulled gently on the agent. "I need you to hold me."

"You do?"

Cassidy nodded. It was strange, but she understood why Alex seemed to be so emotional. Alex had never addressed Dylan as *her* son so directly to Cassidy before. All these moments, to most people they were frustrating; ear aches and principal offices, dishes and even mother-in-laws. Every moment for Alex and Cassidy seemed like the most important moment ever. Perhaps, Cassidy thought, it was because they had just found each other. Or, maybe it was because they had both suffered the fear of losing the other. So many moments, and so many tied to this new family that were a first for them all; maybe that was the reason. It didn't matter. It simply was. "I do, Alex." Cassidy giggled as they began walking again.

"What's funny?"

"I do," Cassidy answered laughing a bit harder.

Alex smiled her understanding. Everything was about to change again and Alex found her heart beginning to race at the thought.

***

"Russ," Alex greeted through the phone as she sipped her coffee.

"Alex. How are you? I heard…"

"Much better, thanks. Cassidy is taking good care of me."

The ambassador laughed. "I am certain. What is it I can do for you?"

Alex sighed. She knew that they could not possibly speak freely by phone for a host of reasons. She still had another week of mandatory rest at home and given the events that transpired on this last trip, she feared telling her family that she would have to leave again. She knew that was an inevitability. "We need to speak. It needs to be soon."

"This is about what we discussed? When?" Alex took a deep breath and the ambassador could hear the tension through the phone line. He returned to the conversation to a less formal tone. "Alex, you need to take it easy."

"It's not that, Russ." She took a deep breath. "Moscow is difficult right now. Any chance of a state side trip?"

The ambassador ran his hand along the top of his desk. He had worked with Alex Toles in the past. He understood if she was asking for a face to face meeting the topic was not typical and not safe, for either of them. "Alex, I have a meeting in London a week from Friday. I know that is almost two weeks. But, that…"

"That's fine," Alex answered. Two weeks was longer than she would have liked, but it gave her some time to plan and some time to allow Cassidy a chance to digest the reality that Alex would need to travel again.

"In fact, there is a dinner that evening. Ambassador Daniels and his wife are hosting. I have it on some authority Jane has been invited. Why don't you bring Cassidy?"

Alex rubbed her temple. The topics she needed to discuss with the ambassador were extremely sensitive. She had to admit, it would be the perfect cover. She and Ambassador Paul Daniels had been friends for many years. They had met at West Point when he was an instructor and Alex had always regarded him as one of the most intelligent men she had ever met. "Russ…"

"I think it might be perfect. The news is a buzz still, you know....about you and the president. He was wildly popular in Europe. It would be...."

The agent sighed. "I'll talk to her."

"Good. It is a good idea on many fronts."

"Perhaps." Alex smiled as she heard the front door opening. "I'll be in touch."

"I will have the invitation sent. And, Alex?"

"Yeah?"

"Whatever puzzle you're trying to solve? It will be there in a week," the ambassador issued her a friendly reminder.

Alex laughed. Russ Matthews, whatever and whoever he was, certainly understood Alex Toles and he was right. This puzzle she was so determined to piece together had been laying in fragments for more years than she wanted to imagine. Still, the longer she waited, the more time people had to move their pieces. "Yeah. I'll remember that," she said as she hung up. Alex wasn't certain anymore who anyone really was or who she could trust. She hoped someone was on her side.

***

"Edmond."

"Jonathan, come in. Scotch?" Jonathan Krause nodded his agreement. "Well, sit."

Jon Krause was still reeling from the loss of his best friend. The decision to assassinate John Merrow was one that his mentor, Edmond Callier, had supported, perhaps even advocated. Now, he sat before the older man; a man he had regarded as a trusted friend; and wondered if the Frenchman felt any differently. He accepted his glass and took a seat, watching as Callier made his way to what Krause called 'the throne'. It was simply a large comfortable chair toward the center of the room. It was a seat that was claimed by only one man in all the years that

Krause had visited this home and that was the man before him. "Merci, Edmond."

"Jonathan, tell me, what brings you here?"

Krause felt his jaw tighten. "How are you?"

Edmond Callier nodded and sipped his drink. "She killed my son, Jonathan."

"I know."

"I suppose you think that is equitable then," Callier spoke quietly.

The CIA agent bristled at the assertion. Elliot Mercier was his friend, a brother of sorts. He may not have been the brother that Krause loved, but he was a kindred spirit, a man who shared a similar path. Krause regarded Mercier much like he did Claire Brackett. Elliot Mercier was a man that had become arrogant and thus careless in his choices. The CIA agent recognized that this arrogance was based on parentage. "I see no justice in meaningless death, Edmond."

"And John's death?"

"It was foolish and unnecessary."

Callier took another sip of his scotch and closed his eyes. "What is it you want, Jonathan? Do you expect me to ask forgiveness?"

"No. But, I wonder how it is you see the picture now."

"I don't trust the admiral, Jonathan. I do not trust that congressman. Claire? The little sparrow…Well, I await her fall."

"I see. And me?"

Edmond Callier finished his scotch and rose from his seat to pour another. "Jonathan, you are like a son to me. You. Ian…..you were…."

"What are you willing to do, Edmond?"

Callier turned and regarded the younger man. "Do?"

"Yes. Do. It is time, Edmond. The world is changing. John, Elliot. For what?"

"What you are suggesting, Jonathan. It is nothing short of the betrayal of our lifetime's work."

"Really? Can you betray a betrayal, Edmond? What have you left to protect?" Krause waited, already knowing the answer. "Edmond?"

"Jonathan, you have nothing to lose."

"I think you will find, Edmond, that I too have something to protect."

"You were wise to make no attachments," Callier pointed out.

Krause had his card to play now and he intended to play it deliberately and carefully. "I have attachments."

"Cassidy."

"Not just Cassidy, Edmond."

Edmond Callier inhaled deeply. "The boy?" Krause nodded. "I see."

"Edmond...."

"What about Ian?"

"He's in. He doesn't know about Cassidy....about...about my son." Krause spoke the words, apologizing in his mind to his best friend. Apologizing for the lie and even more so for the fact that he wished the words were true.

"A son," Callier smiled. "Your son. My daughter. You think this is how we protect them?" Krause tipped his head. "It changes things, Jonathan; doesn't it?" Callier mused.

"What's that?" Krause asked.

"Love, Jonathan. It changes everything."

Jonathan Krause took a final sip from his glass. "Yes. It does."

"Very well. You understand, if we proceed we may have to lose to..."

"We have already lost, my friend. We can only hope to shield them now."

Callier sighed. "And Agent Toles?"

"She understands." He saw the tip of the older man's head. "Yes, she knows about my son. So too I am afraid, does the congressman."

"He is problematic. Not only for us," Callier groaned.

"I agree."

Callier smiled. "You leave him to me." Krause felt a twinge of anticipation. He neither trusted nor did he ever appreciate Christopher O'Brien as anything more than a pathetic liability, in every manner. "Jonathan, whatever comes to pass. There is no rebuilding this bridge once we…"

"*Je préférerais me noyer que prendre ce chemin, un jour de plus* (I would sooner drown than walk this path a day longer). I will be in touch."

***

Sunday, May 4th

"Alex, you need to relax," Cassidy chuckled.

"I can't help it." Alex had been rehearsing her words every way she possibly could. It had been her decision to invite their families over to tell them the news. Cassidy had tried to convince Alex to take it easy. Dylan was feeling better and he was excited about having a secret that Cat didn't know and Alex insisted. Alex was as bad as Dylan when she was excited about something and Cassidy found it heartwarming and sweet.

"It's just Barb, Nick and my mom. I don't really think you need to worry."

"Cassidy," the agent said firmly. "We are telling your mother that we are getting married. I mean, I know she likes me, but do you think that is what she pictured…." Cassidy started laughing and Alex frowned. "What?" the agent asked.

Calmly, Cassidy walked to the agent and kissed her. "I love you, Alex."

"Cass…I don't…"

"Alex, my mother gave you the ring, well the stone. I hardly think she will be surprised."

The agent chuckled slightly. "I don't know what is wrong with me."

Cassidy's eyes twinkled. "You never thought you'd be making this kind of announcement."

"No, I didn't," Alex admitted.

"Well, don't worry," Cassidy kissed the agent's cheek. "Knowing Dylan, your news will hit the airwaves long before you get to tell it yourself."

"You think?" Cassidy raised her eyebrow. "Well, I guess that's fair," Alex said.

"Why is that?"

"Because, Barb will probably have you pregnant in twenty-four hours."

Cassidy leaned her head into Alex's chest and laughed. That was the truth. "If Barb can get me pregnant, we seriously need to talk."

"Who's pregnant?" a voice asked.

"Grandma's here!" Dylan yelled.

"Yes, I see that." Cassidy smiled.

"Alex, did you already get my daughter pregnant?" Rose said seriously, knowing the answer and enjoying rattling the tall agent with every opportunity that presented itself.

"What? No....I....I mean..." Alex stammered.

"Mom, are you having a baby?" Dylan asked.

"What?" another voice called. "Cassidy!" Barb practically screamed as she walked into the room carrying a large plate. "You're pregnant?"

Nick was following close behind and his eyes flew open. "Cassidy's pregnant?"

Alex had turned completely white and Cassidy covered her face, shaking her head. "Why does everyone think I am pregnant?"

"Because," Dylan said, pulling on her slightly. "When you get married you have babies. Right, Cat?"

Cat nodded. "Yeah but your mom isn't married to Aunt Alex."

"Holy Shit!" Nick blurted out without thinking. "Alex....
you're getting married, aren't you?"

"Oh my God," Barb hugged Cassidy.

Alex covered her eyes and finally laughed as Dylan looked
up to her. "Well, Speed....we don't call you Speed for nothing."
He smiled at her, not fully understanding what she meant. "You
sure got everyone up to speed quickly." Dylan grinned wider.
"Well, thanks all for coming," Alex said as Cassidy leaned into
her. "No need to stay. CNN has already broken the news."

"When?" Barb asked.

"When what?" Alex answered with her own question.

"When are you getting married?"

Cassidy just smiled. Dylan looked at the two women he
loved in anticipation. "We really haven't discussed that at all,"
Cassidy intervened.

"Soon," Alex answered.

"Soon?" Cassidy responded. Alex just shrugged. Cassidy
decided to set everyone straight. "All right. Here it is in a nut-
shell. Alex asked me to marry her. I said, yes. I am not pregnant. I have no plans to be pregnant anytime soon. We have
not decided when or where...and to answer all of your questions; if I could I would marry her right now. Now, Dylan...why
don't you and Cat go upstairs and play in your room? Alex, you
wanted to show Nick that plan you've been concocting for a
bar in the basement, and I am ready for a glass of wine."

After a long pause of stunned silence the adults erupted
in laughter. Dylan shrugged his shoulders to his ears and
motioned for Cat to follow. "Welcome to the family," Rose
poked. She hugged the agent. "I'm so glad they found you,"
she whispered. Alex nodded and gestured for her brother to
head for the basement.

"Okay," Barb beamed. "Get the wine. I want details."

***

Alex was lying on the bed in her sweatpants and a T-shirt when Cassidy entered the room. "Quite the day, huh?" the teacher laughed. Alex offered her a weak smile. "You okay?"

"Of course."

"Liar," Cassidy observed. "Spill."

"I'm fine, Cass."

"Alex Toles. Really?"

"Really."

Cassidy crawled onto the bed and rested her head on Alex's chest. "Spill it, Alex."

"Why do you think something is wrong?" Cassidy picked up her head to look at the agent and lifted her eyebrows. "What you said," Alex started.

"What did I say?"

"You know…about…well… you know…"

"No, Alex. What did I say?"

"About…well about babies."

Cassidy was completely perplexed. "You lost me, Alex. When were we talking about babies? And whose babies were we talking about?"

"Ours."

"Ours?" Cassidy asked. Alex shrugged. "Honey, you lost me."

"You said you don't plan to be…"

Cassidy's earlier diatribe suddenly hit her. "Alex?" The agent shifted uncomfortably. "Honey, I was just kidding with everyone."

"Is that how you feel, though?"

"Alex," Cassidy sat up and looked into the agent's eyes. "What is this about?" Alex shrugged again. "Oh no. Spill it, Agent."

"I just thought you wanted to…."

"Of course I want to. You thought I was saying I didn't want to have a baby? Alex, we have talked about this. I just meant….well, I guess I figured that would be something we would talk about in time. That's all. Why did that upset you so much?"

"I don't know." Cassidy raised her brow again. "I guess I didn't realize what it would feel like."

"What?"

"Well...I mean....I guess maybe I just realized...."

"There isn't anything I don't want to do with you. I told you that. I've known that from the beginning. What else is going on?" It was obvious to Cassidy that something else had helped to prompt the agent's sensitivity. When Alex was nervous about work, she always displayed insecurity about their relationship. "Tell me."

"I have to go away next weekend."

Cassidy took a deep breath and held on a little tighter. She closed her eyes. The idea of Alex away conjured images of the agent in the hospital bed. It surfaced all the fear that Cassidy had felt wondering if Alex was even alive. "How long?"

"A few days." Cassidy could not control the tears that began to fall. "Cass?"

"Alex...I'm sorry...I..."

"Actually, Cass, I was hoping you would go with me." Cassidy pulled back in confusion. "Yeah, I need to see Russ. There is a dinner in London next Friday. My friend, Paul, he's the ambassador there. I thought..."

"Alex, aren't you working?"

"I am talking. That's all," Alex promised. "Just a couple of days. We'll be back Monday. I thought, I don't know...maybe if we were away we could talk about..."

Cassidy kissed the agent gently. "Of course I will go."

"Good," Alex said pulling the teacher closer and feeling Cassidy relax in her arms. "Cass?"

"Hum?"

"Is soon okay?"

"Alex, tomorrow would be okay as far as I am concerned."

"Not tomorrow....soon."

Cassidy was exhausted and her body was giving over quickly to sleep. "Whatever you want, Alex."

"Soon."

***

Chapter Twenty-Four

Wednesday, May 7th

Alex thumbed through the pages in front of her, absent-mindedly sipping her coffee. She had been reading and rereading the words for hours, attempting to process what she knew was the truth and reconcile it with everything she once believed. She set the paper in her hands down and grasped the bridge of her nose firmly, letting out a heavy sigh. "Jesus." She took a deep breath and retrieved her cell phone from underneath a large stack of papers. "Fallon?"

"Alex?" Brian Fallon answered with a degree of surprise. "Everything okay?"

"This file…"

Fallon licked his bottom lip and groaned slightly. "Yeah…"

"What exactly did Tate tell you when he gave you this?"

"I already told you. He told me President Merrow was CIA. Alex, you didn't seem that surprised when…"

"I'm not. I told you I suspected that. I just hoped I was wrong." Alex shook her head and picked up one of the papers, tracing several lines with her fingers. "Fallon," she took a deep breath. "Why did Tate want me to see this? There has to be a reason."

"I don't know. He said something about needing to believe in something. Said he and Merrow were friends and Merrow was worried about Brackett."

"The admiral?"

"No."

Alex let out a sarcastic chuckle. "Claire." She laughed a bit more, albeit with contempt. "Got more than they bargained for with her." She lifted another paper and shook her head. "Fallon, I need you to do something for me."

"Whatever you need; you know that."

"Yeah. Listen. I need you to try and get into Tate's personnel files at the bureau."

"What? Why would…"

"There's a reason I got assigned to Tate's division, Fallon. There is a reason, of all the bureau chiefs and assistant directors, in all the agencies, that the president called Joshua Tate."

"Alex, maybe that is just because you *were* assigned to him."

"No. One thing I do know about John Merrow, he was as deliberate as he was cautious. There was a reason for everything he did and everything he said."

"What are you thinking?" Fallon took a moment and let out a slight gasp, "you can't seriously think Tate is a spook too?"

"I'm not even sure we know what a spook is anymore, Fallon. I have someone I need to talk to."

"You are supposed to be on leave," he reminded her.

"Yeah, well…I already told you I have clearance to do puzzles."

"Alex…"

"Just work on it Fallon and keep an eye on our favorite redhead; will you?"

"You think Brackett is up to something?"

"Not a question, Fallon. You already know that." He laughed. "Dig in on Tate. Keep our friend Claire close. I have a feeling someone I know might be able to shed a little more light on this file."

"Who are you…"

"Not important, Fallon. Find anything, call me."

"Alex?" Brian Fallon took a deep breath. "If the president was CIA, what exactly do you think…"

"Politics is business, Fallon."

"Some business."

"Yeah. Call me when you get something." Alex hung up her call and rubbed her eyes with the palms of her hands. None of what the files revealed surprised her; not after her discussion with Jonathan Krause. This had become far more than a case to solve. There were layers here, so many layers. Each layer seemed to do little except to reveal yet another that needed to be peeled away, spawning a whole new set of questions and riddles to be answered. Alex threw her head back and sighed in frustration. What exactly was the CIA, she wondered now? What was the real purpose of anything? She was anxious to see Russ Matthews and more curious than ever about what John Merrow had been involved with. Was he trying to thwart something or was he simply another cog in an ever spinning wheel? Had that wheel become unstoppable? Alex's thoughts were roaming and running as she stretched her neck from side to side in an attempt to relax and order them, her fingers continually pressing her temples.

Two hands gripped the agent's shoulders and began to massage them. "Maybe it's time for a break," a voice whispered. Alex just smiled and let her head fall slightly forward. "Alex...."

"Mm...maybe it is."

"You all right?" Cassidy asked softly.

Alex opened her eyes and smiled. "Yeah. I am. Just tired." Cassidy nodded. "Cass?"

"Yeah?"

The agent sighed slightly and Cassidy raised an eyebrow. "Would you mind if I invited Jane up for the weekend?" The teacher tipped her head in question. "I need to talk to her."

"What aren't you telling me?" Cassidy pursed her lips.

"Nothing, I swear."

"Alex, we agreed, no secrets. No matter what."

"I know. I can't tell you anything. I'm not sure what there is to tell. That's the truth."

"Is this about John?"

Alex guided Cassidy to sit in the chair beside her. "Cass," she stopped and took a deep breath. "I was right. John was CIA."

"When you were in Iraq?"

A heavy sigh escaped the agent and Cassidy closed her eyes. "The whole time, Cass."

"You mean even when…"

"I mean," Alex stopped and pinched the bridge of her nose. "Once you are in; you are always in."

"You know how crazy this all sounds?"

"Yeah. I do," the agent admitted. "Whatever was going on… Jane…"

"Alex, you don't think Jane is involved in…"

"I don't know what I think. Think about it, Cassidy. All these people. They were born into this. It's like some secret society, some bad B movie plot, except it's not. I don't even know what side is what. Who is in for what? Who is reporting to…"

Alex was becoming agitated in her train of thought. This information confirmed John Merrow's betrayal of her trust and that, Cassidy understood, was a painful pill for Alex Toles to swallow. The teacher grabbed Alex's hand and removed it slowly from its position on the agent's face. "Just promise me," Cassidy began when Alex finally fully opened her eyes to look at her. "That you will not rush into some…"

"I promise. Anyway, I was thinking we should see my parents and…"

"You want Jane to go with us to your parents' house?" Cassidy laughed. Alex was nervous about telling her parents about their engagement and Cassidy knew Alex would likely seek any buffer she could.

"No, I thought….maybe a cook-out here, before we go to London on Thursday."

Cassidy nodded. "Mm-hm."

"What?"

"Nothing," Cassidy chuckled as she rose from her seat. "Invite Jane and the girls up for the weekend. I'll call my mother and Barb, but *you* are calling your mother."

"Yeah, but she loves…"

"Nope. Not happening," Cassidy shook her head as she made her way out of the room.

"Great," Alex grumbled.

"Call your mother, Alex," Cassidy called back.

"Yeah. At least I won't have to cook," Alex chuckled.

"No, but you can mow the lawn. Your feet seem to be just fine."

"My feet?" Alex was puzzled.

Cassidy peeked back through the door. "Yes, Alex, your feet. I saw your dance moves with Dylan last night." With that she took her leave.

Alex laughed. "I've got some moves all right," she muttered.

"And the lawn looks forward to them," Cassidy called back. "I'm off to get Dylan. Call your mother."

***

Friday, May 9th

The redhead climbed off of the form lying beneath her and smirked with satisfaction. "You're certain it can't be traced back to me?" he asked.

Claire Brackett let out a roar. "I've told you a thousand times, Congressman, everything is traceable. Why do you care if they trace it to you? They'll know the minute it breaks who was responsible."

"I don't care about t*hem*," he offered, resting his hands behind his head casually and enjoying watching the attractive woman prance about the room.

"People see what they want to see," she said, buttoning her long white blouse to just above her navel before making her way back to the bed. "All we do is make suggestions, Congressman," she purred into his ear and tugged at it with her teeth slightly. "So, they will be heroes or they will be villains. Depends," she cooed and pulled back slightly to regard him.

"And to you?" he asked. "Why do you even care, Claire?"

Her smile widened. "I don't. Perception is power." She ran her fingers down his chest and he shivered slightly. "Control perception, change perception…that is power."

"I thought knowledge was power," he pulled her closer with a smug grin.

She scoffed at his assertion. "Knowledge is really no more than perception." She straddled his waist as he fought to swallow his mounting desire. "Like now, what do you see?" He reached for her and she clasped his hands firmly. "You see power. Seductive, isn't it?" His breath was becoming ragged as the young agent took control. "Be careful, Chris." She leaned back into his ear tracing it with her tongue and whispered to him. "Perception is fickle." He had reached his limit with her games and swiftly grabbed hold of her, thrusting her beneath him in an attempt to assert his control. Claire Brackett licked her lips as her eyes danced in amusement. "That's it, Congressman, you take control."

"I will," he said.

"Your game." He pressed into her and she continued softly, "Just remember, there is a fine line between the victim and the hero." Her words were silenced by the ferocity of his kiss. "A fine line," she muttered as she willingly gave over to his demands.

***

Saturday, May 10th

"Mr. President."

"Admiral, to what do I owe the honor of your visit," President Strickland asked wryly.

"Larry. We need to discuss this upcoming trip you are making to Europe," Admiral Brackett explained.

"What is it that you want, Bill?" the president asked pointedly.

"You need to win over Edmond." The admiral paused for a moment and paced the floor. President Lawrence Strickland watched him closely. There was something slightly different in William Brackett's posture. The admiral teetered on the side of cocky in his usual stance. His gait seemed somehow slower, perhaps even a bit unsteady. "Things," the admiral continued, "circumstances have changed somewhat with our French counterparts."

The president nodded and attempted to suppress his amusement. The president had traveled in this school of fish for many years. He had connections in every corner of Washington and beyond. While he might be somewhat naïve to the tactics of some of the players; he was neither stupid nor uninformed. President Lawrence Strickland could be as ruthless as anyone the admiral had ever met. His ambition combined with his connections made him a potentially volatile player for the admiral. "You are referring to your daughter, I assume."

"Well," the admiral continued. "Claire can be a bit....impetuous. Some of her actions were..."

"Rash?"

"Yes, they were. That is well in hand." The admiral stopped his pacing and sat in a large chair. "There is concern over the movement of materials. Some of the legislation that might complicate that process."

The president fought to contain his obvious delight. Admiral William Brackett needed him and that put him squarely in the driver's seat. "You are referring to the organophosphorus clause in HR1929." The admiral nodded. "And what, Bill, is it that concerns our friends?"

"Not only that measure. Funding initiatives. We have agreements. You must know that. We need clear channels for the movement of funds and technology. Restrictions, oversight on intelligence agencies, these are not measures that bode will with our partners."

The president lifted his chin and tightened his jaw line. "And, why, Bill? Why are we providing this technology? And, to whom?"

"We know Iran is in the business. We know Pakistan is at the ready. We need to be certain that our interests…"

"I see. Yes, I suppose we do, Admiral. Rest easy on the resolutions. I will see to that. As for Edmond, well…I will reassure him."

"I hope so, Mr. President," the admiral offered as he rose to leave.

"Bill?" the president called after him. "Be cautious," he smiled.

The admiral seethed inside. Vulnerability was not something he was accustomed to. His daughter's actions and the man sitting before him now placed him in an unusually precarious position. He nodded his false appreciation at the president's cocky sentiment. "Sir," he answered simply as he took his leave. "Oh, Claire. You had better watch yourself," he whispered aloud as he made his way down the hall.

***

"Alex!" Cassidy called. "Can you get that, please?"

Alex smiled and began to make her way to the front door when Dylan barreled by her. "Slow down, Speed. Where's the fire?" she laughed. He was sliding in his socks across the hardwood floor and opening the door before she could say another word.

"Well, hello, Dylan," Jane Merrow greeted the young boy.

He frowned slightly and then offered her the hint of a smile. "Hi."

"Not quite who you were expecting, huh?" Just then Dylan caught sight of Stephanie and Alexandra Merrow heading up the driveway and he brightened. Jane shook her head and laughed. "Yes, I know. They are far more interesting than me."

"Hi Jane," Alex greeted as Dylan tipped his head backward to meet her gaze.

"Alex," Jane hugged the agent as her daughters finally came even with her.

"Captain," Stephanie winked.

"Hi, Steph. Alex. Dylan, why don't you take Steph and Alex to see Mom?" Alex offered.

He nodded and grabbed hold of Stephanie's hand, leading the pair swiftly away. "MOM!"

Jane laughed. "He certainly has energy."

"Yeah, well, I don't call him Speed for nothing," Alex replied as Jane stepped in through the door. "Where are your bags? You are staying..."

"Yes, Alex. The girls would never have let me get out of *this* invitation. They are in the car," she motioned to the Secret Service agent several yards away. The former first lady narrowed her gaze. "So, what is this all about, Captain?"

Alex directed her friend into the living room and sat across from her. "Maybe I just wanted to see how you were doing." Alex smirked.

"Nice try, Alex."

The agent sighed. "You're right. I need to talk to you about some things. About this Collaborative, as you call it."

"Alex..."

"Yeah, well, I do. But," Alex shook her head and smiled. "That's tomorrow's agenda."

"I see. So what is today's agenda?" Jane asked curiously.

The agent stood and rubbed her eyebrow in thought. "Today is a barbeque."

"Yes, you told me *that* when you called. You really are becoming quite domestic," Jane poked. Alex nodded as she bit her bottom lip gently. "All right, what is going on, Alex? Is everything all right with Dylan? Something happen with that asshole…"

Alex laughed. "No. Nothing like that." Jane raised her hands in questioning and Alex let out a sigh. "Yeah, you know about that domestic thing…"

Jane rolled her eyes. "Was I supposed to buy you a blender or something? Do you even know how to use a blender?"

"Funny. Cassidy has that covered." Jane laughed. "And, you might just be surprised how easily I navigate appliances." Jane raised her eyebrow playfully. "Oh…All right. I asked Cassidy to marry me." Jane stared blankly at the agent. "Did you hear me?"

"Did you just say you asked Cassidy to *marry* you?" Alex nodded and offered her friend a cheesy grin. "Uh-huh, I thought that's what you said."

"I thought you'd be happy," Alex said with disappointment.

Jane chuckled. "I am happy…for you. It's Cassidy I'm worried about."

"What? Why would you…"

"Oh, Alex, relax. Honestly, you are so easy sometimes." Alex sighed in relief. "So, why not just call me? I mean aside from tomorrow's agenda, as you put it. Why invite me and the girls?"

"Because," an approaching voice broke in. "She needs moral support. She figures her parents will behave with the former first lady in the house." Cassidy smiled and reached over to kiss Jane on the cheek.

"Well, whatever I can do," Jane rolled her eyes.

"Where are Steph and…"

Cassidy laughed. "Believe it or not they seemed quite enthralled by Dylan's promise to show them all his *techniques* down on that pool table." The teacher shook her head. "I believe his words were, *I have mad skills?*" Cassidy scrunched her face.

"Well….he…I mean…he is…" The sound of the doorbell was a welcome interruption. "I'll just," Alex started toward the door, "get that now..." Cassidy shook her head again and smiled broadly.

"So?" Jane implored.

"What?"

"Well, please tell me she gave you a ring."

The teacher laughed and extended her hand. "She told you already?"

"Alex is horrible..."

"At hiding things?" Cassidy nodded. "Yes, I know."

"It's beautiful, Cassidy."

"I am glad you are here, Jane." The former first lady seemed slightly puzzled. "And not just for Alex," she continued. "I realize...well, it's not the time for certain things, but Dylan...well, I'd still like him to get to know his..."

"His sisters?" Jane smiled. Cassidy nodded. "I know. And they adore him already." The teacher closed her eyes and felt Jane take her hand. Things sometimes seemed so complicated and so simple all at once. It amazed Cassidy that somehow they had all been brought together. She was no fatalist, but she had to admit it seemed the universe somehow conspired to be certain they would all find each other.

"Come in," Alex encouraged. "You've met Nick and Barb... Jane Merrow, these are my parents, Helen and Nick Toles."

"Pleased to meet you," Jane offered sincerely. "You must be so proud of Alex," she said. "She's always been such a good friend to me, and to John." She grew quiet and Cassidy instinctively rubbed her back, sensing the sadness that lingered.

"Well, yes...pleasure to meet you Mrs. Merrow," Alex's father replied accepting her grasp.

"Just Jane, please."

"Well, why don't we make our way out back?" Cassidy suggested.

The group followed and Nick caught his sister on the way. "Maybe you should tell them alone, Alex." The agent just shook her head. "All right, just be..."

"Nick, whatever he does, he does. This is my home. Mine and Cassidy's. And I..."

Her brother nodded his understanding. "I hope you bought beer. If you don't need one, I think I might."

***

"What the hell?" Brian Fallon rubbed his hand back and forth over his head.

"Brian, calm down," his wife urged.

"Alex is going to flip."

Kate Fallon stared at the television screen and rubbed her own eyes. There were images playing of Cassidy beside several different men and women. She rolled her tongue across the insides of her cheeks and blew out a heavy breath. "Why would anyone...I mean, no one is going to believe," before she could finish an image of Alex flashed onto the screen next to a handsome young Army Officer.

"And the heroic Captain?" a voice said. "Is she truly a hero or just a mourning lover seeking comfort in..."

Brian Fallon had finally had enough and switched the television off. "Brian, no one is going to believe Cassidy was having affairs."

Fallon groaned and laughed at the same time. "People will believe anything, Katie. Anything. It's not the point anyway."

Kate Fallon covered her face. "Are you going to call her?" There was no response as he paced the floor. "Brian?"

"Christ, Katie. Today of all days."

"Why? What's today?"

He collapsed onto a chair and shook his head. He'd spoken to his partner the evening before. "She's got the whole entourage there."

"What?"

"Shit, Katie. I have to call her. If they see any of that before she..."

"Before she what?"

He looked across to his wife before looking to the ceiling and rubbing his hand back and forth over the top of his head some more. "She's telling her parents."

"About them..."

"Yeah." He took a deep breath and reached in his pocket for his phone.

"What do you think she'll do?" his wife asked.

"I just hope she doesn't kill the son of a bitch. At least I hope she doesn't get caught."

***

The day had progressed better than Alex had hoped. Jane's presence kept her father occupied in dialogue and effectively allowed the agent to avoid the entire purpose of the get together. "Alexis," her mother approached. The agent looked to her mother and smiled. "Let's take the boys for that walk down by the stream they keep begging for."

Alex was a bit perplexed. "Now?" Her mother nodded. "Okay..."

The pair excused themselves and walked the short trek to the stream that ran behind the house. Finding a comfortable distance to watch the boys from, Alex's mother began, "Alexis, is there something you want to tell me?"

"What?"

Helen Toles shook her head. "I do realize that you and I have not been close for many years, but I did raise you." Alex forced an uncomfortable grin. "And, I couldn't help but notice," Alex's eyes widened. "The beautiful ring on Cassidy's finger. Or, might I add the slight glow about her."

Alex took a deep breath and released it. "I was waiting for the right moment."

"I know. Look, Alexis," the older woman paused. "Let me tell him."

313

"What?"

"I am assuming everyone else already knows."

"Well, I…"

"I understand. For once, just trust me. Let me tell your father." Alex sighed. "Don't spoil it for yourself." Alex looked at her mother in amazement. "He may not make a scene, but you know he won't give you what you are hoping for."

"I don't understand. Cassidy is…"

"Cassidy is wonderful," Helen complimented.

Alex sighed and lifted her glance to the edge of the stream. "Dylan, not in the water," she called firmly. Helen Toles smiled. "He's just getting over an ear infection," Alex explained before letting out another heavy hearted sigh.

"You can't force him," Helen put her hand on her daughter's back, "or even coax him. Your father is who he is."

"What about you?"

"Oh, Alexis, you are my daughter. You are not me." She paused and watched Dylan and Cat as they searched for rocks. Their laughter was carrying through the air and she nodded as if having a private moment of understanding. "We all have ideas, whether we should or not, about who our children will become."

"I…"

"But, those are our ideas," Helen said with an understanding smile that surprised the agent. "Just because we followed what our parents expected, well, it doesn't mean that is really what we wanted." Alex was puzzled. "I just want you to be happy. It's your life. You have to make it your own."

"He'll never…"

"He may not."

"Mom, Cassidy and I….someday we want to…"

"You are wonderful parents, Alexis. You can't live your life for your father now, or for me. You and Nick….you never did. That's something he just, he can't accept."

A soft buzz in Alex's pocket interrupted them. "Sorry," she said as she noted the number. Her mother just smiled. "I have to…"

"I'll get the boys," Helen offered.

"Fallon?" Alex answered, keeping an eye on her mother in the distance. She watched as her mother wrangled the two friends expertly while attempting to listen to the nervous voice on the other end of her phone. "What did you just say…He what? Where did you hear that…Jesus." Alex pinched the bridge of her nose and shook her head in disgust. "No one will believe it anyway…….What…Me and who?" Alex swallowed hard. "Yeah, I heard you. It's fine, Fallon. Thanks for the heads up. I gotta go."

"Everything all right?" Helen asked as she reached her daughter again with the boys running past them.

"Sure," Alex faked a smile.

"Never a good…"

"I know. It's okay. Just not what I expected, at least not now."

"Work?" Helen asked.

Alex let out a sarcastic chuckle. "I wish it were that simple," she said.

***

"Chairman," Lawrence Strickland greeted his old friend.

"Mr. President," Chairman Stiller acknowledged.

"Sit. Sit. How are things on the hill, Jim?"

James Stiller laughed. "Missing your roots, Mr. President?"

"Sometimes," the president confessed. Unlike his predecessor and in spite of the fact that he relished his new found authority, Lawrence Strickland had enjoyed his days on Capitol Hill. He learned how to attain the things he desired much more quietly than others. Most, including those that had engineered his current placement, regarded the new president as an egotistical puppet. They saw him as a man who in spite of his renowned intellect, was willing to compromise almost anything for a chance to sit on what he considered the world's greatest throne. The pathway to President Strickland's ascension, however, afforded him the opportunity to learn the landscape of legislative politics in a way that few others could claim. He had long standing relationships and his own store of favors owed. "Jim," the president continued. "This resolution…"

Stiller's tensed. "HR 1929," he said with an immediate understanding of this visit.

"Look. You have to admit, the language is broad. Tariffs are high…."

"Mr. President…"

"Jim. I am not asking that you scrap the measure. Just…. take a closer look. Take some time on it."

"I'm surprised you didn't send O'Brien to me."

"Oh? Well, I know that you and John were, well….I know you regarded him highly. I am not President Merrow though. Christopher O'Brien will not be a mouthpiece for my administration."

Chairman Stiller smiled in relief. "I'll see what I can do, Mr. President."

"I appreciate that, Jim. You let me know what you need with regard to the Social Security hearings you have scheduled." It was no secret that Stiller's real passion as Chairman of Ways and Means remained fixed on Social Security, tax and health-care reform measures.

"I will," the chairman responded.

"Good," the president said as he rose to his feet. "Enough business. Bourbon?"

***

"Matt."

"Jon. I hope you understand what you are getting yourself into here," Brigadier General Matthew Waters answered. Jon

Krause nodded. "I don't know exactly what John wanted to talk to me about. We seldom spoke through official channels."

"I know."

"I suppose it was about his..."

"No," Jon Krause stroked his chin. "I know what he wanted to talk to you about," Krause admitted.

"Janie said..."

"There are things that Jane does not need to know. There is a transfer set. Overdue, actually."

"What kind?"

"Biological."

Matthew Waters' expression tightened. He took in a deep breath and released it slowly. "To?"

"Assets in Yemen."

The general paced the floor and shook his head. "I won't ask what the logic in that decision was. So, that is what sparked John's desire to..."

"Matt," Jon Krause stood. "John was working from the other side for years. I didn't know myself...not until I had to make the call."

Matthew Waters turned briskly with an immediate understanding of the CIA agent's meaning. "You set up the assassination?"

Krause closed his eyes and opened them again. "I was charged with making the call, yes. He was supposed to leave by another exit. We planted chatter directly to reach the NSA. He refused the Secret Service request to change exits."

The general rubbed his face with his hands as if to wipe away this new knowledge somehow. "He walked into it, knowing. Why?"

"He was compromised, Matt. That compromised everything he was working on and everyone."

"Why didn't he reach out to me?"

"No. He was more effective where he was. There are others, Matt. More moles than the good admiral is aware of. Things have....well, alliances change. He didn't tell me, not everything, not even when I called. I assumed he would follow the plan. I should have known better. This, well….it has severed relationships or at least severely damaged them. Claire Brackett…I assume you heard about Elliot?"

"I did. Right now this Yemenis transaction is what we need to focus on. If John felt that…"

"I agree. Though, the roots go much deeper than this," Krause offered.

"I am sure."

"Stopping this will not be easy. It's already been delayed. The funds, they should be moving through a French transaction, routed through Nigeria and destined for a Swiss account. The disk with the account numbers will move through the Saudis to the SVR. The merchandise; that disk will move from the SVR to the Saudis."

"What are you thinking? Changing the disks?" Krause nodded. "And how would you do that?"

"We acquire an unexpected asset of our own."

Matthew Waters studied the man before him. "You want to bring Agent Toles all the way in." Krause remained stoic. "I thought you wanted to protect Alex?"

"I do. She's already in, Matt. Strange as it may sound, she's safer immersing herself than skimming the surface."

The general sighed and shook his head, pacing the floor in thought. "What do you need?"

"I'll get the disk with the protocols. We'll need a convincing dummy. Something that will occupy them for a while," Krause explained.

"Have you talked to Toles yet?" Krause lifted his eyebrow. "I see. How do you know she will agree to this?"

"It's in her DNA, Matt."

"You have a plan?"

"I do. The original is in London. I will be there Friday. So will Agent Toles."

"Fine. I'll be expecting your call."

"Expect Alex," Krause answered as he stood to leave.

"Jonathan," the general called back. "Out of curiosity; why was she never brought in before?"

The CIA agent chuckled. "What makes you think she wasn't?" He regarded the general's reaction and shook his head. "She has powerful allies, even she doesn't realize. People who wanted her kept from this life. Even they are not powerful enough to change who Alex Toles is. I'll be in touch."

***

Cassidy sat with the morning paper, shaking her head. "I guess I shouldn't be surprised."

Alex was leaning against the counter sipping her coffee. "I'd like to…" The teacher laughed. "I have to say, Cass, you seem to be handling this pretty well."

The teacher set the newspaper on the table and smiled. "Alex, in the last month I have seen my ex-husband at death's door, been held hostage by a sadistic freak, left my job, moved my entire life, found out my father was an alcoholic….told the truth about a secret I thought I would have to keep forever. Not to mention seeing the father of my son murdered, facing the possibility of losing the person I love more than my own life… and getting engaged." Alex couldn't help but laugh. Hearing Cassidy rattle off the events in their lives like a laundry list made them sound completely absurd. "I don't think there is much Christopher could say or do that could possibly surprise me. None of it is true. He should have been a movie producer with the plots he devises in his head."

Alex crossed the room and took a seat next to the teacher. "One part of it is true, Cassidy."

Cassidy raised her brow and waited for the agent to continue. "Jackson and I, well…when we were at the academy. It didn't last long. We were kids away from…"

"I see," the teacher smiled.

"I hope you're not…"

"Alex, I would hope that neither of us would be threatened by the other's past. Why didn't you tell me last night?" Alex shrugged. "Because he was a man?"

"R.J. was the only…"

"It must have been hard, Alex…I mean, losing him."

Alex's eyes scanned the floor at her feet. "He was one of my best friends, Cassidy. I didn't think anyone knew. I mean that we ever actually," she sighed. "I felt so lost after that day. Sabeen was dead, R.J." She lifted her eyes to the teacher. "He would have loved you."

Cassidy smiled and kissed Alex's cheek. "So, what do we do?"

"Nothing we can do. Though I wish you hadn't stopped me last week when…"

Cassidy laughed. "Is this going to hurt you? I mean at work?"

Alex shook her head. "No. I think it was devised to hurt you."

"I guess it was."

"Are you going to…"

"I am going to make us all breakfast and then you are going to spend the afternoon with Jane while the girls and I take Dylan to the arcade," Cassidy answered as she made her way to the stove.

"Cass?"

"Yeah?"

Alex slipped in behind the teacher. "Let's do it when we get back from London."

"Do what?" Cassidy asked.

"You know."

Cassidy turned in the agent's arms and looked at her in confusion. "No…what are you…"

"Married, Cassidy. Let's get married when we get back."

"You're serious."

Alex nodded. "We can make the plans while we are away this weekend." Cassidy's face contorted slightly. "What?" the agent asked. "I mean, if you don't…"

"Is that really what you want?" Alex smiled. Cassidy returned the expression and kissed the agent. "Okay."

"Okay?" Alex asked hopefully.

"Yeah. Okay."

"Are you sure, Cass…because…"

"I'm sure," she stroked the agent's cheek and turned back to her task. "Now, go pry that son of yours away from his game and save Jane and the girls; will you?"

Alex kissed the top of the teacher's head and bounced off to her assigned task. Cassidy closed her eyes and steadied herself. The congressman's actions, the presence of family, and all of the changes in her life were overwhelming. Almost losing Alex, seeing Dylan with his sisters, it brought reality crashing down on her. She wiped a tear from the corner of her eye and looked out the kitchen window. How was it possible she wondered, that amid so much turmoil she was happier than she ever dreamed possible, and all at once more frightened than she had ever experienced? One thing was clear to her now; life was unpredictable. She was not going to waste one moment of it, not ever again.

***

"Alex, I know what you think," Jane said.

"Jane, he was CIA. How could you not know that?"

The older woman sat silently for a moment contemplating her answer. "I did know."

"Why didn't you tell me when…."

"Oh, Alex," Jane rose from her seat and crossed the room. She stood still for a moment and then turned back to the agent. "Let's take a walk."

"Why?"

Jane looked at Alex and her jaw tightened. "It's a beautiful day, Alex. Let's get some air."

The pair headed out the back door and walked slowly toward the stream. "You think someone is listening? In the house?" Alex asked.

"No," Jane said plainly. "But I think the Secret Service is right out front."

"How long will they stay on full detail?"

"A year, supposedly."

"So…" Alex continued.

Jane let out a heavy breath. "I've always known, Alex… because I am CIA."

Alex stopped abruptly. "What?"

The former first lady laughed. "That is really so surprising?"

"Did he know?" Jane shook her head 'no'. "Jesus Christ. What else don't I know?"

"Alex, the agency is a strange place. It's something we were all born into. We did not all take the same path, however. Even the admiral doesn't know about my placement. That came at my father's reluctant hand."

"So, that's how you know about The Collaborative."

"After you came back from Iraq, John….he was different. I told you that. Things he would say in his sleep. The pieces, well…it was clear that whatever happened there, it filtered from a different source. Matt suspected Admiral Brackett. There are two, Alex; two very different agendas within the intelligence community. Which has the upper hand at any given time dictates many things. The Collaborative is the," she slowed her pace slightly. "It's the business of intelligence, Alex. The money machine. It operates outside presidential findings and legislative oversight."

"The objective?" Alex asked.

"Some would say money. Others would say the national interest. Depends, I suppose, on whom you are asking."

"And you?"

"Me? I thought I left it all behind when I married John. I was low level. Information was my job when I was in film. Collecting it from sources that financed much of the propaganda in the industry. I never expected to return to my roots."

"So why?"

"I guess it's just what I know. I couldn't sit idle while I watched him struggle. I knew he was…he was acting against his own best interest for a long time; walking a tightrope. I could see it. I loved him, Alex, as much as he loved you. I hoped… well, obviously what I had hoped never came to pass."

"How much do you know?"

"Not much. They are cautious and they are connected. My involvement is not so well understood. I simply pass information to the real powers, to Matt, now to Jon. I do know that John was a man of integrity. That, is about the only thing I am sure of anymore."

"SPHINX?" Alex looked to her friend.

Jane sighed. "Only a little bit. You are right, arms trading, drug trafficking….it raised capital."

"For?"

"For more operations."

"Outside of federal funding."

"Correct," Jane confirmed.

"To what end?" Alex asked.

"National security. At least that is the answer you will get."

"How do we stop it?"

Jane stopped again. "Alex, I wish you would let this go. Walk away while you can. Go back to the FBI."

"I can't do that."

The former first lady had expected that response. "I know. But, if you go any deeper, you will have passed the turning back point."

"I already have. Cassidy and Dylan are already at risk. I can't ignore that. What makes you think my walking away would be safer for them?"

"I'm not certain it would be. I just want you to know. What you are uncovering…what you are seeking to do…others have been at this for years, John included. Look at…"

Alex nodded. "What do I leave them, Jane? What does it say about me if I turn the other way?"

"It's a commitment, Alex."

"Commitment doesn't scare me, Jane."

"You can't tell Cassidy everything. It will put her at greater risk."

"No."

"Alex…"

"Jane…It's not up for discussion. I will be cautious. I won't lie to Cassidy. There is no greater commitment for me than to her."

The older woman nodded her understanding. "If you are serious, Alex, you will need to go in as…"

"I understand, part of The Collaborative." Jane nodded. "Call Krause."

Jane closed her eyes. "I wish you would reconsider."

"I wish I could."

***

Chapter Twenty-Five

Wednesday, May 14th

The doorbell interrupted Cassidy's task of packing for the coming trip. She was looking forward to a short getaway with Alex, even if it did entail a stuffy political dinner. She set aside the dress in her hands and headed for the door. She couldn't help silently musing about all the years traveling, attending social functions, meeting foreign dignitaries and world leaders. Most people would find that exciting and intriguing. For a while it had been. She smiled inwardly as she admitted to herself that watching Alex and Dylan engaged in some silly video game was far more exciting and intriguing to her than any trip she had ever taken with the congressman. She shook her head slightly at the amusing thought and opened the door.

"Cassidy..."

Cassidy had to squint in order to process the sight in front of her. "Cheryl?"

"I...I needed..." the woman began to stammer.

"Cass?" a voice called entering from the back door. "Where are you?"

"Come in," Cassidy offered, noting the nervousness in the tall blonde woman. "In here!" Cassidy called to the agent.

"Thought you were going to pack," the agent began as she turned the corner into the hallway. Alex stopped short as the strange sight of her lover and the congressman's girlfriend approached. Cassidy lifted her eyes to indicate that she was just as confused. It was clear to both Alex and Cassidy that the normally poised congressman's girlfriend was shaken.

"Let's go into the kitchen." Cassidy led the woman and helped her gently to a chair. "Cheryl? Are you all right?" The woman looked up to Cassidy with regretful eyes. "Alex, can you get some water?" The agent swiftly complied with the request and handed a glass to the woman.

"Thanks," she said softly, accepting the drink. Alex gave Cheryl a confused and concerned smile.

"What happened, Cheryl?" Cassidy asked as she pulled a chair to sit across from her.

Cheryl's voice wavered. "I always knew, you know? I mean... what's that they say? Leopards don't change their spots; right?" Cassidy inhaled a deep breath and released it. No, they didn't. She could imagine now what might have led the woman to this visit. "I thought that is where he was going....you know? To meet her...somewhere."

"Cheryl," Cassidy began gently. "What happened?"

The woman looked past the teacher and directly at the agent. "I'm sorry." Alex was perplexed. "I can't believe he would go that far." She returned her sight to Cassidy.

"What did Chris do?" Cassidy asked directly, but softly.

"You don't deserve any of this," she said tearfully. "You never did."

"It's okay Cheryl. What happened with Chris?"

"He was with your father," she looked back at the agent. Alex froze as Cassidy's gaze turned squarely to her lover. "I couldn't hear...but this," she pulled a picture from her jacket. "He...." Cassidy looked at the picture and lifted her hand to cover her mouth in disbelief. There was Alex, beautiful and young in her uniform, a handsome young cadet's arm around her. She stood and turned to the agent fully. Alex's jaw was taut to the point that the small veins in her temples has begun to protrude. "I'm sorry," Cheryl repeated.

Alex simply nodded and deliberately began to head for the door. Cassidy patted Cheryl's shoulder as a gesture of comfort and moved to follow the agent. "Alex." Alex was putting on her jacket and had her hand on the front door knob. "Let's just talk about this."

"I have to go."

"Alex..."

"Not now, Cassidy. I have to go."

"Where? Where are you going?" The agent stiffened and began opening the door.

"Alex, we are leaving at six tomorrow."

"I'll be back."

Cassidy reached for the agent's arm and was surprised when she felt Alex's body tighten further in its resolve. "Please...at least let me..."

"Cassidy, not now. I'll be back." With those words the agent was gone.

***

"Ian, are you sure?"

The MI6 agent smiled. "It's there, Jon, at the embassy."

"Matthews?"

"I don't know...wildcard. That's why he's there, though. To retrieve it."

Krause wanted as much information as possible. "Does he know what is on the disk?" Ian Mitchell shrugged. "And Ambassador Daniels?"

"Daniels is the admiral's footman."

Krause bit his lip slightly and padded across the floor to the mini bar in is room. He retrieved a small bottle of scotch and poured two glasses. "So, Daniels has the disk," he surmised his understanding as he handed his friend a glass. Mitchell nodded. "Any idea where?"

"Best guess?"

Krause took a seat and waited for his friend to continue. Mitchell swirled the scotch in his glass and narrowed his gaze. "It will be on his person." Krause scratched his brow. "Problematic. I know," Ian Mitchell admitted.

"Yes, but hardly impossible."

The MI6 agent laughed. "No offense, Jon, I think the ambassador might be suspicious if you moved too close. And just how do you plan on engineering an invitation?"

Krause smiled and traced the rim of his glass with his finger. "I will be accompanying an old friend."

"You're escorting Jane? Is that really wise? I mean…"

"Our friendship is not such a secret in these circles. It creates the opportunity."

"Perhaps, but you still have to get the disk from him. You may be good Jon; Paul Daniels is hardly a novice."

"You worry too much, Ian."

"Maybe…it's a huge risk to do it there."

"No. It is a huge challenge that provides the perfect cover," Krause smiled. He missed these missions. For many years now he had been mainly a broker. He had come to believe that his days of penetrating difficult situations and attaining information without detection were a thing of the past. He had become a businessman of sorts. This mission is what men like Jonathan Krause trained for and lived for; purpose, adventure, excitement, even danger. The fact was that he had an asset he was now eager to employ. "I'm confident we'll be able to make the exchange."

"We? You know I…"

"Ian, you just be ready when I call. I have the disk covered. You worry about those banking transactions."

"What about Matthews?"

"We'll see where his alliances are," Krause said as he finished his scotch. "I'll be in touch, Ian. Just be ready when I call," he repeated.

***

Helen Toles opened the front door and gasped at the expression on her daughter's face. "Alexis?" Alex remained stoic and pushed gently past her mother. "Alexis…"

"Where is he?"

"Who?"

"Where is he?" Alex repeated sternly.

"Your father?" Alex's expression remained painfully grim. "He's in his office." Alex began making her way down the hallway. "Alexis…." Before the older woman could finish Alex had opened the door to her father's private sanctuary.

"Alexis?" he asked in surprise. Alex just tipped her head. "To what do I owe the honor of your visit?" he inquired smugly. Alex shook her head in disgust but still had not managed to speak. "Is this about you and your friend? I told your mother…"

The agent burst out in a sarcastic laugh. "My friend?" She rolled her eyes and bit her lip. "I'm not sure who you mean. No. This is about *your* friend."

"My friend?"

Alex stared at her father harshly. "I almost can accept that you would hate me that much. But, Cassidy; why on earth would you want to hurt her?"

"I have no idea what you are talking about, Alexis."

"Really? I wondered….how it would be that anyone could possibly know about R.J. and me. No one really *knew*. Well, except the person who happened to discover us; once." She paused and watched as her father pushed back a little in his chair. "But, really? You would go to that weasel? What did you think? That it would push Cassidy away?"

"You wouldn't understand," he said pointedly.

"Explain it to me."

"He has a right, Alexis…to be worried about his son." Alex sighed in disbelief. "As I said, you wouldn't understand."

"Christopher O'Brien isn't worried about Dylan or his happiness. He's worried about himself. What *he* wants. Sound familiar to you?"

"You couldn't understand, Alexis; what a parent sometimes has to do. You never cared about your family." Alex shook her head. "I did what I thought was best; for everyone. The truth…"

"Don't you dare talk to me about *truth*. I don't even know who you are."

Nicolaus Toles stared at the woman before him. There was a resolve and a sense of strength in Alexis Toles' posture that he had never noticed. "He is the boy's father, Alexis. You have no right to barge in here and…"

Alex took a deep breath and let it out slowly. "Let me say this so that you understand me….clearly." She walked to the front of his desk and placed her hands squarely on it. "I am going to marry Cassidy. That makes Dylan *my* son. After everything… everything I know, everything your *friend* the congressman has put him through," she stopped and glared at the man across the desk. He was a stranger. She took in another deep breath and shook her head. "Dylan is *my* son. Do you understand me? Not because I gave birth to him, because I would give my life for his happiness. Christopher O'Brien is no more his father than you will ever be mine." She pushed her weight off of his desk and turned to leave. Helen Toles stood in the doorway, her mouth agape. Alex spun on her heels. "You are right about one thing," she admitted. He looked up to her and she nodded. "I never cared much about family." Her father began to let the hint of a smile show when she suddenly continued. "I never knew what it meant to have one until I met Cass." He stared at her. Alex felt a wave of revulsion course through her. "Cassidy and Dylan are *my* family. So, I do understand what a parent will do." She looked briefly at her mother and closed her eyes to gather the rest of her strength before turning back to the stranger across the room. "Anything. You should know; I would do no less for my children, or my wife. I guess we have very different ideas about what that means." She placed her hand on her mother's shoulder and shook her head sadly. "Goodbye, Nicolaus," she said as she left the room.

Helen Toles watched her daughter as she swiftly left the house, never allowing her confident posture to falter. "What have you done?" she asked her husband.

"I did what I had to do," he said without remorse.

Tears had begun to stream down the older woman's face. "She is your daughter," she said achingly.

"No," the answer came. "She is yours."

***

"Yeah. She just pulled in….Are you all right?" Cassidy closed her eyes and sighed. "Why don't you come here...No, my mother will be here. Come and stay with her and Dylan......I know.....I will. I promise. Just think about it." Cassidy placed the phone slowly on the night stand and headed down the stairs. Alex was just walking into the kitchen from the garage as she entered the room. "Hey."

The agent stopped her pace and closed her eyes. "I'm sorry I left like that."

Cassidy deliberately made her way to Alex and gently took the agent's face in her hands. "No. I'm sorry." Alex nodded and kept her eyes closed. "Alex…"

Alex opened her eyes and kissed Cassidy's forehead. "I'm okay." Cassidy looked at the agent skeptically and Alex laughed. "I swear, I am okay." She began to make her way toward the table. "I am a little worried about my mother."

"Yeah, so am I," Cassidy said as she began heating a kettle of water. "I think she is more worried about you though." Alex looked at Cassidy quizzically. "She called me right after you left there." Alex put her face in her hands. "She was….well, Alex…she was a mess. I promised I would call her when you got home." Cassidy made her way to the agent and sighed heavily. "I just called her when I heard the car."

"Probably crazy, right?" Alex began.

"What's that?"

"I don't love the idea of her there with *him*."

"Well...about that." Alex looked up at her lover. "I suggested maybe she come stay here; at least while we are away." Alex didn't respond. "Alex? I hope that's okay. I just..."

"What did she say?"

"She said she would think about it." Alex nodded and sighed again. "Do you want to talk about it?"

"No. Not really. What is there to say?" Alex hung her head. "Probably a lot."

"He said I never cared about family." Cassidy clenched her jaw. "He was right. I didn't. Not until I met you." The teacher smiled. "I am sorry, Cassidy."

"You have nothing to be sorry for, Alex." The kettle began to whistle and Cassidy made her way back across the kitchen.

"Cass...There's....well, there's some things I need to tell you, before we leave. I...I don't know if it will change....what I mean is...you might...." Cassidy lifted a large manila envelope from the far side of the counter. She picked up the mug of tea and handed both to the agent. "What is this?" Alex asked.

"Stephanie dropped that by on her way back to school. Said it was for you from Jane." Alex's gaze narrowed. "I suspect that has something to do with your rambling," Cassidy raised an eyebrow.

"I don't want to keep secrets from you...I don't want you to ever feel you can't trust me and..."

Cassidy raised her hand and knelt in front of the agent. "Your mother told me that she never had been more proud of you." Alex swallowed hard. "That you...you were so confident even though she knew your heart was breaking." Alex fought back the tears that were beginning to well in her eyes. "She said....she said that if anyone understood family, if anyone loved their family...well, she wanted me to know it was you."

"Cass...there are things..."

Again Cassidy raised her hand to stop the agent. "I do trust you, Alex. Whatever it is, whatever you need to do," she hesitated. "I can't promise you that I will never be afraid."

"I know."

"I can promise you that there is no one else for me. This is it, wherever it leads. This is it. This is my family too. You are my..." The teacher's declaration was cut short by a gentle kiss. Cassidy wiped away a stray tear from the agent's cheek.

"You know, Cassidy....everything, all of it; it is about our family...it's..."

"I know." Alex nodded and pulled Cassidy to her. "You are not getting out of that vanilla cake that easily, Alfred."

Alex laughed. "No?"

"Nope. You are stuck with me and doomed for vanilla cake."

"I like everything you make."

"I told you, I am not baking it," Cassidy quipped. "You're the butler."

"Yeah without any culinary skills." Cassidy laughed. "When we get back," Alex said.

"Yes."

"Where?" Alex asked curiously.

"Actually, I was thinking maybe Nick's restaurant."

Alex's eyes twinkled. "Really?" Cassidy nodded. "Any particular reason why?"

"Yes."

"Care to share?" Alex asked, sporting a broad smile of anticipation.

"Well," Cassidy began looking deeply into Alex's eyes. "That's where I fell in love."

"Is that so?"

"It is. There was this beautiful woman. The firelight seemed to dance in her eyes. I remember that I couldn't seem to breathe."

Alex tucked Cassidy's hair behind her ears and smiled. "Lucky woman."

"Yes, I am."

"No...Cassidy, you really do have that backwards." Alex kissed the woman in her arms.

"I think we should get some sleep," Cassidy offered as she made her way to her feet.

Alex took the hand stretched out to her and pulled Cassidy back. "Thank you."

"For?" Cassidy asked. The agent was ready to make a playful remark but the gravity of the day seemed to suddenly hit her and she stopped. Cassidy noted the change of expression. "Alex?"

"For my family."

Cassidy nodded her understanding and kissed the agent's cheek. "You know, Agent Toles," she said as she led the woman up the stairs. "I really do think you have that backwards."

***

Chapter Twenty-Six

Thursday, May 15th

"**J**ane..."

"Jon, listen to me. She is in." Krause smiled. He had little doubt that Alex Toles would feel the need to immerse herself in the task of infiltrating The Collaborative. He also knew that there were things he needed to disclose to the agent. He sensed her apprehension regarding his motives. It was an odd reality that the world of espionage by its nature incited suspicion and at the same time mandated trust between partners. Alex Toles would soon become his unlikely partner. They shared many things in common. This he understood as well. Intellect, a call toward service, and a need for challenge both physically and mentally were attributes that made them both ideal candidates for the work that lay ahead. Moreover, their hearts, while not cold, were not easily commanded by another. His eyes flickered in amusement as their common realities passed through his mind. "Jon?" Jane called to him.

Krause mentally slapped himself for allowing his musings to wander so far. "I understand."

Jane's eyes narrowed. She crossed the room and retrieved an envelope, placing it in his hands. "What is this?" he asked.

She shrugged. "I don't know. Matt gave it to me. He also gave me one for Alex. I had Stephanie drop Alex's off on her way back to school." The CIA agent opened the envelope and studied its contents without expression. "Well?" Jane urged.

He replaced the paper into its shelter and looked at her. "I need to see Toles."

"Well, you will at the…"

"No. I need to see her before the dinner."

"Jon?" Jane inquired, concern coloring her voice.

"Trust is imperative, Jane."

"I do trust you."

"Yes, *you* do, but that is not enough, so does Agent Toles. She is not…" He placed the envelope on a table and considered how to proceed. "Daniels," he paused and took a breath. "We need to retrieve something form him." Jane studied him closely as he continued. "There is something else. Matt thinks there is more information there. Maybe on Daniels' computer."

Jane understood the implication. "You are not going to tell me; are you?" Krause's expression remained resolved and unchanged. "I see," she continued. "Daniels is not a diplomat. That I know. What about Russ?"

Krause allowed a slight sigh to escape his lips. "There are things that are best kept in a very tight circle, Jane. Especially now with what we," he stopped momentarily. "I don't know what Ambassador Matthews knows and what he doesn't. He is no diplomat. No more than John was a politician. We all take our orders from someone. What Matthews' agenda is, what his role is; who his directives come from; I don't have that answer. That is where Alex comes in. No matter, we have a mission and that just got a bit more complicated."

"Is this what John was…"

The handsome agent took hold of both of his friend's arms. "John did what he felt he had to do. It was never about any one exchange, Jane. You know that. I need you to do two things for me." She tugged at her lip with her teeth and waited for his request. "I need you to take something to Alex and I need you to get her to your room tomorrow before the dinner."

"Jon…"

Jon Krause broke into a smile. "You can't protect her from this. Not this. You know as well as I do this is part of who she is."

Jane knew he was right but she wished that Alex would turn away. That had never been Alex's nature, not from the moment the former first lady met the young Army lieutenant. Alex had a fierce determination and loyalty, but also an insatiable curiosity that drove her. She thrived on challenge. It seemed some people were built for this life. Unlike her husband, Alex was one of them. John Merrow was as capable as any man either she or Jon Krause had ever met, but the life he had led was never his calling. President Merrow would have preferred a life flying through the clouds and imagining distant places. Alex Toles was different. She shared the former president's deep compassion, but she possessed a need to search and a need to understand her world that Jane Merrow had seen present in men like the one standing before her. "I know. It's just…"

"If anyone can survive this business, Jane, trust me it is Alex Toles."

The woman laughed lightly and allowed her head to rest against her friend's chest. "I'll make the calls."

***

"You want me to go where?" Claire Brackett asked for confirmation.

"This is not a request, Claire."

"Forgive me, I thought you were less than pleased with my interactions with Dimitri."

The admiral nodded. "You miss the point. You called yourself a cobra. Did you read the story I told you to?" His daughter rolled her eyes. "That's what I thought. The mongoose kills the cobra, Claire. It looks like a cuddly little creature, but when it strikes it strikes without warning and it is lethal. *I* need you in Moscow. This is my directive, not Dimitri's or his uncle's. And, perhaps, just perhaps, sending you will quiet Viktor's need to call in whatever *favor* you owe him now."

Claire Brackett avoided her father's gaze. "What is it you need?"

"I need you to ensure the delivery of a package."

"Call Fed Ex," she mocked.

"You are not as witty or amusing as you think, Claire."

"Fine. What is it?"

Her father just smiled. "The contents are not of importance to you. Just get it into Dimitri's hands. He has a meeting with Colonel Hadad on Wednesday. We are already overdue. Ambassador Matthews will have the package. All you need to do is retrieve it from him in London on Sunday and deliver it to Dimitri in Moscow on Monday. He will, in turn give you a package to deliver to Ambassador Daniels before returning home. That is it."

"And, how exactly will that cancel my debt?"

"It may not. It does put you back in play on *my* terms. It does put you in the middle of a sensitive exchange. Tensions are high. This has been shelved too long and our assets are beginning to grow restless."

"Worried?" she sneered.

"Let's just say I am aware of the consequences should this go awry."

"And?"

"And even you don't want to imagine what those might be. Trust me," he assured her.

She stood and straightened her posture. "Whatever you need, Daddy," she soothed sarcastically as she made her way to the door.

"And, Claire?" She turned with her hand on the door. "Distance yourself from the good congressman." She smirked. "I'm giving you fair warning. He is not the belle of this ball anymore." She nodded her understanding but her dismissal of her father's stern caution was evident.

"Don't screw this up," he muttered as he watched her leave.

***

Friday, May 16th

"Alex, I'm sorry to disturb you."

Alex stretched out on the bed and looked at the clock, 3:30 a.m. "Who is it?" Cassidy grumbled, pulling her pillow a little closer.

The agent kissed her head. "Go back to sleep," she whispered to an already complaint school teacher. "What is it Fallon?"

"Shit, I'm sorry. It's only like 3:30 there, huh?"

"It's okay Fallon. What is it?"

"Look, I don't know if it is anything. But, well…"

"Fallon, out with it already."

"Did you know Tate originally worked for the Department of Treasury?" Alex considered the statement silently. "Did you hear me?"

"Yeah. Secret Service?"

"Says Intelligence Research."

"When?"

"2002 until 2006."

"He worked for FinCEN," Alex surmised.

"What?" Fallon asked for clarification.

"FinCEN. Surprised you never crossed paths with them during your money laundering investigations. Financial Crimes Enforcement Network. Patriot act baby. What about before 2002?"

"Captain, NYPD 1996-2001."

"Interesting."

"Sounds typical," Fallon assessed.

"It does. I wonder, though. What did A.D. Tate do when he left the NYPD until he began with FinCEN?"

Fallon could hear the wheels spinning in his partner's brain. "And?"

"And, I wonder what the good captain did before he became the good captain."

"That's easy. Right here. Lieutenant, 1992-1996. Detective, 1990-1992…"

"Well, I think it might be worth a call. Why don't you call our good friend Detective Ferro? See if he recalls anything about Joshua Tate."

"I mentioned Tate during the Fisher investigation. He never said a word."

"Just check it out," Alex urged him.

"What are you thinking?"

"I'm not really. FinCEN deals extensively with international money laundering. You have to admit. It is interesting."

Fallon laughed. "Yeah, I guess it is. So, uh…set a date yet?"

"Fallon it's 3:30 a.m. and I am in London."

He laughed harder. "Didn't answer my question."

"Don't worry, you'll be on the invitation list." Alex glanced over and caught Cassidy mumbling in her sleep. "I have to go. Call Ferro. See if he can dig a little….and Fallon, just don't schedule anything for the 31st. Tell Kate, she'll remember."

"Why?" Alex started laughing. "That's like two weeks away."

"Can't fool you," Alex poked. "Gotta go. Call you when I get back Monday…and Fallon?"

"Yeah?"

"Nobody knows yet, except Rose…so just…"

"I got it."

Alex hung up her call and crawled back in bed beside Cassidy. In a few hours she would be making her way to Jane's room, though she was certain it was to meet with someone else. She sighed. The envelope Cassidy had handed her didn't tell a full story. It certainly shed a good deal of light on the enormity of what she was entering into. It mapped out a small framework of known entities; businesses, intelligence person-nel, politicians and freelancers that were tied to the known sale of technology, secrets and even drugs. She couldn't imagine how on earth Jon Krause planned to immerse her in this in any believable way, but that was the least of her concern at this moment. She brushed Cassidy's hair aside and snuggled against her with a deep sigh. "I swear," she whispered softly. "I will keep you both safe, no matter what I have to do."

"I know you will," a scratchy voice answered. "Just keep yourself safe too."

Alex couldn't help but smile as she felt the body next to her wiggle closer. Cassidy surprised her in the simplest of moments. "I will."

"I'll hold you to that," Cassidy answered before drifting back to sleep in the agent's arms.

***

"Agent Toles."

"Agent Krause."

"You ready for this?"

"I'm not sure I know what *this* is yet."

Krause nodded and smiled. "You looked at the files." Alex lifted her eyebrow. "So you know Daniels is a player."

"Yeah, apparently."

"Look, Agent Toles....Daniels is set to give Matthews a disk tonight. That's not its final destination. It's marked to be delivered to Moscow where it will pass to an SVR agent who will take it to Bucharest. There he will receive a drive with appropriate bank routing numbers."

"Okay. What is he delivering?" Alex watched Krause carefully. He was difficult to read, but she sensed his hesitancy. "What is he delivering, Krause?"

"Schematics. Locations and schematics."

"For?"

"The placement and use of organophosphorus materials."

Alex pinched the bridge of her nose. "Chemical weapons?" Immediately her thoughts were flooded to an investigation she had been tasked with some years ago. The trail of funds led her to a Somalian fringe group that had gassed its own people. She straightened her posture and pressed down her emotions. Looking at the man before her it was obvious there was more. "What else?"

"Toles." Alex challenged the CIA agent with her eyes. "Protocols," he stopped momentarily and moved to begin a steady pace across the room. "Scientific protocols. I would call them instructions rather than experiments."

Alex was beginning to understand. "You are telling me this disk is a roadmap to some type of biological weapon. Is that right?"

"Yes."

"Who is the buyer?"

"I don't know specifically. It isn't my operation, Toles. That's not how it works. I only know it has been delayed multiple times. It won't be delayed again. I know it is a Yemeni interest."

Alex regarded the man silently for a moment. "Is this what he was trying to prevent?"

"I think so, yes. Though it is obvious he was working things for some time."

"So you want the disk…"

"I want to swap the disk."

"And Matthews?" Alex asked.

"I don't know what he knows. Whatever you can surmise will be a bonus. It doesn't change the objective." He pulled a small disk from his shirt pocket. "This is convincing. Trust me. It will take them some time to realize it's a fake. Daniels will have the disk on him. At least that's what I am given to understand. So, we either switch it on Daniels or we switch it on Matthews. That means we need to get close. Very close."

"Okay. I have some ideas on that front. It is a party after all," Alex smiled. Krause raised an eyebrow. "Daniels is an old friend. I'm discovering a lot about my *friends* these days it seems."

"Well, there's more."

"What?" she asked pointedly.

He handed her a piece of paper and watched her study it without notable expression. "Matt sent that. He has reason to believe there are accounting files here on Daniels' computer."

Alex pressed on her right temple with her thumb. "Do you know where it is? This computer."

Krause got a slight gleam in his eye. "I do."

"And, if one of us were to find this computer; how would we access these files?" He handed her a hotel key card. Alex looked up at him in moderate disbelief. "And this is?"

"Magnetic strip side down on the computer. It will decode the passwords and give access."

"And then?" He handed her a small travel drive and shrugged. Alex couldn't help but chuckle. "You're not kidding." He offered her a sideways glance. "Ideas?"

Krause smiled. "A few."

"Care to compare?" she asked, surprised to find the intrigue of the situation almost as alluring as she found the realities of failure incomprehensible.

Krause smiled. "You are going to have to trust me, Agent."

"You're going to have to earn that, *Pip*."

***

Alex headed straight for the shower when she returned from her meeting with Jon Krause. She'd seen many things in her years of investigative work from the carnage inflicted by terrorists to the sadistic gore of more than a couple of serial killers' handiwork. This was an entirely new world and yet one that felt oddly familiar. She let the water flow over her, attempting to somehow wash away her doubt, and even dampen the tinge of excitement that seemed to be pulsing within her. For many years she had been bound to policy and procedure that she so often found was prohibitive in achieving results. She turned her face upward to the water and stretched. As much as it frustrated her, she understood that there was a need for policy and procedure, checks and balances. She suspected many of the people she was about to encounter had somehow lost sight of that. That was something she never intended to do. She laughed softly as a sudden memory of Dylan passed through her mind. She had something men like Jon Krause did not. She had a reason for her endeavors beyond curiosity, adventure or even duty. She had a family.

The agent continued her routine, drying her hair roughly with the towel before deciding that this might be an occasion to take some time on her appearance. She smirked realizing that Cassidy had never seen her quite as she would this evening. She hadn't shown Cassidy her gown and she wondered what her lover might think. Her cheeks flushed slightly, partly from embarrassment and partly from anticipation of the entire evening.

Cassidy heard the blow drier and turned curiously toward the bathroom door. It was a rarity to say the least. Not that Alex was carefree about her appearance. She normally pulled her hair back and out of the way. It was something she had to do as a runner and in the military and she told Cassidy it just stuck. Cassidy asked her once why she didn't just cut it shorter and Alex just shrugged. "I like it long." The teacher turned back to her own task with a smile.

Alex stepped out of the bathroom and caught sight of her lover across the room. The agent had seen plenty of pictures of Cassidy at events like this evening's, but none did the sight before her justice. Cassidy turned and immediately captured the agent's stare. Alex was certain the lump in her throat would choke her. Cassidy was in a fitted, deep red evening gown. Her hair was lifted in a swirl and soft tendrils hung to each side. She stood at least an inch and a half taller than usual and the simple pearl necklace she wore highlighted the top of her cleavage. "My God," was all Alex managed.

Cassidy smiled softly. Then she allowed her own eyes to fall over the agent. Alex was, as Cassidy often mused, riveting. That was the only word she could find to describe Alex Toles. The agent could be wearing her uniform, a suit, or a pair of sweat pants and Cassidy found herself riveted. Each represented a different side of the complex woman she loved and Cassidy cherished every part of Alex. Slowly, she crossed the room and lifted her hand to Alex's cheek. "You are beautiful, Alex."

The agent could feel the heat rising between them. Alex's hair cascaded over her bare shoulders freely. Her black gown nearly touched the floor, but the long, narrow slits that ran up each side gave an enticing view of the agent's long legs. Cassidy caressed the agent's shoulder and she felt her hands unconsciously begin to glide along Alex's long frame. The agent closed her eyes and tugged at her bottom lip. She sensed, more than felt Cassidy reaching for her and slowly responded with a soft kiss that quickly deepened. Cassidy broke away and caught her breath with a desperate giggle. "I am going to go get those earrings on now."

"Uh huh," Alex choked slightly.

"Did you see Jane?" Cassidy asked, her back turned again in an attempt to regain control.

Alex came up behind her and nuzzled her neck. "Cass?"

"Yes?"

"Do you know how beautiful you are?"

Cassidy moaned softly, "Alex...."

"I know," Alex sighed. "But this is to be continued."

The teacher turned and smiled. "You like this better than that denim shirt, huh?" she raised her eyebrow playfully, knowing that a shift in their mood was needed. Cassidy had no real desire for anything but Alex at the moment and she suspected her fiancé felt the same way.

Alex shook her head. "No."

"Really?"

"But, I would love to see you in that little apron you have that..."

"Alex Toles!" Cassidy scolded with a beaming smile. "What has gotten into you?"

"Nothing," Alex said innocently. "But, I was thinking…"

Cassidy burst out laughing. "You are impossible."

"Yeah, well. I would really rather just stay here." It was true. Alex had to admit, nothing in her world could ever fill her the way the woman who now stepped into her arms could.

"I'll take that as a compliment."

"You should," Alex said offering her lover another kiss. "You just remember when those drunken diplomats start trying to woo you away…."

"*Woo* me away?" Cassidy bit back a laugh, realizing that there was actually a tinge of apprehension in the agent's voice.

"What's so funny?"

"Alex, you are so silly sometimes. Only one person has ever *wooed* me at all."

"Yeah, who is he so I can set him straight?"

"Just some crusty old butler."

"Hmmm….can he cook?" Cassidy shook her head. "Is he a rich butler?" Cassidy shook her head again. "So my competition is a…."

The agent was hushed immediately with a kiss. "I love you, Alfred."

Alex smiled. "You ready?" Cassidy nodded.

"Alex?"

"Yeah?"

"Remember, to be continued."

Alex shut the door behind them and tried unsuccessfully to hide her grin. She had several missions to complete and she was suddenly extremely eager to move the evening along so she could get to the most important one of all. The one that she expected would take much longer and offer far greater reward than any file retrieval or diplomatic ball ever had.

***

Chapter Twenty-Seven

"Ambassador," Alex greeted her old friend.
Ambassador Paul Daniels stood a solid 6'3. He possessed a charming smile and piercing blue eyes that immediately engaged even his greatest critics. Alex often likened him to a storybook knight in shining armor. He was as charismatic as he was good-looking. She pondered the notion that she might be standing in front of a real life James Bond. He narrowed his gaze playfully at the agent before quickly relaxing his expression and taking her into a hug. "Captain Alexis Toles, quit the formalities," he laughed.

"It's good to see you Paul," she smiled. Inside her stomach was in knots. She had always regarded Paul Daniels as a friend. He was a man she had known for years, but now she found herself wondering; had she really known anyone? She clasped Cassidy's hand a bit tighter as reality passed through her thoughts. "Paul, this is…"

"Cassidy. So nice to meet you," he took her hand and kissed it.

"They certainly have taught you manners here," Alex chided.

The ambassador laughed. "You'd better keep an eye on this one, Cassidy. She is quite the handful."

"Yes, she is," Cassidy smiled.

Alex shook her head. "Alright, I see where this is going. Has Jane arrived yet?"

"Just before you actually," he responded. "I was surprised to see her escort."

"Well, they have known each other for years, Paul."

"Yes, so I have heard. You don't..."

"No business tonight, Ambassador," Alex winked.

"I can't say I blame you," he answered, gazing a little too long at Cassidy for Alex's liking. Just as Alex was about to reassert her presence Jane turned the corner beside Krause.

"Alex," Jane hugged the agent and then followed the same action with Cassidy. "I am so happy you decided to make the trip."

"How could I turn *this* down?" Alex raised an eyebrow, soliciting a hearty laugh from both the ambassador and the former first lady.

"Paul," an attractive brunette grasped the ambassador's arm.

"Ahh...Alex you remember Karen?"

"Certainly," Alex accepted the woman's hand.

"Lovely to see you again, Captain. I almost didn't recognize you out of your uniform."

"Karen Daniels, this is my," Alex paused and looked at Cassidy for a moment who tugged at her bottom lip to suppress her growing smile. "This is my fiancé, Cassidy O'Brien."

The ambassador tipped his head as his wife took Cassidy's hand. "Well, I guess we have plenty to celebrate then. Nice to meet you, Cassidy," she winked.

"Well, what do you say we get these ladies something to drink to celebrate?" Daniels suggested. Krause nodded and began to follow. The ambassador turned when he noticed Alex was not accompanying them. "Captain Toles?"

"What?" Alex shrugged. "I heard you say you were going to get the ladies drinks." Alex looked at herself as if giving an inspection. "Are you saying I don't qualify?" Cassidy shook her head slightly. Alex most certainly did qualify, more than qualify in Cassidy's mind.

"I plead the fifth," the ambassador joked.

Alex gave Cassidy a light peck on the cheek and turned to follow the ambassador and Krause. "Russ here yet?" Alex inquired.

"No, I expect him soon though," Daniels responded.

"So, how are the boys, Paul?" Alex asked as they made their way to the bar.

"Excellent! Jake is playing lacrosse. You wouldn't believe him." Alex smiled and allowed her gaze to drift slightly to their other companion.

"You have two sons, I understand?" Krause joined the conversation.

"Yes, Daniel and Jake. Jake is sixteen this year. Hard to believe. Umm Alex, wine or..."

"White, both Cassidy and I."

Daniels turned to Krause. "Jane will take white as well."

"And you? What is your poison Mr. Krause?" the ambassador inquired.

"Scotch."

"I figured as much," he replied handing each their glasses. "Shall we?"

"The boys are not into these functions I take it?" Alex asked as they rounded the corner. "No, no....you know how kids are."

Alex laughed. "I am learning, yes. Dylan just turned seven. Seeing Alexandra and Stephanie, I can't imagine Dylan when..."

"I understand. It goes so quickly," the ambassador paused for a moment. "I am sorry about the president, Alex. I know you were very close."

"We were," she said softly. Alex scanned the room casually and caught sight of a man approaching. He was precariously juggling several drinks and she smiled inwardly at the opportunity. So far, her plan was lining up just as she had hoped. She looked to Krause briefly as they approached their awaiting group, hoping he would read her signal clearly. In less than an instant Krause had repositioned himself behind the ambassador, pretending to notice someone in the crowd. Alex stepped forward and allowed her heel to extend slightly. With a thud the man flew into Alex, sending both their drinks flying and dousing the ambassador thoroughly in white wine. Alex winced slightly at the contact but then immediately recovered.

The commotion caught the attention of their waiting party. Within seconds Cassidy was at Alex's side having noticed her grimace of pain in the distance. "Are you all right?" Cassidy asked.

"I'm fine, though Paul here seems to be doubling as a wine cask."

"Funny, Captain," he looked at her in mock annoyance. "I need to change this jacket." Alex promptly grabbed the back of it and slipped it from his shoulders. "Thanks," he said.

"Least I can do" she said as she folded it over her arm.

"You want to see the pictures of the boys?" he asked. Alex smiled. "Follow me."

Krause struggled to contain his momentary pride in Alex's flawless execution. He too was slightly wet from the gin and tonic the man had been carrying. "If you'll excuse me, I think I need to clean this up just a bit," he explained.

Alex followed Ambassador Daniels up a winding stair case and into his office. The ambassador made his way to the bathroom at the far left of the room and pointed to his desk. "That's Jake there on the right," he pointed. "I'll be right back."

Alex quickly retrieved the small hotel key card and laid it on the computer as Krause had instructed. "God, Paul, he has to be almost your height already," she said, keeping the conversation normal and light. Krause appeared in the doorway just as Alex was reaching into Daniel's jacket pocket. She nodded affirmatively in his direction and met him at the door, quickly handing him the disk in exchange for the fake.

"Yeah, he is huge, isn't he?" the ambassador answered.

Alex quickly made her way back to the desk and lifted the picture studying it. She let her eyes momentarily drift to the computer that was rolling through a series of screen changes. Looking back at the picture she smiled wondering what Dylan might be like at that age. The last time she had seen Jake Daniels she figured he had been about eight. Just then the ambassador appeared in a clean shirt, attaching his cufflinks. Alex set down the picture as he began to move closer. She grabbed the wet jacket and made her way toward him. The last thing she needed was for him to go anywhere near the computer screen. Now, she simply needed to get him out of the office. The rest would be up to Krause. "You probably should hang that up," she arched her eyebrow at him, handing him the jacket.

"You are learning, there, aren't you Captain?" Alex laughed and headed back toward the desk, hoping that her task had been successful. Seeing the password populate, she retrieved the card, placed it back in her dress and picked up the picture of Jake a final time. Daniels emerged from the bathroom again, placing something in the pocket of his new jacket and regarded his friend holding the picture. "Seems everything has changed for you," he observed.

Alex took a deep breath and set down the picture. "I guess it has. Maybe it's changed for all of us," she offered.

He nodded. "I knew John a long time. He was a good man."

Alex gave her friend a cockeyed smile. "The man I knew was a good man as well."

Daniels put his arm around Alex and led her out of the room. She followed, taking only a brief pause at the top of the stairs to signal Krause that he should proceed.

Alex looked across the large ballroom to see Cassidy engaged in a conversation with Ambassador Matthews as her friend Paul Daniels headed straight for them. For a moment she wondered how they had reached this place, this moment. Cassidy was laughing and Alex felt the gravity of her mission momentarily replaced by a warmth that traveled through her entire body. Even in the distance she could feel Cassidy's presence as it filled the room. "She is very beautiful, Alex," a voice said softly.

Alex closed her eyes and nodded. "Yes, she is," she whispered as Cassidy turned slightly to offer her a loving glance. The agent sighed. "I have to keep her safe, Jane." Jane's only response was a firm but loving grip of Alex's shoulder. With an audible exhale Alex began to slowly and deliberately cross the large room. Now she would need to engage Russ Matthews. She hoped that he would somehow convince her that he was on the right side of things. She shook off the thought, asking herself if she even knew what the right side of things was anymore. Keeping her focus on Cassidy, she mused that if she ever needed a compass for what was right, it was standing just a few feet away.

***

"Well, well, if it isn't the sparrow." Ian Mitchell watched as Claire Brackett entered the hotel. "Now what has Daddy charged you with?" He lifted his phone and placed the call.

"What is it?" Krause answered quietly as he placed the small travel drive into his pocket and turned off the computer. He kept his peripheral vision keenly attuned to his surroundings as he meticulously sifted and replaced papers on the top of Ambassador Paul Daniels' desk.

"Guess who is in London?"

"Sparrow," Krause guessed. He carefully placed the ambassador's chair back in its original position and headed for the door.

"You knew?"

"No, but I expected. Just watch her. This will not be her final destination," he replied. "Wherever she goes, Ian…follow. Just because he sent her doesn't mean she'll follow what he prescribed." Krause made his way to the staircase and scanned the scene unfolding below. Alex was leading Ambassador Matthews toward the small foyer, engaged in conversation. She was a natural. Jane and Cassidy were standing near the middle of the room. Two magnificent women, he thought. He watched as Ambassador Daniels leaned toward Cassidy as if to imbue her with some secret and struggled to contain his laugher. 'Not a chance in hell,' he mused to himself. Deliberately, he made his way to the women. "Sorry about that," he offered as he slipped a hand around Jane's waist.

"So, Mr. Krause," Daniels began, keeping close proximity to Cassidy. "What brings *you* to London?"

Krause answered smoothly. "I had an invitation I couldn't pass up."

"Is that right?"

"Of course."

Daniels studied Krause. He had only crossed paths with the agent a few times in his career. Paul Daniels prided himself on being the consummate spy, the perfect agent, and a master at subterfuge. He could assess a person readily at a distance and within moments determine weakness, strength and concoct the perfect scenario to endear himself. Krause's cool exterior and natural composure matched the ambassador's effortlessly. "I suppose this is boring for you, given your line of work," the ambassador grinned. If he had hoped to provoke Jonathan Krause, he had seriously miscalculated.

"Oh, I don't know, Ambassador. Business and diplomacy are not so different. I would say we share many things in common." Krause smiled and glanced at Cassidy.

"Perhaps," Daniels responded. "Why don't we head toward the dining room? See if we can't find that agent of yours?" he smirked flirtatiously to Cassidy who simply nodded politely.

"What do you think?" Jane whispered to Krause as they followed.

"Smug enough to make a mistake," he answered. Jane smiled. "We'll see what Alex gets from Matthews."

"Did you…"

"We got what we came for. Let's see if we make the bonus round. Sparrow is here," he said softly. Daniels turned to the pair following behind and Krause offered him a steely gaze. 'We'll see,' Krause mused as the ambassador turned his attention back toward Cassidy, 'what you are hiding, Ambassador.'

***

"I thought we were set to meet in Moscow."

"Plans change, Sparrow."

"What is you want Dimitri?"

Dimitri Kargen lifted his finger to his lips and pondered his response. "You will recall that we had an agreement."

"There is no need for pleasantries. What is it you desire?" she asked.

"What is it your father asked of you?"

"I think you know. Simply to deliver a package from the ambassador to you."

"And, does that make sense to you, Claire? Why send Ambassador Matthews here to retrieve the package at all? Why not simply send you in the first place?"

"I am sure he has his reasons."

"Mm. Yes, he does not trust our good ambassador. Perhaps for good reason," Kargen said.

"So? What then?" she walked slowly toward her Russian compatriot.

"I want you to go home. Wait a day and return to the states. I will deal with the ambassador."

Claire Brackett smirked. "My father will not like that."

"You will tell him that I already intervened. That Matthews had already passed the goods to me."

"And what about what you are supposed to give to me?"

Kargen wet his lips. "There is nothing. Daniels has already received those files."

"All right," she answered as she moved closer to him. "Why do I have the feeling there is more that you want, Dimitri?" she asked as she allowed her hand to graze the opening of his shirt. He allowed her hands to roam but made no move to further engage her advances. "Your friend; it is time for him to deliver."

"You mean the congressman," she hummed in his ear as she circled him.

"I do. He will announce his intention to run for your senate."

"And why should you care about the good congressman's political future?"

"I don't. Our contact in the states will assist in the financing of his endeavor," he explained.

"Oh," she let out a seductive laugh. "You're using him as a funnel."

"It's time, Sparrow. Tell the admiral I had already secured the goods from Daniels, and deliver the message to Mr. O'Brien."

"Things for the congressman have been a bit strained. What if he refuses?" she asked.

"That would be unwise."

"And that is all you desire, Dimitri? Like my father, I am your errand girl?"

He snickered. "You are many things, Sparrow. This is not the small errand you suggest. You will have to decide who you wish to serve."

"That's easy," she whispered, moving close enough to his face that their breath began to mingle. "There is only one person worth serving, Dimitri and only one person worthy of trust." His eyes began to flicker with excitement as he allowed her to continue her seduction. "If you care to pay attention," she offered with a bite on his neck. "I will introduce you."

***

"I hope I am not intruding."

"Nonsense," Rose McCollum answered. "Cassidy will be glad to know you took her up on the offer."

"I am not certain how Alexis…"

Rose smiled at Alex's mother. "Alex will be relieved to know that you came." Helen smiled sadly.

"Grandma?" Dylan called as he entered the room.

"Yes, Dylan?"

As Dylan came closer and took notice of Alex's mother his pace quickened. "YaYa! You're here!"

"Well, hello, Dylan," she smiled sweetly.

He walked directly to her and studied her pensively for a moment. "Are you sad, YaYa?"

"Why would you ask that Dylan?" she smiled.

"You look like Alex when she's sad."

For the first time in several days Helen Toles felt genuinely happy. "I am all right. Thank you for worrying." He nodded. "How are you?"

"Okay."

"What is it that you wanted, honey?" Rose asked gently, noting a hint of sadness in his eyes.

"Can we call Mom?"

"Honey, it's late where Mom and Alex are right now. They'll call you when they can. They had a dinner to go to tonight."

Dylan hung his head slightly. Helen watched him closely and her eyes narrowed but her smile grew. "You missing someone a little?" she asked him. He just shrugged. "I see. What if I let you in on a little secret even my daughter doesn't know?" Dylan brightened. She beckoned him closer and whispered in his ear. "I will bet you some chocolate ice cream that I can beat you on that pool table downstairs." His eyes widened in amazement and Helen winked at him, "but it has to be our secret." He nodded enthusiastically. "So, you want to go rack those balls? I'll bet Alexis taught you that."

"Yep. I can do it. Alex usually breaks though."

"Does she? Well, all right then, you go set that table up and I will be down in a few minutes." Dylan nodded and started to run off and stopped suddenly. "What is it?" Helen asked.

"Are you gonna stay here tonight, YaYa?"

"Actually, Dylan I am going to stay the whole weekend if that is okay with you."

"Then I can show you the Batcave," he said excitedly.

"I'd like that," she winked. Dylan nodded and scurried off. "He is quite something," Helen laughed.

Rose beamed. "Yes, he sure is. And he loves Alex."

"I can see that," Helen sighed. "I wish I knew..."

A hand came to rest on Helen's shoulder and Rose gave her an understanding squeeze. "Far be it from me to advise you where Alex is concerned..."

"No...please. She adores you. It's..."

"Helen, the truth is I love Alex as if she were my own. I really do. It's funny. I could see it almost from the moment she arrived. The way she looked at Cassie. The way she could seem to calm Cassie. Dylan, well...they were inseparable almost immediately. I can't imagine this family without her. So much that they have been through in such a short time. I almost can't remember when Alex wasn't here." She chuckled affectionately. "And, I know...I know Alex loves me too, in her own way." Rose watched as Helen nodded knowingly and with evident sorrow. "But, I am not her mother. She only has one mother. Whatever has happened, Helen, well...I can tell you this; she loves you and she needs you. It's a lot of change for all of them."

Helen nodded. "I know."

"What do you say you go show Dylan a thing or two so we can get what I imagine will be an evening full of superheroes over with and move onto a nice glass of wine?"

"Sounds perfect. Rose, thank you for..."

"Don't thank me. Last time I watched Dylan I was plagued by nightmares of being Catwoman. I still haven't recovered."

Helen laughed. "Hence the wine?"

"Exactly," Rose winked. They started toward the stairs when Rose stopped momentarily and grasped Helen's hand. "Remember, this is your family too." Both women smiled. Helen Toles had much to learn about her daughter and her life. She was determined that she would have that chance.

***

"So, Alex, we both know you didn't come all the way to London for dinner."

"No, I didn't."

"Well, what's on your mind?" Ambassador Matthews asked.

"You mentioned ASA at John's funeral."

He took a deep breath and let it our slowly. "Yes, I did."

"What could he be trying to stop, Russ?" she asked somewhat pointedly.

Russ Matthews considered the expression in Alex's eyes. She was guarded, but clearly concerned. He scratched his brow and leaned in closer. "You know. This is not the place, Alex. Not here."

"I don't know."

"Alex, these walls have ears. Do you understand me?"

Alex took a deep breath. "I think I do."

"John had access to a lot of things, Alex...and not just as the president." Alex's expression remained unchanged. "You are not surprised by that. You are here with Krause and Jane. So, there is little I can say that you haven't already surmised."

"There is a lot I don't know, Ambassador," Alex said bluntly.

"There are people that do not see things the way we do."

"And who might the 'we' be in this?" she asked.

"Not here, Alex. Tomorrow, take Cassidy on the tour of The Tower. Break away and meet me at the Salt Tower. 2:00 p.m."

Alex pulled her concentration from him as she saw Paul Daniels approaching beside Cassidy. "I'll expect you have something worth the effort," she said flatly as she flashed a smile at the oncoming pair.

"Some things are as you suspect, Alex. Some may not be." He let a slight laugh escape him and changed the course of the conversation. "Well, if I knew all it took to get you to cross the pond was a fancy dinner, Agent Toles, I would've made the arrangements long ago."

"Something tells me she's not here for our company, Russ," Paul Daniels surmised, giving Cassidy a wink.

"Well, you two certainly aren't as pretty or as interesting." Alex took Cassidy's hand. She leaned into Matthew's ear as she walked away. "I am beyond suspecting. 2:00 p.m."

***

Chapter Twenty-Eight

Alex was grateful that Cassidy had opted for an afternoon of shopping with Jane in lieu of her proposed sightseeing trip. She realized that Cassidy suspected there was an ulterior motive in her proposal for the day. Attempting to fool Cassidy in any way was generally a futile effort. She laughed at the thought as she traversed the South Wall of the Tower of London toward her intended destination. She stopped briefly to regard the iron sculpture guarding the entrance and allowed her thoughts to travel momentarily backward in time. Looking out over the expanse of the tower's property she sighed. Power had always been dressed up as protection. This fortress was as much about power as it ever had been about protecting a nation. Its walls stood tall, for centuries they stood at a staggering height. Even now this place emanated a feeling of power, regardless of the fact that it was dwarfed by the monoliths surrounding it. She took a deep breath and made her way into the building.

There was no one in the small room except a tall figure in a long black trench coat. She chuckled. "Glad you made it," he said. Alex came even with him to look into a mirror. It provided a ghostly illusion of living inside the Salt Tower as a prisoner. "Eerie, isn't it?" he suggested.

"A bit. Why here?"

Russ Matthews turned and looked into Alex's steel blue eyes. Her resolve and her skepticism were equally evident. "Do you know, Alex, what this building was originally called?"

"Did you bring me here for a history lesson, Ambassador?"

He nodded and sighed. "Perhaps a history lesson is called for, Agent. Humor me. This is one of the oldest parts of this fortress. It's stood for nearly eight hundred years. Do you know what it was originally called?" Alex pursed her lips and shook her head. She was already growing tired of her friend's cryptic game. Matthews laughed. "Julius Caesar's Tower." Alex stood stoic. "Aside from the fact that it is generally quiet here this time of day, I thought it a good place to speak; instructive."

"Interesting," Alex said quietly. "While I am fascinated by history I am far more concerned with the future."

"Yes, well, Alex...Most times the answers to the future can be found in the past," he offered as he began to pace the room.

"Perhaps. You are the one that came to me first, Russ. Obviously, something concerned you about John's death, about..."

"A great deal concerns me."

"I'm sure. Being a CIA agent in an embassy must come with a great deal of expectations," she concluded.

He turned slowly. "There are always expectations. The question is whose expectations you choose to meet."

"And whose expectations are you rising to, Ambassador? You didn't travel to London from Moscow just to dine with our friends either."

"No. I suspect that you already know why I am here, or at least you think you know." The ambassador took a deep breath and returned his focus to the mirror. "Can you imagine, Alex, being trapped in here? In this space? Left to ponder your fate without any control?" Alex did not answer his rhetorical diatribe. "When this was built England was Rome. No longer content to simply fortify its defenses. No longer at peace with the idea of prosperity for its people." He turned and faced her. "Caesar had everything a man could ask for. The more he acquired, the more he seemed to require. King, emperor, supreme leader, general, none of it was enough. There was more and more and more until…"

Alex exhaled forcefully. "I understand your point. That does not help me…"

"Alex," he began softly. "Rome is no longer limited to one hemisphere or one continent. Caesar is no longer one man."

"I understand. What does that have to do with John? With you?"

"We are headed for a collapse, Alex. John could see it. I can see it." He stopped for a moment and gathered his thoughts. "We thought we were the walls, Alex. That's what we were told. We were the walls that protected the mighty fortress. We aren't. We might as well be locked in this tower." Matthews stopped again and licked his lips. "This transaction, the reason I am here. It can no longer be prevented. Not, at least, at this juncture. The consequences of interrupting it I fear, would be far greater in scope than the risk of allowing its completion."

Alex bit her lower lip gently. If her efforts with Krause were on target, the transaction that Matthews spoke of now would be interrupted. She considered in her mind what the ambassador might fear more than the technology for biological weapons in unpredictable hands. "What about SPHINX?" she asked.

Matthews sighed and looked back in the mirror. "Ghosts," he whispered to himself.

"Russ? What do you know about SPHINX? If it is still an operation that…"

The ambassador turned on his heels swiftly. "Alex, Sphinx is not an operation."

"What are you talking about? I've read the files. It was the operation that John was charged with in Iraq…that our team…"

Alex watched as he shook his head and interrupted her. "Yes that is all true. But, Alex…Sphinx, Sphinx is a person."

"What are you…."

"No one knows who Sphinx is. Well, no one at my level. Not even John, though I suspect he was close to that discovery."

"You're telling me…"

"This is not simply about selling secrets, Alex. Believe me. The Russians are unpredictable right now. The French are at odds with what our friends here in London and at home propose. John was close, too close."

"Who killed him?" she asked.

"I suggest you speak to Krause about that."

"I will do that. That does not answer my biggest question. Whose expectations are you…"

"Alex, I have reached the point that John reached long ago. The only expectations I can hope to rise to meet are those of my own conscience. I don't expect you to believe me or understand. The answers you seek are found in the past. That I know. If you want to change the course of the future you are going to have to travel places that…"

"That is not very specific."

He laughed. "Alex, no one in this business is ever given specifics. You know that. It's plausible deniability. The only people who know the specifics you speak of are locked in fortresses much like this, nearly impenetrable and obscured from sight."

"Nothing is impenetrable," she said assuredly.

The ambassador offered her a genuine smile. "People did not want you in this game, Alex."

"What people? You mean John?"

"No. I don't. Maybe at one time."

"Who?" Before he could answer she continued, "and more importantly, why?"

He shrugged. "Maybe to protect you in the beginning. Now?" He laughed. "Probably to protect themselves."

"You're not going to tell me."

"Callier. You should speak with Callier. If you want answers… that is the place to start."

"Who is…"

"He may not be Sphinx, but he almost certainly knows who is. If he doesn't, he may be the only one that can help you uncover it."

"What about you?"

"ASA is an issue. Ivanov…"

"Victor Ivanov?" Alex sought clarification.

"Yes."

"What does the head of ASA have to do with all of this?"

"He has as much to do with this as anyone. And, if I am right…more to do with John's assassination than anyone… even Admiral Brackett."

"Are you telling me that the admiral was complicit in John's death?"

"Speak to Krause. He obviously trusts you. I only know John suspected the attempt on his life was imminent. What he told Krause, I don't know. Callier is key, Alex." He began to head toward the exit and stopped. "Follow the money. That is what John was doing. I have a different course I have to take."

"Russ…what about Cassidy and Dylan? O'Brien…"

He took a deep breath. "Alex, Cassidy and Dylan are tied to all of it. They are tied to you. Cassidy and Krause…well…"

"You know?"

"News travels fast. For what it is worth, you have powerful allies," he told her.

"I don't…"

"It's not my place, Alex. Whatever you think you know; John was your ally, not your adversary. Jane…I suspect even Krause. If Cassidy has a chance at being safe it is with you. It isn't her safety I fear for."

Alex nodded her understanding. "I appreciate your concern," she said somewhat incredulously. "I can take care of myself."

"Yes. Don't be foolish. O'Brien's carelessness in France is child's play compared to what you are choosing to immerse yourself in. You are right to keep a close eye on the sparrow, but even she is far more of a pest than a threat."

"Sparrow?"

"The admiral's daughter."

"Claire," Alex spoke in a hushed tone.

"Everyone has their sign, Alex, their handle. And, this I will tell you…their sign has its purpose and reason," the ambassador offered as he turned to leave.

"And what is your sign?"

"Crow," he answered. Alex nodded and chuckled to herself, considering the absurdity in all of this. "I wonder what they would call me?" she mused aloud.

"Spider," the answer came in the distance. "You are the spider."

***

Monday, May 19th

"You all right?" Cassidy asked the agent as they turned the corner onto their street.

"Yeah, why?"

"I don't know. You've been quiet all day."

"I'm just tired."

"Alex, you don't have to tell me anything. I just worry about you sometimes. Are you worried about seeing your mother?"

Alex drummed her fingers on the steering wheel and Cassidy reached out to take hold of the agent's hand. "I just don't know what to say," Alex confessed. Cassidy was certain that their weekend in London had produced its share of stress and questions for Alex. She could read the expression in Alex's eyes as the agent rolled through her thoughts. Alex Toles' mind was seldom, if ever, silent. The only times Cassidy ever saw Alex truly at peace were when she was playing with Dylan or sleeping beside Cassidy. Sometimes, even in those moments, Cassidy would notice Alex's thoughts straying and turning wildly. Alex was curious about everything and she sought answers to every question that posed itself in her life. There was one thing that Cassidy had grown to realize very clearly; nothing unsettled Alex Toles as much as dealing with her parents seemed to.

The discovery that her father had engaged in any meeting with the congressman had not only angered Alex, Cassidy knew it had demolished any hope of reconciliation. Alex was compassionate, but she had very definite ideas about right and wrong and she was nothing if not devoted to those she loved. Her father's betrayal ironically coincided with the establishment of a renewed relationship with her mother. Cassidy was fully aware that Alex was perplexed by the situation. The agent was confident in her abilities to solve daunting mysteries in her work, but her relationship with her mother remained an enigma. "Alex, why don't you just tell her how you feel?"

"I'm not sure I know how I feel."

Cassidy stroked the back of Alex's hand with her thumb and thought silently for a moment as the car rolled to a stop in the driveway. She tightened her hold and directed Alex to look at her. The apprehension in Alex's eyes pulled at her heart and she sighed deeply. "I think you do know. No matter what happened in the past, your mother loves you....and you, you love her. I see it every time you mention her. She is here. She came here. That should tell you something. Just tell her the truth. Tell her what you feel."

"I'm not sure I..."

Cassidy pursed her lips and then began opening her door. "Tell her you love her, Alex. I'm betting those are words you really need to say."

"I don't..."

"Yes, you do know how. You'll feel better once you do."

"I don't think I can forgive him," Alex muttered.

"I know," Cassidy answered. She stretched up and kissed Alex on the cheek. "Just don't miss an opportunity and end up struggling to forgive yourself."

Alex nodded. Somehow Cassidy always seemed to understand what Alex needed, both what she needed from Cassidy and what she needed from herself. The trip abroad had opened doors for Alex. She was beginning to see the outline of a very complex picture. She didn't like what was developing, but that was a puzzle she felt assured she would be able to complete in time. And, the inescapable truth was, no matter the risks, she enjoyed the challenge. What awaited her beyond the door she now opened completely dumfounded her. She thought it was almost strange that what she now confronted in her professional life posed potential dangers to millions; to everyone; yet the challenges of building her family had become the mission she viewed with the greatest sense of urgency. "Thanks, Cass," she whispered.

Cassidy just smiled. "Let's go."

***

"What did you find?"

"Well," Detective Pete Ferro scratched his forehead, "nothing that knocked my socks off."

"So, you think Tate just made a natural move to the Secret Service?" Fallon asked.

"I didn't say that. He was well respected here, Fallon...and well liked. I didn't know him. He garnered a lot of respect after the World Trade Center bombing in '93. Guess he liaised with the FBI. Made some in roads for the department with the federal services. You know how it can be."

"That's it?" Fallon asked.

"No one seems to have much to say about Captain Tate, Fallon. One interesting fact I did overturn."

"What's that?"

"When he left the department it wasn't for the Department of Treasury or the Secret Service."

"There is a gap..."

"From what I heard he was headed to DSS," Ferro explained.

"He worked for the Department of State?"

"Not that surprising."

"Why wouldn't that be in his file?" Fallon wondered aloud.

"Who knows? I didn't find anything nefarious on Tate. The people who did know him well at all seemed to respect and trust him. If they didn't, they sure as hell weren't sharing that with me," Ferro said.

"Anyone say what his role was at DSS?"

"No, just that they heard he was headed there. It's not that shocking. Diplomatic Security Service had more hands in the game in '93 and 2001 than most realize. You still suspect he is involved with the congressman?"

"I don't know what I think." Fallon shook his head in frustration.

"Well, I will dig a little more. Don't count on too much. Blue blood runs thick."

"Yeah, I remember."

"Be careful, Fallon. I don't know what you and Toles are into, but whatever it is it seems to cross every line imaginable."

"If there are any lines to cross," Fallon responded.

"Check out the DSS thing. I will ask a few more questions here. Just don't expect much. His father was a detective in Brooklyn. It's in his blood."

Brian Fallon nodded. "Understood."

***

Alex walked into the kitchen where her mother was sitting with Rose over a cup of tea. "Did you finally get him to bed?" Rose asked.

"No," Alex answered, grabbing a Diet Coke from the refrigerator. "Cass is trying to settle him down. I think I was just making it worse," she shrugged.

"He's just excited you are both home." Rose winked and patted Alex's shoulder. "I'll go see if a double team from Grandma can help." Alex just smiled as Rose strolled away leaving the agent alone with her mother.

"How are feeling?" Helen asked.

Alex let go of a heavy sigh and looked up at her mother. "I'm fine. Tired. I'm more concerned about you."

Helen Toles' nose crinkled slightly as her lips curled into a soft smile. "I'm all right, Alexis." She took her daughter's hand and began contemplating her words when Alex spoke.

"I don't think I can forgive him," Alex said so softly the words were barely audible.

Her mother nodded her understanding. "I don't think I can either."

Alex looked up in surprised pain. As angry as she was she did not want to come between her parents. "I…"

Helen shook her head and rose from her seat. "There is no excuse for what he did."

"I don't want…"

"Alexis," Helen took a deep breath and turned around. "Alex," she said reclaiming her seat. "Your father is who he is. I'm not sure I know who that is right now. After more than fifty years I suddenly feel like I am looking at a stranger. I will not lose my children to his arrogance," her voice dropped. "Or to his ignorance."

Alex pinched the bridge of her nose and took a deep breath. "Mom?" Helen looked across to her daughter. "Cass and I… we decided not to wait. So much has happened. I almost lost her once already and then with me getting, well…I want you to be there. I mean, what I mean is," Alex shook her head in frustration. She closed her eyes and recalled Cassidy's advice. "It's going to be simple and small at Nick's place." She looked at her mother who was offering her a gentle smile. "I want…I'd like it if you would be there with us, with me."

"Of course I will be there. It isn't everyday your only daughter gets married."

Alex was amazed that her heart had begun to beat double time and that she could feel tears stinging the back of her eyes. For so many years the woman in front of her seemed an opponent of all the agent loved and believed in. Alex suddenly realized how much her mother's approval still meant to her. "I know you are not really that comfort..."

"That may be true, Alexis. It isn't what I pictured." Helen chuckled. "What I pictured isn't what matters. I spent the last few days with Rose and with Dylan. I realized what a wonderful woman you have become. They love you."

"I love them."

"I know you do. It's your family," Helen said somewhat sadly.

"Yes, they are," Alex agreed. "But, they're not my mom." Helen was stunned. "I love you too, Mom. I'd really like you to be part of that family." Cassidy had just reached the doorway to the kitchen and she smiled.

"I love you too. I'd like that."

"Well, I'm glad that is all settled then," Cassidy's voice broke the emotional tension. "I don't want to have to explain to your son why YaYa isn't here. He's been going on and on about his secret with YaYa for the last fifteen minutes."

Helen attempted to hide her grin. "What secret?" Alex asked. Her mother just shrugged.

"Alex, if she tells you it won't be their secret anymore," Cassidy whispered in the agent's ear loud enough that Helen could hear her.

"Yeah...well my job is uncovering secrets, you know."

"Umm...right now I'd say your job is bringing those bags upstairs," Cassidy winked at Helen.

Alex got up from her seat. "Yes, dear."

Cassidy leaned up and kissed her cheek. "I'll be up in a few minutes."

"Take your time. You are staying tonight, Mom?"

"If that is all right with you."

"I'd like that," Alex offered as she made her way out of the kitchen.

"Thank you, Cassidy," Helen said.

"What are you thanking me for?"

"I think you know."

Cassidy took hold of the older woman's hand. "Helen, Alex loves you. She may not always know how to say it, but she does."

"I know," the soft reply came. "She loves you Cassidy... more, I think, than even she can understand." Cassidy blushed. "Remember that. Alexis is..."

"You don't need to worry about me. I know who she is. I know how she is. It's not what I expected either," she giggled and saw Helen's eyebrow raise. "Well, it isn't. But, I love her. She's...well, she is everything to me," Cassidy said plainly.

"I can see that. You are everything to her."

"I know. She missed you, though. I think she is just realizing how much. I'm glad she has her mother back."

Helen rose from her chair and looked down at the woman who had captured her daughter's heart. "I guess I got the bonus." Cassidy was confused and Helen laughed. "I ended up with three daughters and I only had to give birth to one." She bent over and kissed Cassidy on the forehead. "I'll see you in the morning."

Cassidy watched her future mother-in-law leave in awe. She pushed her chair in and shut off the lights, taking her time to climb the stairs and looking over the house that had quickly become a home. So many questions rolled through her mind. How would she tell Dylan about his father? When would she tell him? What would he think? What would happen when her ex-husband found out that she had married Alex? How much danger were they in? How much danger was Alex in? Question after question. She flipped off the hallway light and peered into their bedroom. Alex had fallen asleep lying on top of the bed, still in her clothes. A peaceful calm swept over Cassidy, quelling all of her fears and quieting all of her questions. She looked down the hall to receive a slight wave from her mother as she entered one of the two extra bedrooms. She couldn't predict anything. The answers were all here, all quietly retiring just like the questions in her mind.

***

"I'm not certain this is the time to announce a campaign, Claire."

"You sound as though you think you have some choice in the matter."

O'Brien shook his head. "There is no logic in it."

"No one cares about your logic," she laughed heartily. "Dimitri was very clear about his expectations." She sipped her glass of wine and kicked off the heels that had managed to fatigue her feet. "You know who to see about the accounts?"

"I do. I'm not sure that is the best idea now either."

"Well, it may not be your ideal, Congressman. Doesn't matter, just do it."

"What about you? He just sent you back to face your father empty handed, other than a message for me?"

She leaned her head back and closed her eyes. "Never said I was empty handed."

"Care to share?"

"No," she replied.

"And what if I refuse?"

"It wouldn't be the first stupid thing you've done, but it would be the last," she smiled.

O'Brien bristled. "Fine. So we are clear…"

Brackett open her eyes and exhaled. She set down her glass and pushed the congressman back into a large chair, straddling him. "Oh, set me straight, Congressman. Please," she gushed.

"You are not telling me everything."

"No," she nipped at his ear, "and you should be glad."

"Your father…"

She slowly traced his neck with her tongue before placing her lips just above his. "My father will not be a concern to you any longer."

"Your father concerns everyone, Claire," he answered with a heavy breath.

"Mm," she cooed. "Things change," she whispered and kissed him soundly.

***

Thursday, May 22nd

Alex walked carefully along the railroad tracks until she caught sight of the large abandoned building. She scanned it, considering what it might have looked like in its glory days. Whatever Jon Krause wanted to discuss, it was clear that he was taking every possible precaution. It had taken Alex nearly twenty minutes to traverse the wooded railroad tracks before she finally reached the abandoned station. The façade remained intact, but it was adorned now by a plethora of colorful images and messages. She paced along the cement and looked out at the littered woods below. A faint shuffling ahead captured her attention. She gently moved a large beam of wood aside and entered an expansive room. "This your idea of first class travel?" she goaded the CIA agent.

"See you found it."

"Yeah, not for lack of looking. What the hell possessed you to choose this place?"

"No one comes here, Alex, save maybe an addict now and then. The woods of Willimantic are hardly the hub of espionage."

"No, I don't suppose it is. This is the place time forgot. So, what is it? You find something on that disk?"

Krause sighed. "I found what I expected to find. Matt has it. What I found from Daniels' computer was more enlightening."

"Speaking of enlightenment, *Pip*. Why is it that Russ Matthews thinks I should ask you about John's assassination?"

"Probably because I arranged it," he answered as a statement of fact.

"What?"

"I think we both know you heard me clearly."

"What the hell?" Alex felt a fury build within her. "You didn't think that was pertinent to tell me? Jesus, does Jane know?"

"She has an idea." Alex rubbed her face with her hands violently. "Before you start making assumptions, Agent Toles, you should now that John was fully aware of the plan. I spoke with him after I made the call."

"What are you telling me?"

"I'm telling you it was his choice. I planted the chatter that Brady picked up. Secret Service approached him to change exits. He refused."

"Why? You are telling me he walked knowingly into an ambush. Why?"

Krause nodded. "He had things to protect. With him gone, those things could no longer be used as leverage."

Alex licked her lips. "Why didn't you tell me this when you came to me?"

"I would have preferred not to tell you at all," he admitted.

"Not exactly a great way to engender trust."

"I have my reasons."

"I'm sure. What about this Callier?" she asked.

"Give it time, Agent. What exactly did Matthews tell you?"

"Not much actually. Two things I found interesting."

"Oh?"

Alex turned from him and began to mill about the room. "He told me Sphinx is a person," she paused for a moment. "He told me they call me the spider." She turned slowly on her heels to face him. "Now why, I wonder, would anyone feel the need to give me a handle? Just what the hell is going on?"

"You've had a sign since you were assigned at the Pentagon, Alex. Anyone considered a potential ally or adversary is given one."

She chuckled sarcastically. "Why do I think there is more to it than that?"

"Probably because there is. They didn't deem you Spider for no reason. You're resourceful and creative."

She rolled her eyes at his assessment. "Matthews said that there were people who didn't want me in this. I thought he meant John." She stopped and regarded the man before her. "That isn't who he was talking about; was it?"

"No, Alex. A lot of people wanted you kept at bay. You got too close too many times when you were at the NSA. That's why John supported your move to the FBI. He thought you would be safer. But, I don't think that is what Matthews was referring to. I think he was talking about your father."

"What does my father have to do with any of this? He runs a medical supply company."

"Oh, come on, Alex. You don't really think O'Brien ran off to your father for some kind of dirt on you just on the spur of the moment? How would he even know to do that?" Alex covered her mouth and shook her head in disbelief. "I didn't know myself. That is the truth," Krause continued. "I knew Carecom was a major donor to many of our candidates. I knew he helped navigate the establishment of the accounts and that he donated privately to certain campaigns when asked. He has ties to Callier, to the admiral. Callier let it slip once during your investigation into the Somali gas attack that he asked your father to compel you into a new line of work"

"My father does not make my decisions. How would my father get mixed up in this, Krause? He never even served. For God's sake he went to Harvard Law School. He's an Ivy League brat."

Krause let out a heavy sigh. "I don't have that answer, but he is. Your father has major contracts with the military, surely you knew that."

Alex stared at him blankly. She had never taken any interest in her father's business dealings. As far as she was concerned he ran a successful small business. "I never really paid it much mind."

Krause nodded his understanding and continued. "The documents on Daniels' computer....they identified a source, an individual with the means to transport goods safely through customs and even across hostile borders."

"Sphinx?" Alex asked.

"No. I was not even aware Sphinx was being used as a handle. Until, last night this person was known only as The Broker. In the note that John left me about Dylan, he mentioned The Broker. He had been unable to identify....Alex, The Broker... he's your father."

Alex stood frozen in place. "What are you telling me, Krause?"

"It gets worse."

"Of course it does."

"The protocols, we interrupted those. But, there is something we didn't know. There is a shipment...it's already in process. Looks like it is heading into Northern Africa under the guise of measles vaccinations."

"And what is it?"

"My best guess?" Alex nodded. "Small pox strain."

Alex pressed on either side of her forehead forcefully with her fingers, covering her eyes. She let out a rush of breath and shook her head. "My father is involved in this?" Krause kept his gaze focused and unwavering. "Jesus. Why didn't you tell me, Krause?"

"I told you; I didn't know."

"No, you didn't know he was this 'Broker', as you call it. You knew he was involved. Don't you realize this could put Cassidy and Dylan at even greater risk? You want me to trust you? All these secrets. God." She pinched the bridge of her nose again and took a deep breath. "Between your secrets and my father's lies…"

Krause moved closer and looked directly at Alex. He softened his voice slightly and hoped that she would hear the truthfulness in what he was about to say. "Listen to me. I would never put Cassidy or Dylan, for that matter, in danger. Not ever." Alex did believe that, but she had no intention of ceding her ground. He needed to understand that she was his equal. He nodded his understanding of her stance. "Alex, not every lie that is told is done so with malicious intent and not every secret is sinister. You know that. Sometimes we make the best choices we can to prote…"

"Yes, I know. To protect what we love. I do know. I also know that secrets and lies have a way of being discovered. When they are, and trust is broken; we often lose far more than what we sought to protect. You have some loyalty…"

"We all have something to protect in this. All of us. What that is will determine where we fall in this game, that and how far we are willing to go."

She sighed. "All right, *Pip*. You didn't call me here just to unveil this epiphany about my father. What is it?"

"I need you to get access to his office. Some of the logs that we were able to trace; the messages to Daniels originated from his home."

Alex let go a chuckle of disgust. "You might have guessed that I am not speaking with my father." He raised his brow and Alex shook her head. "Fine. I'll figure it out. How soon?" He looked at the floor. "Great," she sighed. "What am I looking for?"

"Cargo container numbers, shipping manifests, I'm not sure exactly, Alex. You'll know when you see it. It's slated from Boston. The departure date was unclear, so…"

"I got it. And if I find the information? Then what?"

He shrugged. "We stop it."

Alex laughed. "Just like that?" Krause shrugged again. "I'll see what I can find, but I want you to do something for me," she said.

"What is that?"

"If you want me in this, Krause…you are going to have to start telling me everything. I mean it. No secrets, no lies. You find out from Mr. Callier what you can about my father."

"That's it?" he asked.

"No, there is one other thing…"

***

Chapter Twenty-Nine

C assidy and Dylan were engaged in a packet of homework when Dylan suddenly looked up to his mother. "Mom?" Cassidy directed her attention to him.

"What, Dylan?" Dylan kept his eyes focused on his finger as it made swirling patterns across the kitchen table. "Dylan?"

"When you and Alex get married," he stopped and shook his small head.

"Dylan, what is it?" He shrugged. "You can tell me, sweetie."

He kept his eyes down and shrugged again. "Well, Cat gets to carry your rings and Uncle Nick will be with Alex. I have to sit with Grandma."

"What do you want to do?" He shrugged again. "I see." She lowered herself to her knees in front of him and brushed a tear from his cheek. "Dylan," she sighed. "Do you want to stand with Alex?" He would not meet her gaze and began tugging at his bottom lip. "Mm-hmm; why didn't you just tell me that, sweetheart?" Another shrug prompted Cassidy to envelop him in her arms. "You were afraid you would hurt my feelings?" She felt his affirmative nod against her as his tears broke forth. "Oh, Dylan...it makes me very happy that you love Alex so much. I would love for you to walk with me, but I understand if you want to be with Alex."

"But I do want to be with you, Mom."

Cassidy sighed. "I know you do. It gets complicated, huh? Listen, I don't want you to worry about this, okay?" He looked up to his mother a bit sheepishly. "We'll work it all out. I

381

promise. All that matters to me is that I have you and Alex. If it was just the three of us there I would be happy." She kissed him on the forehead and wiped his remaining tears. "I love you more than anything Dylan. All that matters to me is that you are happy. Okay?" He nodded. "So, you let me worry about this. I promise we will make it all work somehow." She ruffled his hair slightly. "What do you say you and I go grab a pizza together? Alex will be home late. Just you and me."

"I have to finish my math," he reminded her.

"Yes, you do. How about this?" Dylan looked at his mother hopefully. "You work on that and I will go order us a pizza. That way it will be here by the time you are done. Then, maybe I will let you show me what YaYa taught you on that pool table." Dylan's eyes grew wide. "Mm-hmm. Mothers have a way of finding these things out," she winked. His small mouth flew open wide. "Oh, don't worry," she assured him. "Your secret is safe with me." Relieved, he cast his eyes back on his homework. Cassidy shook her head in amusement as she watched him. He was truly the light in her world. She'd meant what she had said. For Cassidy, all any wedding needed to consist of were the two people who mattered most to her. She had suggested a ceremony at Nick's restaurant because she knew the sentiment would mean a great deal to Alex. It never occurred to her that Dylan might feel torn between them. She was certain Alex had not entertained that notion either. Dylan's need to be close to Alex reaffirmed what she knew; they were already a family.

***

Alex took a seat at a small table in the corner of the café and ordered a cappuccino. She stretched her neck from side to side, attempting to relieve her tension. A waitress appeared and placed two napkins on the table, sliding one slightly forward before placing the agent's drink on the other. "If you need anything else."

"I will let you know," Alex answered. She retrieved the cup and casually took a sip before turning over the napkin closest to her. She continued toying with the napkin, sipping her cappuccino for several more minutes until the waitress returned.

"Anything else?" the waitress asked.

"Yes, another one. To go please, and the check." The waitress nodded her understanding. Within a few moments she returned and placed a covered cup and the check on the table. Alex laid down a ten dollar bill and wrapped the coffee cup in the napkin she had been fiddling with. She made the short trek to her car, throwing the small package she was carrying into the first garbage can she passed. Reaching her car, she signaled a left into traffic and followed the street for several blocks before pulling into the parking lot of Fast-Go Dry Cleaners. She rolled her eyes slightly and opened the door. "Picking up," she said. The small dark skinned man behind the counter gestured to a door on her left. She nodded her understanding. "I really hope you got all the wrinkles out," Alex remarked sarcastically.

"A few at least," a voice answered.

"It's hotter than hell back here. What is this all about Taylor?"

"I thought it best we take care. What happened with Krause?"

Alex rubbed her brow. "Lots. What did you find out about my father?"

"Not much. Carecom is like every other company. There have been no red flags that sent the NSA into overdrive. Political contributions are typical."

"Yeah, well...that may be, but there's more to it."

"Probably," he admitted. "You actually trust Krause? Alex, the man..."

Alex folded her hands and brought her thumbs to her temples. She needed to make a decision. How far should she let her old friend Michael Taylor in? Given all she now had learned, was it possible that Taylor was not completely truthful about his own motivations? She drew in a deep breath, tightened her lips and then looked at him directly. "Do I trust Jon Krause? The truth?" Taylor nodded his encouragement. "I have my reasons, Taylor. Yes, I trust him."

Taylor's surprise was evident. "How do you know he isn't playing you?"

"I suppose I don't. He has nothing to gain by doing that. Not that I can see."

"What aren't you telling me?" he asked.

"Quite a lot actually," she said. "You first. Why all these hurdles? What did you find?"

"I didn't find much on your father. Fallon met with his detective friend. Got some interesting information. I did a little digging. Well, actually a lot of digging…on your old boss."

"Tate?"

"Yeah. Seems Tate did go to the Secret Service and work within FINcen. Thing is, he was still on the payroll at State."

"What are you talking about? Tate worked for the State Department?" Taylor arched his brow. "Doing?" she asked.

"Classified. So highly classified that I had to make a personal plea to Secretary Carver. Who, reluctantly, released a few files to me," Taylor told her.

"And?"

"He worked on a project, Alex. A joint DOD, State Department project."

"And?"

"The project name was SPHINX."

Alex nodded. "I see."

"That's it? He worked on a project we were assigned to three years later. You don't find that odd?"

"No, I don't. It makes perfect sense, actually," she responded.

"All right. What the hell is going on? I'm not as sold on your new friend's motives as you seem to be."

"I'm not certain I know anyone's motives at this point, Taylor." Alex was about to cross a line she had hoped she would never have to choose to cross. So far in her career she had managed to avoid deception. Now, all things considered, she needed to immerse herself fully. In this case, that meant deceiving her old friend. "Taylor, Jon is Dylan's father." She let the words pass, feeling at least somewhat relieved that they were not a total lie.

"You are telling me that Krause and Cassidy..."

"Look, if you trust me...trust this; Jon Krause, whatever his past, whatever his connections, loves my family as much as I do. So yes, I trust him."

"Did you ever consider that might make him more of a threat?"

"I have. Believe me. I have. If you trust me, Taylor, you will trust me on this judgment. I don't like it, but everything in me tells me to trust him."

Taylor groaned but conceded his defeat in the matter. "So, what do you make of Tate?"

"I don't know. It fits. Makes sense why John would want me assigned to him at the bureau. If he knew about SPHINX then he would be able to deter me from investigations leading in that direction."

"What else?" Taylor inquired sensing there was more.

"I need you to focus on chatter surrounding Northern Africa. Shipments, medical but with a darker..."

"I think I understand."

"Taylor, listen to me. John was CIA. I am betting Tate was working under agency directives as well. My father is bankrolling at least some of this. I still think O'Brien's accident...well, there is more there. Why try to kill a congressman? As a fall guy? What could he possibly have done or not done?"

"I suspect he was playing both sides."

"Of what? He may be an asshole, but he isn't a complete idiot."

Taylor laughed. "Well, that's a glowing appraisal," he said. Alex smirked. "Suppose that the movement of money and shipments was compromised or hindered by legislative restrictions. Let's just say O'Brien made promises in too many directions."

"Yeah, but politicians do that every single day. I agree, but there's more, Taylor. Brackett didn't shack up with him for no reason. And it isn't just because she arranged that accident."

"How do you know she…"

"Oh, she did. I don't need a smoking gun to know that. She's vested in him and believe me, he is not her type. She's getting something or she is wanting something from him. There's more. I have other fish to fry this week," Alex explained.

"I heard."

"Yeah, well. Unfortunately, Cassidy will be dealing with most of that situation with our mothers. Look, Taylor, this shipment that's slated for Northern Africa. It looks like it may be a biologically engineered…"

"Christ almighty, Toles. Who would…"

"Who knows?" Alex admitted. "We'll figure that out later. Right now where it is going, how it is going and when it is going have to be the priorities. Get Brady on that. Anything at all. My suggestion?" He waited for her to continue. "Get a tap on my father. Hone in on Carecom."

Taylor nodded. "And Tate?"

"Time will tell."

"If you find this shipment you're going to need a way to stop it. You want Brady…"

"No."

He took a deep breath. "Krause."

"Taylor, it's what he does."

"And you?"

Alex just smiled. "It's what we do," she thought silently.

***

"Hey," Cassidy greeted. She rolled over and allowed her eyes to adjust to the figure entering the bedroom.

"Sorry it's so late," Alex apologized as she took a seat on the edge of the bed. "Didn't mean to wake you," she said as she kissed Cassidy's forehead.

"You didn't. I actually just got Dylan down about an hour ago."

"Why? Is he feeling okay?"

Cassidy jostled herself over toward Alex. "He's okay. Why don't you go get changed and come to bed."

"Oh no. What's going on?"

"Alex, it's fine. Go get changed." Alex shook her head, kicked off her shoes and positioned herself against the headboard, pulling Cassidy into her arms. "Nice try. You never let Dylan stay up this late. What happened? Wait...he didn't get sent to the principal's office again or..."

Cassidy giggled. "No. Although he ate so much pizza it might be considered a crime."

"I missed pizza?"

"Mm-hmm." Alex kissed the top of Cassidy's head. "There's some left for you."

"You are the best, Mrs. O'Brien." Alex paused. "By the way, what are you going to do about that?"

"About what?"

"You know? The Mrs. 'thing'," Alex explained.

"The Mrs. 'thing'? If I'm not mistaken I will still be a Mrs."

"Yeah, I guess you will. But we haven't talked about that. I mean, are you still going to be Mrs. O'Brien?"

Cassidy sat up and offered Alex a cock-eyed smile. "I suppose I hadn't really thought about that." Cassidy could see the pained expression that Alex tried to conceal. "But no, Alex. I will not still be Mrs. O'Brien. What about you?" Cassidy tried not to laugh. "Technically you will be a Mrs. too, you know."

"Yeah. I guess so. I mean...do you want me to be Mrs. McCollum?"

Cassidy tried not to erupt in a roar of laughter at the question. She could hear the strain and yet the sincerity in Alex's voice. She took a deep breath to quell her threatening out-burst and pretended to consider the question carefully. Alex's eyes seemed to get wider by the second and Cassidy decided to relieve her anxiety. "Mrs. McCollum is my mother," she winked and kissed Alex's cheek. "No, love. I do not want you to be Mrs. McCollum. I prefer you as a Toles." Alex smiled in relief, but Cassidy had no doubt that had she asked Alex to take her name, the agent would have done so without any hesitation. "Brings up some things we need to discuss," Cassidy said.

"Oh? Did you want to wait or…did you…"

"Alex, I told you before I would marry you right now if I could. No, I don't want to wait. But, Dylan…"

Alex felt a sudden rush of fear sweep through her. "Does he not want us to…"

"No, no," Cassidy sighed. "He wants to stand with you at the wedding."

"He's walking you…"

Cassidy nodded. "About that…"

"No," Alex was firm. "Cass, you are his mom. He needs to be…"

Two warm hands suddenly held Alex's face gently and stopped her speech. "He needs to be with both of us. He loves you so much, Alex. I knew that, but today…he just…he needs to know you want him to be part of your…"

Alex closed her eyes and nodded. "I guess I never even thought about that. I just figured he would want to be with you."

"I know."

"Cass, aren't you going to be disappointed if he doesn't walk you down the aisle?"

Cassidy blew out a heavy breath. "A little," she admitted. "Alex, if…"

"Listen, why don't you let me work on this, okay?" Alex offered. "I am going to my mom's tomorrow. Let me take Dylan with me."

"Are you sure? Don't you want to spend some time alone with her?"

"Cassidy, I should have thought of this earlier. I cannot subject my son to shopping with you and Rose and Barb all day tomorrow. That's just cruel." Cassidy smacked Alex playfully. "Well, it is."

"Um, you are shopping with Helen."

"Yes, but the operative word in that statement is *you*, meaning me. I won't be parading in and out of dress shops all day cooing over shoes and jewelry and hair styles. Me, it's one and done. You know you and..." Alex's rant was abruptly ended by Cassidy's kiss.

"You may not be cooing, but you will be with Helen, so my guess is more than one before you are done," Cassidy poked.

"Still more fun."

"Yes, I am sure that is true," Cassidy conceded.

"I'll talk to Dylan."

"If he wants to stand with you; I really am okay with..."

"Just let me work on this, okay?" Alex pleaded quietly. "You still didn't answer my question."

"What question?"

"What are you going to call yourself?" Alex asked.

Cassidy pursed her lips. She loved to tease Alex and this seemed a perfect opportunity. "Hum," she considered the question as she positioned herself to straddle the agent's hips. "I suppose I will call myself Cassidy."

Alex narrowed her gaze at her lover who was concentrating on the buttons of Alex's blouse. "Yeah, but what about what your students will call you?"

"Don't have any of those to worry about right now," Cassidy answered, lowering her lips to Alex's neck.

"What about what your driver's license says?" Alex asked.

"Doesn't renew for six years," Cassidy continued her assault.

Alex was determined that Cassidy would not distract her, but the gentle caresses and kisses trailing down her body were making it increasingly difficult for her to form a coherent thought. "Okay...what about what..."

"Alex," Cassidy pulled herself up to look into her lover's eyes. "Why don't you just ask me what you want to ask me?"

"I don't..." Cassidy raised her eyebrow and Alex sighed. "I don't care, Cass. It doesn't matter."

"Yes, you do." Cassidy kissed the agent. "And, for the record Agent Toles, I can't tell you how much it means to me that you do care."

"I want you to do whatever makes you happy."

"You make me happy," Cassidy answered. "It's going to take some getting used to. I've been Mrs. O'Brien for a long time."

"You can be Ms. McCollum, you know?"

Cassidy shook her head. "No." She kissed the agent passionately.

"You can be Cassidy McCollum-Toles."

Cassidy scrunched up her face. "Sounds like a disease. No." She kissed the agent again.

"Cass are you sure you want to be..."

"Alex?"

"Yeah?"

"When we have a baby, what do you think his or her name will be?"

"I don't know."

"I think," Cassidy stroked the agent's cheek, "we both know it will be Toles. So, I think you have your answer." Alex smiled broadly and Cassidy arched her brow. "What?" Cassidy inquired.

"Nothing," Alex answered. She pulled Cassidy into a gentle kiss. "I just had this thought of our kids' friends calling you Mrs. Toles."

"Our *kids*, huh?" Cassidy smirked and Alex nodded. "Well, guess I will be busy then. Better make the most of our alone time now." She started to kiss Alex when she felt Alex pull away slightly. "What's wrong?"

Alex sat up and sighed. "What about Dylan, Cass? You can't change your name. I mean, he's an O'Brien. I don't want him to feel like…"

Cassidy kissed Alex gently. "I love you."

"What?" Alex asked in confusion.

"Well, I do." Cassidy tucked a lose strand of hair behind Alex's ear. "We'll cross that bridge when we come to it. But, the answer is the same. I am not going to stay Cassidy O'Brien. I don't know why I never changed it before."

"I do," Alex said. "Dylan."

Cassidy closed her eyes. "You're right. It was Dylan. But Alex, in a week…in a week I will be Mrs. Toles, not Mrs. O'Brien. Dylan will understand." Alex nodded with some sadness. "Alex?"

"You know I wish he could be a Toles. I mean…he is, but…"

"I think all you need to do is tell him that," Cassidy suggested. "Now," she said softly. "You don't have many more chances to make love to Cassidy O'Brien."

Alex's eyes took on a playful twinkle. "Seven days, seven nights."

"Six, actually. Better get started."

"I wonder," Alex mused as she placed Cassidy beneath her.

"What do you wonder?"

"What it will be like to make love to Cassidy Toles."

"Like nothing you have ever," Cassidy was lost to her lover's kiss.

"I have no doubt," Alex whispered. "I could make love to you forever."

Alex's hands were drifting sensually and softly over Cassidy's hip. Cassidy sighed and wrapped her hands around Alex's neck. "I may have to test that theory," she whispered. Her words were stopped by a long kiss that deepened gradually and set her ablaze. Alex began kissing her neck and Cassidy stopped to pull the agent back. She searched the blue eyes above her and had to close her own. "*Je vais consacrer le reste de ma vie a t`aimer* (I will spend the rest of my life loving you)," she promised.

Alex just smiled. Often she found that there were no words adequate to convey the depth of her feeling for the woman in her arms. Cassidy was nothing less than her world. When Alex held Cassidy everything faded away. There was no fear, no sadness, no questioning. There was comfort and completion in the connection they shared. Alex intended to show Cassidy how much the love between them meant to her. She caressed every inch of the woman she loved, slowly, tenderly, and lovingly. Every time she touched Cassidy it felt like the first time. Her mind went silent and her body hummed with energy. The sound of Cassidy's sighs, the feel of her own heart thrumming in her chest, the scent of Cassidy's shampoo, the way that Cassidy would reach for her, the expression of love that emanated in the beautiful eyes that searched hers; all of it carried Alex away and she was content to lose herself completely.

"Alex," Cassidy called softly as Alex's lips trailed over her stomach. "Please…" Alex reached for Cassidy's hands and suddenly felt transported to the first time they had made love. Alex had struggled to surrender. Somehow Cassidy understood. She reached for Alex's hands and held them tenderly. No one had ever reached for her that way, wanting only to love her and reassure her. It was such a simple gesture yet it meant everything to Alex. She felt Cassidy's hands in her own and looked up at the expression on her lover's face. Cassidy sensed Alex's gaze and opened her eyes. "I love you, Alex."

Alex tightened her grip on the hands she held and continued her gentle exploration. She felt Cassidy's hips rise to meet her and the teacher's fingers reflexively grasp her hand as the waves of passion crested and fell. "I'm here," Alex whispered as she slowly lifted herself to look into Cassidy's eyes. She felt Cassidy draw her closer and laid down to pull the teacher onto her chest. "Thanks," Alex whispered.

"I didn't do anything....*yet*," Cassidy chuckled through a yawn as she drew small circles on the agent's skin.

"Yeah, you did, but if you have something else that...Cass?" Alex ran her fingers through Cassidy's hair. "Perfect," Alex sighed in contentment.

"What?" Cassidy mumbled.

Alex just shook her head and snuggled closer. "Nothing," she answered. "Go to sleep." She felt Cassidy's breathing even out and closed her eyes. "Yep, this is perfect."

***

Chapter Thirty

Saturday, May 23rd

"I'm glad you brought Dylan."

"Me too," Alex agreed. Dylan was walking slightly ahead of the pair down the street. "Wait there, Speed."

"So?" Helen asked.

"What?"

"What do you mean, what? What are you going to wear, Alexis?" Helen asked as they caught up with Dylan.

"I don't know what I am going to wear."

"You are supposed to wear a dress," Dylan said.

"Who says?" He shrugged. "Well, I don't know. I don't think your mom expects me to wear a dress."

"Yeah but she says you are beautiful in a dress." Helen sniggered at the statement.

"She does, does she? When did she say that?" Alex asked, genuinely curious.

"When you came home. She says you would look good in a paper bag too."

Helen covered her face to conceal her amusement. "Your mother did not tell you that," Alex said definitively.

Dylan just shrugged. "Me and Cat heard her tell Aunt Barb," he explained.

"A dress, huh?" Dylan smiled and nodded. "Hum." Helen looked at the pavement, still attempting to hide her grin. "Oh, all right. You all win." Helen looked up and smiled. "But no frill, Mother. I mean it. I hate…"

"Yes, Alexis. I do recall your feeling on frills."

"We have a stop to make first, though." Helen looked to Alex about to question her. "I have to get a ring. Might be help-ful," Alex winked.

"Any ideas?" Helen asked.

"Well, a few." She stopped in front of a jewelry store. "I fig-ured Dylan could help." Dylan smiled. "What do you say? You help me out?" He nodded. "Excellent."

***

"You really think this is a good time to announce a senate bid?"

"I don't think I have much of a choice in the matter," O'Brien answered.

"I have to say I am surprised with the timing."

"What timing?" the congressman asked.

Nicolaus Toles sipped his glass of bourbon and stroked his chin. "You mean, you don't know?"

"Know what?"

"Your ex-wife and my daughter…"

"The whole world knows that, thank you."

"I guess you didn't make the guest list either," the older man laughed.

"What the hell are you taking about? What guest list?"

Alex's father shook his head and patted the congressman's hand. "Seems my daughter is making a…well, an honest woman out of your ex-wife."

"What?"

"Oh, don't worry, Congressman. I'm sure it will have no bearing on your future. If they want you in, you have nothing to fear. I'll get your funding. They'll engineer the votes."

O'Brien rose to his feet. His voice dropped as he battled his rising anger. "Are you trying to tell me Cassidy is getting mar-ried?" Nicolaus Toles raised his glass in a mock toast. "What the hell is she thinking?"

"Oh, my daughter can be quite persuasive, Congressman."

"Are you attending this debacle?" O'Brien asked.

"No."

"What are you going to do about it?"

"Marriages are not part of my obligations," he answered.

"What exactly are your obligations, Mr. Toles?" O'Brien inquired with disgust.

"Above your pay grade, O'Brien," he responded, rising to take his leave. "I suggest you worry more about your campaign and less about Alexis' love life with your ex-wife."

"Bitch," he muttered.

Nicolaus Toles stopped abruptly and grabbed the congressman by the collar, lifting him off his feet. "Let me make something clear to you, Mr. O'Brien. I may not approve of many of my daughter's choices. She is many things, many things... and all of them...you listen to me," he tightened his grasp, "all of them put you to shame. You are a weasel, O'Brien. Tread lightly. You have no idea who you are dealing with." He set the man down, straightened his suit and smiled politely. "Just do as you are told," he said as he turned to leave. "I'll be in touch."

***

Alex walked into her parents' house as Dylan regaled her mother with another story. The day had been far more enjoyable than she had imagined. There was something comforting about being with her mother. Alex hated that she would have to deceive the woman even in the slightest sense. She reached in her pocket and pressed a button on her cell phone. "I have to take this," she said as she lifted the phone from her pocket.

"Go ahead," Helen said. "I'm going to walk Dylan across the street and introduce him to Mrs. Montgomery." Alex looked at her mother inquisitively. "Oh, Alexis, you know Carol. She's seen you all on the television."

Carol Montgomery was ninety-five and had been a fixture in the neighborhood since Alex and Nick were young. Alex nodded her understanding as her mother scuttled Dylan though the front door. If she hadn't known better she would have sworn that her mother was deliberately giving her space. She shook her head to clear that notion and made her way to her father's study. As she expected it was locked. She reached in her jacket pocket and pulled out a pen. She twisted the bottom, removing the small curved torsion wrench and placing the pick into the lock before leveraging slightly to release the pin. She sighed in relief as the door opened.

Alex stopped momentarily to scan her father's study. She memorized the room inch by inch as quickly as she could. She noted where there were books, shelves, awards and pictures and then made her way to his desk. She wondered how brazen her father might be about leaving information accessible. She spent a few moments looking at the desktop then popped the lock on his file drawer and thumbed quickly through the files. One caught her attention immediately. She retrieved it, pulled the small camera from her pocket and quickly photographed all of the pages. Nothing screamed at her. She closed the drawer and shook her head.

Alex knew her father. She hated to admit they were alike in many ways. If he had placed calls or emails, or even kept files here, he would be reticent in their protection. As she prepared to leave, an object on the corner of the desk captured her attention. She lifted it and allowed her hand to trace the faces hidden behind the glass. It all seemed so long ago, a different lifetime. She went to set it down and noticed the cardboard backing of the frame was bulging slightly. Gently she slid the back from the photograph and retrieved the paper that resided within. It was folded crisply, but appeared rather worn. She opened it and studied it for a moment. She closed her eyes and folded it again. She did not place it back in its home, opting instead to place it in her pocket. She stopped briefly to commit her surroundings one last time to memory before leaving the room. She hadn't found what she had come for, but she had found something. What it meant, she wasn't certain. She hoped Krause might be of help and she prayed that Brady and Taylor would find the shipment bound for Northern Africa in time.

***

"Cassidy, it's beautiful," Barb complimented. "What's wrong?"

"Honestly?" Barb nodded. "I don't know, Barb. Part of me just wishes we were doing this alone, no real festivities."

"Any particular reason?"

Cassidy gave a sad smile. "Dylan, mostly...but, I don't know. I know it's small...it's selfish of me. No matter what Alex says I know she really wants this."

"I think all Alex really wants is you," Barb offered gently.

"I know, but I do know her. She gets this glow about her when the subject comes up. I would never deny her that."

"Maybe that glow is because she thinks she is doing it for you."

Cassidy chuckled. "Partly, only partly."

"Is Dylan upset about something?" Barb asked.

"No. He just wants to be with Alex...you know."

"Umm, I think I do," Barb conceded and took hold of Cassidy's hand. "Cassidy..."

"I know. I'm being silly."

"No, you are being human."

"I guess," Cassidy sighed. "You really think she will like this?"

Barb laughed. "Sorry, the idea of Alex wearing a wedding ring; just not something I ever pictured." Cassidy nodded. "If you really want it to just be the two of you, just tell her."

"No. This really does mean something to her. You should have seen her bouncing this morning, trying to get Dylan to move it." Cassidy shook her head in amusement. "It was adorable."

"Adorable? Alex, adorable?" Cassidy winked. Barb looked back at the simple platinum ring. "She'll love it."

"Barb?"

"Yeah?"

"There's something else I need to ask you, before my mother gets back."

"What is it?"

Cassidy sobered. "I have to tell you something and this isn't how I planned it, but…"

"Cassidy, what? You can tell me anything."

"I know that."

Barb squeezed her friend's hand in encouragement. "I can't tell you everything, but…Chris, he isn't…he's not Dylan's father." Barb stared blankly at Cassidy. "Okay…say something."

Barb gathered her thoughts for a moment. "Good?"

"Good?"

"Yeah, good. No offense Cassidy, but I hate that guy." Cassidy laughed. "You don't have to tell me anything ever, but you can tell me whatever you need to. I hope you know that."

"I do. I do know that. The reason…I have an appointment with my lawyer Monday. I haven't told Alex. I want to talk to him about custody and Dylan. If anything were ever to happen to me," Cassidy's thoughts trailed off as she saw her mother approaching with the clerk. "Well, I would want Dylan with Alex."

"I understand."

"Barb, his father is not an option. If anything ever….given everything that's happened…"

"You don't even need to ask. You know Nick and I love Dylan. I swear he and Cat are more like brothers anyway."

Cassidy had already expected that response, but hearing it lifted an enormous weight off of her shoulders. Since her abduction and Alex's injury, she had been doing a great deal of thinking about Dylan and his future. It didn't seem to her that this was the right time to try and explain his paternity to him. He was only seven. While she hated feeling that she was being dishonest, she did think he needed to mature at bit before he could fully understand the situation. She was prepared for the conversation if it needed to happen sooner and she feared it might.

Her conversation with Alex the night before about Dylan's name and Dylan's response to all the changes in their lives only solidified her decision. She would need to challenge Christopher O'Brien on Dylan's paternity if she and Alex had any hope of gaining full custody. That was no longer a choice. There was no trust left to exist in the man she had once shared her life with. She hated to imagine what Christopher O'Brien might do in response. That could not deter her. She was fully aware that Dylan had not just accepted Alex; he had invited Alex into his life every bit as much as she had. He wanted Alex to be his parent. Cassidy intended to make that a reality in every way she possibly could for both her son and for Alex. She would not risk her ex-husband's continued interference. "Thanks," she said softly as her mother returned.

"So?" Rose asked. "Is it a winner?"

Cassidy smiled and looked back at the ring. "It is."

"Good, we still need to find you a dress." Cassidy rolled her eyes. "Something that will knock the knickers off that agent of yours."

"What decade are you in?" Cassidy quipped.

Barb could not contain herself and looked at Rose. "Oh, I'm pretty sure with all their tomfoolery her knickers will be off by the first toast."

"Don't encourage her," Cassidy warned her friend. "And, tomfoolery? Really? What have you two been doing? Watching old reruns of Ozzie and Harriet or something?"

"I think we already know what Miss Preggo here has been up to," Rose laughed.

"What?" Barb cracked back.

"Mm-hmm...and *I* actually have been watching *The L Word*, if you must know," Rose offered slyly.

"You have not," Cassidy said pointedly.

"And why not?" Rose answered in kind. "I was curious."

Cassidy covered her face with her hands as Barb broke out into a hearty laugh. "I really don't want to know," Cassidy cringed.

"I do," Rose poked.

"Mom!"

Rose patted her daughter's back. "You are so easy."

"Yeah, well," Cassidy shook her head. "I don't know why anything you say surprises me."

"Neither do I," Rose winked. "So, dresses then a glass of wine?" she suggested.

"I think at least one of us will be forgoing that," Cassidy put her arm around Barb.

"Yes, well, it appears I will be the designated driver on this adventure," Barb interjected. Cassidy opened her mouth to say something and Barb held up her hand. "No, no...I assure you, you will get to return that favor in the future." Cassidy arched her brow. "Yep. I think we will leave Auntie Alex with babysitting duties; you know...prepare her. You can drive Rose and me while we baby shop for *you*. And then we will toast *my* day of freedom while you sip seltzer and chauffer."

"Have this all planned out; do you? Or are you psychic and didn't tell me?" Cassidy laughed as her mother smirked.

"I don't need a crystal ball to see that future," Barb responded as she headed for the door. Cassidy just rolled her eyes. "I'm so glad everyone seems to know my future."

Rose put her arm around her daughter as she accepted her bag from the clerk. "I told you; you are easy."

Cassidy just laughed. "Let's go. I think I need that glass of wine."

***

"Sparrow."

"What is it you need, Dimitri?"

"You delivered the message?"

"Of course."

"Good. We have a situation. I need you to handle it," he said.

"Oh? And what kind of situation do you need me to handle?" she purred into her phone.

"The House."

Claire Brackett stretched her tall frame. "When?"

"He'll let you know. Do not tell your father, Sparrow."

She chuckled. "Oh, Dimitri, are you worried about Daddy?"

"Heed my…"

"Relax," she moaned.

"Very well. Go prepared."

"Never took you for a boy scout," she mocked him. "You of all people know I am *always* prepared."

"We'll see," he responded before dropping the call.

*****

"Thought we could talk over an ice cream. What do you say?" Dylan nodded his agreement enthusiastically. "The usual?" Alex asked. He nodded. "All right. Two hot fudge sundaes with extra whipped cream coming up. Why don't you go find us a seat and I'll be there in a minute." Dylan scurried off while Alex stepped to the counter to order. She hoped that she could coax the truth from him. She knew Cassidy was touched by Dylan's affection for and desire to be with Alex, but it was also evident that Cassidy was a bit hurt. Alex understood. Dylan was the center of Cassidy's world. They were the center of Alex's. Somehow she needed to find the middle ground. She was learning more and more every day that navigating a family required its own brand of diplomacy.

Alex set down the ice cream sundaes and took a seat across from Dylan. "So, what do you think, Speed? You think Mom will like the ring?"

Dylan nodded as he spooned his sundae into his mouth. "Yeah, and your dress," he giggled slightly.

"Is my dress funny?" Alex asked as she took a bite of her own ice cream. Dylan shrugged and started toying with the cherry on top.

"Dylan, don't play with your food," she warned him gently. "So, my dress isn't funny then?"

"Nah."

Alex swirled her ice cream around in the dish. "Are you excited about the wedding?" Dylan tipped his head slightly. "Speed?"

"I guess," he said.

"Something you want to talk about?" she pried. He shook his head.

"You know your mom is really looking forward to you walking her down the aisle." Alex paused. "Even if it is a really short aisle," she joked.

"I guess."

"Speed? Don't you want to walk with your mom?" He shrugged. "Hey, I know you love your mom. What is it?" He looked up at her as tears formed in his eyes. "Dylan, what has you so upset?"

"Your family stands with you, right?"

"Sometimes they do." He shrugged. "Dylan?"

"I'm not really your family."

"What?" Dylan twirled his ice cream in the bowl. Alex scooted her stool closer. "Why would you say that?" she asked, feeling as if her heart had just broken.

"Cause...I'm not."

Alex sighed. "I thought you wanted Mom and me to get married?" Alex noted his tears beginning to escape. "Dylan, I love you as if you were my own son. I told you that. Wedding or not I would still want you to be my son."

"Jason says steps have to say that, but blood is thicker than water and steps are just water. His brother told him. That's why you have Nick and Mom has me. He has a step mom and a step dad. You don't marry the kid, you marry the mom."

"Jason from soccer said that?" Dylan nodded. Alex thought for a moment. 'Kids,' she griped to herself. "Well, Aunt Barb is standing with your mom and they aren't *blood* related." Dylan looked at her closely. "Do you remember when I asked you if I could marry Mom?" He nodded. "You do? Well, I did that because we are a family. We all fit together, you and me and Mom. As far as I am concerned you walking your mom to me is the most important job in the whole wedding." He looked at her curiously. "But, I think I understand and you are right, Dylan."

"I am?"

"Well, most people think of weddings as about two people. So, Jason is right, but he is also very wrong." She looked at the small boy across from her and smiled. "A lot of times when people get married it is just the two of them. You really can only marry one person at a time, and I can't marry you Dylan," she joked lightheartedly. "You are too young for me and that would be weird. You're my son." He tried not to laugh. "But, you raise an interesting point. When someone like me marries someone like your mom, it isn't really only two people; is it?" He crinkled his mouth slightly. "I have an idea. You are going to have to help me with it and we will surprise Mom." He looked up hopefully. "That is if you still want me and Mom to get married? Because, Speed, you have to want that too." She could see the answer plainly on his face. "Okay, then how do you feel about talking in front of everybody?" He shrugged. Dylan was outgoing much like his mother. "Good. So, new plan...but you still walk Mom." He nodded.

"Will Mom be mad?"

Alex smiled at him in reassurance. She had been giving the situation a great deal of thought all day and she was quite proud of the plan she had devised. She had shared some of her thoughts with her mother after their lunch while they watched

Dylan on a nearby playground. Alex could tell her mother was touched by her idea. Helen had assured Alex that Cassidy would be moved by it as well. Dylan's concerns were not exactly what she had expected, but she understood his feelings. He needed to be a part of this in a very tangible way, not as a token. "Ready for the plan?" He nodded vigorously. "Okay, here it is…"

***

"You did well, Ambassador."

"I did nothing, Dimitri…but act as the gopher I am," Russ Matthews responded.

"Nonsense, this was an important mission. You know what is at stake," Dimitri said.

Matthews sighed. "I do know what is at stake. I wonder how we justify the risks."

"Well, Ambassador, we all know these are necessary evils to keep control. You know that as well as anyone."

"Giving terrorists the means to use biological…"

"Don't be naïve, Ambassador. They have the means to acquire what we have provided from any number of sources. Best it be us so that we can ensure containment."

Matthews laughed sardonically. "Containment?"

"You would do well to remember why you are here," the SVR agent reminded Matthews.

"Oh, I am more than aware why I am here, Mr. Kargen. I just wonder when we will all accept the fact that we are dinosaurs in a new age." Kargen looked at the Ambassador harshly. "Oh, come now, Dimitri. This is a new world. Control and containment are illusions. What is to come is inevitable."

Kargen stood stoically. "What is to come is whatever we decide it will be. We are the commanders."

Matthews shook his head. "You know what happens when you try too hard to maintain control, Dimitri?" the ambassador asked as he looked across Red Square. "No? Control is

406

the pretext for containment, no? There is only one outcome, Dimitri, only one." Dimitri Kargen remained expressionless. "Fools; that is what we are. Collapse is the inevitability in all of this."

"You have lost your courage and your conviction," Kargen said simply.

Matthews' caustic reply came swiftly. "Con artists can have as much conviction as any commander I have ever known. As for courage, well...I suppose we will all need that soon enough," he remarked as he began to stroll away. Ambassador Russ Matthews combed his thoughts as he made his way through the square. "Going to take a lot more than courage," he said quietly as he continued forward. "I just wonder how many more casualties we will suffer first," he mused. Heaviness overtook him as he studied the historical sites in the heart of Moscow. Now, he would simply wait and watch until he was called upon again.

***

Tuesday, May 26th

"I have to say I was surprised you wanted me here already."

"It's not about the wedding, Fallon," Alex said.

"So what is it?" he asked as they walked toward the stream that abutted Alex and Cassidy's property.

Alex took a seat on a large tree stump near the water's edge. "Dylan loves to sit here and skip rocks," she said softly.

"Alex?" Fallon asked with some concern.

She skipped a rock across the water's surface. "Fallon, I think you are probably the only person I can be certain of right now."

"What's going on?"

Alex closed her eyes, threw her head back and pinched the bridge of her nose. She was about to invite Brian Fallon into a world the likes of which she could barely fathom. If he accepted, it would mean immersing himself in a culture that defied the logic she knew he relied on so heavily throughout his career. Worse still, it would mean secrecy, deception, and danger. "Look, before I tell you anything; there are things you need to understand. And, if you choose to accept what I am about to ask you," she stopped and momentarily reconsidered her actions.

"Toles? What is it?" She did not answer immediately, staring out at the ripples in the water and shaking her head. "Whatever it is; I'm not afraid to…"

"You should be. I am," she warned.

"I didn't choose this profession to walk away when it got nasty or when it got dangerous. There are always risks, Alex. We both know that. Exposing the truth, protecting people, that…."

"Fallon, if you choose to follow me into this you are going to discover that truth is not a two sided coin." She stood and regarded him closely. "Even a coin has multiple dimensions. Truth is like that. Heads or tails, Fallon?" She shook her head. "Which is right and which is wrong? All about perception."

"What are you talking about?" he asked in confusion.

"You know when I first started working as a profiler I realized quickly that most times the people I was chasing didn't view their actions as wrong. You can call it justification or rationalization. You can call it whatever you like. I had to learn to walk in their truth in order to discover their secrets, uncover their weaknesses, and root them out. They were easy. Serial killers, warlords, drug dealers, even terrorists. They existed in small networks, seldom elaborate. No matter how intelligent or how creative; they were easy to expose. Their agendas were clear; money, idealism or sex. It was all self-gratification. This… this is…"

"Alex," he moved toward her. "I can't walk away from this. I won't."

She grimaced at his statement and clasped his arm. "I know. I just need you to understand, this is totally off the grid. *Do you understand?*" He searched her for her meaning silently. "Nothing to Tate, nothing to Taylor, and nothing to Kate. As far as any of them know nothing has changed with your allegiance, your objective…"

"I understand. Now tell me what you need."

Alex pulled out a piece of paper and unfolded it. She handed it to Fallon and watched him study it. "They are coordinates. Code names and coordinates."

"For what?" he asked.

She shook her head. "That I don't know yet. At least not all of it. Some were easy to discern. Many are embassies. A few are military bases. Some, well…they seem to be in the middle of nowhere, or in the middle of a major city; but obscure. Moscow, Berlin, Paris, London, even Washington all appear on that list. But there is no landmark to correspond. It's dead space. A residential neighborhood, a street."

"Maybe it's just…"

"No, it is something, Fallon," she said as she began to pace toward the water's edge. "I found that in my father's office." She noted his silence. "On that paper, scroll down to where the words begin to appear. You see The Broker?" She gave him a moment. "Keep reading down.

He began to recite the list, "Crow, Fox, Goddess, Griffin, Hawk, Peddler, Phoenix, Sparrow…"

"Spider," she said.

"And?"

Alex turned. "Spider, Fallon. That is *me*. I am the spider."

"What are you talking about? Are you trying to tell me you have been agency all…"

"No. I didn't even know about it until I was in London. At first I thought Matthews was bating me, but Krause confirmed it."

"I don't understand."

409

"I don't either. Not totally anyway. From what Krause told me I was assigned that handle when I entered Intelligence. Doesn't make sense. That note is older than…"

"Maybe Krause is lying," he interjected.

"Could be," she admitted. "If he is, he is trying to protect me from something."

"That's a shift," Fallon noted.

"I'm not so sure about that either. The Broker, Fallon," she inhaled deeply and expelled her breath with force. "The Broker is my father." Fallon's face went pale. "Tell *me*. Krause and I, we stopped an exchange in London; made a switch if you will. There will be fallout. There's another scheduled. Krause thinks it's biological. He believes my father is engineering the transportation and probably arranged the money chain. Seems my father's company is more of a front than a business."

"Your father is CIA?"

"Didn't say that," she answered. "I don't really know who we are dealing with. Yes, most are agency. Krause, Matthews, Ambassador Daniels, and John….but it isn't formal channels doling out orders or missions, Fallon."

"Then who?" he asked.

"Jane and Krause call it The Collaborative."

Fallon rubbed his face vigorously with is hand. "Jane? As in Jane Merrow, the former first lady?" Alex just raised her brow. "Jesus Christ, Alex."

"Gets worse, Fallon." He shook his head. "You'd better sit down." Fallon complied and sat on the tree stump. "Look, what the overall objective is in this, I don't know. I do know that the president….John…was working from within much longer than most knew. He was close to something. He got too close, slipped his hand…"

"With you, you mean?"

Alex shook her head. "That didn't help. He didn't place me at Cassidy's just to take care of Fisher. He was worried about their safety."

Fallon was confused. "About Cassidy's? Why? Because of O'Brien?"

Alex took a deep breath. "He hated O'Brien near as I can tell. O'Brien's placement wasn't his choice." She skipped another stone and then turned back to him. "Yes, Cassidy...but also Dylan. He wanted them protected. He needed someone he could trust implicitly. He just never counted on..."

"Okay, but..."

"Fallon...Dylan," she nodded and then smiled. "Dylan is John's son." Fallon looked as if he had not heard the words correctly. "You heard me correctly. The details really don't matter. It's true. Dylan is Cassidy and John Merrow's son."

Fallon put his face in his hands and digested the information. "Who knows?"

"Other than Cassidy and I?" He nodded. "He did. Jane, Krause and Rose...now you. That's it." He sighed. "There's one more thing. You know O'Brien shot me." He looked at her severely. "He showed up at the house after. Cassidy just....she lost it. She told him he's not Dylan's father."

"He knows? Shit...Alex..."

"Nah...long story. Bottom line? He thinks Krause is Dylan's father. Now, so does Taylor." Fallon shook his head in disbelief. "I know it's all crazy. I trust you, Brian. You need to know what is at stake. These people are dealing in chemical weapons, biological agents and God only knows what else. That alone would be reason enough for you to walk away. I can't. It's my family; more than I knew. With my father involved, I have to..."

Fallon turned and looked at Alex. "Alex, I'm in."

She nodded and handed him another piece of paper from her pocket. "Memorize that number, Fallon."

"What is it?"

"It's a pin code to a warehouse in Baltimore. That's all I know. Krause will be in touch. You will need that. Once you commit it to memory, burn it." He swallowed hard and nodded.

"What about you? What did you make of Tate being at State?" he asked.

"My best guess is he is agency. At some point he made that turn. Makes sense. John trusted Tate. So we watch. And we watch Taylor. I made the suggestion that he focus Brady on chatter surrounding Northern Africa and a shipment. You need to keep looking into O'Brien's accident. I still think there is more there. Watch Claire and be mindful of everything. Taylor can't know you are working with Krause and me. You are the wild card." Fallon nodded.

"What are we hoping to do?" he asked.

"Break them apart, expose them, whatever we have to do to shut down this Collaborative. First we have to figure out what their end game is and who they really are."

"More stressful than a wedding," he cracked.

"I definitely would not say that," Alex smiled.

"Alex, no matter what…"

"You listen to me, Fallon. The moment I think your family is in any danger you are out. No arguments."

Fallon's frustration was evident. "So you can risk your…"

"No, Fallon. My family was already at risk. Dylan's at risk just by who he is. Now, with my father in the mix…I have no choice. You cannot hide from these people and you can't run from them. You *do* have a choice. I am letting you make it for now, but I will not let you risk Kate or the kids. It's not worth it. If I had a choice…"

Brian Fallon saw the array of emotions cross his partner's face. "Agreed," he conceded. "Now, uh…how do you feel about bachelor parties?" he lightened the conversation.

"About the same as I feel about frills," she laughed as she led him up the hill. She was relieved to have someone she trusted completely on her team. As they made their way back toward the house, Alex captured sight of Barb and Rose and realized Brian Fallon's presence was welcome for more than professional reasons.

***

Chapter Thirty-One

Thursday, May 28ᵗʰ

"Getting nervous?" Rose asked her daughter. Cassidy just smiled as she poured them each a cup of coffee. "Alex left early this morning," Rose changed the subject.

"Yeah. She's been preoccupied all week," Cassidy offered.

"You think she's anxious about the wedding?"

Cassidy sat down and shook her head. "No. I don't. At least not yet."

"You worried?" her mother inquired.

"About the wedding? No. About Alex? A little."

"Cassie? It's not just that, is it?"

"No. I met with Steven on Monday." Rose was unsure what Cassidy was driving at. "Steven Richards." Steven Richards had handled Cassidy's divorce. "About custody of Dylan," Cassidy explained.

"I see. And?"

"Well, he expects what I expect. One way or another there will be a challenge to Dylan's paternity. Whether Chris drives that or whether I have to."

"Chris already knows, doesn't he?" Rose sought confirmation.

"Yeah, he knows. But, you know Chris. This will not be about Dylan's best interest." She sipped her coffee slowly and closed her eyes in thought. It didn't matter what Christopher O'Brien did. Cassidy was resigned to her decision. "Doesn't matter, Mom. I had him start the paperwork. I'm seeking full custody of Dylan."

"What does Alex say?"

"She doesn't know yet," Cassidy answered.

"You haven't told her? Cassie…"

"No, not yet. I also spoke with him about Alex."

"You mean that Alex would receive custody should anything happen to you."

"Yes. Challenging the paternity also paves the way for adoption. If Alex would want that."

"What do you mean *if* Alex would want that?" Rose looked at her daughter carefully. "You don't think she would?"

Cassidy shrugged. "I do, but I would never assume."

"And you haven't said anything to her?" Cassidy shook her head. "Don't you think you should?"

"I will, tonight. It's sort of my wedding present." Cassidy laughed. "Kind of a stressful wedding present, huh?"

"Oh, I don't know about that," Rose reassured her. "I'm pretty certain there isn't anything you could give Alex that would mean more to her."

"I hope so."

Rose grinned. Alex had shared her plans for Dylan's involvement in the wedding ceremony with her earlier in the week. All Cassidy knew was that Dylan would be walking her down the aisle. Alex explained that she had spoken with Dylan, that he understood it was a very important job, and that he was a very important part of their ceremony. Cassidy accepted that explanation happily. Rose almost started to laugh. Cassidy was really the only one in the family that remained in the dark other than Cat. At first, Rose had cautioned Alex that Dylan might let the cat out of the bag, but Alex seemed completely confident in her grandson's ability to keep the changes a surprise. To her astonishment, he had. In fact, he seemed to beam with pride in the trust Alex had placed in him.

Rose watched as her daughter contentedly sipped her morning coffee, noticing how Cassidy's ring glistened in the sun. She marveled at the way Alex and Cassidy seemed to consider the other so thoughtfully and with such care. "I am happy for you, Cassie," she said with emotion.

Cassidy saw the tenderness in her mother's eyes. "I know." She smiled. "You love her almost as much as I do," Cassidy chuckled.

"Probably so. If I was thirty years younger you might have some competition," Rose chided.

"Yeah? I think that's enough *L Word* episodes for you, Grandma." They both burst into laughter. "Thanks, Mom."

"For?"

"Oh, I think you know. Watching Alex go through what she has with her father. Well, I just know how lucky I really am."

"Cassie, believe me when I tell you; you *are* very lucky." Cassidy started to laugh at her mother's response when she noticed that Rose had a tear in her eye. "You are lucky to have found someone that makes you so happy. But, believe me when I tell you that I am lucky too. I'd like to take all the credit," Rose arched her brow playfully, "but the truth is that you were a compassionate child who has turned out to be an extraordinary woman. Not every parent can say that." Cassidy was dumfounded at her mother's heartfelt compliment. "I may tease you relentlessly, but I am always proud of you. Your father would be too. If you want my opinion, biased as it may be, Alex won the jackpot when she found you and Dylan."

"Mom, I…"

Rose kissed her daughter's cheek as she made her way to her feet. "There is no one in this world I love more than you Cassidy Rose. Not a soul. I would move heaven and earth to see you happy. I just didn't have to." She pulled her daughter to her chest. "You found what we all dream of. Just hold onto it."

"I know that it isn't exactly what you would have expected," Cassidy admitted.

"No, Cassie, it is much more."

"I love you, Mom."

"I know. Now, finish that coffee so we can get moving," Rose redirected the conversation. Cassidy wiped a tear from her eye as she contemplated her mother's words. She didn't see her mother do the same as she made her way to the sink. Rose looked back at her daughter with a sense of immense pride. She was certain that Alex and Cassidy had many hurdles ahead of them. That was life and their life was not like other couples' in so many ways. But, their devotion to one another was unique. It gave Rose more than hope for her daughter's future. It gave her confidence that whatever might come to pass, Alex and Cassidy would endure.

***

Claire Brackett moved inside the abandoned building on L Street slowly. "This must be good," she said as she entered a small room.

"Claire," the man answered. "Nice of you to show."

"Can't say as I expected to see you any time soon," she dripped with insincerity.

"Yes, well…things have changed." He handed her a paper. "That is an address and a container number."

"I can read," she shot back at him.

"You will need to be cautious, Claire. The contents are hazardous."

"All right. Why the rush?"

"Toles is on this already. Agent Brady put her on the path this morning. You need to move." He handed her a small case. She opened it and regarded the series of needles laid out inside. She took a deep breath with a sudden understanding of the potential danger.

"Prussian Blue. Let's hope you won't need them," he said. "I am sending Agent Anderson with you." She looked to him with alarm as the second agent appeared. "He will not enter, but he will be in constant communication. He knows the landscape."

"He's NSA," she said skeptically, warning the tall, muscular man before her with her eyes.

"He's ours. They have no idea what they are walking into. You do. You have the advantage, but you need to move now."

"I don't like it," she said definitively, still staring at the man before her. Agent Marc Anderson towered over the smaller, older man that stood at the room's center. His seemed to almost glisten where the light from the cracks in the window boards filtered onto his dark skin. He watched her appraisal of him. His short sleeved, white T-shirt accented his muscular features and he could see her appreciative gaze. "Don't worry," the agent assured. "You'll be safe with me."

Claire Brackett stared at him. "If I were you, Agent Anderson...I would be the one that would worry," she hissed. "One move that I don't like..."

"You are spunky," he allowed a smile to escape.

"Relax, Claire," the older man intervened. "And, get used to it. You and Anderson will be seeing a lot of each other."

She seethed at the remark. "We'll see."

"No. It wasn't a suggestion. It isn't a request. It's a fact. Go. Anderson knows the drop plan."

Reluctantly, Brackett moved to follow her new partner. She turned back slowly. "One day she will figure it all out, you know," Brackett gloated.

"Perhaps," he said. "Not today."

***

"Toles...let me go in," Krause urged.

"Now how does that make sense?" she asked. "If anything happens and I do get stopped...at least *I* have a chance of leaving quietly, without any altercation. My name alone gives me an advantage. It is a Carecom facility after all."

Krause hated to admit that Alex was right. "I don't like it. We don't even know what the package is."

"No, we don't," Alex agreed. "All the more reason we need as many advantages as we can get." He nodded with apprehension. Alex opened the car door and adjusted the feed in her ear. Krause opened a small netbook on his lap. "Listen," she said as she exited the car. "Remember what I asked you…"

"I'll have you on screen the entire time, Toles. The first sign of trouble and…"

Alex smiled genuinely. "I almost think you are worried there, Pip."

"You just watch yourself," he instructed. Alex smiled and headed toward the rear of the warehouse, adjusting her side arm under her sweater. "Watch yourself, Toles," he muttered.

***

"I'm not certain what Dimitri is up to," Admiral Brackett said.

"You know he is just Viktor's errand boy, Bill," Callier responded.

"Yes, well, I am fairly certain he has Claire in his pocket. She came home empty handed."

"The Russians don't trust Matthews either," Callier surmised.

"No. Merrow did."

"Umm…how close was he?" Callier inquired.

"Too close," the admiral answered. "I need to know, Edmond. Which side of this you come down on."

Edmond Callier smiled confidently. "The same as I always have, just as you. What choice do we have?"

"And Krause?" the admiral asked.

"He'll fall in line."

"You seem rather sure of that. He and Merrow…and now the boy."

"Krause is secure, Bill," Callier assured. "When the time comes he will stand firm. I have no doubt." Admiral Brackett took a deep breath. "You want to make the call?" Callier asked.

"I think it had best come from you at this juncture, Edmond."

"Very well."

***

Claire Brackett moved cautiously through the narrow hallway toward a large steel door. She paused briefly to look side to side where two corridors met. Seeing that her pathway was clear she continued forward. '4-1-1-2-1-2' she punched the numbers into the keypad and the door clicked. "Showtime," she whispered.

***

Alex watched as Brackett entered the room. She followed behind and grabbed the door just before it shut. "You getting this?" she asked quietly.

"Yeah, I see her," Krause responded.

"At least she was kind enough to let me in," Alex joked.

"Just keep your distance. Let her lead," he instructed. Alex did not answer. She positioned herself behind a loader and watched the younger agent search an aisle loaded with steel containers. "Toles," Krause broke in. "I mean it, just watch for now." The sound of the car door opening startled the CIA agent. "What in the hell?"

***

"What am I looking for, Anderson? None of these are numbered," Brackett griped.

"It will be small. Look for a red stamp on the front. USMED," he answered.

Several yards away Alex ducked behind a pallet full of packing materials. She crouched as low as her body would allow and listened carefully. Brackett, believing she was alone spoke again. "USMED?"

"Think about it, Brackett," Anderson replied.

She shook off her question and continued her search. Alex kept her gaze locked on Brackett and attempted to scan ahead for a secure pathway to follow. She heard Krause's question. "What in the hell?"

"What?" Alex asked in a whisper. "Krause, what do you see?"

"Brady," was his response.

"You see Brady?"

"Yeah, he's next to me."

"What in the hell?" Alex now repeated.

"What are you doing here?" Krause asked the NSA agent.

"Listen to me, Krause, we don't have much time," Brady answered.

"What are you talking about?" Krause asked.

Alex tried to discern the conversation in the car while keeping tabs on Brackett. "She's moving, I gotta find an avenue."

"Get her out of there now," Brady demanded.

"What?" Krause shook his head. "Why would I do that?"

"It's not biological, Krause. Get her out of there. It's Cesium-137."

"What are you talking about, where did you…"

"Doesn't matter now. Later…she's not prepared. Get her out of there."

Krause recognized the tension on Brady's face. "Toles, leave it. Get out of there now."

"Are you insane?" Alex responded. "I am not letting Claire Brackett get her hands on any kind of weapon."

"Toles!" he shouted. She did not respond. "Shit!" He reached in a bag behind his seat and handed Brady an ear piece. "You watch her and tell me where she goes."

"Where are you going?" Brady asked.

"To get her," Krause responded.

***

"What the hell are you doing, Brackett?" Alex asked herself.

422

"Toles!" Krause's voice bellowed through the earpiece. "Stay where you are." The decibel of the agent's voice in her ear was maddening and she loosened the device slightly. "Do you hear me?"

"Shit. She's grabbing something." Alex moved carefully around the corner of a large crate. "No way, Brackett. Not this time." Alex moved closer, swiftly and silently until she was directly behind her former lover. "Didn't your daddy ever tell you it's not nice to take other people's things," Alex breathed in the redhead's ear.

"Miss me?" Brackett fluttered her eyelashes as she turned.

Alex scoffed at the notion. "Sorry."

"Oh, now Alex, did you want something?" Brackett smiled seductively.

"From you?" Alex asked. Brackett smiled and placed both of her hands on Alex's chest. "No," Alex said pointedly. "Just for you to leave."

"Oh, come on, Agent; before we even dance? I mean shouldn't I get at least one before you are off the market."

Alex arched her brow and rebuked the woman's suggestive offer with a smile of disdain. Brackett shrugged and turned back toward the container. "Step away from the container Brackett, or we will dance."

"Promise?" the redhead dripped with excitement. Alex watched as Brackett reached forward. She grabbed the redhead's fore arm and spun her around swiftly. "OOO....Alex, I forgot how forceful you can be," she growled as she began to raise her hand toward Alex's neck.

"Too bad I didn't forget how overanxious *you* are," Alex shot and swiftly caught Brackett's hand, pulling it behind her back.

"Like the rough stuff, huh?" Brackett winced. "That teacher must have some talent. Never would have guessed that from her ex-husband." Brackett moved her left leg sideways and swiped Alex off balance. Each now stood staring at each other, warring with their eyes and words and seeking to anticipate the next move.

"Leave Cassidy out of it," Alex hissed. She saw Brackett's kick in motion and caught it in the air. "That all you got?" Alex asked. Brackett chuckled but her anger was growing hotter. She swung at Alex with her right hand. Alex avoided the contact and placed a kick to the younger woman's thigh. She continued forward and placed another kick against Brackett's opposite hip, knocking her backward. "Don't test me, Claire," Alex warned. She moved toward the container as Krause reached the door.

"Brady, I need a code," Krause said. Brady shook his head. "Brady!"

"I don't know. Can you pry off the panel?" Brady suggested.

Krause looked at it closely. "Yeah, I think so." He heard the sound of crashing behind the door. "Shit. TOLES!!" he screamed in the earpiece.

"Kinda busy right now, Pip," she answered accepting a kick to her ribs.

"What the hell is going on?" Anderson yelled into Brackett's ear. "Just get the damned package!"

"Working on it," Brackett answered just as Alex managed to land a punch to her left cheek.

"Pull your sidearm, Brackett!" Anderson demanded.

"No, no," she soothed. "This is my show."

"Show, huh?" Alex licked her lips. "You are a piece of work, Claire." Alex moved closer and tipped her head. "Just curious; what is it you see in that asshole anyway?"

"Jealous?" Brackett asserted as she threw a punch at Alex.

"Did you get it off yet?" Brady asked Krause.

"Yeah, shit....does Brackett know what is in there?" Krause asked.

"No idea," Brady answered.

Alex gave Brackett a cocky smile. "Why do you want that case so badly?" she asked in the hopes Claire Brackett would give up the contents.

"You don't even know what you are after," Claire cooed.

Krause pushed the door open and Alex turned slightly to see him approaching when she felt a hard kick to her abdomen. Brackett flew toward the small container and grabbed it. Alex reached her feet. She grabbed another box and slid it across the floor, sending Brackett and the case crashing to the ground. Immediately she was in motion toward them both. "NO!" Krause's voice bellowed. Suddenly, two strong arms had hold of Alex as Brackett made it to her feet. Brackett fumbled with the container in her hands and then sprinted away. Alex struggled to free herself from Krause's grasp. "Let her go, Alex."

"What the hell are you doing Krause?"

"Did it open?" Brady asked with urgency.

"What?" Alex asked, hearing his question in her ear.

Krause loosened his grip and put his hands on his knees to catch his breath. "Did the container open?" Brady asked from his location.

"Why?" Alex questioned. "What the hell is going on?"

"Cesium, Toles." Krause regained his footing. "Cesium-137."

"You let Claire Brackett leave here with nuclear material? Are you insane?" she asked. "What the hell were you thinking?"

"You asked me something the other day," Krause answered.

"What the hell does that have to do with this?" Alex demanded.

"Everything," he said calmly. Alex looked at him and shook her head.

"Krause, you and Brady just let Claire Brackett leave here with the key ingredient for a dirty bomb."

"Yeah, I know. But we know what it is and we know who took it. We'll find its destination, Alex," Krause said calmly. "And you'll live to do that."

Alex pinched the bridge of her nose. "Jesus."

"We need to make sure we weren't exposed," Krause said.

"The case wasn't open," Alex said definitively. "Looks like I'll be home late again," Alex shook her head.

"At least you'll be home. Thanks for that, by the way," Krause said.

"What?" Alex asked as they walked toward the exit.

"I really would hate to tell Cassidy why you were glowing in the dark at her wedding. Much less why you failed to show up." Alex laughed. "Next time just listen to me," he suggested.

"Don't count on it, Pip," she answered.

"I'm not," he admitted assuredly. "I'm not."

***

Alex stretched out on the bed and closed her eyes. "You okay?" Cassidy asked.

"Hum? Yeah, just tired," Alex answered.

Cassidy sighed and sat down on the bed. "Alex, I need to talk to you about something before tomorrow. You'll be at Nick's and I'll be at the hotel…"

Alex opened her eyes at the seriousness in Cassidy's voice. "What's wrong?"

"Nothing," Cassidy answered. "Nothing is wrong. I just." She took a deep breath. "Alex, can I ask you something?'

"You can ask me anything."

Cassidy was suddenly very nervous. "I met with my lawyer on Monday." Alex was puzzled. "About custody of Dylan."

Alex sat up. They had discussed this, but she did not want to press Cassidy on the issue. "You did?" Cassidy nodded. "And?"

"We both know that Chris is likely to make it, well…messy." Alex chuckled. "I started the process. Whatever happens, I want him with us, where I know he is safe and where I know he is happy." Alex nodded. "There is something else though." Alex looked at Cassidy curiously. "Well, we will likely have to establish that Dylan is not Christopher's biological son. He won't relinquish rights; you know that. Even if he doesn't exercise them."

"I know. Are you okay with that, Cass?"

"Yeah, I am." She moved closer to the agent. "Alex, once that happens. I...well..."

"What is it?"

"I want to know if you would want to adopt Dylan." Alex lost her breath. "You don't have to answer now. It will take months before..."

"He would be my son," Alex said quietly.

"Legally, yes."

Alex looked up. "What if he doesn't want that?"

"Well, I don't think that is a concern, Alex. I truly don't."

"You would really want that?" Alex asked.

"Of course," Cassidy said.

"Thanks, Cass."

"For?"

"For being you." Cassidy smiled and kissed Alex's forehead. "My last chance you know," Alex said.

"Last chance for what?" Cassidy asked.

Alex smirked. "Last chance to make love to Cassidy O'Brien."

"Oh, I guess it is, isn't it?" Alex raised her brow suggestively. Cassidy kissed the agent's neck and began caressing her sides. Alex winced and jumped. "Alex?" The agent smiled sheepishly. Cassidy lifted Alex's T-shirt and her mouth flew open at the sight of the black and green bruise that adorned Alex's rib-cage. "What the hell happened?" Cassidy asked.

"It's nothing," Alex said. "I've had worse. I'm fine."

"I call bull shit," Cassidy said somewhat harshly.

"Honest, I am okay."

"Yeah...you're not shot. I wouldn't call this okay," Cassidy asserted. "Just tell me that the other guy is worse off."

"Oh, I am sure she is," Alex said with some satisfaction.

"She?"

Alex sighed. "Umm...Brackett."

"You fought with Agent Brackett? When? Why?" Alex pinched the bridge of her nose and Cassidy took a deep breath. "You know what...I don't want to know."

"No, you don't," Alex said. "Now, come on; where were we?"

"Ohhhh no….*that* is nasty. Your ribs aren't even fully healed from France. No way."

"Cass…"

"Uh-uh. Sorry, Agent…you will just have to wait for Cassidy Toles."

"You are not serious?" Alex complained. Cassidy fluffed her pillow and laid down on her side.

"Cass? Come on, you are not really mad; are you?"

Cassidy turned over and looked at Alex. "No, Alex. I'm not mad." She caressed the agent's cheek. "It scares me sometimes. Seeing you hurt…"

"Cass, it's just a bruise."

"This time," Cassidy's voice dropped.

"Hey," Alex lifted Cassidy's eyes to her own. "I'm not going anywhere." Cassidy sighed and Alex could feel her tension. "Cassidy, listen to me. Sometimes, yes…I might get a bit banged up. It happens. Trust me when I tell you I have people watching my back. I've got way too much to live for."

"Good," Cassidy said as she planted a light kiss on Alex's lips. Alex tried to pull her closer but Cassidy pulled away. "Before you say it…no, I am not angry. But I fully intend to have you one hundred percent Saturday. No arguments."

Alex conceded her defeat. "At least, just let me make love to you," she practically begged.

"Nice try, Agent." Cassidy gently patted Alex's stomach. "You have the rest of what had better be a very long life to make love to me. Tonight, just hold me. Okay?"

Alex immediately heard the fear break through Cassidy's voice. She wrapped her arms protectively around her lover and mentally slapped herself for not just listening to Krause. It was selfish. She couldn't deny that she had taken some pleasure in her altercation with Claire Brackett. Whatever momentary satisfaction she felt earlier had evaporated the moment she saw the fear in Cassidy's eyes. "Cass?"

"Hum?"

"Still want to marry me?"

Cassidy pulled the agent's arms around her firmly. "Yes, Alex. The answer will always be yes."

Alex took a deep breath. "Je t'aime, Cass."

"Je t'adore. Go to sleep."

***

Friday, May 30th

"Hey," Krause greeted Alex. "How are you feeling?"

"I'd feel better if Brackett didn't have her hands on Cesium."

He acknowledged her feeling with a smile. "We'll find it, Alex."

"How do you think she knew? My father?" Alex asked.

"Maybe, maybe not. She could have gotten the same info as Brady."

"Except I think she knew what it was," Alex explained. Krause shook his head. "I swear to God…"

"How are the ribs?" he inquired.

Alex rolled her eyes. "Sore. Not as sore as Cass was when she saw the bruise last night."

"Ouch," he chuckled. "What did you tell her?"

"The truth, just a really slimmed down version."

"I'm headed back to D.C. tonight," he said. Alex looked at him as he stared out the front window of his sedan. "Callier made contact with Ian. Something is going down. I need to meet with the admiral."

Alex nodded. "Are you going to see Cass before you leave?"

"I don't think so."

"Why not?" she asked.

"Not my place, Toles."

Alex sighed. "I disagree." He looked at her. "Look, I'm not going to lie to you. I still don't know what to make of all of this. And, truth be told I am still not convinced you are being totally honest with me. But," she looked at him and smiled. "You compromised a mission for my safety yesterday. It's not the first time you have compromised yourself. You love her. I get it."

"Toles…"

"Krause, you mean something to Cass. Maybe it isn't what you wanted, but you do. I'll never understand how she ended up with O'Brien."

"Neither will I," he conceded.

"Point is, she is the best judge of character I know. Save that jerk. And frankly, I think she figured him out long ago and just couldn't admit it to herself. At least call her."

Krause was surprised. "You are lucky."

"I know," Alex said.

"Listen, Toles…when that disk we switched gets to….when they realize…they are going to think it was Matthews who made the switch."

"I know," she admitted.

"Then you also know what might happen." She nodded. "If the admiral is expecting me, it's likely they suspect something already." Alex closed her eyes and sighed. Russ Mathews was a friend. "What they'll do…"

"I know. For whatever it is worth I think he expects it," she said.

"You'd better go, Toles. You have a big day tomorrow," he grinned.

"Yeah, I do," she laughed.

"What?" he asked.

"The last few weeks I seem to be saying 'I do' all the time. Like it's rehearsal or something." Krause laughed. "Call Cass, wish her luck."

"Why? Think she needs it?" he joked.

"Developing a sense of humor?" Alex snapped back.

"Don't tell anyone."

"Your secret is safe with me, Pip."

"Take care of her," he said as Alex exited the car. Alex just smiled. Krause gripped the wheel and started the ignition. "Now Admiral, let's see what you are planning," he mused.

***

The black phone that sat on the corner of the large wooden desk rang. A hand reached slowly over and lifted the receiver. Landline; that was not a good sign. A steady man's voice came through immediately. "There's been a fracture. Time to call in The Broker."

A forceful sigh escaped through a painful silence. "I understand," was the only response.

"Sphinx must be ready," the voice demanded.

The hand holding the black receiver tightened its grip. "I'll take care of it."

"Quickly," the voice responded.

Slowly the receiver fell back to its home leaving only the hollow echo of a dial tone to linger. "I'll take care of it."

***

Chapter Thirty-Two

Saturday, May 31st

"My God, Cassidy," a voice called softly. "You look gorgeous."

Cassidy turned and offered a slightly embarrassed smile. "Let's hope your sister feels that way," she said.

Nick shook his head. "I hope it's okay. Barb didn't want to let me in. I had to bribe her."

Cassidy laughed and motioned to her future brother-in-law to sit. "How is Alex?" she asked.

"Pacing."

"I know this will sound crazy, but I miss her."

Nick reached for Cassidy's hand. "It's not crazy at all. Cassidy?" She smiled at him and raised her brow. "I want you to know how much you mean to this family." Cassidy tilted her head in confusion. "I'm sorry about my father. I tried."

"Nick…"

"No, please. Let me say this. Growing up, Alex was my best friend. I got picked on a lot. I was small. Alex, well, she never let me feel small." Cassidy watched as Nick's emotions threatened to overtake him. She had noticed from the first time she had met Alex's brother how much Nick adored his older sister. Cassidy understood how the tension in the Toles family created a lingering sense of loss and sadness that plagued all of them over many years. She listened intently as Nick continued. "Having Alex in my life, in Cat's, everyone being together, my mother with Alex; I don't think that would have happened without you. You gave me my family back."

Cassidy took a deep breath. Nick was very much like his sister. Not everyone saw the side of Alex Toles that revealed her innocence and tenderness. Cassidy witnessed it in every moment, even when Alex seemed to exude strength and purpose. With Cassidy, Alex's deepest fears and desires were always exposed. Family meant the world to the man before her, just as it did to her lover. "Nick," he looked at the sparkling green eyes that held his. "I didn't give you your family back." He started to protest and Cassidy placed her hand on his cheek. "You and Barb, Cat, and now Helen; you complete what Alex brought to both Dylan and I. Alex gave me the family I didn't even realize I was missing. For whatever it is worth we have fallen in love with all of you."

"You know, I knew she was in love with you the first time you came here," Nick confessed. "I even told her so. She denied it. Too soon. You were straight. I was crazy." Cassidy laughed. "I had walked out to check on you. You had your eyes closed. Alex was just watching you." Cassidy pushed back her tears. "I'd never seen that expression on her face before. She was smiling, just watching you. I just wanted you to know. Barb and I...we love you. You are my sister. I would do anything for you and Dylan."

"I know that," she said. "I feel the same way." Sensing a need to shift the conversation, Cassidy stood. "Speaking of my son," she said. "Where is he?" Nick tried to hide an impish grin. "I know that look," Cassidy chastised him. "What are you and Alex up to?"

"Nothing," he feigned innocence. Cassidy narrowed her gaze. "Honest, nothing. Last I knew Dylan was with The Rev."

"You'd better save the good reverend. You know Dylan," she suggested.

"Right," he agreed. "He's probably with Alex by now. I'll make sure he makes his way here."

Cassidy watched as he scampered out the door, passing her mother and Barb with a toothy grin. "Okay, you two," Cassidy warned. "What is going on?"

Rose beamed with pride as she looked at her daughter. "Cassie, Alex might just pass out when she sees you."

"Nice try, Mom. Alex has been in far more stressful situations."

Barb shook her head. "I wouldn't be so sure about that," she remarked.

"Someone please tell me what is going on," Cassidy looked at Barb. "Neither your husband or my future wife are very good at hiding things." Cassidy rolled her eyes. Alex might be completely in command professionally, but at home she was constantly caught with her hand in the proverbial cookie jar. "I've seen that grin plenty. What is Alex up to?"

Rose walked to her daughter and took Cassidy's face in her hands. She could sense just a hint of actual fear in her daughter. "I can't tell you that and neither can Barb," she said plainly. "I will tell you that she loves you…And that she is downstairs fiddling and fussing with anything she can get her hands on."

Cassidy tried to remain stoic but failed. "Just tell me this; am I going to cry and ruin all this mascara?" Both women shrugged. "Great," Cassidy sighed.

"There is no way you are making it through that ceremony, no matter how short without crying and we all know it, so just forget about the mascara," Rose counseled her daughter. "And I will tell you this…" Cassidy perked up in curiosity. "I wouldn't be surprised if you fall over when you see her either. She is beautiful."

Cassidy's expression softened. "Yes, she is."

***

"Alexis, stop fidgeting," Helen giggled.

Alex rubbed her temple with her thumb. "I don't want to screw anything up."

"Are we talking about the vows or the marriage?" Helen asked with a smile.

"Both."

"Want to back out?" Helen asked with as much seriousness as she could muster.

"What? No!"

"Alexis, relax. Cassidy is head over heels in love with you."

Alex smiled and shook her head. "I know. I still can't believe it though."

"She is a remarkable woman," Helen complimented.

"Yeah, she is."

"But then, so are you." Alex was stunned. Her mother continued without missing a beat. "You are Alexis. You always have been. Beautiful, smart…sensitive." Alex bit her lower lip. "Oh you might think you hide that well and you probably do from most people. You've always been sensitive, Alexis. You used to bring home every injured animal you found and try to nurse them back to health. Cats, birds, squirrels; I swear your father and I thought we were raising a future zookeeper." Helen watched as the pained expression fell across her daughter's face. "He does love you, Alexis. I know you don't think so. I understand why you would think that, but today of all days; don't you doubt that. Today is about love. Today is the day to be that sensitive little girl."

Alex took a deep breath and stilled herself. "Thanks, Mom." Helen just smiled.

"Alex!" an exited seven year old bounced into the room. "Whoa!" he said as he caught sight of her.

"What?" she asked him with concern.

"You are so pretty," he said innocently.

Alex tried to remain serious. "Does that surprise you, Speed?" she asked, forcing down her laughter.

"Nah. You're always pretty, just not as pretty as Mom."

His statement ended all hope of containing her amusement and she moved to envelop him in a bear hug. "That is the truth if ever I heard it," she conceded. "Your mom is the most beautiful woman I've ever seen."

"Yep," he said proudly.

Alex stepped back and regarded him. She hadn't seen him since Nick took him to get dressed. He was wearing a small black tuxedo, complete with a black vest to match. What captured her attention immediately was the bow tie around his neck. It too was black, but it sported a repeating pattern of a yellow Batman logo. She straightened it and looked at him with pride. "You look handsome, Batman," she complimented him.

"Mom picked it out for me and Cat."

Helen watched as Alex closed her eyes and intervened. "Speaking of your mom, Batman; we'd better get you to her. Alex needs to go."

He nodded his understanding, but stopped short before leaving. "Alex?" he whispered to her.

"What is it, Speed?"

"The Rev says I can say..."

"You say whatever is in your heart," Alex squatted to meet his eyes. "Mom and I will be right there with you the whole time."

"I won't tell her," he promised as he turned to follow Helen out the door. Alex just winked. She could not imagine a sweeter child.

"Okay sis," Nick called as he entered with Cat. "Any last words?"

Alex laughed. "You have the rings?"

"Everything is all set," he answered.

"Let me see them," she squinted in disbelief. He shook his head. "Aww, come on, Nicky."

"No way, I have my own wife to deal with. I'm not dealing with yours too. She already knows you are up to something."

"What does she know?" Alex asked.

"Nothing, but she knows you. No deal."

"Cat, help me out," Alex pleaded to her nephew. Cat looked at his father, turned back to Alex and shrugged.

"Come on Cat," Barb called. "You come wait with me. I have the rings anyway."

Alex grumbled. "It's time," Nick put out his hand.

"Nicky?"

"Yeah?"

"Did you see her?" Alex asked as they made their way toward the beach.

"Yep."

"How was she?" Nick looked at his older sister and smiled. "Well? Is she okay?"

"You are a lucky woman, Alex," was all he said as they reached their destination.

"I am; huh?"

***

Dylan burst into the room where Cassidy was. Cassidy wasn't certain she had ever seen him so excited. A wide smile graced his small face as he walked tall in his tuxedo. "Look at you," she said.

"Hi Mom," he greeted her. "I like your dress."

Cassidy didn't know how it was possible, but she was certain that the smile on her face had grown even wider. She motioned to her mother and Helen to give them a moment alone. "Thank you," she said to him, patting the seat beside her. "Come sit with me for a minute."

He complied happily and looked up to a pair of eyes quite similar to his own. "Alex looks pretty," he told her.

Cassidy nodded. "I heard."

"Mom?"

"Yes?" she answered, taking a moment to straighten the small bow tie that seemed determined to remain slightly cock-eyed. He smiled at his mother and reached in his pocket to retrieve a slightly crumpled blue ribbon. "What's this for?" she asked.

"It's my lucky ribbon," he said. "Grandma said you had to have something old, something new and something blue."

Cassidy bit her lower lip. She recognized the ribbon and she was astonished at her son's thoughtfulness. "This is your Field Day ribbon," she observed.

"Yep. Remember?" he asked.

"I do remember. Alex came to our house the day you won this." She felt a tear grace her cheek.

"Yep. It's good luck," he said. "Mom? Why are you crying?"

Cassidy wiped the tear from the corner of her eye with her thumb. Her mother was right. She hadn't even made it to Alex and she was already crying. A soft chuckle escaped her lips and she kissed her son's forehead. "Thank you, Dylan." Dylan smiled and hopped to his feet.

"Going somewhere?" she kidded with him as the door opened.

"You ready?" Rose prodded.

Dylan put out his small hand and Cassidy accepted it. He pulled on his mother's hand slightly. "What is it, sweetie?"

"You're the best mom, Mom," he whispered.

Cassidy could feel herself beginning to tremble from emotion. "And you are the best Speed Racer," she winked as they made their way down the stairs.

***

Cassidy reached the doorway and looked out at the scene before her. She could not see Alex immediately with everyone already standing. What she could see nearly left her breathless. There were square, white bricks embedded down the makeshift aisle, separated by a fine line of sand. The chairs were a simple white wood. Along the sides of the aisle were flower sprays of pink, white and green that matched Cassidy's bouquet, each with a starfish in front of them. A small arch stood at the front of the walkway with simple greenery adorning it. "She was out here most of the day yesterday with Nick, Brian and the boys," Barb whispered as Brian Fallon escorted Rose to her seat.

Cassidy took a deep breath and inhaled the ocean air. "It's exquisite," she said softly, scanning the faces that had turned in their direction.

"Wait til you see Alex," Barb whispered as she stepped off.

Cassidy waited a moment and patted Cat's back. "Go on, Cat," she said. He began his slow pace down the short aisle and Cassidy looked down to her son. "Shall we?" she asked, accepting his arm. He smiled up at her proudly and began to lead her the short distance ahead. She looked to her left and saw Jane with the girls and smiled. When she turned back, she could see only one face. Alex was standing next to Nick. Cassidy nearly stopped in her tracks. Alex's hair fell softly over her shoulders in loose curls. Her white dress dropped to a low 'V' where it was adorned by a simple beaded pattern. It fell perfectly over Alex's frame, accentuating her athletic curves. Cassidy swallowed hard as she struggled to keep moving.

Dylan looked up at his mother and smiled. "Pretty, huh?" he said as quietly as he could. Cassidy snapped out of her haze and looked down at him with a nod before returning her sight to the woman she loved.

A few paces away Alex was silently praying that her knees would not buckle. She felt her brother's hand press into her lower back as a means of support. "I told you," he whispered, "lucky." Alex watched as Cassidy and Dylan stepped forward. Cassidy's hair was swept up, much like it had been in London. She was breathtaking. Her dress was simple and elegant. The strapless top was form fitting and changed dramatically at the waistline where it fell in what looked like soft waves until it just brushed the sand. Alex smiled and let out a shaky breath as the pair approached. She took Cassidy's hand and looked deeply into the bright green eyes that held the secrets of her soul. She felt as if she should say something, but she was completely lost just drinking in the sight before her.

The reverend struggled not to laugh himself at the pair before him. He had known Alex since their days in Iraq. The healing and the love that he felt in the presence of the two women was not something he had encountered often. He looked briefly at the array of smiling faces behind the couple and then at Dylan. "Today," he began. "I have the pleasure of joining not two souls, but three." Alex broke out into the widest smile Cassidy had ever seen and Cassidy narrowed her gaze slightly in questioning. Alex just clasped her hand a bit tighter. "When any two people come together it is very special. It is the beginning of a family. Today, we have a family that seeks to come together before us all to pledge their love and devotion to one another. Dylan," he began. Cassidy looked down at her son curiously. "Your mother and Alex came here today to make a commitment to one another in front of their friends and family and God. You are part of your mother and Alex will now be a part of you both. Do you want to commit to this family that your mother and Alex are here to create?" Dylan nodded and The Rev opened his eyes a bit wider.

"Yes," Dylan answered. Cassidy and Alex both smiled.

"And what do you promise to bring to this family?" he asked.

Cassidy looked at Alex in amazement, knowing now that this was the secret she had been keeping and gaining a new understanding of how Dylan accepted his role so enthusiastically. She looked down at her son as he cleared his throat and tried not to giggle at the evident seriousness in his expression. He nodded to The Rev. "Go ahead," the reverend encouraged.

"I promise to love Mom and Alex," he said. "Mom is the best mom. She's the best at video games, she makes the best tacos, and she always makes me feel better," he paused. His declarations were so innocent and so honest it was difficult not to giggle, but his tone was thoughtful and it was obvious he had practiced his words. Rose felt Helen grab her hand as Dylan raised his eyes to his mother and then to Alex as he continued. "But Alex is the funniest. She knows how to make perfect cereal, and she keeps me and Mom safe. She's our protector." Alex and Cassidy exchanged a glance as both accepted there would be no holding back tears. "I promise to try and listen and to protect both my moms. Most kids only get one. I get two." A soft laughter erupted behind him, but Dylan was not fazed. He looked at Cassidy. "I love you Mom," he said and then he turned to Alex. "I love you too, Mom," he said plainly. A tear rolled over Alex's cheek and Cassidy wiped it away.

"We love you, Dylan," Cassidy said.

Dylan smiled and looked back at the reverend. "You had something you wanted to give your parents?" the reverend asked. Dylan nodded and Rose and Helen stepped forward with two small boxes.

Cassidy looked to Alex with her question. Alex shrugged. This was news to her. "Think you are the only one who can keep secrets, huh?" Helen whispered in Alex's ear as Rose raised an eyebrow.

Dylan opened the first box and turned to Cassidy. Rose helped him pull out a delicate necklace with half of a heart as a pendant. At the tip was a diamond and a ruby. Cassidy smiled, immediately understanding the significance. It was adorned with both Alex and Dylan's birthstones. Helen opened the second box and helped Dylan retrieve an identical necklace with one exception. At its tip lay a diamond and a sapphire. The reverend accepted this and nodded again to Dylan. Dylan looked at his mother first. "This is from me, Mom. It's half my heart. It's the part that I give to Alex, so that you can keep us close." Cassidy could not imagine how a seven year old had come up with that sentiment on his own, but the expression on her mother's face conveyed clearly that it was indeed her son's basic idea. She bent down and Rose removed her pearls so she could help Dylan fasten the necklace around his mother's neck.

Cassidy kissed his cheek. "I love you so much, Dylan," she whispered in his ear.

Dylan was elated as he turned to Alex. Alex was completely overcome by the turn of events. She looked at the boy before her and shook her head in awe. "This is for you, Alex. This is the half of my heart I give to Mom, so you can always keep us close." Alex bent over and Helen fastened it around her neck.

"I'm so proud of you," Alex whispered to him.

"Dylan has given you both something very special," the reverend began, "to remind you that you are all a part of one another. Do you accept his offering?" The Rev winked and both women understood their part.

"We do," they answered.

"Now...Dylan, your Mom and Alex have both accepted you as part of them. Now it's time for them to become your moms; officially," he winked.

Dylan nodded and accepted a kiss from each of the women beside him before accepting a hand from Helen and Rose. "I get an extra Grandma too," he said innocently. "'Cept she's a Yaya." The comment received a burst of affectionate laughter from all who heard it as he moved to sit between his two grandmothers.

Cassidy squeezed Alex's hand. She silently wondered how she would get through her vows. Dylan's words were embedded in her heart. Having him stand with them and make his own commitment to their new family; knowing that he wanted to do that; it overwhelmed Cassidy with joy and with pride. Alex felt Cassidy stroke the back of her hand and sighed. She hadn't known what Dylan intended to say. She could never have imagined the way it would fill her heart.

The reverend began the formalities. Cassidy wasn't certain she had heard any of his words. The sound of his voice gently calling her name signaled her that it was time to speak her vows. She looked at Alex and took a deep breath. The warmth of Alex's hands in her own and the gentleness in the blue eyes that she adored calmed her. "Alex…I've tried to think of all of the right words to say to you today. Truthfully, I think that what we share exists beyond words. I remember the very first time you brought me here. When you came into my life, you changed everything. You opened my eyes to a world I had only dreamed could exist. You accepted me. You loved me without any questions or any expectations. That night, as we sat here, I lost myself in your eyes. I've lost myself there every day since and I don't ever want to return. I watch you with Dylan, how you playfully encourage him, how he looks to you to guide him and I am grateful for whatever conspired to send you to us. I cannot imagine our lives without you. When you hold me I feel safe and I know that I am home. When I look at you the past fades away and I find myself thinking of our future together. The family I know we will build. The love I know we will continue to share. I know all of our roads will not be easy. Some might feel like mountains, but I promise you that I will always be beside you. I will always be faithful to what we share and I willingly give you all that I am; my mind, heart, body and soul. I love you more than any vow could ever express and I thank you for sharing your life with me."

Alex searched Cassidy's eyes as her tears fell silently. She had expected Cassidy's words to amaze her. Now, it was her turn. She breathed out audibly and felt Cassidy's grip tighten in encouragement. "Cass…I am not a poet. I planned what I was going to say. I even practiced it. But then I listened to Dylan and I realized I could never really plan what to say to you. And those words, well," she took in as much air as her lungs could hold and closed her eyes to gather herself. She opened them and looked lovingly at the woman before her.

"There isn't anything more important in my life than you and Dylan. Not one thing. A lot of people don't believe in love at first sight. I didn't. I'm not even sure I knew what love was. I remember when you opened your door that day in New York. I can't really explain it. I didn't think much about it then, but I have thought about that moment every single day since. If you hadn't opened that door. If I had never been sent there…You said everything changed when I came into your life. The truth is Cass, my life began the day we met. Everything before that is like a shadow. With you, well…"

Alex began to choke up and Cassidy smiled. "I know," she whispered.

"You are my life, Cassidy. I can't say I couldn't love you more because I seem to love you more every single day. I would do anything to keep our family safe and happy. I know sometimes I am not the easiest person and I know sometimes I might fall short. I promise you this, you have all of me. Every part. And, you make me better just by being in my life. I listened to Dylan today and I could hear you. It's no wonder he is so bright and so loving. That's you. I see you in him every day. I know I will see you in all of our children. And, I want you to know that I think about our life all of the time. I never thought I would need a family, but now, being with you, building a family with you and Dylan, it's all I want. I love you, Cassidy. I'll never be able to tell you how much, but I promise I will try to show you for the rest of our lives." Alex reached across and wiped away Cassidy's tears. She caught a glimpse of Barb who was smiling, but she could see the tear stains on her sister-in-law's cheeks.

"Do you have a symbol of your commitment that you would like to share with Alex?" the reverend asked Cassidy.

"I do." She accepted the ring from Barb and turned toward Alex. "Alex, I give you this ring as a symbol of my love and fidelity. As a reminder of the laughter, the pain, the challenges and the joys we will share. It is a perfect circle. It is endless and unbroken. My love for you is endless and my commitment can never be broken." Alex swallowed hard as Cassidy slipped the simple, platinum ring on her finger.

"Alex? Do you have a symbol of your commitment you would like to share with Cassidy?"

"I do." Alex took the ring she had chosen with Dylan's help from Nick. She turned to Cassidy and paused. Cassidy's eyes seemed to dance in the sun. "God, you are beautiful," she said aloud, receiving a chuckle from all present. "Well, she is," Alex proclaimed. Cassidy bit her bottom lip gently, amused and touched by Alex's candor. Alex cleared her throat softly. "Cassidy, I spent a long time wondering what kind of ring I should get you. I walked back and forth and I couldn't decide. Dylan pointed to this ring and immediately I knew. It sparkled, just like you. I said you are beautiful; you are. I give you this ring as a symbol of my love and fidelity. It is a perfect circle. It is endless and unbroken. My love for you is endless and my commitment can never be broken." Alex slipped the ring on Cassidy's finger with shaky hands. "I love you, Cass," she said simply.

"I love you," Cassidy answered, forgetting that anyone else was present.

The reverend smiled and lifted his hands. "Alex and Cassidy have declared before you and before God their love, devotion and commitment. May they be blessed with the richness of family and friends to love and support them on their journey. Now, before you all and before God, by the powers vested in me by the State of Connecticut, I declare you legally wed spouses and partners for life....That means you should kiss your wife, Alex," he nudged.

Alex grinned and took Cassidy's face in her hands. They stood silently for a moment looking at one another, neither caring who was present or how long they waited. This was a moment for only them. It would pass quickly and both felt the need to commit it to memory. A smile overtook them both and Alex guided Cassidy's lips to her own. She closed her eyes and inhaled the emotions coursing between them. "How'd it feel to kiss Cassidy Toles?" Cassidy asked quietly.

Alex kissed Cassidy again. "Like coming home," Alex whispered.

***

Chapter Thirty-Three

Alex pulled out Cassidy's chair and was ready to take her seat when she noticed a small bottle on her chair. "What's this?" she asked. Cassidy shrugged. Alex set it on the table and studied it for a second.

Cassidy giggled. "It is a beach wedding, Alex. It's a message in a bottle. Maybe you should open it," she suggested.

Alex raised her brow and pulled out the cork. She fished inside to pull out the rolled parchment. "Did you put this here?" she looked to Cassidy. Cassidy just shrugged again. Alex unrolled the parchment and read the inscription. She read it several times and then turned to her wife. "Cass?"

"Yes?" Cassidy smiled flirtatiously. She expected her note would get an interesting reaction from her new wife.

Alex leaned over for a searing kiss. "Get a room." Barb laughed as she passed by. Alex ignored her and pulled away slightly only to kiss Cassidy again.

"Remind me to leave you notes more often," Cassidy laughed.

"You just make sure I am the only one you ever leave a note like that for," Alex said.

Cassidy spun the ring on Alex's finger. "I don't think you have anything to worry about." She kissed Alex on the cheek.

"Mom?"

"Hey, sweetie." Dylan wiggled in between his parents. "Thank you for what you said today Dylan," Cassidy said. "What made you think of giving us necklaces?" she asked curiously.

He made his way onto Alex's lap. "I didn't. It was YaYa's idea. I was thinking of what to say. They let me practice...when she and Grandma took me to pick up my clothes. You know?" Cassidy nodded her encouragement. "Well, I don't have anything to give you or Alex. So, I said I would give you both my heart. Then I said you could have the part that takes care of me and Alex could have the part that protects me. YaYa said that was beautiful and it gave her the idea."

Cassidy saw the wave of emotion in Alex's eyes. "It is very beautiful, Dylan, and it was a wonderful idea."

"Yep," he said proudly. "Grandma and YaYa thought so too, so YaYa said she would talk to her friend. And you know what too?" Cassidy shook her head. "She got a really cool bracelet there. You should go see it!" he said excitedly.

Alex was curious. Her mother always wore jewelry and Alex never paid any of it much mind. "Why is it cool?" she asked him.

"Cause...it has a stone for you and Uncle Nick, Aunt Barb, Mom, Cat, and me....and YaYa says she'll have one for Cat's brother or sister...and mine too someday."

Cassidy pulled Dylan onto her lap, kissed his forehead and looked at Alex. "Go see your mother." Alex nodded and started to leave. She stopped and rolled Cassidy's note back up, placing it back in the bottle and raised a brow at her new wife. "That's later. After the vanilla cake you promised," Cassidy winked.

Alex chuckled and bent over to kiss Dylan on the cheek. "Save me a dance?" she whispered in his ear.

"Sure thing, *Mom*," he said playfully.

Cassidy started laughing at the expression on Alex's face. Alex huffed jokingly and Dylan gave her a toothy grin. "Oh God." Cassidy rolled her eyes. "Twenty minutes married and already you are sporting her grin. You really are a Toles," she said as she ruffled his hair.

***

"There's a problem," Viktor Ivanov said.

"What are you talking about?" Admiral Brackett asked over his secure line.

"The protocols are not complete."

Brackett ran his hand over the top of his head. "Impossible. Perhaps you should talk to your nephew, Viktor. He did send my daughter home, assuring her he was in control."

"Are you suggesting that Dimitri is somehow involved in this?" Ivanov's voice dropped.

"He is the one who retrieved the disk."

"From your ambassadors," Ivanov bellowed. "This will not stand."

"Are you threatening me?" Admiral Brackett asked.

"Threats are words. This is beyond threats. Your people have compromised us again."

"Watch yourself, Viktor. You don't know who is responsible. I would advise you to use caution," Brackett warned. "You should be careful who you recruit and mindful of who you attempt to intimidate." Ivanov laughed at the admiral's assertion. "Viktor," the admiral cautioned. "Calm down. We must proceed carefully. The future of our work is…"

Ivanov interrupted the admiral. "The future of our work lies in the past."

"What are you saying?"

"Tried and true, Admiral. We will return to our roots."

"Viktor!" There was no response. "Viktor!" Admiral Brackett dropped the receiver and placed his face in his hands. He understood the implication in Viktor Ivanov's words. The fracture was complete. The past had returned. What had taken years to fully cultivate now lay in waste. The worst of it; Ivanov was not wrong. This new world needed a new order. History often repeats itself for someone's specific reason and Admiral William Brackett was certain the past would now return to haunt them all.

***

"Mom?"

"Alexis," Helen smiled and placed her glass of wine on the table to hug her daughter. "It was absolutely beautiful."

"Thanks," Alex said. "Thanks for helping Dylan."

"Oh, I just made a suggestion, Alexis. Really, it was all inside of him. He is a very thoughtful young man."

"Yeah, he is. He's like his mom." Helen agreed. "He was pretty excited about this bracelet you got. I think it meant a lot to him to be included." Alex's voice dropped to a whisper, "it means a lot to me too."

Helen sighed and put her arm around her daughter. "You know, Alexis…Dylan and Cat, they are both very smart young men. I look at them and then I look at you and your brother. Time passes quickly. You shouldn't waste it." Alex was a bit confused by her mother's musings. "You know what struck me the most about your vows, all three of you?" Alex shook her head. "Most couples talk about each other. And, Alexis…I have been to many weddings with children involved, none where they were included." Alex studied her mother. "All of you talked about family. The family you have, the family you want to build." She smiled at her daughter and pointed to the bracelet Dylan had referred to. "Dylan gave you and Cassidy something so that you could always carry each other. Even when you are apart, you are connected. Made me think that I never want to forget again that I carry each of you with me. We lost too much time, Alexis. Someday soon I will add another stone for my newest grandchild." Alex smiled. "And," Helen continued as she retrieved her wine. "I am betting that I won't be the only one adding another stone in the not so distant future." She pointed to Alex's necklace. Alex shook her head. "Don't worry," Helen said giving Alex a light peck on the cheek. "I made sure my jeweler knew to expect you." She laughed and walked away. Alex stood dumfounded.

"What did she just say?" Barb asked, coming up behind Alex.

"I thought you were bad," Alex said.

"Me? Why? What did I do?" Barb asked seriously.

Alex rolled her eyes. "Twenty minutes married and my mother already has Cassidy pregnant." Barb howled in laughter. "Laugh it up."

Barb shrugged. "At least we're consistent!"

Alex just rolled her eyes again. She made her way back towards the table she was sharing with Cassidy and stopped. Cassidy was standing surrounded by Dylan, Cat and the Fallon brood. Dylan and Cat were engaged in telling some animated story. Cassidy was listening intently and smiling. She was everybody's mom. Alex laughed thinking it was no wonder her wife had become a teacher.

"You okay?" Rose asked.

"Yeah," Alex chuckled. "No," she corrected herself. Rose was perplexed. "Better than okay," Alex smiled. "Much better than okay."

***

"All right, Admiral. What was so important that you needed to see me late on a Saturday night?" Jon Krause asked.

Admiral William Brackett sat in a large leather chair sipping a glass of scotch. His expression was somber. His demeanor was quiet and reserved. From Krause's perspective the admiral looked as though he had just suffered a great personal loss. Krause wondered momentarily if Claire Brackett had finally crossed one too many lines. The admiral gestured to the table at the far side of the room. "Pour yourself a drink and sit down Jonathan," he said. He closed his eyes and leaned back against the large chair. Krause followed the admiral's suggestion, pouring himself a short glass of scotch before taking a seat on the opposite sofa. "How are you, Jonathan?" the admiral asked. The sincerity in the older man's voice sounded almost fatherly.

"I'm fine, Admiral," Krause replied as he studied the man.

Admiral Brackett opened his eyes and leaned slightly forward. "Hum. Honestly, Jonathan…How are you?" Krause was puzzled by the question and shook his head slightly in confusion. "Come now. You lost your best friend and your son's mother married today, if I am not mistaken," he said gently.

Krause nodded. "I'm not sure what any of that has to do with why I am here," he said.

Admiral Brackett sighed and leaned back again. "I had a best friend, Jonathan," he said. "He was really my brother, more of a brother than either of the two that shared my parents." The admiral sipped his scotch. "I was in love once. I mean, really in love." He smiled. "And, we both know I have a daughter. So, answer me truthfully for once. How are you?"

Krause swirled the scotch in his glass. "Angry that my brother is gone," he said without any evident emotion. "As for Cassidy and Dylan, well…They are getting something far better than I could ever give them," he said simply.

Admiral Brackett smiled. "Agent Toles is a unique breed, Jonathan. It wasn't always that way you know." Krause watched the admiral closely as the older man rose to his feet and walked toward a book case. "I used to read to Claire when she was small. Whenever I was home I would read to her. Always stories that I thought would help her to understand life a bit. The notion that heroes are made and not born. The idea that loyalty is precious." The admiral shook his head. "I'm not sure what she heard in those stories. I wonder if she listened at all." Krause was beginning to wonder if in fact something had happened to the younger Brackett. The admiral pivoted and faced Krause again. "We've suffered a fracture. Not even a fracture, actually. The framework we have built….it's in pieces. Shattered."

"Admiral?"

"The Russians have moved on their own. There was an interruption in an important trade. One that was several years in the making. I don't know where the breech occurred. London, Moscow…it's unclear."

The picture was become clearer. Krause was certain that the admiral was referring to the disk he and Alex had exchanged. "Sir, one transaction or trade…"

"Oh, it isn't just one, Jonathan. The cracks have been appearing for years. Maybe John was on the right track, I don't know."

"What is it…."

"Jonathan, the Russians will begin a new alliance of sorts. They will revert. Do you understand?" Krause searched the admiral for his meaning with his eyes. "Do you know how long it has been since we have worked separately? I mean the Russians, the British, the Germans, the French and us?" Krause remained still. "Hmm," the admiral chuckled. "More than seventy years, Jonathan. More than seventy. This? All you have come to know began amid war. War that shook the entire earth. What it produced required control. Quiet and careful control."

"I'm not sure I understand," Krause admitted.

"All the details aren't important," Admiral Brackett sighed. "You will no doubt learn them all in time now. The fracture, that is important. We've had to make some changes. How Viktor and the Russian contingent of our organization respond will determine many things. Where they strike."

"You think that Ivanov is going to retaliate? Against who? This is not America versus the Soviet Union. We are not in the 1950s or even the 1980s," Krause observed.

The admiral tipped his head. "Yes, Jonathan. The question isn't if they will retaliate, it is when and how. And when they do, well…I suggest you brush up on the history you mentioned." Krause swallowed hard. He could see the concern in the admiral's eyes. "This time, I am not certain that we are playing in the same orchestra. We may be looking at the same piece of music, but we exist under separate conductors."

"What is it that you need from me?" Krause asked.

"I need Agent Toles." Krause's expression hardened. "Edmond has made a call, Jonathan. One I had hoped we would never have to make. Everything has changed. The sides we take now, well....there *are* sides to choose."

"I'm not certain," Krause said, "that I understand what those sides are, Admiral. I can assure you that Alex Toles will not choose any side that compromises her family or her beliefs."

The admiral nodded. "That is precisely why I need her."

"And the sparrow?"

Admiral Brackett shook his head sadly. "She has chosen a different path."

"And you are prepared for what that might mean?" Krause asked. "I'm not certain that I could do what you are suggesting as a father."

"No. But, it is not my choice to make. It was hers. She prizes nothing beyond her own ascension. That only ever leads to one's destruction." Krause nodded his understanding. "Today, we live in a new world. To most people it will seem exactly the same, but trust me, Jonathan, it will not for long. Everything has changed."

"What exactly do you want from Agent Toles?"

The admiral sat back in his large chair and closed his eyes. "That will become evident soon enough. You will know without me needing to explain. She will be faced with a choice. It will be your decision which way to guide her."

"And if I choose to guide her away?" Krause asked.

The admiral shrugged. "That is your choice, Jonathan. I will not force you now. I will not force Alexis." Krause roused at the admiral's use of Alex's name and made an immediate mental note. "But, you should know...both of you; there will be clear enemies to combat. The kind you both once believed you were fighting. Some will seek to rebuild the past. That will be the choice; the past or a new future."

Krause leaned back into the sofa. He looked across to the admiral who was clearly lost now to his own thoughts. He was not certain what he made of this. It was clear to him that whatever The Collaborative had been, however it had been formed, it no longer existed. He took a deep breath, feeling assured that he had been right. He had sensed it when John Merrow decided to walk in front of an assassin's bullet. The wheels had begun to spin at a frenetic pace and he knew then the only thing to stop the out of control ride would be a crash. That was happening now. It had been inevitable. He simply did not expect it so soon. What would be rebuilt, that was what the admiral was referring to. This was the opportunity men like Matthew Waters and John Merrow had sought. It was the opening he and Alex Toles needed to discover why The Collaborative was formed and to trace its roots so that they could pull them out. It also presented a new set of questions and perils he could not predict. "Oh, Alex," he thought silently. "I hope you are ready for this." He took another sip of scotch as he sat in weighted silence with the admiral. "I hope I am too," he admitted to himself.

***

"Hey, Speed." Alex took a seat next to Dylan. She looked out at the small dance floor. Nick had cleared a space near the outdoor fireplace that Cassidy loved. Cassidy was dancing with Nick and laughing. Barb was sitting nearby with Cat, her mother and Kate Fallon. Rose was engaged in a lively discussion with Jane and Stephanie Merrow. "Getting tired?" He shrugged. "Too much cake?" Dylan giggled. "You bored?"

"Kinda," he admitted.

"Well, it's almost all over," she said. The truth was that Alex was tired herself and she was anxious to spend some alone time with Cassidy. The note her wife had scribbled and placed in the bottle on her chair had piqued her curiosity. But, there was one thing she still wanted to do. One thing that, at this moment, eclipsed everything and every person surrounding her; every person but one. "You know," she said getting back to her feet. "You called me Mom, earlier." Dylan looked up at her wondering if he had done something wrong. Alex smiled at him and put out her hand. "I'm pretty sure you promised me a dance. I've already danced with my wife. I'd really like a chance to dance with my son." Dylan smiled. He had danced with Cassidy, danced with his Grandma and his YaYa, danced with Stephanie Merrow and danced with Cat and the Fallon kids to all kinds of songs. He was tired from all the excitement, but there was one person he had waited all night to dance with and she was standing before him now. Alex nodded to the disc jockey as the song playing faded and led Dylan to the dance floor. "I picked this song for you, Speed. Someday, when you are older and you listen to it, I hope you will know why."

Cassidy watched as Dylan looked up to Alex. Alex had only told her that she had picked a special song that always made her think of Dylan. The sound came through to Cassidy's ears and the words made her smile from within. *Never Alone*, that was the name of the song Alex had chosen. She could see Alex singing the words to Dylan. She felt a hand on her shoulder and clasped it. Somehow she knew that it would be Jane. "She loves you both so much," Jane said. Cassidy just smiled, unable to speak. She watched Alex playfully twirl Dylan and saw him laugh. Then she saw Alex motion to her. "Go," Jane whispered.

Cassidy closed the distance between them and looked at Alex. "Last dance coming," Alex said. Dylan was ready to walk away when Alex grabbed hold of him and lifted him onto her hip. "Oh no, Speed. We started this day as a family and we are ending it exactly the same way." Cassidy touched Alex's cheek lovingly as Alex pulled her closer. "I hate these shoes," Alex said, kicking them off. Cassidy laughed and kicked off her own. That sent Dylan into his own fit of giggles. The Beach Boys started playing and Cassidy shook her head. "Hey! It's a beach wedding," Alex explained. "Besides, what *would* I do without you?"

"Less dishes?" Cassidy raised her brow.

"Yeah and you'd eat less tacos," Dylan said plainly. All three began to laugh.

Rose put her arm around Helen and sighed. "I'm not sure I have ever seen two people who belong together as much as those two."

Helen nodded. "I never thought I would see Alexis so happy," she said. They both scanned the faces surrounding the family on the dance floor and realized everyone was having the exact same thought. Alex and Cassidy and Dylan looked as if they had always been together. It was something no one could explain and no one needed to.

Cassidy was signing slightly off key as she and Alex simultaneously lifted Dylan off the dance floor. He laughed and when his feet hit the floor again, he crossed his heart theatrically, singing the chorus he had only just heard. Alex lifted him back to her hip and she and Cassidy put their arms around him as the song wound into its final chorus. "Thank you for being my family," Alex said to them both.

Cassidy smiled. "Thanks for being my moms," Dylan said as he and Alex both flashed Cassidy a huge grin before singing the last chorus to her.

"You are both crazy," Cassidy laughed. "But I love you both," she said as the music ended.

"Perfect way to end the evening," Alex observed. Dylan hugged them both. "You have fun with Cat," she said. "Mom and I will pick you up tomorrow afternoon." Dylan nodded and skipped over to Barb and Cat. "So you ready to blow this beach party, Mrs. Toles?" Alex asked.

"Are you going to carry me over the threshold?" Cassidy bantered.

"I'm going to carry you over more than one threshold," Alex countered.

Cassidy flushed slightly. "In that case, let's get a move on, Alfred."

"Wait!" Alex ran over to the table and came back with Cassidy's message in a bottle. "My wife left me an important message. Wouldn't be good if I forgot it."

"What kind of message did she leave you that is so important you had to run?" Alex whispered something in Cassidy's ear. "I thought marriage was supposed to end all of that nonsense," Cassidy submitted.

"Oh? You haven't met *my* wife," Alex said as they began to make their final exit.

"No? What's she like?" Cassidy asked, curious how Alex would answer.

Alex stopped abruptly and turned Cassidy to face her. "My wife?" Cassidy nodded. "She is the most amazing person I have ever known. Frankly, I don't think I deserve her, but I thank God every day she thinks so."

Cassidy kissed Alex soundly, receiving a host of whistles. "She sounds wonderful. But I think you should know," Alex listened carefully as Cassidy continued, "that my wife takes my breath away every time I see her. And I know I don't deserve her, but I am grateful she loves me."

"She does," Alex said with a kiss before gently pulling Cassidy forward. No one stopped them. It was more than clear where they were headed and that the festivities had ended. A quick kiss on the cheek from Rose, a whistle from Nick and Alex was opening the door of a ridiculously decorated SUV for Cassidy. "What the hell were they thinking?" she shook her head as she got in. Cassidy was doubled over in laughter by the time Alex got in the driver's seat. "What? What is it?" Cassidy pointed to the dashboard. "What in the hell?" An action figure of Agent Mulder from the *X-Files* was secured to the dashboard holding an action figure of Agent Scully across his arms. The note in front of it read: *The truth is out there, Agent. Just hope you know where to look.* "I'm gonna kill him," Alex said before she erupted in laughter.

✳✳✳

Nicolaus Toles walked through his house slowly, sipping a glass of red wine. It hadn't changed much over the years. He turned down the hallway and slowly allowed his eyes to follow the array of portraits on the walls. It was almost as if he was traveling back through time. He stopped halfway down the narrow corridor and stared at the face of a young girl. She was missing her front tooth in the portrait, but she smiled with pride; no care or worry about the gaping hole in the front of her mouth. He laughed, remembering the day she had lost that tooth. She was chasing the neighbor's dog, determined that she could catch him on her own when she tripped over one of her brother's toy trucks and landed squarely on her face. He shook his head. He recalled she didn't cry. She didn't yell at her little brother. She'd been wiggling that tooth for weeks and now it was in her hand. "Look, Daddy!" she screamed to him.

"What happened?" he asked when he saw the trail of blood running down her lip.

"Tooth fairy is coming!" she exclaimed. Her brother ran over to inspect the damage to his sister. She showed him her prize happily. "Look Nicky! That means the tooth fairy comes!" His eyes got wide as his sister bent over to him. "And you get half of whatever she leaves."

"Why does Nicky get half?" her father asked.

"Cause, silly, his truck made me lose my wiggly tooth! Come on Nicky," she grabbed her brother's hand. "Let's go show Mom!"

Nicolaus Toles raised his glass to the little girl. "Never change," he whispered. He continued his slow pace, sipping his wine and studying the changing faces on the wall until he reached his study. He paced around the desk and took a seat. He picked up a pen and began scribbling a note; occasionally sipping from his glass as he combed through his private thoughts. After several minutes he scrolled his signature and placed the note in an envelope, addressing it simply. He unlocked his file drawer and thumbed through some folders until he found what he was searching for. He dropped the envelope inside, closed the drawer and locked it. Closing his eyes, he allowed a deep sigh to pass his lips and took the final sip of wine from his glass. "Never change," he whispered.

***

Alex opened the door to the suite she and Cassidy were sharing and nearly dropped the bucket of ice she was carrying. Cassidy was standing near the large window, looking out at the water. She still had her wedding gown on and the moonlight through the window highlighted the soft curls that fell to the side of her face. Alex set down the bucket and moved behind her, taking Cassidy gently into her arms. Cassidy leaned back into the embrace. Alex looked out at the moon over the water. It was mesmerizing, but it did not hold a candle to the woman in her arms. "Cass?"

"Hum?"

"We're married," Alex whispered.

"I know," Cassidy smiled and held Alex's hands around her.

"Is it weird?"

"Being married?" Cassidy asked as she gently caressed Alex's arm.

"No," Alex kissed her wife's head. "I'm supposed to come in here and ravish you, right?" Cassidy just giggled. "I keep thinking about Dylan. Is that weird?"

"I don't think it's weird at all," Cassidy assured her. "It's one of the reasons I love you so much."

Alex sighed. "I can't believe what he said. He's just...God, Cass. I was so proud of him."

Cassidy turned in Alex's arms. "I know. Me too. You gave him that chance, Alex. It meant so much to him, and to me. Dylan is lucky to have you in his life."

"You know, my mother seems to think I am going to have you pregnant on our wedding night," Alex smirked.

"In that case you'd better call Mulder and Scully down there on the dashboard," Cassidy laughed.

"Oh, I don't know, if I try all the things on the note my wife left, I think I might just have a chance."

"Well, you know, it seldom happens the first time, Alex. You'd better be prepared to try a whole lot."

Alex cupped Cassidy's face in her hands. "No time like the present," she said. She kissed Cassidy and felt Cassidy fall into her.

"Good start," Cassidy whispered into Alex's ear. She kissed Alex's neck and lingered there.

"Oh God, Cass…"

Cassidy had lost all thought. Her hand was slowly tracing Alex's cleavage and her kisses were trailing swiftly behind each caress. Alex wanted to speak. She had been waiting to make love to Cassidy all night, but she was helpless when Cassidy touched her. That was something she prayed would never change. "Alex," Cassidy began as she moved around her wife. Cassidy slowly began to unzip Alex's dress and push it gradually off her shoulders. "I didn't write that note about you making love to me." Alex closed her eyes as she felt Cassidy's hands tenderly stroke her back. "You still have no idea," she kissed Alex's shoulder and she circled back to face her wife, "how much I love you." Cassidy traced the outline of Alex's face and led her slowly to the bed. She hovered over Alex and smiled. "You think I can tell you somehow," she said.

"Cass, you are a poet compared to me." Cassidy shook her head and kissed Alex. "Well, you are," Alex insisted.

"No. I told you. What I feel for you…I told you, it exists beyond words." Alex closed her eyes and struggled to catch her breath as she felt Cassidy's kiss reach the top of her breast. Cassidy said nothing. Her hands delicately touched every inch of Alex's skin. Her exploration of Alex's body was so slow and so complete it was almost painful; almost. It was a torture that Alex hoped would never end. Alex ran her hands over Cassidy's back and reached the zipper of her dress. She need to feel Cassidy close to her and as always, Cassidy immediately understood and lifted herself so that Alex could free her of her confines.

Cassidy's hair was still swept up and Alex drank in the radiant glow that emanated from her; the moonlight brushing her skin, the flickers of passion that danced in her eyes. "You do," Alex whispered.

"I do what?" Cassidy asked as she admired the beautiful face looking up at her.

"You sparkle," Alex smiled.

Cassidy gave a soft chuckle. "I think you are in love, Agent Toles."

"Yeah?"

Cassidy raised her brow. "Maybe," she said as she kissed Alex and resumed her tender and loving exploration of the woman beneath her.

Alex thought she might die from anticipation. She could feel the warmth of Cassidy's body gliding softly against her own. She could feel the beat of Cassidy's heart when Cassidy pressed up against her. Soft kisses descended gradually down her hip and Alex could no longer remain silent. "Cass..." The sound of urgency in Alex's voice increased Cassidy's own desire and she moved to end Alex's suffering. She felt the need to see Alex, to look in her eyes. Her touch gently increased and she lifted her kiss to Alex's lips. For once Alex was not content. She turned them both. Cassidy felt Alex's hand travel slowly down her body, stopping only occasionally to solicit a response and an appreciative moan from Cassidy. "I need you," Alex confessed. Cassidy looked into Alex's eyes and kissed her slowly.

"You have me, Alex." Cassidy closed her eyes as Alex brought her over the first threshold, just as she had promised. Cassidy whispered Alex's name as Alex's body began to submit to Cassidy's touch. It was enough to push Cassidy over the edge again and she held onto Alex more tightly than she ever had, looking into Alex's eyes, riveted, transported, most of all loved. "Alex," she managed as her tears began to flow freely.

"I'm right here, Cass." Cassidy collapsed into Alex and held her close. "Cass?"

"I just can't believe it sometimes, Alex."

"What?"

"I don't think most people ever find what we have. I really don't," Cassidy admitted. "I can't imagine ever living without it again."

"You don't have to," Alex assured her wife.

"So, what was it like?" Cassidy asked, finally relaxing in Alex's arms.

"What?"

"Making love to Cassidy Toles."

Alex unclipped Cassidy's hair, removing the pins she could see and gently prompted it to fall. "Cassidy, making love to you is always new for me. But, I love that you are Cassidy Toles."

"Good."

"Cass?"

"Yeah?"

"Do you think we succeeded?"

"Succeeded?"

"Yeah, you know...I'd hate to disappoint my mom."

Cassidy laughed and propped herself up on her elbow. "That *would* be terrible."

"I think we should try again," Alex smirked.

Cassidy shook her head. "You are incorrigible. I am happy to be your test subject, but I think YaYa might have to be disappointed on this one," she winked and kissed Alex's cheek.

"Well, no harm in trying."

"No harm at all," Cassidy agreed.

***

Epilogue

Tuesday, June 3rd

Cassidy sat at the kitchen table perusing job postings for local schools. Alex was at work. Dylan was at school. Life was quiet. Life was wonderful. She looked at the ring on her finger and pondered how happy she truly was. There were still things that she needed to resolve. Custody of Dylan was paramount on her list. She had Alex's full support and they had wonderful people behind them. She had no doubt that with the love of her family and friends, she and Alex would be well on their way to establishing the family they both desired; a family free and clear of the influence of her ex-husband. She took a sip of her iced tea and returned to her task when the ringing of her cell phone startled her. "Alex?"

"Yeah, it's me."

"Hey, are you okay?" Alex did not respond immediately and Cassidy knew something was wrong. "Honey?'

"It's my father, Cass."

"What, did you see him or something?"

Alex took a deep breath. "Cass, I'm on my way to my mom's. Is there any way you can get Dylan and pick up Barb and Cat and meet me."

"Alex, what is going on?"

"Cass....my father is...he's gone."

Cassidy was confused. She knew Helen's insistence on supporting Alex had caused tension in Alex's parent's marriage. They had been together over fifty years, married for forty. She couldn't imagine that Nicolaus Toles would leave his wife. "He left?" Cassidy asked.

"No, Cass. He didn't leave. He died. He's gone," Alex said softly.

"What?"

"Mom came home this morning from Nick's and found him in his study. Looks like he had a heart attack, maybe a stroke." Cassidy was at a loss for words. She ran her hand over her face. "Cass, can you? I mean can you get Dylan early and pick up Barb and Cat? I just talked to Nicky…I just…I'm closer…I…"

"Of course. Whatever you need me to do. You know that. Alex? Are you all right?"

"I don't know, Cass. I really don't know."

"I'll be there as soon as I can, okay? I love you."

"Okay. I love you too."

***

Friday, June 6th

"How are you feeling?" Cassidy asked.

"Numb," Alex answered.

Cassidy understood. She looked over at the casket and shook her head in disbelief. A week ago they we preparing for their wedding. Now they were standing in a receiving line at a wake for someone Alex loved. It made Cassidy angry. Alex's life was suddenly upside down. "You know, whatever you decide; I will support you."

Alex smiled at her wife. "I know that," she said. She was dreading making pleasantries with her father's business associates. She didn't want to imagine who might make an appearance today. She had talked at length with Krause the night before. What should she do? He seemed certain that her father's death was no accident and no heart attack. This was the choice the admiral had assured Krause that Alex would face. Should she take the helm of her father's company? It presented problems and possibilities.

Initially, she had completely disregarded the idea. But, after talking to Krause, she had begun to consider the possibility. "Right now," she said to Cassidy, "I am mostly worried about Mom."

Cassidy took Alex's hand and squeezed it gently. "I know." She looked a few feet away to see Helen looking at the casket that held the man she loved. The visual made her weak. She recalled her own father's death and witnessing the grief in Helen's eyes, Cassidy could only imagine what losing Alex would feel like. "I love you, Alex," she said as the first wave of condolence givers streamed in.

Alex smiled and pulled Dylan against her hip. "Wanna know a secret?" she asked her wife. Cassidy nodded. "There *is* one thing that makes me smile."

"What's that?" Cassidy asked.

"I am going to introduce you and Dylan to every person who walks through this line as my wife and son." Cassidy couldn't help but smile. There was a slight twinkle in Alex's eye as she shared her secret. Cassidy was certain that Alex would do exactly that.

***

Three hours into a long afternoon Helen Toles was fading. Alex was showing clear signs of exhaustion. Dylan and Cat has taken up residence in the far corner of the funeral parlor with Barb's iPad and everyone's blessing. Cassidy was pleasantly surprised that Jon Krause had made an appearance and had decided to stay. He was sitting in the corner with the boys keeping a close eye on each passersby. Cassidy knew there was more than a personal interest at play in his presence, but she could also see the genuine concern he had for both Alex and Dylan. It surprised her a bit at first, but then she recalled the phone call he made to her the morning of the wedding.

Her old friend didn't have much to say. He did say that it was Alex who told him to call. He was quiet for a long moment and then he said something Cassidy was certain she would never forget. "You know, I loved you when we were in France. Maybe I never stopped. The truth is Cassie, Alex is lucky to have you. But, I think you are lucky to have her too. If I could go back and do it all over? Everything in my life? I'd take a page from Alexis Toles," he told her.

Cassidy turned to Alex. The steady stream of visitors had tapered and she felt the need to see Dylan. The atmosphere had unsettled both the boys. "Honey?" Alex smiled. "I'm just going to check on Dylan while there is a lull, okay? I'll be right back."

"Tell him we are almost done and I know YaYa has ice cream," Alex said.

Cassidy patted Alex's hand. "I will do that." She nodded to Helen and Nick and headed for the boys and their unlikely adult companion.

Alex took the moment to close her eyes and take a deep breath. She heard the voice next to her that was speaking to her mother. It sounded familiar and she opened her eyes. "What the hell are you doing here?" she hissed. Helen's eyes flew open as she realized suddenly who was standing before her. Already exhausted and emotional, the older woman started to lose her balance. Alex grabbed hold of her mother's arm as Barb flew in from a few feet away. Alex stepped away slightly. "Get. The. Hell. Out of here."

Krause saw Cassidy jump to her feet. "Stay with the boys," she issued her statement as an order. Before he could protest she was gone.

"I am telling you...leave," Alex said as quietly as she could manage.

"Oh, Agent Toles...your father was one of my most avid supporters. After all, in a way we are family now. I simply wanted to pay my respects....Cassidy," he acknowledged his ex-wife as she approached. "Congratulations, by the way."

Dylan had caught sight of the man talking to his mom and Alex and he sprinted away. "Dylan," Krause jumped up. "Cat, stay here," he said. "Dylan, wait." It was too late, Dylan had made his way to his family. He saw his YaYa first. His Aunt Barb was sitting beside her and she looked very upset. Then he saw Alex. He moved toward her. Nick tried to catch him, but he pulled away forcefully.

"Hey, buddy." Congressman O'Brien took the opportunity for all it was worth and put his hand out to Dylan. "How are you?"

Dylan pushed himself up against Alex and felt her hand come to rest on his shoulder. "Did you know Alex's dad?" Dylan asked skeptically.

O'Brien crouched to the boy's height under the steely gaze of two very protective mothers. "I did. And, Alex is your friend, right? So..."

"Alex isn't my friend." Dylan looked at his father harshly.

Cassidy heard Krause's voice in her ear and felt his hand on her shoulder. "I tried." She patted his hand as reassurance and kept watch on her son.

"No? I thought that you and Alex..."

"Alex is my mom," Dylan said definitively.

"Now Dylan," he began.

Cassidy had reached her limit with her ex-husband and she stepped forward grabbing his arm. "If you will excuse us," she said as she pulled him away.

Krause immediately started to follow and Alex stopped him. "No. I'll go. She needs to handle this. Let her." Alex followed Cassidy's path and stopped in the small doorway. She could see O'Brien and she could hear Cassidy clearly.

"Cassie, you look well."

"Cut the shit, Chris. What exactly do you think you are doing?"

"Offering my condolences of course."

"Just leave, Christopher. Leave my family alone. If you ever cared a thing for me or for Dylan, just go."

"I have a right to see my son."

"Well, you certainly choose interesting times to exercise that right. Which is one reason I am exercising mine to end it."

"Excuse me? Cassie, you really should rethink the people in your life."

Cassidy laughed. "I did that, thank you. I walked away from Cassidy O'Brien. I much prefer Cassidy Toles."

"Well, that is very nice for you, Cassie. Dylan is still an O'Brien."

"Actually, he's not."

"Well, maybe not technically. He may be a Krause, but in the eyes of anyone who matters he is an O'Brien."

Cassidy nodded and then smiled. "I guess you haven't gotten the news. Should be delivered any day."

"What are you talking about?"

"You'll see," she smirked and started to turn away. Deliberately, she turned back. "Oh, and Dylan? He's not a Krause." O'Brien's ears perked. "He's a Toles, just like both of his parents. His choice, not mine."

"You don't even know who Alex Toles is," he said smugly.

Cassidy pursed her lips in amusement. "Of course I know who she is, Christopher." He was ready to speak when Alex appeared. Cassidy smiled and held out her hand to Alex. "She's my wife. Now, I really don't care why you came. I think it's clear that no one wants you here. I'd hate anything to taint your image." She raised her brow and gestured toward the door.

"Watch yourself," he said as he walked through the door. "You don't have anyone to protect you now."

Cassidy shook her head. "I don't have anyone to protect me?" She rolled her eyes.

Alex exhaled and pulled Cassidy to her. "He wasn't talking about you, Cass."

"What?"

472

Alex kissed Cassidy on the forehead and then glanced at the door the congressman had just exited through. "I'm going to do it."

"Do what?"

"Take my father's role over at Carecom."

"Alex, are you sure you…"

Alex nodded. "Yeah. I am. I promise you, Cass; you never have to worry about being protected. You or Dylan." Cassidy smiled as Alex's arm wrapped around her and they began to head back to their family. "A Toles, huh?" Alex asked.

"Yep, think all of our kids should have the same name as their parents."

Alex nodded as Dylan sprinted for them. "I couldn't agree more."

"So, what now?" Cassidy asked.

"I have no idea," Alex confessed. "But, we Toles stick together." Dylan pressed against Alex as Cassidy moved to take Helen into a hug. Dylan tugged Alex's hand. "What is it, Speed?"

"Can I be a Toles?"

Alex glanced over at the shiny metal box that held the man she once called her hero. She smiled and looked at Dylan, suddenly secure in her decision. "You already are, Dylan. You already are."

CPSIA information can be obtained
at www.ICGtesting.com
Printed in the USA
LVHW031531060619
620404LV00035B/599